# 主体性的生成与危机：

## 现代中国文学生产的文化政治

The Making of Subjectivity and Its Crisis:
On the Cultrual Politics of Modern Chinese Literary Production

王晓平 著

厦门大学出版社
XIAMEN UNIVERSITY PRESS

国家一级出版社
全国百佳图书出版单位

**图书在版编目(CIP)数据**

主体性的生成与危机:现代中国文学生产的文化政治/王晓平著.—厦门:厦门大学出版社,2016.12
ISBN 978-7-5615-6297-0

Ⅰ.①主…　Ⅱ.①王…　Ⅲ.①中国文学-现代文学-文学研究　②中国文学-当代文学-文学研究　Ⅳ.①I206.6

中国版本图书馆 CIP 数据核字(2016)第 257599 号

| | |
|---|---|
| **出 版 人** | 蒋东明 |
| **责任编辑** | 孟令娟 |
| **美术编辑** | 李夏凌 |
| **责任印制** | 许克华 |

| | |
|---|---|
| **出版发行** | 厦门大学出版社 |
| **社　　址** | 厦门市软件园二期望海路 39 路 |
| **邮政编码** | 361008 |
| **总 编 办** | 0592-2182177　0592-2181406(传真) |
| **营销中心** | 0592-2184458　0592-2181365 |
| **网　　址** | http://www.xmupress.com |
| **邮　　箱** | xmupress@126.com |
| **印　　刷** | 厦门市明亮彩印有限公司 |

| | |
|---|---|
| **开 本** | 720mm×1000mm　1/16 |
| **印 张** | 22.5 |
| **字 数** | 405 千字 |
| **版 次** | 2016 年 12 月第 1 版 |
| **印 次** | 2016 年 12 月第 1 次印刷 |
| **定 价** | 68.00 元 |

厦门大学出版社
微信二维码

厦门大学出版社
微博二维码

# 目 录

# Introduction

# Three Trends in Recent Studies of Modern Chinese Literature and Culture

As an academic discipline or field, the study of modern Chinese literature and culture in North America has seen profound changes since the late 1980s, culminating in a "theoretical turn" in the field. This new situation has produced an array of works that can be broadly classified under "cultural studies." Compared with the field in Chinese mainland, which still stresses empirical research, in North America this theoretical turn is marked by a conscious application of various cutting-edge theories in scholarly studies that support their theoretical frameworks. Many of these works follow postmodernist and post-structuralist trends, especially in the early period of the turn. The arrival of the global media age and the ensuing media studies fever has been accompanied by the emergence of a new tendency that emphasises studying literary and cultural texts and phenomena from the perspective of cultural production. The scholarship in the field has generally followed the theoretical paradigm-shift seen in the Anglo-American world: from structuralism to post-structuralism, from historicism to new historicism, and from modernist-oriented new criticism to postmodern, postcolonial criticism. Recent years have seen the emergence of a renewed interest in historical experience, which in turn has proven conducive to the formation of a hermeneutical paradigm.

## 一、Postmodern Approach and Postcolonial Criticism

Postmodern theory holds that various "grand narratives," such as modernity and revolution, in their teleological narrative of a linear, progressive modernity, all disregard the plurality of historical experience and repress alternative choices and opportunities. As a counter-move, postmodernists stress local experience, "suppressed voice," and exploration of "plural modernities."[①] This tendency in the field manifests itself mainly in critiques of the "May Fourth Paradigm" as a master narrative, and the argument for "repressed modernities" existing in the late Qing period.

David Wang has strongly advocated this thesis over the last decade, especially in his work *Fin-de-siecle Splendor : Repressed Modernities of Late Qing Fiction*, 1849-1911.[②] In this highly influential and inspiring book, Wang argues that promising sprouts of incipient modernity burgeoned in the late Qing period, but were either eradicated or repressed following the May Fourth transformation. In challenging the orthodox view of May Fourth literature as the beginning of modern Chinese literature, this thesis provides many insights for studying late Qing literature.

Over the years, however, challenges have arisen to Wang's thesis, in particular regarding its concept of "modernity." Disparaging the May Fourth pursuit of (literary) modernity, Wang persistently contends that in their effort to save and change China, writers of the period passionately and blindly embraced any "newness" from the Western world, yet their "discourse of the modern" was less modern than that of the late Qing period, which was imbued with an energetic spirit of experimentation. Yet if the modern or modernity only refers to the new and the innovative, we might say the modern has appeared numerous times in human history, and the term therefore becomes vacuous.

The crucial point lies in identifying modernity. Anthony Giddens defines it as the emergence of industrialisation, imperialism, nation-states, etc.,

---

① Best, S., Kellner, D., *Postmodern Theory : Critical Interrogations*, Houndmills: Palgrave Macmillan, 1991.

② Wang, D. D., *Fin-de-siecle Splendor : Repressed Modernities of Late Qing Fiction*, 1849-1911, Stanford: Stanford University Press, 1997.

terms that for the most part refer to concrete institutions or historical phenomena,[1] while Jameson connects it with the new, capitalist mode of production.[2] In terms of cultural modernity, the "modernness" of the May Fourth period lies in the spread and entrenchment of modern Western ideas (science, democracy, liberty, equality, individualism, etc.), which formed the base on which intellectuals envisioned a modern world for the Chinese. In the West, modern ideas had become institutionalised in the course of fundamental social, political, and cultural changes over hundreds of years; for China, the pursuit of modernity as new set of social and economic as well as political and cultural institutions by which to reorganise the nation and society in a belated industrial stage had substantial significance: it was not blindly dreaming up something that was "new" in a merely discursive sense.

However, confusion between the substance and the discourse of the modern is evident throughout the book's discussion of four fictional sub-genres. In the analysis of chivalric and court-case fiction, on one hand, Wang acknowledges that the writers "continued under the spell of traditional concepts of legitimacy";[3] on the other hand, he proposes that "by flagrantly playing with the complicitous relationship between law and violence, between justice and terror," fiction "marks a radical re-thinking of legitimacy, whether imperial or ideological."[4] Rather than serving as a form of literary modernity, however, this cynicism showcases the bankruptcy of imperial legitimacy, calling for a modern replacement. Likewise, depraved novels are said to "anticipate a new epitome of concepts such as self, sexuality, and gender in the May Fourth period," contributing to the intense

---

① Giddens, A., *The Consequence of Modernity*, Stanford: Stanford University Press, 1991.

② Jameson, F., *A Singular Modernity: Essay on the Ontology of the Present*, London: Verso, 2002.

③ Wang, D. D., *Fin-de-siecle Splendor: Repressed Modernities of Late Qing Fiction*, 1849-1911, Stanford: Stanford University Press, 1997:121.

④ Wang, D. D., *Fin-de-siecle Splendor: Repressed Modernities of Late Qing Fiction*, 1849-1911, Stanford: Stanford University Press, 1997:120.

interest in desire in the latter period.[1] Yet the sexual promiscuity that imbues these novels neither offers nor heralds more equal gender relations. Thus, the word "anticipation" here does not connote a causal relationship, much less denote a modern form of literature. Here, the application of Foucauldian discourse of genealogy might be confounded with an examination of the origin itself.

Similarly, chivalric and court-case fiction is viewed as foreshadowing later concerns with patriotism, altruism, and the forms of brotherhood exemplified in revolutionary literature, a view that is also based on thematic similarity. Undoubtedly, certain elements of traditional ethics persisted in the later revolutionary era; yet this does not testify to their modernity, which is defined much more by qualitatively different elements that emerged during the epistemological shift. In a similar vein, the "moral ambiguity" illustrated through the cynicism, exaggeration, and vulgar disfiguration of reality in exposé novels is not in itself the manifestation of literary modernity,[2] but only reveals an anxiety mired in the Hegelian "unhappy consciousness" that leads to, but has not arrived at, the stage of new reason.

In a nutshell, while self-consciously westernised writing is only one of several forms of literary modernisation pursued at the time, this does not mean that the seeds of modernity would sprout from indigenous sources. The author's key concept of "involution," defined as the failure of a social or cultural pattern to transform itself into a new pattern, implies an inability to break away from tradition to achieve modernity. Put differently, most of the aforementioned novels stood at the crossroads of the traditional and the modern, but lost the competition with other emerging literary voices and experiments and were ultimately forgotten. This failure of metamorphosis from traditional to modern cannot simply be attributed to external social-political pressure, especially in light of the fact that the cultural market was

---

① Wang, D. D., *Fin-de-siecle Splendor: Repressed Modernities of Late Qing Fiction*, 1849-1911. Stanford: Stanford University Press, 1997:50, 52-61.

② Wang, D. D., *Fin-de-siecle Splendor: Repressed Modernities of Late Qing Fiction*, 1849-1911, Stanford: Stanford University Press, 1997:186.

still relatively autonomous and was not subject to complete political control in late Qing and Republican China.

Among the four subgenres, only science fantasy bears the clear imprint of modernity. These works appealed to readers by dramatising new social-political ideas that combined knowledge of modern Western concepts and indigenous utopian traditions to depict scenarios that were often unimaginable in that society. Most of them were written only after Liang Qichao's 1902 promotion of a "new novel," which aimed to propagate new Western ideas, especially political ideas calling for more enlightened and equal socio-political relations and the establishment of a "new morality." Thus, this brand of fiction does not demonstrate involution, but rather is the beginning of a revolution deriving its inspiration from imported "new" ideas to experiment with literary modernity.

Through discussions of Chinese representation and conception of history in the 20th century, David Wang's most recent work, *The Monster That Is History*, *History*, *Violence*, *and Fictional Writing in Twentieth-Century China* explores the violence and brutality of 20th-century China through a critique of enlightenment, rationality, and revolution as discourses or movements that re-envisage history in the image of a monster.[①] In a formal analysis that sees both literature and cultural phenomena as linguistically structured texts, David Wang tries to relate various sorts of violence to tradition, modernity, and Chinese identity, with a view to opening "a new critical dimension by looking into the rich repository of Chinese historiographical imagination."[②]

For this purpose, the author intentionally does not differentiate between the related subjects of history and representation, and modernity and monstrosity. This exercise is legitimised by the post-structuralist discourse to which David Wang subscribes, in which history is nothing but

---

① Wang, D. D., *The Monster That Is History: History, Violence, and Fictional Writing in Twentieth-Century China*, Berkeley: University of California Press, 2004.

② Wang, D. D., *The Monster That Is History: History, Violence, and Fictional Writing in Twentieth-Century China*, Berkeley: University of California Press, 2004:5.

representation; it also shows the imprint of postmodernism, in that "postmodernism is a response to a crisis of representation, and loss of faith in the truth-claims of representation."[①] Thus fiction is sometimes treated as journalistic reporting. Undoubtedly, handling texts as sociological documents or even historical fact lead to engaged and meticulous reading of various texts that debunks their ideological underpinnings, but the conflation of literary texts with historical documents is problematic, and can lead to erroneous conclusions.

Meanwhile, the question of the nature of modernity remains unclear; for instance, what constitutes the "modernity" of the violence, the "bodily rupture," or suicide that occurred in the modern era? The disenchantment with historically radical ruptures accentuates the critics' wholehearted embrace of continuity, yet this sometimes ends up creating another myth and neglecting the particular and the non-identical in history. The connection between violence and modern, and the entanglement of revolution and modernity, call for more historical explication. Relying on thematic resemblances alone might also lead to an over-deterministic and teleological narrative. For instance, if May Fourth literature was believed to be directly responsible for the rise of communist literature, the argument needs a historical study to explain how the former developed into the latter and under what political-cultural conditions.

The postmodern-postcolonial paradigm often engages in deconstructive analysis. The deconstruction of colonialism relies much on textual analysis, in which we continuously witness a shift from historical-social examination to discursive analysis, from interrogations pertaining to political economy towards questions regarding cultural identity.

Deconstruction, as it is commonly held, involves the close reading of texts in order to demonstrate that any given text has irreconcilably contradictory meanings. David Wang's first book, *Fictional Realism in Twentieth-Century China*, *Mao Dun*, *Lao She*, *Shen Congwen*, typically

---

① Dirlik, A., Contemporary Challenges to Marxism: Postmodernism, Postcolonialism, Globalization, *Amerasia Journal*, 2007, 33(3):4-5.

applies deconstructive skills to challenge officially-sanctioned hegemonic realism as a unified discourse,① and forcefully downplays mimesis in favour of mimicry. For instance, David Wang points out that Lao She's stories, rather than faithfully representing reality, "indulge in emotional spectacle, gestural hyperbole, and verbal extravagance,"② revealing through melodramatic or farcical literary technique the absurdity of Chinese reality. The book also stresses that reality is always mediated in the text:there is "a fantastic inscription of textuality and memory in a past which is always already mediated" in Shen Congwen's "self-reflexive display of nostalgia."③ By demonstrating that there are many polyphonic, often irreconcilably contradictory elements contained in the stories of these writers, the monolithic discourse of realism is dismantled.

What should also be pointed out is that the various "realistic representations" that emerged in specific historical and political circumstances profoundly self-problematise the claim of fidelity to the real. Lu Xun acknowledged that he was not totally faithful to the real; instead, in order to adhere to the order of the revolutionaries, he deliberately added a tinge of hope by contriving a detail at the end of his story—here the writer had self-consciously explored other possibilities of reality beyond any orthodox discourse of realism. Lao She's comic effects were also deliberately intended; he surely would not concern himself with any taboos of "realistic description." In this light, the monolithic discourse of realism did not have ideologically hegemonic effects on these writers; therefore, the object of deconstruction points more to the discourse of realism than to the "realistic" texts themselves. In short, the deconstructive impulse is led more by an urge to find textual evidence to support its predetermined argument than by

---

① Wang, D. D., *Fictional Realism in Twentieth-Century China, Mao Dun, Lao She, Shen Congwen*, New York:Columbia University Press, 1992.

② Wang, D. D., *Fictional Realism in Twentieth-Century China, Mao Dun, Lao She, Shen Congwen*, New York:Columbia University Press, 1992:15.

③ Wang, D. D., *Fictional Realism in Twentieth-Century China, Mao Dun, Lao She, Shen Congwen*, New York:Columbia University Press, 1992:21.

the motivation of literary study itself. The inadequate attention given to historical experience as the condition and context of the text can therefore result in a neo-formalist approach.

David Wang's three books can be seen as a coherent entity that applies postmodern epistemology to reflect on existent scholarship and remap the literary and cultural contours of modern China. They are coherent in the sense that the crisis of modernity leads to a challenge to its value-system, which furthermore leads to a re-evaluation of tradition; meanwhile, the loss of faith in modernity's truth-claims of representation leads to a re-examination of literary realism, which was the most-often used vehicle to represent reality.

As noted, postmodern-oriented postcolonial criticism disclaims any essentialised identities, and tends towards "a preoccupation with fluid, unstable, and hybrid identities of borderlands against the claims of stable political and cultural entities."[①] Thus Rey Chow sets out to deconstruct "Chineseness" in her various books, revealing the historical untenability of westernised third-world intellectuals' clinging to the illusion of return to a "pure ethnic origin."[②] In *Primitive Passions: Visuality, Sexuality, Ethnography, and Contemporary Chinese Cinema*, especially, the myth of origin as a traditionalist, essentialist discourse is legitimately debunked. But the critique often stops short of further explicating historical experience apart from discourse-deconstruction. For instance, if, as Rey Chow acknowledges, subjectivity "is not individual but an effect of historical forces that are beyond any individuated consciousness,"[③] where this collective-based consciousness lies needs to be clarified.

Postcolonial criticism often collaborates with Western feminism to

---

① Dirlik, A., Contemporary Challenges to Marxism: Postmodernism, Postcolonialism, Globalization, *Amerasia Journal*. 2007, 33(3):5.

② Chow, R., *Primitive Passions: Visuality, Sexuality, Ethnography, and Contemporary Chinese Cinema*, New York:Columbia University Press, 1995.

③ Chow, R., *Woman and Chinese Modernity: The Politics of Reading between West and East*, Minnesota and Oxford:University of Minnesota Press, 1991:xii.

assert its critical edge. In her path-breaking (in terms of application of critical theory) work *Women and Chinese Modernity: The Politics of Reading between West and East*, which is an interpretation of history based on literary analysis with the instrument of power-relationship analysis, Rey Chow argues that women were "othered" for exclusion from the nation by the modernising drive that claimed to enlighten and liberate Chinese women. As a reflection, Rey Chow proposes the possibility of a reconstruction emphasising the female body and sexuality that are repressed in world history.[1]

These arguments are inspired by a (postcolonial) feminist stance that asserts women's rights and calls attention to their repressed status. But what feminist discourse often overlooks is that the well-being of women is always subject to socio-economic conditions. Instead of exploring real historical experience, it often projects later insights back onto the historical site. A case in point is Rey Chow's argument that when young Chinese men in May Fourth theatres adopted Western feminism to substantiate their attacks against the Confucian establishment, it was "another way in which Western fathers subjugated and colonized non-Western women."[2] Here the efforts of progressive Chinese intellectuals to liberate women from traditional oppression are not sufficiently acknowledged. Rather than assuming that there should be a postmodern feminism actively working at that time, it is necessary for us to keep the historical context in mind and focus on historical investigation; for example, to inquire why and how women were excluded from history, and under what conditions they could have avoided exclusion; or, in what historical circumstances the open staging of the female body and sexuality was possible, if it was really possible. Leaving these questions unexamined, merely holding the postmodern feminist stance verges precariously on anachronism.

---

[1]　Chow, R., *Woman and Chinese Modernity: The Politics of Reading between West and East*, Minnesota and Oxford: University of Minnesota Press, 1991: xii.

[2]　Chow, R., *Primitive Passions: Visuality, Sexuality, Ethnography, and Contemporary Chinese Cinema*, New York: Columbia University Press, 1995: 138.

The other side of this ahistorical critique of women's roles in society based on the contemporary standard of postcolonial perspective is aggrandisement. Nicole Huang's work *Women, War, Domesticity: Shanghai Literature and Popular Culture of the* 1940*s*, which studies Shanghai literature and popular culture of the 1940s, inflates the role of women writers in the occupied area to the extent of lionising them as the heroes of cultural construction in the era, and argues that their production was a cultural resistance and ethnography of the Chinese people.[①] Essentially middle-brow in nature, this new boudoir literature, focusing on life in a certain class stratum, has much less to do with ethnography; it is located in a different position within genre hierarchies in comparison to the literature of cultural resistance.

In short, this trend of postmodern methodology with postcolonial critique has a tendency to embrace new historicism, which ostensibly reads texts in its contexts. Still, this study of context is not an exploration of historical genesis but an interweaving of various personal relationships, debates, memoirs, and diaries, with a tendency to project the scholars' historically-conditioned vantage-point back to the historical objects. Inspiration from the postmodern-postcolonial critical paradigm has brought many insights into modern Chinese studies; however, the various flawed arguments that have resulted also underscore the necessity to recall and reflect upon the validity and applicability of theories when applied to the study of modern Chinese literature and history.

## 二、Studying Works within the "Field of Cultural Production"

The key to genuine historicising is to explore the historical conditions and situation that explain the origin and development of a historical phenomenon. A case in point is the study of literary institutions, which are constantly changing in the frame of a cultural field. This kind of

---

① Huang, N., *Women, War, Domesticity: Shanghai Literature and Popular Culture of the* 1940*s*, Leiden and Boston: Brill Publishers, 2005.

contextualised study can avoid the pitfalls of postmodern, imaginative historiography.

More than three decades ago, Leo Lee took notes of the structural context of literary activities. One feature of his classic *The Romantic Generation of Modern Chinese Writers* that distinguishes it from previous works is its interest in literary industries.[①] In his delineation of the cultural arena and the rise of professional writers within it, Leo Lee's work implied the idea that a shared understanding of the role of the writer and the function of literature constitutes a cultural institution.

The attention to cultural industries was continued in Perry Link's seminal work studying "Mandarin Duck and Butterfly" writers.[②] Edward Gunn's *Unwelcome Muse: Chinese Literature in Shanghai and Beijing*, which studies Chinese literature in Shanghai and Beijing during the Resistance War, also investigates this cultural field,[③] but remains a form of traditional historical account by generally defining the field in terms of geographical area. Political conditions are only treated as background, and Edward Gunn disavows any interests in the sociology of literature. The 1990s has seen the emergence of a clearer intent to delve into specific historical formations and practices based on studies of relational nexus and structural context.

In *High Culture Fever: Politics, Aesthetics, and Ideology in Deng's China*, Jing Wang argues that her study of cultural experiments in contemporary China intends "to examine it in the changing context that yields different, and perhaps conflicting, vantage points";[④] this, however, is less a study of literature per se than of cultural politics. Lydia Liu in

---

① Lee, L. O., *The Romantic Generation of Modern Chinese Writers*, Cambridge, Mass.: Harvard University Press, 1973.

② Link, P., *Mandarin Ducks and Butterflies: Popular Fiction in Early Twentieth-Century Chinese Cities*, Berkeley: University of California Press, 1981.

③ Gunn, E., *Unwelcome Muse: Chinese Literature in Shanghai and Beijing*, 1937-1945, New York: Columbia University Press, 1980.

④ Wang, J., *High Culture Fever: Politics, Aesthetics, and Ideology in Deng's China*, Berkeley: University of California Press, 1986:6.

*Translingual Practice: Literature, National Culture, and Translated Modernity—China* also aims to "enter the changing field of meaning in relation to other discursive constructs" and believes that "it is only with reference to the performability of such relations that a particular construction is meaningful in its context."[①] Nevertheless, the various subjects in her project, "literature, national culture, and translated modernity," are different in nature.

In recent years, the tendency to integrate studies of cultural industry, or broadly speaking, industrialised culture, with analysis of literary works and cultural phenomena has become more salient, demonstrating increasing attention to the perspective of cultural production as a "field." Leo Lee's new book on Shanghai's modern urban culture is one of the first studies of this kind, aiming to explore "what may be called the cultural imaginary, which was a contour of collective sensibilities and significations resulting from cultural production."[②] For this purpose, Leo Lee not only continues with his earlier interest in the industrial aspects of cultural production, but goes a step further in heeding "both the social and the institutional context" of production, such as the cultural and industrial institutions of the publishing and film industries. This approach sees urban culture as the result of a process of production as well as consumption, which involves the development of new public structures and spaces that serve as material background for new forms of cultural activity.

Nicole Huang's *Women, War, Domesticity: Shanghai Literature and Popular Culture of the* 1940s follows the same direction. It studies Shanghai literature and popular culture during the period of Japanese occupation in the 1940s, and includes an examination of the emergence of the women's print culture, especially the features of women's popular magazines. Its contextual discussions underline the analytical importance of the "field of cultural

---

① Liu, L., *Translingual Practice: Literature, National Culture, and Translated Modernity—China*, 1900-1937, Stanford: Stanford University Press, 1995: 197.

② Lee, L. O., *Shanghai Modern: The Flowering of a New Urban Culture in China*, 1930-1945, Cambridge: Harvard University Press, 1999: 63.

production."

However, lest literary studies become sociology, it is important to connect texts and contexts organically rather than mechanically. Currently, the two theoretical foci in the field, namely modernity and literature (or literary modernity) as an institution, play mediating roles in this connection: by focusing on modern literature as a new socio-cultural institution, they offer genuine means to achieve this synthesis.

Shu-mei Shih's methodology in *The Lure of the Modern : Writing Modernism in Semicolonial China* is a contextual study combined with an intrinsic analysis. She states that her intention is to chart "the interrelatedness between these extrinsic conditions and the intrinsic aspects of writing style, particularly in terms of the stylistic and aesthetic propensities."[①] For this, she has tried to define the positions of the writers in the context of the field of cultural production in order to contextualise, for instance, the rise of jingpai writing by reinvestigating the immediate post-May Fourth cultural formation. Nevertheless, the way she ties these two aspects together, through the different attitudes of writers towards cosmopolitan culture and colonial culture, leaves out many writers who belong to the two schools she studies but who do not show the same degree of "modernist techniques." Also, this framework, on its own, cannot account for textual features.

With the coming of a media-centred age, media studies have become a favourite subject, and one in which the tendency to study cultural production in its own right is particularly evident. For instance, film studies of recent years have reached a consensus that the aesthetic features of individual films result from the mixing of directors' own idiosyncratic input with the forces of contemporary industrial modes of production, and therefore they cannot be considered solely on the basis of auteur theory. Hence Zhang Zhen's *An Amorous History of the Silver Screen : Shanghai Cinema*, which studies early Chinese cinema, claims to combine "aesthetic analysis and semiotic

---

① Shih, S., *The Lure of the Modern : Writing Modernism in Semicolonial China*, 1917-1937, Berkeley: University of California Press, 2001:257.

*exegesis in relation to both larger textual or intertextual systems.*"① This should be regarded as a breakthrough in Chinese film studies，which previously either focused on state policies or merely discussed directors' individual styles. But while Zhang Zhen acknowledges that "the sociological and historical landscape I delineate along the way should not be construed as the separate means or the end of the cinematic experience as the two are inexorably interwoven，" her analytic procedure follows Hans Ulrich Gumbrecht's proposal，tying in "the interests in textual 'meaning-constitution'" with "the concern for the body and other physical and material properties of signification."② From the perspective of this methodology，multifaceted film culture contributed to "the production of a sociocorporeal sensorium and a broadly defined vernacular movement."③ The method is still a corporeal-materialist approach that is situated mid-way towards a historical hermeneutics，with the result that Zhang Zhen's concept of a "vernacular modernism" does not fully account for the aesthetic characteristics of early Chinese films.

A few works have more or less successfully accomplished the two-end interpretation. The issue of literature as an institution in the field of cultural production in terms of the sociology of culture is the principal concern of Michel Hockx's *Questions of Style*：*Literary Societies and Literary Journals in Modern China*，which studies modern literary societies and literary journals.④ The work most saliently focuses on the institutionalised aspects of cultural production. Michel Hockx is conscious of applying Pierre Bourdieu's theory of "field of cultural production" to analyse literary institutions. Instead of treating literature in an unmediated relationship with

---

① Zhang，Z.，*An Amorous History of the Silver Screen*：*Shanghai Cinema*，1896-1937，Chicago：University of Chicago Press，2005：xxviii.

② Zhang，Z.，*An Amorous History of the Silver Screen*：*Shanghai Cinema*，1896-1937，Chicago：University of Chicago Press，2005：xxviii-xxviv.

③ Zhang，Z.，*An Amorous History of the Silver Screen*：*Shanghai Cinema*，1896-1937，Chicago：University of Chicago Press，2005：xxx.

④ Hockx，M.，*Questions of Style*：*Literary Societies and Literary Journals in Modern China*，1911-1937，Leiden and Boston：Publishers Brill，2003.

society, Michel Hockx sees the field as a privileged context for interpreting literature. The study's use of the Bourdieusian terminology, such as habitus and hierarchies, and its attention to distinct trajectories of writers and their activities, opens a broader horizon on literary activity and production.

The major invention here is a new concept of style, which refers to a conglomeration of features involving language (form and content), lifestyle, style of organisation of literary activity and production, and style of publication.[①] This concept is helpful in switching attention to the collective features of literary production, but its framework may also be overloaded with too many heterogeneous elements, making it difficult to analyse either individual works or general phenomena.[②] This departure from Pierre Bourdieu's theory, which was intended as a development through adaptation, might not have entirely attained its goal.

A minor problem, acknowledged by the author, is the work's emphasis "on literary practice, on the activities of the people involved in literary production, rather than on analysis of the text they produced."[③] Put other way, his analysis complements textual analysis rather than replacing it. Yet, by leaving out the consideration of individual texts, its value in judging literarity, or literariness, as Pierre Bourdieu in his theory has promised us, is greatly decreased. Generally speaking, however, Michel Hockx's shift in focus from author studies to the economic aspects of literary production, as well as the readers' role as consumers, pilots a new, heuristic, and sociological direction.

Within the distinct trend towards studies of "field of cultural production," Yvonne Chang's *Literary Culture in Taiwan:Martial Law to*

---

① Hockx, M., *Questions of Style:Literary Societies and Literary Journals in Modern China*, 1911-1937, Leiden and Boston:Publishers Brill, 2003:13.

② It is made more confused by its integration into a larger concept of "normative form," defined as "a constellation of style, language, context and personality." Hockx, M., *Questions of Style:Literary Societies and Literary Journals in Modern China*, 1911-1937, Leiden and Boston:Publishers Brill, 2003:221.

③ Hockx, M., *Questions of Style:Literary Societies and Literary Journals in Modern China*, 1911-1937, Leiden and Boston:Publishers Brill, 2003:6.

*Market Law* tries to address these shortcomings by comprehensively and proficiently applying Pierre Bourdieu's theory.[①] First，changes in the political parameters of Taiwan occupy an important place in her discussions of the shifts in Taiwan's cultural field，which wrought profound changes in its literature. Second，Yvonne Chang makes a careful categorisation of different positions that correlate with different types of political/cultural capital and interplay with each other. Third，in studying the paradigm-shift of cultural production since the 1980s，she points out that the entire cultural field has gradually freed from political subjugation and gained relative autonomy，with a new cultural principle of legitimacy superseding political principle. Meanwhile，writers' production was increasingly subjected to the mandate of market forces as a "heterogeneous principle." Fourth，she investigates both elite literature and popular cultural products and explores their mutual influences and penetration. In elaborating these ideas，the book focuses on such key concepts as hegemonic discourse，hierarchy in genre and style，and autonomous/heteronomous principles of hierarchisation. The last but not the least distinct feature of the work is that Yvonne Chang incorporates ideological analysis，in particular class analysis，in her discussion of the different positions. In short，Yvonne Chang adds depth to the scope opened up by Michel Hockx.

The application of the theory of "field of cultural production" to the study of literary arts can explain the production of texts within certain political circumstances and in specific cultural fields，and to a certain extent literary characteristics of texts，and thus has received increasingly favourable consideration in recent years. Nevertheless，its exclusive focus on the relatively-fixed structure of the field prevents it from serving as a dynamic model that explains historical experience，and therefore from fully explicating the aesthetic details of cultural works，or how individual works can transform the field. In order to grasp structural transformations in the cultural fields in their historical motions，therefore，this methodology needs

---

① Chang，Y. S.，*Literary Culture in Taiwan：Martial Law to Market Law*，New York：Columbia University Press，2004.

to work in tandem with another perspective that has gradually emerged as a third trend in our field.

## 三、The Practice of Historical Hermeneutics

Marston Anderson's *The Limits of Realism : Chinese Fiction in the Revolutionary Period* can be seen as the beginning of this new theoretical direction.[①] Through "a kind of archaeological investigation," Marston Anderson explores the connotations of realism as situated in theoretical, and more importantly, historical contexts, thus differentiating it from various other kinds of realism (classical, critical, revolutionary, and socialist) in other periods. It goes a step further towards a historical explanation.

A flaw of the book is that it falls short of fully explaining the metamorphoses of realistic writings. Marston Anderson follows the conventional argument that modes of realistic writing changed because the "old realism came finally to seem powerless to repair the cultural schism that opened in China after the fall of the traditional world order."[②] This explanation is only a partial and subjective observation. Perhaps it is less the intrinsic shortcomings of any brand of realism per se than historical forces that spurred these variations in style. Here, the historical experience is not merely the context, but more fundamentally becomes the subtext. For instance, the reason for the disintegration of old realism with the emergence of the crowd and then the masses is not merely the force-play within the texts, but needs to be investigated by studying the historical experience crystallised and articulated in the texts. In these texts, the individual is first inundated by the ignorant "crowd," and then the crowd is replaced by the revolutionary "masses." In other words, explaining aesthetic details of texts requires combining analyses of literary contents and historical subtexts in an

---

① Anderson, M., *The Limits of Realism : Chinese Fiction in the Revolutionary Period*, Berkeley: University of California Press, 1990.

② Anderson, M., *The Limits of Realism : Chinese Fiction in the Revolutionary Period*, Berkeley: University of California Press, 1990:202.

organic way.

Wang Ban's *The Sublime Figure of History : Aesthetics and Politics in Twentieth-Centary China* proposes that a "sublime figure" defines and circumscribes the making of Maoist revolutionary discourse,[①] revealing hidden links among official ideology, mass psychology, and individual aesthetic experiences. Wang Ban's psychoanalytic approach, which delves into psychosomatic aspects to account for the interplay between the political and the aesthetic, is both refreshing and problematic, mainly because the Freudian and Lacanian models of psychological interpretation cannot be assumed to be historically scientific and universal. Wendy Larson thus challenges Wang Ban's holistic assumption that erotic desire was transformed into revolutionary passion under Maoism, which is the key premise of the author's whole elaboration.[②] Consequently, although the book ostensibly refutes the prevalent cold-war assumption that a mechanical brain-washing took place in Mao's China, it in fact never departs from this mode of thinking (e.g., he also holds that social ritual mimics "the psychic operation of hypnosis"),[③] but merely contributes to a more psychoanalytical affirmation of the thesis. Why and how the sublime effects were widely produced and accepted, and the collateral issue, why and how they were debunked and became disenchanted, are the content of real historical experience, but are not treated. Wang Ban's linking of the individual body and the body politic mainly by philosophical and literary discussion, but not by historicising the doubtable causal link, causes a short circuit in his line of reasoning.

Indeed, organically integrating internal analysis and external explication requires attending to the dialectics of form and content. In this regard, the

---

① Wang, B., *The Sublime Figure of History : Aesthetics and Politics in Twentieth-Century China*, Stanford : Stanford University Press, 1997.

② Larson, W., Review : the sublime figure of history, *Comparative Literature*, 1998,50(2):191.

③ Wang, B., *The Sublime Figure of History : Aesthetics and Politics in Twentieth-Century China*, Stanford : Stanford University Press, 1997:217.

same author's new book, *Illuminations from the Past: Trauma, Memory and History in Modern China*, progresses further in this direction.[①]

The book can be read as a succinct cultural history of modern China in the past century. As historical catastrophes characterise modern China, its literary writing is underscored by traumatic experience. The author's approach is to see through the textual surface into the historical depth by analysing how literary expressions articulate the historical unconscious. Thus, he either examines the modes of representing catastrophic histories in Xiao Hong's novels, or explores the decline of history and the loss of communal value in the age of commercialisation in Wang Anyi's (auto-) biographical novel, both of which chronicle the historical development of Chinese modernity. This approach is not only helpful for understanding how the texts represent history, but is also instrumental in exploring how historicity can be textualised and visualised. This analysis relies not on discussions based on a historiographical imagination, but on the articulation of the historicity of representation and the representation of history through the mutual mediation of texts and historical experience. In this way, it represents a departure from Wang Ban's earlier methodology and a step closer to historical hermeneutics.

To pursue historical hermeneutics is to inquire why and how different class consciousness (refracted by the habitus and in the writing practices of individual writers) and historical conditions circumscribed writers to recognise the political situation and propelled them to carry out their aesthetic ideal, leaving traceable signatures and imprints in their works waiting to be deciphered. To put it in another way, the semiotic system of literary texts is broken down to show history and politics, just as history and politics are examined to make them speak to the semiotic system.

In this respect, Zhang Xudong's *Chinese Modernism in the Era of Reforms: Cultural Fever, Avant-Garde Fiction, and the New Chinese*

---

① Wang, B., *Illuminations from the Past: Trauma, Memory, and History in Modern China*, Stanford: Stanford University Press, 2004.

*Cinema* provides a reference point for this double analytic movement.[①] The work is a discerning analysis of theoretical debates, modernist poetry, fiction, and Chinese new cinema in the 1980s. It applies a dialectical framework to the relationship between aesthetic modernism and political and economic modernity, which contextualises the internal structure of aesthetic texts.

The most promising prospectus that this method brings to literary studies is evident first and last at the textual level: by inexorably historicising, it can explain the most idiosyncratic aesthetic details. In an analysis of the image of the hero "Grandpa" in the film *Red Sorghum*, for instance, ZhangXudong sees him as an expression of historical "truth-content": while on the one hand he embodies "a new, far more dynamic historical agency, whose recognised value is unmistakably spelled out as commodity" with even a fascist impulse in the reform era, he on the other hand "transgresses not only peasant ethics but the capitalist rationale of the social organisation of labor and profit making as well," with its "source of productivity and enjoyment" coming from "a transformed and motivated communal life, from a deep-seated value system reinforced by a new enthusiasm for action and adventure, from something benign that, once reactivated, would create a spectacular world of its own,"[②] which articulates the political unconscious of the new era. In short, it is an expression of an ideology as well as a utopia. Here historical hermeneutics translate, or decode, a work (either realistic or modernist) as an account (either through conscious expression or unconscious crystallisation and articulation) of historical experience. Through a virtuoso hermeneutical drill, the socio-political, the historical, and the aesthetically textual finally illuminate each other.

This approach carries over to Zhang Xudong's most recent book,

---

① Zhang, X., *Chinese Modernism in the Era of Reforms: Cultural Fever, Avant-Garde Fiction, and the New Chinese Cinema*, Durham: Duke University Press, 1999.

② Zhang, X., *Chinese Modernism in the Era of Reforms: Cultural Fever, Avant-Garde Fiction, and the New Chinese Cinema*, Durham: Duke University Press, 1999:324.

*Postsocialism and Cultural Politics: China in the Last Decade of the Twentieth Century*, which can be seen as the continuation of the former book in its discussion of China's culture since the 1990s.[①] Zhang Xudong employs here a new term, "postsocialism," to define contemporary China's social-economic as well as cultural configuration. Chinese postsocialism is articulated in the cultural arena mainly through the discourses of postmodernism and nationalism, which not only play discursive functions, but also are mediated by the coexistence of multiple modes of production and socio-cultural norms, thus mixing different "temporal-historical structures."[②] Aside from discussing intellectual discourses vis-a-vis the national and global overdeterminations of the making of the 1990s intellectual field, Zhang Xudong analyses various narrative possibilities of this postsocialism. Examples include the relationship between mourning and allegory in Wang Anyi's literary works, between the "demonic realism" and the "socialist market economy" in Mo Yan's fiction, and between the construction of a collective memory and the assertion of a unique cultural/political legitimacy in the cinematic discourse of two films. Throughout the book the analysis triumphantly demonstrates "the way in which readings of novels, films, social and political texts, and the polemics around them" is "positioned to illuminate each other."[③]

These three methodological trends bear out the fact that in recent years the concepts of "modernity," "modern," and "modernism" have become self-renewing focuses for scholarly contestation in this field.[④] In various ways, scholars try to explicate the intricate connectedness, or organic relationship, between modern China's political-social modernity and literary modernity.

---

① Zhang, X., *Postsocialism and Cultural Politics: China in the Last Decade of the Twentieth Century*, Durham: Duke University Press, 2008.

② Zhang, X., *Postsocialism and Cultural Politics: China in the Last Decade of the Twentieth Century*, Durham: Duke University Press, 2008:188.

③ The remarks are made by Fredric Jameson; see the back cover of the book.

④ Wang, D. D., A Report on Modern Chinese Literary Studies in the English Speaking World, *Harvard Asia Quarterly*, 2005,9(112).

The "Chinese modern" was a process of nation-state building to which more than a century of revolution and modernisation efforts contributed. The contention for the Chinese modern involved not only struggles between different political forces, but also a vying for legitimacy between different versions of modern Chinese literature as conceptual and social institutions. Chinese literary modernity thus contains not only different literary narratives such as enlightenment narrative and national-salvation narrative, but also involves the establishment and institutionalisation of divergent modern modes of cultural production, and the development of differing forms of modern popular culture. In an effort to study these diversified conditions and contending voices coexisting in the tumultuous age of modern China, with its rapid and radical restructuring of cultural fields and shifting paradigms of cultural production, the application of Pierre Bourdieu's theory of cultural production has in recent years been gradually combined with the approach of historical hermeneutics to evolve towards a more dialectical and comprehensive interpretive methodology in studying modern Chinese literature and culture.

## 四、Structural Outline of This Book

The title of the present book points to the thesis which constantly appears in this collection. The five parts of the main body showcase the application of historical hermeneutics in studying modern Chinese literary production.

In the first part "Realism Unbounded," I analyze two significant modern Chinese female writers, Xiao Hong and Ding Ling, whose literary outputs both concern the predicament of Chinese "new women" and their ways of emancipation in modern China. Thanks to the differing social-political environments they lived in, the writings assume very differing outlooks. In the Japanese-occupied area of Northern China, Xiao Hong's fiction shows the hard, tragic life Chinese (rural) women in particular and the masses in general had endured; whereas in the KMT-controlled area and the CCP-dominated regions, the changing contents and styles of Ding Ling's stories reveal the ever-shifting social concerns and political strategies for her to deal with the dilemma of Chinese " new women" within diversified cultural-political frameworks and structural institutions. The diversified life trajectories of the two writers also deliver two distinct paths a Chinese "new woman" could take and their entirely different outcomes.

The second part discusses two popular writers in the 1940s of China, Wumingshi and Xu Xu, whose stories are said to be breaking through the boundaries between elite literature and folk culture. Through an ideological dissection of the textual evidences, I suggest that either the "modern literati novel" or the "modern tales of the strange" they create inexorably shows the impossibility of realizing the ideal of cosmopolitanism in the era, which led these liberalist intellectuals fall into desperation and orchestrate these phantasmogoric works for psychological compensation. The result of their literary fantasies could neither be simply called romanticism nor modernism.

Part three would delve deeply into a renowned writer Eileen Chang's fictional works to find the cause of the symptom of cultural nihilism within the ostensible cross-cultural transaction appeared in her "boudoir stories," which shows a strong matrimonial complex and identity anxiety. It is not merely a personal dilemma or a gender-related issue, but brought about by the vulnerability of a particular class in a merciless era.

From the aforementioned parts, we have witnessed that the divergent narrative strategies arise from diversified class habitus and political consciousness. Thus part four takes two case studies to further exemplify this rule. Under the middle class' or bourgeois consciousness, Mei Niang's fiction shows the double pitfalls that Chinese "middle class" women inexorably fell into in the occupied regions, whereas Ang Lee's rendition of Eileen Chang's story *Lust*, *Caution* orchestrates an idiosyncratic ethnography through piling up the agony and predicament of this particular class.

Realism is unbounded and multi-dimensional, depending on the varying social-political circumstances; modernism and romanticism in its Chinese soil would sometimes transform to be "modern literati novel" or "modern tales of the strange" out of an idiosyncratic "political unconscious"; in an ostensible cross-cultural transaction, traditional "boudoir stories" containing matrimonial anxiety would also transmogrify to bring out a modern sense of cultural nihilism; under certain class consciousness, narration of the life of the middle class would harbour idiosyncratic cultural-political connotation. Ultimately, it is the "subjectivity" of writers that overdetermines the production of their literary outputs. However, the nature of the subjectivity is worthy of further diagnosis. Thus the last part of this manuscript would go ahead to undertake an examination of two cultural moves in the 1940s: in the "liberated area," Zhao Shuli produced "problem stories" for the sake of peasants' aesthetic disposition, which was taken as an excellent embodiment of Chairman Mao's proposition for establishing a "national form." They both envisage a profound scenario of building a homogenous literary community in order to advance their particular cultural-political agenda.

As a conclusion, I would reflect upon the origin of modern Chinese literature, in particular musing on the historical specificities of "high-brow," "low-brow," and "middle-brow" literatures in modern China. After exploring the issues from both chronological and synchronic perspectives, it suggests that these concepts are not only related with canonization, legitimation, and cultural hegemony; but in modern China, they are also closely tied in with the issue of class structure. In particular, Chinese "middle-brow" literature is intimately correlated with a sentimentalization of an essentially political issue, which is a displacement of social-economic elements and a moralization of conservative move. Throughout the critical inquiry, we witness that the various ways to negotiate with or to design the "new culture" that the writers faced were expressed as, and incarnated in, the form and the content of their stories through the refraction of their class consciousness, thus the three key terms of subjectivity, class consciousness and identity are closely tied in with each other when we read into the texts to appreciate the cultural politics of modern Chinese literary production.

# Part I.

## Realism Unbounded

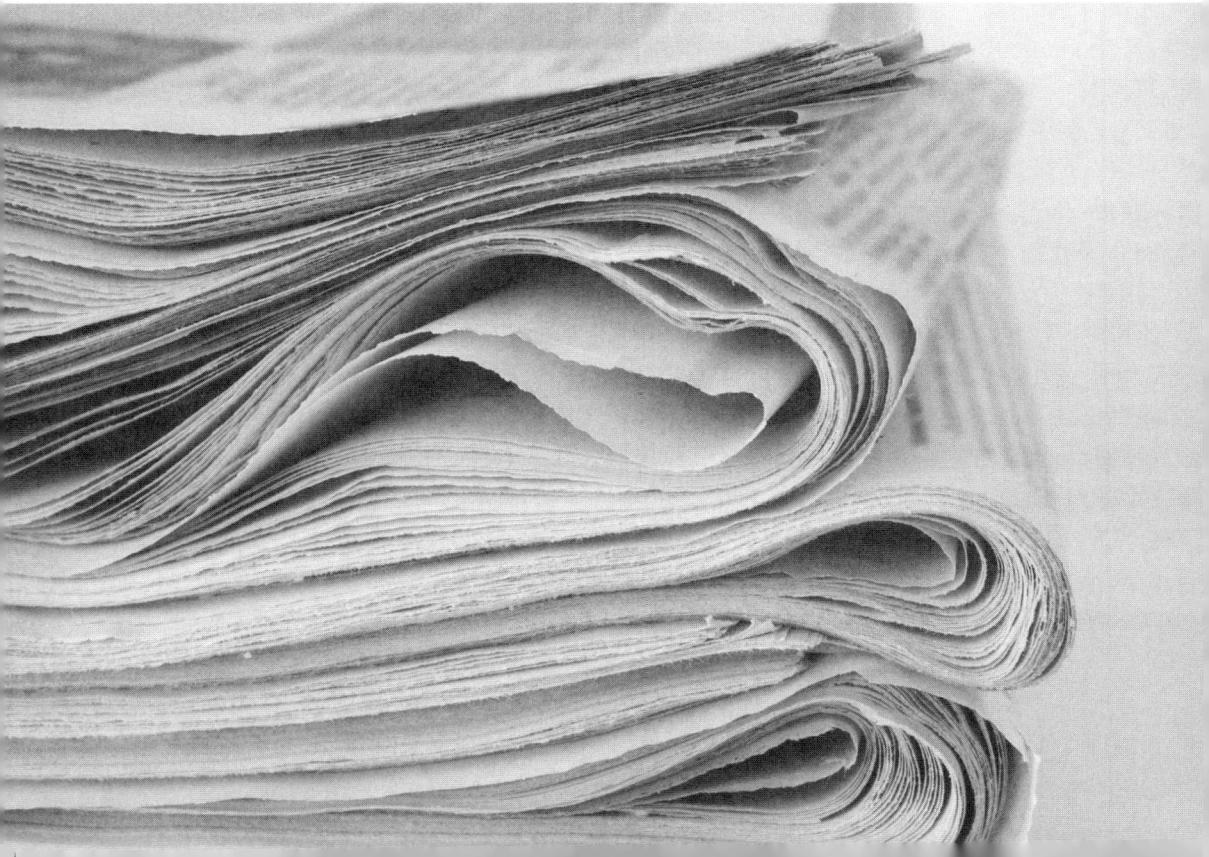

# Chapter One   A Homeless Soul and a Misplaced Nostalgia Exiled Experience and Xiao Hong's Diasporic Literature

2012 marked the centennial of birthday of the famed modern Chinese female writer Xiao Hong (1911-1942). Whereas she is always regarded as one of the most talented writers (or even the utmost one) of the "group of Northeast writers" (东北作家群), the appraisement of her writing of fiction is not only susceptible to the vicissitude of political situation and cultural atmosphere, but also is differing with different critical perspectives. This to some extent is attributable to the fact that she is a writer of multiple hues and talents: she had been the core member of the "Lu Xun faction" (and later the "Hu Feng group") of leftist writers, and one of the originators of the "Resistance Literature," and was also the pioneer of the "poeticized stories" (诗化小说) popular in the latter half of the 1940s; she even tried the water of "satire literature," a trend in her time.

But in the English world, apart from Howard Goldblatt's 1976 biographical study of the writer, until now there is no significant works studying this important writer. Howard Goldblatt's work integrates the writer's life experience with her literary creation, but this was done in a less integrated way. [1] The book is divided into seven chapters. The first six chapters follow her trajectories of exile, and the title of each chapter is mostly geographical name; only the final chapter is clearly devoted to "Xiao Hong and Her Craft." This biographical framework, as well as its analytical tool which is mainly the traditional approach of New Criticism, might not reach the objective of fully investigating the writer's literary achievement.

---

[1]   Goldblatt, H., *Hsiao Hung*, Boston: Twayne Publishers, 1976.

Yet as a pioneering research, it did a fabulous job of effectively ushering in another talented writer into the pantheon of modern Chinese literature.

This chapter, by dialectically correlating the writer's works with her life experience and the historical conjuncture, tries to offer a new interpretation of the writer's literary creativity. I choose this way of contextualization not merely because the writer's literary trajectory, including the frequent shifting of her intellectual-political positions between humanist and humanitarian concerns, is closely tied in with the real occurrences throughout her personal life—most of her stories can find their direct origins in, or inspirations from, her individual sufferings in society; but also both the ingenuities and shortcomings of her writings can ultimately find their explanations from the subtext of the historical experience. Only through this procedure, can we understand why she was often wavering between differing choices and oftentimes apparently made miscalculated decisions, which finally cost her life; and why this incompetence in recognizing social-political conflicts and contradictions sometimes left fissures in her works, which then became thematically incoherent. Based on this study, I suggest that not only is her tragic experience a microcosm of the besieged "new women" in particular, and the radical epochal change in general, but the dilemma of her always miscalculated choices and the predicament of her literary creation incisively show the divergence between the May Fourth "New Literature" and the "post-New Literature."

## 一、The Beginning of an Oppressed "New Woman"

In 1911, the year when the last "feudalist" Qing dynasty was overthrown, Xiao Hong was born in a county of Heilongjiang province in Northeast China. The county was a typical Chinese town of the time. The quintessential feature is its backwardness and the conservativeness of its residents due to the long-term isolation of this small town and the ingrained peasant mentality of the populace. The then named Zhang Naiying was the first child of her well-to-do landlord-gentry family, but she did not enjoy the prestige this identity might confer upon her. Instead, in her memory, all family members—except her grandfather—were not friendly to her. No matter whether the writer's own accounts of her father and her stepmother are facts or simply a refraction of (and so a distortion by) an innocent child's eyes, they indicate her alienated experience with the family members; she apparently felt her needs for love and warmth. It was her grandfather that introduced her to classical poetry, during which she showed a particular taste for nature poems.

But her grandfather needed to spend a lot of time taking care of his sick wife, so Zhang Naiying often experienced loneliness. Nevertheless, when she grew up, she still claimed that "I learned from my grandfather that besides coldness and hatred, life also had warmth and love. And so, for me there is a perpetual longing and pursuit to find this warmth and love."[①] In addition to her personal distress, this desire was also cultivated by her direct association with the sufferings of peasant folks around her. However, this longing and pursuit was often stymied and frustrated in the writer's short life, as men's maltreatments and betrayals more often than not went hand in hand with her. This unfortunate experience only strengthened her longing for individual security and personal happiness. Like many writers of the time, she received the baptism of the momentous New Culture Movement in her young age. She took part in demonstrations against the Japanese encroachments when she was in the First Municipal Girls' Middle School of Harbin. This doesn't necessarily show that she had a strong political consciousness, but her patriotic awareness was largely propelled by the popular New Culture concepts at the time, including radical anti-traditionalism, anti-imperialism, and gender equality and freedom in marriage. She also cultivated a fondness for the "new literature," especially those of romantic writings, by her reading of the literary supplement of a local new-styled newspaper *International Gazette* (《国际协报》). But when the idealistic, innocent girl implemented the ideas in reality, she met her first disaster in life. Just before she graduated from the school, to work against the arranged marriage by her parents to a warlord's son, she left

---

①  萧红:《永久的憧憬与追求》,《报告(创刊号)》,1937 年 1 月 10 日,74.

home and school with a young man. But when she went together with him to Beijing several months later, she found that he had wife and child. She was pregnant now and was abandoned. Economic predicament forced her to return to her home in January the next year. Seen as a shame of her family, she was imprisoned in her house for ten months. When she escaped from the family, her father declared publicly the severance of her family relations. The life after this was too harsh for a woman at the time: she found no help from relatives, friends, and schoolmates in Harbin. Feeling that there was a great distance between her and the outside world because of this betrayal by her father, lover, and friends, she felt alienated and disillusioned. After Nora left home, there was no much room to roam: Chinese society was not rationalized enough to offer enough social space for women to explore, as a result they had few choices. It was also around this time that the Mukden Incident broke out (on September 18th, 1931), but her sense of personal agony probably prevailed over this national tragedy at the time.

Her life after this was miserable: finding a cheap hotel run by a White Russian, she was still unable to pay her rent. Worse, she was addicted to opium and probably occasionally sold her body for life necessities. Arguably this was one instance of the cases that would happen, and which did happen, after Nora left home. Fortunately, the bleak outlook was turned around by the editors of the newspaper that she was fond of, to which she had written for help. Finding a pregnant woman trapped in a dire existence, they managed to deliver her out of the hands of the ruthless hotel proprietor. One of them is Xiao Jun (1907-1988), a writer from a peasant family of a small county of Liaoning, one of the three Northeast provinces, who soon became her lover.

## 二、Left-Leaning Stories with Strong Humanist Concerns

In 1933, Xiao Hong coworked with Xiao Jun to produce a collection of stories and essays, *Trudging*(《跋涉》). These stories generally can be read as leftist stories popular at the time. In *The Death of Wang Asao*(《王阿嫂的死》), the titled peasant woman is found not in the field, but in her bed as

she is seriously ill. She confesses to a sister Wang who comes to see her that
she was kicked by Landlord Zhang the day before because her pregnant body
forced her to take a rest in the field. "It's a karmic entanglement—the baby's
daddy died at the hands of Landlord Zhang, and I just know that the same
thing will happen to me. No one can escape the clutches of the landlord."
Then we are informed how her husband died: he was murdered by the
landlord who asked his lackeys to set fire to his house when he was asleep at
home, because his wild behavior out of his indignation over the act of
withholding his one-year wages by the landlord (in the excuse that his
carelessness led the landlord's horse accidentally lose its leg when it
stumbled on a rock) horrifies the latter. The reaction of the landlord after
this murder is vividly presented,

> After a while, Landlord Zhang made an appearance: looking like a sinister hawk
> flapping its wings, he strode over from the front village, flyswatter in hand, eyes
> bulging, snorting through his nose, and oozing airs of superiority.[1]

He asks her not to cry, and orders the burial of the bones of her
husband. This is seen by the masses as a benevolent deed while his crime is
unknown. He then "turned and strode back to the front village, waving his
flyswatter like a wand that could drain the blood from the villagers' bodies."
The caricatured description is filled with sarcastic connotations.

The text is composed mostly of the scenes in which the reactions and
discussions of the ignorant yet benevolent village folks are presented. We are
thus informed that Wang Asao had three children, but they all died (the
causes are not informed). The gruesome scene before she dies is reminiscent
of many similar pictures of women's bloody death during childbirth in the
writer's later stories: she "was lying on the kang(炕), her final labored wails
filling the small room. Her body was covered with her own blood, and there
in the midst of all that blood a tiny, brand-new creature was fighting for its
life."[2] It shows the author's particular concern over women's suffering in

---

①    萧红:《萧红卷》,傅光明编,太白文艺出版社 1997 年版,第 18 页.
②    萧红:《萧红卷》,傅光明编,太白文艺出版社 1997 年版,第 26 页.

procreation. As a prototypical leftist story at the time, the story, with its graphic scenes and weighty tone, effectively transmits the author's message of cruel class oppression.

It is easy for us to find strong doses of class conflicts in this category of stories, but what also stands out is a humanist concern. This should be understood in conjunction with her life experience to this moment. Her father, who often appeared to her as avaricious, mean, and cruel, generated in her a bitter feeling of injustice. And the kind-hearted folks who led a squalid and miserable life around her brought about her great sympathies. This spontaneous tender feeling for the social outcast, when combined with her own wretched experience thus far, undoubtedly contributed to her sense of merciless class division and oppression. This pre-theoretical recognizance did not necessarily lead to revolutionary thoughts, but her humanist feeling undoubtedly led to her pro-leftist inclinations and a strong humanitarian spirit, to be shown in these early stories.

While these writings about the miserable destiny of the subalterns are technically mature and thematically persuasive, when the writer shifts her attention to the awakening of the peasants and the fights of the revolutionary, the plots appear less plausible. *Flying-Kite Observation*（《看风筝》）is a typical case of this category. An old man's daughter dies in an incident when she is working in her factory; the father seeks for compensation for several days, yet achieves nothing. Besides, his son has not returned home for three years since he was out. We are told that his son, busy in promoting revolutionary messages to the oppressed, neither knows the tragedy of his family members, nor does he care for it. This is because, the narrator informs us, "he has numerous fathers; he takes every sufferer' father as his father; once he thinks of these fathers, there is only one road, one authentic road." The revolutionary disregards his father, even when he accidentally chances upon the latter one day. When this insensible man preaches to the villagers, sometimes "his hands raise high and then put down, which probably means exploitation; sometimes he raises his hand gigantically to the high, which probably means (to them) not to be oppressed." And the reaction of the countrywomen to be awakened by him is less credible, either, "I had been a cow and horse for a life. Haha! When the time comes I would be a man! I've been enough to be a beast." The whole story reads like a parody of this category of work, written by a demagogue from the ideologically opposite rank. This is probably due to the writer's lack of real experience of the subjects. Consequently, the writer's knowledge of the social injustice, like many leftist writers at the time, although touches on the primordial political consciousness of class oppression and exploitation, was still coated with a spontaneous humanitarian feeling and humanistic concern, rather than undergirded by a rigorous class analysis.

## 三、Heteroglossia of Multiple Contradictions in *The Field of Life and Death*

The collection was soon banned by the Japanese occupants. When the political situation became too tough for them to live there, they left for Qingdao in May 1934. With the help of a friend, Xiao Jun edited the literary supplement of a local newspaper. Their lives improved to some extent, and Xiao Hong was able to devote most of her time to writing. It was around this time, when she was 23 in the road of exile, that she completed the novel *The Field of Life and Death* (《生死场》), her first novel.

For left-wing scholars, the novel records vividly "the initial stages of awareness and resistance of the peasants."[1] But for other critics, because in it only "less than one-third of this short novel" that "concerns the Japanese at all," the target of this "story of struggle" lies elsewhere.[2] Undoubtedly, the novel had helped to promote the patriotic anti-Japanese sentiment of the populace, which should be seen as what it (at least partially) aimed at. Yet, the debates regarding its overarching thematic concern fell into a pitfall, because there are multiple concerns in the novel, which are not coherently connected but are intricately in conflict with each other.

The narrative structure of the novel is composed of two time periods.

---

① 　王瑶:《中国新文学史稿》,新文艺出版社 1953 年版,第 53 页.
② 　Goldblatt, H., *Hsiao Hung*, Boston: Twayne Publishers, 1976:45.

One takes place ten years before the Mukden Incident，another immediately after it. But the diegetic space is strictly confined in a village of the Northeastern area. The first ten sections lay out the contour of the major characters through exemplifying their behavior and manners. Via the last transitional section of the tenth，which narrates："The hill in the village and the stream at the foot of the hill remained the same as ten years before…In the village the cycle of life and death went on exactly as it had ten years before；"[①] the remaining seven sections turn to the changed life of the peasants with the coming of the Japanese. A narrative without a closely-knitted central storyline，in most times the novel only presents episodic daily life events.

Let us read the beginning of the 11th section carefully，which reads："one snowy day a flag never before seen by the villagers was raised and began to flutter under the open sky…The villagers were wondering：'What is happening now? Has the Chinese nation had a dynastic change?'"[②] And let us consider all the episodic anecdotes in the novel thus far. A clear message will come out：the cycle of "life and death，" just like the cyclic "dynastic change，" is the prevailing leitmotif of the first part，which then sets the stage for the development of the serial. In this first half，the writer aptly presents a rural world in which suffering peasants barely eke out a tremendously difficult life.

For the villagers of the area，lands and livestock are always their property，and indeed for them "life has always been a bitter struggle" and their "attitudes towards life reflect the harshness of their existence."[③] It is in this sense that Howard Goldblatt perceptively notes：though "a few characters rise to the surface as their stories are told，but it is the village and not any particular person or family that is being portrayed，a community in

---

① Xiao，H.，*The Field of Life and Death and Tales of Hulan River*，Goldblatt H. and Yeung E. Trans，Bloomington：Indiana University Press，1979：72.

② Xiao，H.，*The Field of Life and Death and Tales of Hulan River*，Goldblatt H. and Yeung E. Trans，Bloomington：Indiana University Press，1979：73.

③ Goldblatt，H.，*Hsiao Hong*，Boston：Twayne Publishers，1976：45.

action, as it were."[1] However, this does not mean the characters are less important or their activities can be neglected, as we can see that the paramount issue that receives the most extensive treatment is the suffering of women. The women's tortures are mainly shown through numerous painful births, their maltreatment by men, and their ensuing suicide, sickness, and death. The most macabre one is the gradual process of dying of Yueying, the most beautiful woman of the village, out of paralysis and careless abuse by her husband. The scene is graphically presented, leaving the strongest visual impression on the readers. Their sufferings are also displayed in their loss of their children: Golden Bough's baby daughter is casually dashed to the ground by her husband (due to his poverty and his incapability in raising the baby); Second Aunt Li has a miscarriage; Mother Wang's three-year-old daughter also dies by her incidental disposal (she mistakenly throws the baby to the haystack, where there is a rake under it), and her grown-up daughter dies heroically in the resistance; the old woman from north village loses her son in the resistance fights.

That the author stresses the suffering of women who are oppressed by men is surely bearing a heavy dose of the memory of her own experience. Noting her intentional management of the narration to convey this message, Lydia Liu aptly points out that "the few deaths of men are meaningful if they affect the lives of the women." For instance, "when Golden Bough becomes a widow and is forced to make her own living, we are not told when, where, why, or how her husband died, whereas the manner of women's deaths, such as Mother Wang's suicide, receives extended treatment."[2] In this narrative, on the one hand, women's tragic destinies in the hierarchical gender relation are mainly represented as being caused by the (male) peasants' backwardness, their ignorance and narrow vision, which is overdetermined by the patriarchal "feudal" system; on the other hand, what

---

① Xiao, H., *The Field of Life and Death and Tales of Hulan River*, Goldblatt H. and Yeung E. Trans, Bloomington: Indiana University Press, 1979:46.

② Liu, L., *Translingual Practice: Literature, National Culture, and Translated Modernity—China*, 1900-1937, Chicago: Stanford University Press, 1995:204.

the narrative presents, or the impression it gives the readers, is mainly their animalistic existence due to their poverty and animalistic instincts. Especially in terms of the latter one, which is exemplified by rural women's experiences of sex (their physical desire rather than emotional passion), the message is emphatically articulated through Golden Bough's affair with a man (who eventually becomes her husband) in the field. Her experience is shown as a cycle,[1] but what the narrator tries to pinpoint seems to be that "the female body serves the interests of men,"[2] as evidenced by the conclusion that Golden Bough makes: "men are heartless human beings, a feeling shared by the rest of the village women." Here, the narrative attributes the causes of the "women problem" to the peasants' poverty, ignorance, and eventually to the "problem of men." Couched on the peasants' own petty existence, the narration at most articulates an enlightenment discourse of the ignorance of peasants due to the evilness of the patriarchal system, including the gender inequality.

But in addition to this message, which seemingly prevails in the first part of the novel, there is another message about class conflict that is handily released, through a separate chapter mainly, which is full of symbolic connotation. Mother Wang, out of her demanding debts of land-rents to the landlord, has to sell her aging horse to the knackers. The "emotional intensity" as well as its "starkly hideous scenery" of this episode is noted by critics,[3] yet its symbolic import and its structural position in the text are not sufficiently explicated.

When "they drew near the slaughter house…the city gate was now directly ahead. Mother Wang's heart turned over." The narrative voice, a seemingly narrated monologue, informs us,

---

① Liu, L., *Translingual Practice: Literature, National Culture, and Translated Modernity—China*, 1900-1937, Chicago: Stanford University Press, 1995:206.

② Liu, L., *Translingual Practice: Literature, National Culture, and Translated Modernity—China*, 1900-1937, Chicago: Stanford University Press, 1995:206.

③ Liu L., *Translingual Practice: Literature, National Culture, and Translated Modernity—China*, 1900-1937. Chicago: Stanford University Press, 1995:50.

Five years ago it had been a young horse, but because of farm work it had been
reduced to skin and bones. Now it was old. Autumn was almost over and the
harvesting done. It had become useless, and for the sake of its hide, the master had to
send it to the slaughterhouse. And even the price of its hide would be snatched away
from Mother Wang's hands by the landlord. [1]

Mother Wang's farm work relies on the cooperation of the horse. But
now she has to sacrifice the latter to pay for her rent. Class oppression and
exploitation is worsened to such an extent that to drag on a living she must
sacrifice the most precious personal belonging—she had developed an intense
emotion with the living stock in years of labor. The latter also has an
emotional attachment to her: when she leaves, the horse also follows behind
her.

Not knowing what was happening, it was heading for home. Several men with
their hideous faces came running out of the slaughterhouse, prepared to lead the horse
back in. Finally the horse lay down at the side of the road…There was nothing Mother
Wang could do but walk back into the courtyard, and the horse followed her back in.
She scratched the top of the horse's head, and slowly it lay down on the ground,
seemingly about to go to sleep. Suddenly Mother Wang stood up and walked briskly
towards the gate. At the head of the street she heard the sound of a gate slamming
shut.

…She wept all the way home until her two sleeves were completely soaked with
tears. It seemed as if she had just returned from a funeral procession. [2]

Mother Wang's emotional torture and psychological paralysis are
touching. Symbolically, she has just attended a funeral of her companion,
almost one of her family members: she has raised it, taken care of it, and is
also benefited from it. Now since she vicariously kills it, it is tantamount to
a symbolic action to take away her own life force. "The sound of a gate
slamming shut" behind her is a strident blow signaling her own doomed

---

① Xiao, H., *The Field of Life and Death and Tales of Hulan River*, Goldblatt H.
and Yeung E. Trans, Bloomington: Indiana University Press, 1979: 32.

② Xiao, H., *The Field of Life and Death and Tales of Hulan River*, Goldblatt H.
and Yeung E. Trans, Bloomington: Indiana University Press, 1979: 33-34.

destiny, which is enforced and precipitated by the incarnated evil, the landlords.

> A servant from the landlord was already waiting by the door. Landlords never let even a single penny go to waste on the peasants. The servant left with her money.
>
> For Mother Wang, her day of agony was all for naught! Her whole life of agony was all for naught.[①]

That "Her whole life of agony was all for naught" is predetermined by the landlords who "never let even a single penny go to waste on the peasants." Therefore, the novel shares the view of Xiao Jun's novel *Village in August* that "there were more evil forces afoot than those which had customarily tormented the peasants since time immemorial;"[②] although for Xiao Jun, this evil force refers mainly to the Japanese invaders, which was shared by most of patriotic writers at the time and quite fit in with the discourse of the mainstream resistance literature; whereas for Xiao Hong, in addition to the peasants' ingrained traditional mindsets brought about by the patriarchal society, the evil force has also an incarnated form. It is in this sense that she shows her courage to present life "as it is" rather than just follows the "call for arms" of the epochal "main melody" like other writers.

But if Mother Wang has no choice but to sacrifice the living stock at this moment, in real life in the following days she still takes care of Yueying before the latter hopelessly dies, and even has the courage to fight against this oppressed life imposed by the oppressors. She has encouraged her second husband, Zhao San, to join bravely in a rebellious scheme against rent-accretion. Although shortly later, she has tried to kill herself by taking poison because she learns that her son by her first husband, being one of the "Red Whiskers," is executed by the government; it is only now that we learn her life experience: earlier she has divorced her former husband because of his abuse; when her suicide fails, she has taught her daughter to avenge for her brother. Her courageous behavior is also greatly admired by her

---

① Xiao, H., *The Field of Life and Death and Tales of Hulan River*, Goldblatt H. and Yeung E. Trans, Bloomington: Indiana University Press, 1979:34.

② Goldblatt, H., *Hsiao Hung*, Boston: Twayne Publishers, 1976:47.

husband Zhao San, so even though the latter mistakes the death of the boy
to be an outcome of his desire to keep a woman (a fantasy by himself),
when he recalls Mother Wang's tenacity, "he could not help but feeling
admiration for the boy," because "at least no one had dared to bully him
while he was a bandit."

But this latent plotline about a series of Mother Wang's experience,
together with the episode about Zhao San's aborted scheme of violent
rebellion against landlords' increased rent, both of which contain the
ideological information about class conflicts, is overshadowed by the
secondary theme of the novel, the nationalist resistance, which is assumed
mainly by the personae of Zhao San. The latter's scheme of riot, though
aborted because of a real incident of mistakenly-committed misdeed in the
first part of the novel (taking a thief to be the one sent by landlords to burn
his house, he accidentally kills him), becomes another subtle yet also
important plot-point that leads to the development of the second part of the
novel, in which he repudiates his weak mind of "conscience" towards the
landlords and strengthens his national consciousness to fight the Japanese.
The raison d'être of this new type of resistance is also offered: the Japanese
deprive the villagers' means of living by forbidding them raising livestock
and farming the land, thus driving them to rebellion; and they kill numerous
villagers, some of whom are their relatives. But the most often noted episode
by scholars is still Zhao San's suddenly raised national consciousness.

> Zhao San knew only that he was a Chinese. No matter how many times other
> people explained things to him, he was still unsure as to what class of Chinese he
> belonged. …but he now represented the progress made by the entire village. In prior
> days he had not understood what a nation was. In prior days he could even have
> forgotten his own nationality! [1]

The nationalistic discourse transpired from this statement (and from the
overarching actions occupying the second part of the novel) obviously
displaces the message of class conflicts expressed dexterously yet forcefully

---

[1]    Xiao, H., *The Field of Life and Death and Tales of Hulan River*, Goldblatt H
and Yeung E. Trans, Bloomington: Indiana University Press, 1979:86.

in the first part. As if to legitimize this displacement, we are informed that although he has been oppressed to such an extent——to be considered as a rebel, he "was still unsure" that he was oppressed by another class! Indeed, although this barely plausible mind now finds its incarnated enmity—the Japanese, this shifted priority that suddenly covers up the class problem is a miscalculated choice. Obviously, the writer's treatment of these two social contradictions is not skillful and balanced, thus the transition from one social contradiction of class conflicts to another contradiction of national conflicts appears abrupt and haste, without logical consistency and thematic coherence. Perhaps the only connection between the two parts lies in the fact that the much-stressed persistent cycle in the first part has implied that if there is no fundamental transformation of the agricultural society and its ingrained and exacerbated class exploitation, a national resistance would not by itself bring about a qualitative change of the peasants' mindsets and their customary behavior, including the patriarchal practice of subjugating women. But now let us temporarily shift our attention to her way of dealing with this secondary motif: national resistance, in the second part of the story.

In general, the writer's description of the peasants' spontaneous resistance against the Japanese touches on the issue of peasants' awakening to a political consciousness, or sends out a message that "nationalism enables the poor village males to transcend their class status by giving them a new identity."[①] This is particularly shown in the character of Two-and-a-Half Li, who had not been willing to devote his aged goat for the sacrificial ritual of the peasants' oath of resistance; but after his wife and daughter are killed by the Japanese, he is finally willing to give up his cherished goat—although only by entrusting it to a friend—to join the ranks of the fighters. The awakened nationalist consciousness even beckons women into its ranks (because their husbands or their scions are killed by the Japanese): they reply to Zhao San's call to arms against the Japanese with the oath, "Yes,

---

① Liu, L., *Translingual Practice: Literature, National Culture, and Translated Modernity—China*, 1900-1937, Chicago: Stanford University Press, 1995:208.

even if we are cut into a million pieces."

It is the consensus that because the writer neither had resistance experiences, nor did she has any direct knowledge of the atrocity of the Japanese, that her description of the resistance is not convincing. Nevertheless, her incompetence in treating material is not merely because of these empirical matters, as writers do not necessarily always have to engage personally and directly with the war. And we can also note that her presentation of stories about the Japanese ferocity, though often not done through vivid representation of bloody scene merely via vicarious retelling or simply through a sentence of message (for example, "Two-and-a-Half Li's pockmarked wife was killed. Tunnel legs as well"), still can effectively convey the messages of the evilness of the Japanese—thus the peasants' lack of choice but to revolt. Especially since the contemporary readers had their pre-knowledge to imagine the real happenings through the succinct information, due to the bombardment of such descriptions rapidly emerging at the time, the literary effect is not necessarily compromised. The story's problem lies elsewhere—in its diversion from the subject by inserting a message which is not closely knitted into the plotline of a gradually intensified resistance.

This message is conveyed by Golden Bough's experience of being forced to sell her body, when she leaves the village to the city of Harbin to seek job opportunity, where she finally settles down to mend the clothes of customers. Obviously, as noted, the placement of this episode here only "effectively destroys what little intensity of feeling the author has created against the Japanese."[1] What we need to ask, however, is why this bizarre design? Would not this gifted writer realize the existence of this jarring juxtaposition?

Obviously, here the writer includes some autobiographical elements, and her presentation of this dire picture, a disappointing episode, is divergent from many works of resistant literature at the time which single-mindedly eulogize resistant efforts. The complex and conflicting message is

---

[1]    Goldblatt, H., *Hsiao Hung*, Boston; Twayne Publishers, 1976:49.

best conveyed by the woman's painful proclamation.

> Golden Bough snorted, "I used to hate men; now I hate the Japanese." She finally reached the nadir of personal grief: "Do I hate the Chinese? Then there is nothing else for me to hate."[1]

What this complaint articulates is that she now hates the Japanese and the Chinese (men) simultaneously. The inclusion of the element of a leftist story[2] here has lent it to some controversial interpretation,[3] for it seemingly presents an ironic picture of the resistant ranks: are the Chinese men, or better, the Chinese society, with its patriarchal gender relations and class oppression and exploitation, less evil than the Japanese (colonization)?

What these viewpoints bypass, however, is that it only reveals the fact that without a fundamental adjustment of class hierarchy and the change of patriarchal system that undergirds this structure, the national consciousness is still a vulnerable political awareness. The new collective national identity irrespective of class distinction will not by itself solve the social inequality. However, what compromises the narration here is that it does not show how this concern over the existing unfair gender inequality, which is predicated upon the class hierarchy, could be organically integrated into the resistant efforts. For the latter, the message is sometimes rambling and not cohered with each other: Two-and-a-Half Li who goes to pursue the resistance is for the revenge of his wife (and child) who are subjected to the atrocity of the Japanese, but this important reason is only briefly mentioned; and sometimes the message does not exist at all: as said, Zhao San in the first part of the novel has tried to revolt against the landlords, but in the second

---

① Goldblatt, H., *Hsiao Hung*, Boston: Twayne Publishers, 1976: 100. With my slight modification of the translation, it is more literally faithful to the original text.

② In addition to her own tragic experience, we need to note that she is merely "sharing the fate of other hapless women who have reached life's lowest rung." Goldblatt H., *Hsiao Hung*, Boston: Twayne Publishers, 1976: 49.

③ For instance, see the relevant discussions of the novel in Lydia Liu, *Translingual Practice: Literature, National Culture, and Translated Modernity—China*, 1900-1937.

part the landlords appear nowhere.

All these drawbacks that impair the artistic unity of the novel are not merely out of the writer's careless negligence, but it is probably because the writer did not know how to correlate the three aspects of the social contradiction at the time—patriarchal gender inequality, (which is undergird by) class oppression, and nationalist resistance (which helps to lessen, but not to solve, the two other problems)—organically in her mind and in her work. Put in another way, the writer's unclear differentiation of the priority (and her incapability to look into the innate correlativity) of the three aspects of the major social contradiction of the time led to the heterrogloss— thus the aesthetic incoherence—within the text.

## 四、Humanist Concern in *The Bridge* and *On the Oxcart*

In the second period of her creative career, the writer kept her spontaneous humanist spirit unabated. This brought out some touching pieces.

Around November 1934, because the newspaper where Xiao Jun worked experienced serious financial crisis, and because their earlier contact with Lu Xun (1881-1936), the giant figure in modern Chinese literature, they received the latter's favorable response and left for Shanghai after their five months stay in Qingdao. In November 1936, *The Bridge* (《桥》) was published. It includes mostly sketches, but the only two short stories included, with their symbolic skill and subtle yet touching humanistic leitmotif, both show excellent literary quality. It confirms the writer's continuous concerns over the life of the subaltern and the oppressed, but what is outstanding is her particular emphasis on human dignity and humanistic values.

*Hands* is about a country girl's experience of discrimination in the school by classmates and teachers around her. Cherished the only educational opportunity her family gives her among her brothers and sisters, she works hard with a strong will; yet with little help from the others, the many difficult issues she faces in her studies prevent her from achieving what she desires. Furthermore, her humble family background—she is from a dyer's family—together with her blackened hands out of her tough labor, becomes her original sin. She is evaded by her elitist classmates, only allowed to sleep on a hallway bench, and becomes the target of their satire and teasing. The epitome of the social pariah, she is refused to enter the elite club—though nominally she is given the opportunity of receiving a proper education. A stringent class-divide still exists despite the rhetoric of equality. What makes us moved that contributes to its literary effects, in addition to her naivete, is her all-forgiving, and even self-effacing manner. She never shows resentment towards those snobbish people. Her experience not only reveals the omnipresent class division (in the form of discrimination between the superior and the inferior, in terms of intellect and social status) in the society, but also bespeaks the predicament of the "New Culture" enlightenment program which falls short of attaining its proclaimed goal of an authentic equality among all people. When the headmistress says "when one is filthy, her hand is also dirty," we cannot help but thinking of the other way. Obviously, only in a different social structure can her treatment and destiny be fundamentally altered.

*The Bridge* uses a physical object that appears as the transitory medium between a boy and his mother (a nanny for a social rich) and between the poor and the wealthy of the divided local community as the symbolic vehicle to deliver its central theme about class hierarchy. A dilapidated bridge across a ditch, with only two railings remained, prevents the crisscrossing of the river between the two separated banks, where people of differing class strata reside respectively. "If only the railings, too, had disappeared, then she would have felt easier about it; then she could believe that the ditch was a natural one, and that man would be powerless to conquer it." This epigraphic sentence has invited much critical attention, but has not received full explication. If the ditch is "unnatural," then it is manmade, and it implies that men can and should clear away the arbitrary obstacle. This sort of symbolic language is used cleverly throughout the text, a narrative that focuses on the nanny's attitude towards his son and the child of the rich whom she helps to raise.

The mother is forced to steal food for her child; her monotonous muttering is sentimental though it might appear a little unnatural: "You poor little devil, in your destiny there should have been a bridge." The wish that her child can cross the divide, to evade his predetermined destiny, is conveyed vicariously. When her son is beaten by the child who she helps to raise, she dares not to intervene publicly; but when the reverse case happens, she has to chasten harshly her sweetheart. However, it is the new bridge which now seemingly connects the divided that leads to the tragedy, which implies the superficial and ineffective vehicle to patch up the deep, wide chasm, the gulf between classes. When at the end of the story she learns that her son falls into the river because of his eagerness to meet his mother, the description of her reaction is short and non-melodramatic, nevertheless it successfully captures the rarely-noticed yet cruel daily happenings of the society, and the woman's guilty feeling of being a mother who had been forced to abandon her child; a touching atmosphere is produced accordingly. Alternating between short narrative and long, sensitive psychological movement ( through interior monologue and psychonarration) of the mother as the single protagonist, with a poetic language in her characteristic episodic plot structure, the prose is well-written. While containing leftist message, it bears a strong tone of liberal humanism, which subtly yet emphatically poses the question: how to redress substantially the inequality between the rich and the poor.

However, this apparent humanitarian concern frequently shifts to a humanistic spirit, which we can clearly witness in *At the Foot of the Mountain* (《山下》), a story written in 1933 and included in a later collection. Here the message of class inequality is toned down, while the self-dignity of the poor is standing out. A story about a maid servant's sense of pride out of her dismissal from her duty by her host family (due to her mother's mistake in heeding to her jealous neighbor's advice to require an unreasonable increase of salary), it shows the author's interest lies less in the social problem of class politics than in the humanistic concern over the moralistic value of the subaltern. Between September and October of this year, Xiao Hong published five stories and sketches, which later on were collected in *On the Oxcart*, coming out in public only in the middle of 1937. Among them, the title piece stands out as the one bearing the strongest social concern. The story within the story is delivered by the heroine, Sao Wuyun, a maid employed by the maternal grandfather of the narrator (who is a girl and a relative of the driver of the ox-driven cart). In the cart, she tells the girl and the driver the tragedy of her husband, a soldier. It invites the readers' interest by keeping the emotional intensity of the woman and the suspense about her husband's destiny unabated; only until the end the enigma is vicariously revealed in a totally unsentimental way: he was executed on site, before the band of deserters that he leads met the same punishment. The juxtaposition of a barely noticed tragic drama with the straitened rural life that the heroine and the coach driver drag on, shows a skillful manipulation of literary technique to bring out messages of social criticism. This story about the dire reality of the people living in a circumstance of rampant warlordism in North China is a representative piece of "critical realism." It also shows the inheritance of the tradition of "native place literature" (乡土小说), which was initiated in the early 1920s, and has been popular ever since.

As said, the short stories in this period show a strong humanist concern, though they are not very different from her stories of the earlier period which apparently stress class conflicts. What this indicates, however, is the ambiguous distinction between stories with the spirit of liberal humanism and stories with leftist information. It is hard to separate the two, which is not merely because in modern China, they both fundamentally narrate the lamentable, unfortunate life of the downtrodden and the oppressed, thus both belonging to the category of "critical realism"; but it is also because Xiao Hong, as a writer with a spontaneous humanistic feeling and little equipment of theoretical knowledge of class politics, stops exploring further areas apart from what she observed within her own (somewhat narrow) life circle—the latter of which, furthermore, mainly comes from her childhood experience. Without a broadened social experience and without taking part in the dramatically shifted social reality, the largely unchanged pattern shows a predicament difficult to break through. Now we will turn to the analysis of this category of stories.

Although Xiao Hong then found a sense of home under Lu Xun's indulgence and care, her relationship with Xiao Jun was worsened. The emotional crisis forced her to leave for Japan in the summer of 1935. This self-imposed sequestration ended when she learned of Lu Xun's death on October 19. After returning to China, she re-established her ties with Xiao Jun, and for a while they were in friendly union. Acquiring acquaintance with more friends, Xiao Hong had been in high spirits for a moment. But Xiao Jun's male-chauvinistic manners remained, and she was abused quite often. With the outbreak of the full-scale Resistance War, they moved to Wuhan. The city had just become the new center for literary activities. The Chinese Writers' Anti-Aggression Association that was just established there advocated writers' active participation in frontline and village life. But Xiao Hong's idea was different. While many other writers held that to keep being separated from the wartime reality and to remain in the city would be a great obstacle for them to be in touch with the people, Xiao Hong believed that "life is everywhere." For her, even "taking refuge during an air-raid alert is a part of wartime living conditions" for "the problem is that we haven't grasped its significance."[1] However, her works during this period did not fulfill the promise.

Because of Xiao Jun's enthusiasm for joining real resistance activities, Xiao Hong had to accompany him to Linfen, Shanxi province, to work in the People's Revolutionary University. It is here that Xiao Hong met Ding Ling (1904-1986), a veteran May Fourth writer-turned party's cultural worker. Xiao Hong's experience apparently reminded the latter her own earlier days, and they became closely associated. Nevertheless, Xiao Hong never thought about becoming a revolutionary soldier. One month later, the bombing of Japanese airplanes forced them to leave again. As the university headed towards Yan'an, Xiao Jun again pondered the possibility of becoming a fighter in real life. Longing for a peaceful and secure life, Xiao Hong urged him not to go, but to no avail. She ended their relationship and formed a new

---

[1]  Goldblatt, H., *Hsiao Hung*, Boston: Twayne Publishers, 1976:80.

liaison with another writer Duanmu Hongliang（1912-1996），and they soon got married.

In April，this new couple was returning to Wuhan. Later，in Xi'an，they again met Ding Ling. Xiao Hong refused again the latter's invitation to go to Yan'an，due to its harsh material environment and her long-term skepticism of any political forces. She finally went to Chongqing by her own，as her new husband had arrived there earlier，but Duanmu Hongliang had been tired of her. When she arrived there，she gave birth to a dead infant. She lamented that "I am always walking alone... It's as though I am fated to walk alone"[①]；nevertheless，it is aptly noted that it is "her peculiar brand of tunnel-vision" that lends her many problematic choices "a degree of inevitability."[②]

In Chongqing，she had produced a story collection *A Cry in the Wilderness*（《旷野的呼喊》），and a first draft of her autobiographical "novel" *Tales of Hulan River*（《呼兰河传》）. Overall，the stories included in *A Cry in the Wilderness* display the writer's efforts to contribute her energy to war efforts，to join the currents of resistance literature yet without doing simplified propaganda. Nevertheless，the mediocrity and lack of meaningful theme of these stories show the impossibility to achieve the goal without experiencing intimately the new social reality emerged.

The title piece of the collection is a long short story that vicariously touches on the subject of resistance，yet it is a dramatic regression compared with her first novel. In terms of theme，it is very ambiguous. In all aspects，it reads like a conflict between filial love and nationalistic consciousness. The father loves his son，and has an anxiety over the possibility that the latter has joined the resistant guerilla. In the beginning，there is a long digression describing the mother's activity of praying for his son's safety（she makes sacrifice at the family altar）. This episode might partially aim to strengthen the anxiety of the family's，especially the father's，sense of distress over the safety of their son；but perhaps the writer devoted too much of her personal feelings out of empathy. After this digression，the plot finally develops

---

① 梅林：《梅林文集》，力生书局 1955 年版，第 35 页.

② Goldblatt，H.，*Hsiao Hung*，Boston：Twayne Publishers，1976：87.

further when the son returns home informing his parents that he was only away for hunting. When the father knows shortly later that his son is actually employed by the Japanese to construct a railway, he even feels proud of him, because to him his son becomes a wage-earner. But this presentation is in conflict with his nationalistic consciousness, as shown earlier in his monologue over the courageous behavior of the patriotic guerilla fighters. Yet, we are even informed that the father feels his son being "far-sighted, considerate, and capable," and boasts it to the villagers. However, it turns out that his son is indeed an underground fighter who is working secretly to explode a train. When the father is informed that his son is arrested by the Japanese, in the mood verging on madness, he staggers out searching for his son in a blooming windstorm. But what does his cry in the wilderness signify? It seems that the author does not see very clearly the relation between the parental love that she aims to eulogize and the patriotic resistance she vicariously presents, to the extent that it becomes a paradox or an ethical dilemma between individual love and national sacrifice, which reminds us her early unsuccessful story *Flying-Kite Observation*.

At most, the story can be read as a transformation of a man with weak patriotic consciousness to one with an awakened political awareness, as a result of the unexpected experience of his heroic son; but this message is very weak. This surmise is partially justified by the other stories in the collection, which have more salient thematic motif of resistance. Still, they are all digressive and ambiguous. *Yellow River* (《黄河》) is apparently also related to the resistance motif, yet in the rambling and aimless discussions between a boatman and a solider, mostly about their daily lives, we can hardly pinpoint any central concern. Except in the last dialogue, in which the soldier is being asked: "If China wins this time, will the ordinary people lead a better life?" With the soldier's confirmative answer, the exchange barely gives out a feeble patriotic message. But the story might be more aptly interpreted as expressing an anxiety over the import of the resistant efforts, which is also conveyed in another story, *Vague Expectations* (《朦胧的期待》). It tells of an innocent maid's longing for marrying herself to her boss' bodyguard. In her night dream about his return from the front lines, she is informed by the latter that "I've come back to establish a home for us; from today on everything will be fine." This is followed by a self-contradictory sentence:"We had to win; how could we have lost? It doesn't make any sense!" She then "had a gentle smile on her face." The "story" might also be interpreted as an anxiety over the prospectus of the war, in particular over the destiny of the couple, but it has no salient central leitmotif. The writer's ineptitude in representing the wartime society furthermore is exemplified in her last novel *Ma Bole* (《马伯乐》). On the surface, it is a work of satire literature, which is generally regarded as following Lao She's style of lampoon. Yet, the protagonist that she aims to satirize lacks the literary "typicality," which probably is due to the fact that the writer merely based her model on the persons around her. However, while the latter might be vulgar, they don't necessarily have any representative value in terms of "national character." Simply put, the protagonist Ma Bole is not a "typical" member of the wartime petit-bourgeois intellectual class stratum that the writer intended to portray. Because Xiao Hong did not have much opportunity to observe the newly developed character of the intellectual class except those around her narrowed circle, her work did not leave strong impression on the readers, now and then.

## 五、*Tales of Hulan River* and a Dispossessed Nostalgia

With the death of Lu Xun in 1936, Xiao Hong lost not only her surrogate father, but also her intellectual mentor. As observed, throughout her life, she did not join any political party, nor was she active in any significant literary organization, which was quite unusual for most of writers at the time. Apparently, Ma Bole's "flight from the war, from the family, and mainly from reality" (words of Goldblatt's; and we should add one, flight from politics), is shared by the writer herself, which proves to be more tragic than the character, however. Indeed, in the third and also the last period of the writer's life, Xiao Hong furthermore struggled to retreat to her own narrowed life space for security and peace. However, as most part of China was under imperialist colonization and in Resistance War, this individualistic consideration not only did not bring to her what she desired, but also led her to various irresolvable predicaments, and finally cost her life. In the wartime reality, there was no peaceful place for an ordinary couple. Disregarding the advice of most of her friends, when Chongqing was subjected to the Japanese's air-attack, in the spring 1940 she again decided to flee, now to Hong Kong, where it turned out to be the locale of her premature, tragic death.

There, *Spring in a Small Town* (《小城三月》) is the writer's last creation, which is beautifully written yet has no much significance, as it is basically a simple story about a semi-traditional fille's unfulfilled love towards a stripling, who is a "new youth," her forced betrothal to an ugly man, and her sickness and death out of the unrequited longing and sorrow. No matter whether the theme of the story is regarded as a traditional one of a-beauty-meet-a-talent, or as a May Fourth enlightenment narrative about the awakened dreaming of the modern, it was not new and freshing any more. While it can also be afforded to an allegorical reading—by telling us a story of an immature death of an energetic youth, a buried and passed spring, it signifies the unfortunate destiny of the unblessed modern surrounded by a traditional social web—the story is better to be read "literally": Xiao Hong's re-rendition of the centuries-old narrative is probably a nostalgic lamentation of her own unfulfilled yearning for love.

This sorrowful tune extends into her last masterpiece, *Tales of Hulan River*. Fundamentally a cultural critique founded on a personal memory of childhood experience, it has two observational angles: one is the adult narrative, which is premised upon the other angle of the children's horizon. This narratological setup simultaneously strengthens and undercuts its thematic effectiveness.

The first chapter lays out the general natural and humanistic environment of the small town. Symbolically, in the very start it is presented as a "frozen land." This apparent presentation of a still nature soon turns to a mapping of the cultural physiology of the country folks and their way of life. Four cases of instance vividly show the local people's tradition-bound mentality and the idiosyncratic mannerism that it brings about：firstly， their ignorance and refusal to accept new knowledge and modern practice， as illustrated by a modern-styled dentist's experience of changing to become a midwife in order to make a living because of her lack of customers； secondly， their want of rationalization and the more problematic， their ways to adapt the new to meet the old， are presented through an anecdotal tale：while the "agricultural school" nominally "is for the study of raising silkworms，" it is humorously revealed to be just a place that "when autumn arrives the silkworms are fried in oil， and the teachers enjoy several sumptuous meals；" the third case which occupies the largest textual space none other than bespeaks their fundamental life philosophy：an attitude of passive existence， avoiding any challenge and new way of thinking， evading real praxis but engaging in pleasure-seeking idle talk， as typified by their ways of dealing with a mudhole that lies in the road， which is a topic of idle conversation but never the object of a concerted action； and finally， their ingrained habitus of dragging on a muddled life by self-cheating， which is represented by their handling of an infected， dead swine that is reminiscent of "the emperor's robe."

This emaciated life philosophy is further revealed as being premised upon a tedious life cycle of "birth， age， sickness， and death，" which， however， has more imprints of an agricultural society than being a universal form of life. This is evidenced by the two forms of reproduction：physical reproduction and men's self-reproduction， which are closely intertwined with each other， as illustrated by three incidents—a murder case in which two apprentices fight for the owning of a woman in the dyer's workshop and as a result， one kills the other； the scuffle between two employees of a bean-curd workshop accidentally breaks the leg of a donkey， which is a big event for a woman who is the mother of the man breaking the donkey's leg. Her eyes become blind out of her long-time crying—this is because the donkey is the key instrument for physical reproduction； and finally， the starved-to-death of a bastard child. The backwardness and the muddled life of the local community in this way are shown to be both the result and the cause：the suffocation of one's desire， the ignorant way to live one's life， and the retarded development of relations of reproduction are all correlated with each other. They are a social totality that is hard to be separated.

This centuries-old, persistent totality facilitates the growth of a mentality of resignation: "man lives to eat food and wear clothes"; and, "when a man dies, that's the end of it." They holding such an attitude is not because they do not cherish life, but because they are forced to drag on such a listless living. Nevertheless, they do want to enrich their life; the way they achieve this, however, is again to do a self-benumbing job of building magnificent ornament-houses for the dead, and to pay much emphasis on eating. The description of the selling and buying of flat cakes, dough twists, rice puddings, and bean-curds presents a seemingly self-fulfilled, highly-poetic, simple and naive, idyllic way of life, the norm of an agrarian, pre-industrial society. Even the natural scene of the phantasmagoric change of the shapes of "fire cloud" provides an enjoyable leisure picture for the carefree form of life. "Spring, summer, autumn, winter—the seasonal cycle continues inexorably, and always has it since the time immemorial," the narrator laments; only the last sentence of this chapter offers an ominous tone:"Those who have not yet been taken away are left at the mercy of the wind, the frost, the rain, and the snow…as also always."

The second chapter delves more into the spiritual world of the people by presenting vividly various forms of local customs and numerous festival parties. Ostensibly, it is "more about ghosts and goblins than about people, more a tale of superstition and fear than the interaction of human beings"[1]; however, the interaction of human beings, especially the gender relations in which women are always subordinated to men in matrimonial affairs, leading a less-than-happy life, is aptly presented everywhere. The seamless integration of the sorrowful women affairs with the apparently boisterous folk customs skillfully presents the local world as a "natural," long-perpetuated social totality.

With a change of narrative persona from the third-person one to the first-person, the narrative turns from a "custom study" to the human society and in particular to a more intimate personal world. The third chapter

---

① Goldblatt, H., *Hsiao Hung*, Boston:Twayne Publishers, 1976:107.

delivers the narrator's remembrance of her close relations with her grandfather—his love and care to his innocent, little granddaughter in the cold and stifling household, as well as the latter's childish psychology of curiosity and her eagerness for love. Like the first two chapters, here the secular affairs are oftentimes observed from a child's perspective, and because of this the text is filled with a lively atmosphere.

In the following chapter, however, this child's perspective is mixed up with an adult's narrative (though still couched in a first-person narrative) of the downfallen condition of the family garden—which is a "natural being" yet a cultural symbol traditionally signifying the flowery prosperity and sophisticated cultivation of the gentry-class world. A specific reference is applied to a steel plow, the most important tool for production in the agrarian society.

> I don't know why, but the steel plow didn't look as though any new life was associated with it; meanwhile, it was falling apart and covered with rust. Nothing was born of it, nothing grew from it—it just lay there turning rusty. If you touched it with your finger, flakes fell to the ground, and although it was made of steel, it had by this time deteriorated so much that it looked as though it were made of clay that was on the verge of crumbling to pieces. When viewed alongside its mate, the wooden trough, there was absolutely no comparison—it was covered with shame. If this plow has been a person it would doubtless have wept and wailed loudly: "I'm made of better stuff than the rest of you, so why has my condition weakened to it present state?"
>
> Not only was it deteriorating and rusting, but when it rained, the rusty pigment that covered it began to run, spreading with the rain water over to its companion, the hog trough, the bottom half of which had already been stained the color of rust. The finger of murky water spread farther and farther away, staining the ground they touched the color of rusty yellow.[①]

The symbolic message is more than clear: a corrupted and outdated mode of production not only is deteriorating, but also stains and corrupts the land and the people. This natural-historical object is undergoing its

---

① Xiao, H., *The Field of Life and Death and Tales of Hulan River*, Bloomington: Indiana University Press, 1979:209-210.

"shameful," "rusting" and disintegrating period.

Just like this listless, still object, we are informed that "my home" is also "a dreary one." This is the refrain the narrator numerously articulates. In addition, the country bumpkins who live in the three dilapidated old rooms attached to the house lead a squalid existence; they depend on the nature to get food (they are quite happy with the mushroom growing up in the roof of their rooms, not heeding to the possibility of poisonous elements within); they are selfish and parochial; and their stoical way of life contains a deeply concealed, hopeless sorrow.

> Their songs (during and after they're making the noodles) were not an expression of the joys of their work; rather they were like sounds of someone laughing with tears in his eyes.
>
> Stoically they accepted their hardships: "You say that the life I live is a pitiable one; well, that's all right with me. In your eyes I am in mortal danger, but my life gives me satisfaction. And if I were not satisfied, what then? Isn't life made up some of pain than pleasure anyway?"①

Their negligence of the dangerous condition of the dilapidated house is not out of their manliness, but it again is a result of their shortsighted, self-conceited life philosophy. "As for the question of whether or not the building would someday collapse, and whether it would bring good fortune or ill to those inside, that was considered by everyone as something too far in the future to warrant any thought."②

Having laid out the general lifestyle and spiritual world of the county folks, in which their vulnerable character of an ingrained inertia and weak-mindedness are once again stressed, chapter five through seven is devoted to three concrete case studies of their mentality and behavior, in which a macabre murder stands out.

We are already informed at the end of the fourth chapter the background

---

① Xiao, H., *The Field of Life and Death and Tales of Hulan River*, Bloomington: Indiana University Press, 1979:218.

② Xiao, H., *The Field of Life and Death and Tales of Hulan River*, Bloomington: Indiana University Press, 1979.

of a carpenter's family, in which there is always a sorceress-dancing being performed there, a superstitious practice for the health of its matriarch. The sounds of drums were mournful, which "confused one's sense of time." We are told that on the surface:

> This family was more blessed than any other in the compound, with its three generations living together. Their family traditions were the best defined and the neatest: they treated one another with respect; there was mutual understanding and good feelings among the siblings, and a great deal of love between parent and child.[①]

Nevertheless, beneath this exemplary surface, there are always internecine fights among siblings, which is the characteristics of traditional Chinese extended household in which several generations live together. Although this "model household" leaves almost everyone the impression that "providence has smiled on old Hu's family, and one day wealth will come to them as well," a gruesome incident narrated in detail in chapter five offers an appalling case of the maltreatment and final murder of a child bride by superstitious convention. She is abused merely because her robust appearance and bold manner contradict the concept that the tradition holds for a newly married woman, thus a process of disciplinarization is regarded as a necessity—this was a usual practice perpetuated in traditional China, and most of the wrongdoers themselves had undergone the same "training" when they were newly married to the family. They are both the victims and the injurers: the sufferings are oftentimes the perpetuators of their own destiny, out of the traditional mindset. Here, a subtle exposure of the ignorance of the neighbors is also presented with their curiosity and cold indifference towards the public punishment of the young girl. The episode is reminiscent of many May Fourth enlightenment stories which were popular two decades ago before this novel was written.

The next chapter is about "a family outsider," Second Uncle You, whom the writer had described in an earlier story with that title. Although the man is a close relative of the narrator's father (and in reality the

---

① Xiao, H., *The Field of Life and Death and Tales of Hulan River*, Bloomington: Indiana University Press, 1979:220.

author's, too), his now resourceless status contributes to his downtrodden life in the household. He himself also seems to yield to the concept that destitute man owns no rights to many things. Still, his sense of bitterness bears a subtle tone of class resentment.

> …He started cursing even smaller things…if there were birds flying overhead and something dirty landed on his sleeve or somewhere, he would shake it off while he turned his head towards the sky and spoke to the birds that by that time had already flown by,
>
> "You dirty…hah! You sure know how to aim, right here on my sleeve…what are you, blind? If you have to drop something, then drop it on someone who's wearing silk or satin! Drop it on me and you just waste…you bunch of crippled beggars…①

But in actuality he is a kind-hearted man with an innocent animism. He refrains from eating lamb because in his childhood, his life has been saved with the help of a goat's milk. What he demands from the family is respect from the others; which, just like love and care is what the narrator (a persona of the author herself) desperately longs for, he substantially lacks. If the family buys something and does not give him a share or a portion, he would vicariously rebuke; but if he is given, he would say: "Your Second Uncle You does not eat it, you take it!" He steals some things from the host to sell in order to get some pocket money, yet when the cases are juxtaposed with the child narrator's own analogous deeds, both feel greatly embarrassed; the comic effect of which dispels any moralistic qualms that might emerge.

The last person being introduced is about a poor mill worker, Feng Waizuizi, or Hare-lip Feng. He is honest and very nice to the child narrator. But the most important thing about him is that he is courageous enough to acquire a beautiful and robust wife from a peasant family, which invites the indignation of almost all (apart from the grandfather who apparently harbors sympathy towards him). They had praised the woman for her appearance before, but now they charge her for not obeying women's virtue. Defying traditional customs strong-mindedly, the woman unfortunately dies when

---

① Goldblatt, H., *Hsiao Hung*, Boston: Twayne Publishers, 1976: 72-73.

she gives birth to a second son. The caring husband shows a tenacious perseverance against all odds to raise their scions. Humbleness they may be, what is outstanding is the will of the subaltern to live a decent life and their unyielding self-respect. Humanistic sentiments over human dignity prevail over any humanitarian concern.

Taken all these together, this beautifully written novel of "poetic prose" is a study of local customs and morals with mild sarcasm and humor. What the novel falls short of portraying, however, are the social-historical elements that lurk behind and overdetermine all these lamentable creatures. To be sure, the narrative sometimes vicariously touches on this "unspoken history": Underside Second Uncle You's pitiable existence is his traumatic personal memory of the Russian invasion of his homeland during the Russian-Japanese War in his childhood. Whether there is certain causality out of this for his despicable status in the household we are uninformed, yet his suddenly emotional burst to tears—which is quite unusual given his daily carefree and cynical mannerism—bespeaks a large territory that is concealed in the darkness and mysterious to us. Whether it is due to the author's childish innocence at the time (we have to remember that the "novel" to a large extent is an autobiography) when she was not intellectually mature enough to know his history, or it is due to the author's incapability to dissect the origin of his double-sided character, in any case the readers share an impression of a man worthy of pity and sympathy; but that is the only thing we get.

To be sure, the author leaves many traces that expose the social reality of class exploitation, such as the following description of a ledger in the fake house for the dead: "A look at this ledger shows that there is no haphazard accounting of debts in the nether world, and that there is a special type of individual whose job is to manage these accounts." It "goes without saying" that the master of the grand ornament-house is a landlord. But these intermittent narrations are merely appearing as careless comments not seamlessly knitted into the structure of the text, which thus could be completely omitted.

Not only do the peasants here appear their own enmity, but the writer

also sees the peasants themselves as their only true hope for betterment.
What we can get from the descriptions, as a result, is a list of adjectives
about the personalities of the peasants, which is mixed up with virtues and
drawbacks. Premised on a culturalist perspective, this narrative
fundamentally sticks to the enlightenment discourse of the New Culture
Movement. Thematically, when compared with the first part of *The Field
of Life and Death* and her numerous early stories about peasants' lives, this
novel also implies a reticent regression, or involution, of the author's views
in regard to the unyielding spirit of the downtrodden. Therefore, although to
a great extent it successfully "put under a microscope the entire town, and
by extension much of early twentieth-century Chinese rural society in the
Northeast,"[①] this work has much more aesthetic value (in the sense of being
a poetic "pure literature" or "belles lettres") than a masterpiece of
ethnography that trenchantly takes a social-historical study. Put in another
way, the ultimate reason for its incapability to achieve its potential still lies
in the culturalist discourse that the writer relies upon. To be sure, this was
probably what the author intended in the very beginning: it was a nostalgic
remembrance of her childhood experience for her self-solace in a very painful
moment, when she reluctantly came to the end of her life in her sick bed.

## 六、The Premature Death of a "New Woman"

Xiao Hong had long been weakened by her long period of wanderings
and bad health. Leaving her cohorts in the hinterland, in Hong Kong she
again became desperately lonely and gravely ill. In late 1941, she was helped
by a foreign friend to enter the Queen Mary's Hospital. Shortly later, on
December 8, the Japanese attacked Hong Kong (which unraveled the curtain
of the Pacific War) and soon occupied it on the Christmas day. In January
1942, she received a lethal surgery for suspected throat tumor, and died nine
days later out of throat infection. "To die like this…my heart is heavy" was
her last word.

---

① Goldblatt, H., *Hsiao Hung*, Boston: Twayne Publishers, 1976:108.

Ironically, she died in colonized Hong Kong almost nine years after fleeing from Japanese-occupied Manchuria. There was no way for an individualist to seek a room of her own for peace and security in the merciless modern Chinese society. Xiao Hong's vulnerability shown in her early wretched existence (in terms of both physical and emotional disasters) confirmed her own naïveté and unworldly behavior. She was partially responsible for her own tragedy: her self-imposed isolated life cost her life.

Xiao Hong has written in the wake of the Resistance War, "For me, it always comes down to the same thing: either riding to an alien place on the back of a donkey, or staying put in other man's home. I am never keen on the idea of homeland. Whenever people talk about home, I cannot help being moved, but I am perfectly aware that I had become 'homeless' even before the Japanese set their foot on the land."① Indeed, for a homeless soul, her road in exile was endless before the nation-state was liberated and the national identity of its citizens was solidly founded. Holding no firm belief in any political doctrine, she was always in exile—sometimes self-enforced—and ultimately a humanist and an individualist who had tried to seek "a room of her own," yet the merciless Chinese society did not allow her to do so. A gifted talent—she learned writing all by herself—she left many masterpieces in her short-term tragic life of exile, works ranging from outcries for weapons to dispossessed nostalgia for a lost homeland; yet her reluctance to delve into the deep water of wartime exigency also compromised her literary efforts and sometimes jeopardized the aesthetic unity of her fictional works. Her tragic, exiled experience is symbolic of the dilemma of Chinese "new women" in particular, and the predicament of the New Culture agenda in general.

---

① 萧红：《萧红全集》，哈尔滨出版社 1991 年版，第 105 页.

# Chapter Two　From Feminist to Party Intellectual? Identity Politics and Ding Ling's "New Women Stories"

## 一、Introduction

Ding Ling (1904-1986) was the pioneer of Chinese feminist writing in the post-May Fourth era, the effects of her sensual writing on female emotions and women entangled in love rippling across society. In the 1930s, however, she became increasingly left-leaning, and after Mao's 1942 Yan'an Talks she became a staunch Communist writer, completing her famed novel, *The Sun Shines over the Sanggan River* (《太阳照在桑干河上》). Nonetheless, her concerns over the "women's problem" ran throughout her career. How did Ding Ling negotiate her feminine and feminist concerns with the movements for nationalist salvation and mass revolution in her literary works? What psychological trajectories had she experienced? This chapter tries to place her works in sociohistorical context, in order to find the motivations underlying her dramatic changes. It suggests that the four stages of development Ding Ling experienced before 1949, with respect to both personality and literary style, represent a shift in her intellectual commitments, and thus the transformation—or perhaps the formation—of her identity.

An introduction of the life and upbringing of Ding Ling as a "new woman" is necessary. Born Jiang Wei in Hunan province to a gentry's family in rapid decline, Ding Ling faced adversity during her childhood. Her father died when she was three; he had studied law in Japan, though this foreign education brought him little economic return. Her mother, a young widow, persevered through life with a strong will. While also teaching elementary school，she enrolled in a new-styled normal school—both rare and courageous at the time.

Influenced by her mother's spirit of independence and anti-traditionalist views，Jiang Wei could identify with the ideals of the May Fourth Movement. She joined student demonstrations，listened to patriotic speeches，and attended anti-imperialist meetings. At fifteen，she cut her braid and taught abacus at a night school for the masses. In 1922，with an anarchical impulse，she left Hunan. Hereafter she went back and forth between Shanghai，Nanjing，and Beijing，observing intellectual life along the way. During this period she became enchanted with the idea of anarchy，thereafter changing her name for simplicity. In 1925，she fell in love with Hu Yepin（1903-1931），a penniless poet at the time. Out of economic necessity she tried to enter the film industry but failed. And so，she began writing.

## 二、A Bewildered Feminine Woman in Anarchism Belief

Until 1929 the writer saw herself as a feminine woman，an identity based on taking men as her other，the result of a patriarchal society. During this period，she began to identify with the anarchist movement（无政府主义运动）. The anarchists regarded themselves as independent from conventional moral codes；sanctioned by the social structure of the traditional world，they shed their names，left their homes to pursue higher education，and engaged in free love（自由恋爱），viewing marriage as a traditional institution that needed to be repudiated. Their practices constituted the first wave of Chinese sexual emancipation，homosexual love representing another part of their erotic utopia. With this，Ding Ling had formally joined the Anarchist Party. The radical trends among the youth of the period in mind，we can begin to explain the "women's problem" described in her stories from this era.

The aborted dream of becoming a movie star gave Ding Ling the opportunity to witness a number of sexual and under-the-table negotiations and exchanges，as described in *Mengke*（《梦柯》），her first published story in 1927.[①] The heroine

---

① 丁玲：《梦柯》，《小说月报》，1927 年 12 月 10 日.

begins an innocent artistic student who leaves school out of indignation at
the molestation of a model by her teacher, only to lose herself in society in
her efforts to find a job fit for her; in the end, she becomes an actress,
selling her body and her soul. Exactly what becomes the last straw is not
apparent, yet the readers can feel that society, mercenary and degraded, is
most responsible. The accelerant to this transformation is her experience in
her wealthy aunt's family. Her cousin Xiaosong is a newly returned overseas
student with new ideas and a lifestyle that attract her, but he turns out only
to be a debauchee. Upon finding out the truth, Mengke leaves her aunt's
house. Out of her sense of being betrayed as well as the economic
imperative, she turns to the degraded movie industry.

Mengke's series of experiences show the predicament of the Chinese
"new women," promoted as a modern idea by the New Culture Movement.
Although the degradation associated with her status is explainable by a lack
of social rationalization, the new woman herself is at least partly responsible
for her own weakness: she is unwilling to "open a school or factory" (as she
almost surely lacks the capability) or to shift to a new school, and she
acknowledges that becoming a nurse or a child bearer may be out of reach.
This is a dilemma for a particular class: As a lower middle-class girl who is
reluctant to accept the old-fashioned traditional marriage that her parents
offer, she is left to face a new social setting in which women are no more
than fetishized commodities. But once this new woman leaves her family,
she has few alternatives to choose.

*The Diary of Miss Shafei*(《莎菲女士的日记》), written the following
year, is a typical case of anarchist life.[1] Shafei is "away from home, and
living by herself … not enrolled in the university"; together with her
girlfriend, they have "few or attenuated family connections," and moreover,
"these young women rarely have family or given names, but take
unconventional westernized ones… surviving anonymously and precariously
in the interstices

---

① 丁玲:《丁玲文集》,湖南人民出版社 1983 年版. Unless otherwise specified, all the
stories discussed in this chapter are included in this collection.

of the huge city."[1] Economically, morally, and spiritually, they are alone. Shafei's tuberculosis metaphorically becomes a token of a restless passion, shown in the form of her psychosomatic impulses and dreams of a freewheeling utopia. The illness exempts her from work, providing an opportunity for her to project her fantasy into an anxiety about the impossibility of establishing a female subjectivity.

Her attraction to Ling Jishi, a handsome gentleman from Singapore—bearing a semi-Chinese and semi-Western air, seems an enigma for scholars: it is a "perverse passion"; "while she indulges in feverish fantasies of longing for him, she realizes at the same time that he is unworthy of them."[2] What triggers her revulsion is seemingly a spiritual elevation that rejects his carnal and material enjoyment, as well as the bad habitus born from his dual identity as a semi-traditional gentry man and a Western-styled flaneur.[3] When this revulsion becomes closely intertwined with her sexual fantasy, it brings about in her a split between body and soul, reason and passion. When she has satisfied her sexual fantasy of acquiring this man, she thinks she has won a battle against men. And yet, she cannot help despising herself—despite her victory in her battle with men, she is losing her war with herself.

Does Shafei pursue a pure love? She refuses the genuine pursuit of another lad, Wei Di, and regrets that he does not understand her. But she acknowledges that she does even not understand herself. To solve the puzzle, we need to return to Ling Jishi: this dream, for money, for a comfortable life, and for a journey to officialdom, is the ideal of a Chinese middle-class that few at the time could afford. That he keeps with the social expectations of his class with some residually corrupt gentry-class habits

---

① Feuerwerker, Y. M., *Ding Ling's Fiction: Ideology and Narrative in Modern Chinese Literature*, Cambridge, Mass, and London: Harvard University Press, 1982:28.

② Feuerwerker, Y. M., *Ding Ling's Fiction: Ideology and Narrative in Modern Chinese Literature*, Cambridge, Mass, and London: Harvard University Press, 1982:28.

③ See the oft-quoted her psychological movement on Ling Jishi, in 丁玲：《丁玲文集》,湖南人民出版社 1983 年版,第 71 页.

points less to his own "dirty" soul than to the semi-modern conditions of
society. Thus the problem seems to lie in Shafei herself: her split psychology
originates from her incapability to differentiate, on the one hand, her true
necessity of that which even she herself might not be consciously aware, and
on the other hand, the false desire and will that she clear-mindedly notices.
As such, her anxiety is less because "she was only partially freed from the
traditional institutionalized modes of womanly behavior,"[1] as she can easily
satisfy her physical desire at any time; what matters is that, for her real
identity, she is seeking that which sexual satisfaction cannot grant her, and
she complains that she has no time to contemplate crucial issues about "her
body, her reputation, and her future."[2]

This negligible phrase offers us some hints, and yet its decoding still
requires historical context as the subtext. We need to ask: if her "love"
towards Ling Jishi is consummated, exposed, and even acknowledged, then
what would be the outcome? Even if her reputation were not sacrificed, for a
flaneur who has enjoyed the reputedly freestyle way of Western life and is
also familiar with debauched Chinese custom, she would have little
opportunity to be his lawful wife, as many wealthy men at the time kept
concubines. And even if this privilege were granted and her "body" were
saved from being humiliated as merely a mistress, the prospect of her
"future" Would look gloomy. Such is the ultimate, yet deeply concealed
reason for her anxiety—her angst about her dignity and social status that she
herself would not like to acknowledge. Tani Barlow' description of Ding
Ling's life at this time echoes many aspects of Shafei: "She had indeed
achieved a life of independent personality, but she found that freedom under
those   circumstances   offered   neither   livelihood   nor   even   a   socially

① Feuerwerker, Y. M., *Ding Ling's Fiction: Ideology and Narrative in Modern
Chinese Literature*, Cambridge, Mass, and London Harvard University Press, 1982:44.

② Feuerwerker, Y. M., *Ding Ling's Fiction: Ideology and Narrative in Modern
Chinese Literature*, Cambridge, Mass, and London Harvard University Press, 1982:74.

recognizable role."①

### 三、A Social Critic against Mercenary Market and "Political Reactionary"

In her second period, the author identifies herself less as a feminine woman, but more as a social critic, as one who critiques the mercenary market—the commercialized cultural industry in which cultural productions are nothing but cheap commodities. More importantly, she takes the dark reality and the "political reactionary" as her antagonistic other. Again, her personal experience facilitates this change. Her husband Hu Yepin had been radicalized: he entered the executive committee of the League of Left-Wing Writers and became chairman of the Committee on Worker-Peasant-Soldier Literature. Ding Ling had less interest in revolution at the time. While he attended secret party meetings, she stayed at home writing stories on the contradiction between revolution and love. As a result, the scenes of life shown in these stories are generally regarded as not authentically representing the true experience of the revolutionaries.

The first story is *Wei Hu*. Later on, Ding Ling admitted that she did not intend to make Wei Hu a hero, nor did she plan to write about revolution. What she wanted to do was "merely to write about a few pre-May 30th characters," yet she "discovered [herself] that it was only a very vulgar story fallen into the trap of the love and revolution conflict."② The problem with this formulaic pattern is not the subject itself, to be sure, but how to represent the historical experience of this entanglement. This story fails to offer a genuine picture for either of the two dimensions of this conflict.

---

① Barlow, T., *I Myself Am a Woman: Selected Writings of Ding Ling*, Boston: Beacon Press, 1989:24. This is not merely a coincidence, as Tani Barlow notes that the writer "borrowed heavily from her own experience," "the wasted efforts" of her "anarcho-feminist years."

② 丁玲:《创作的经验》,天马书店 1933 年版,第 24-25 页.

The transformation of the heroine from an anarchist girl to a lover of a revolutionary seems less plausible. Lijia and her liberated female friends are art students, and they bear all the features of the Chinese anarchists at the time. Although it takes two-thirds the length of the story for her to claim her love with revolutionary Wei Hu, the readers do not see what triggers her love, except that she appears tired of the lifestyle of her friends, who in her views merely enjoyed what they themselves considered free love in a state of bewilderment.

The remaining section, devoted to their passionate life, is similarly lackluster, showing no more than embraces and kisses. What adds to its flavor is Wei Hu's reading of poems. Wei Hu's departure from his sweetheart seems to be the result of the inexorable contradiction between love and revolution, something at odds with what we might expect of the subject. For youthful idealists, love and revolution are often seen as mutually beneficial rather than reciprocally deconstructive. So why is there such a difference? Though this incompatibility exists for only a short period, between 1927 and 1930, it should again be understood with the socio-historical context in mind. After the massacre of the leftists in 1927, the radical intellectuals, if they were to take part in revolutionary work, would have kept in a state of "white terror" (白色恐怖) in which they could lose their lives at any times. It was often impossible for them to have love and revolution simultaneously; in order to protect their lovers, many found it better to involve themselves in the work alone rather than bringing their lovers in. Moreover, because middle-class women were generally less interested in politics, the lovers of the revolutionaries plausibly came from the laboring masses. But with the spread of radical ideology, and with the changing of the political situation as time went on, love and revolution would seem less incompatible; especially after the outbreak of the Resistance War, they indeed increasingly appeared to work hand-in-hand in literary works.

At the same time, theoretically, the incompatibility of the two at this time reveals the conflicts between the May Fourth discourse of free love prevailing in the 1920s and the leftist discourse of revolution gradually emerging late in the decade. In the view of this emerging discourse, the dominant discourse of free love at the time was a manifestation of bourgeois culture, for it was individualistic and egocentric, and intended only for the middle class. At this point, as a new ideological force the discourse of revolution aimed to usurp the power of the discourse of free love to become culturally dominant. It is thus also out of necessity that revolution prevails over love in the story.

The triangular contradictions among love, revolution, and literature receives a different treatment in the following two stories, both entitled *Shanghai, Spring 1930*. Let us begin from the second story. Seemingly a moderate redress of the preceding story's problem, the male revolutionary protagonist now endeavors to convert his bourgeois lover to the revolutionary ranks. But he appears too clumsy to do this: he never preaches an ideological message to her, and he only invites her to attend his meeting on trivial, daily work. Even when the efforts fail and she leaves him for a rich youth, he rests assured that she is again happy. In repudiating the possibility of ideological interpellation, and, with the plot of the partnership between his comrade and a female bus conductor, in implying that only people in the same class can have the same class consciousness, be in a harmonious love, and join revolution together, the writer shows the inexorable divide between classes, which is wrong in the view of revolutionary ideology. In acknowledging her life of happiness—a state of false consciousness—the meaning of revolution is also dubitable.

On the surface, the first "Shanghai, Spring 1930" departs significantly from Ding Ling's previous two stories, as the heroine Meilin transforms herself from "a complacent mistress into active revolutionary."[1] But her "awakening to the truth of her own situation and to the need to reach out for other means of self-fulfillment," which provides "the prime motivation

---

[1] Feuerwerker, Y. M., *Ding Ling's Fiction: Ideology and Narrative in Modern Chinese Literature*, Cambridge, Mass, and London: Harvard University Press, 1982:56.

*force" for plot development, is not convincing.* [1] The reason is that, given
that her decision to be a mistress of a male writer is rooted in the May
Fourth tide of free love, nothing of revolutionary tenet can be regarded as
the reason for her leaving. Instead, we can only infer that her leaving is
because, for her, life with him appears tedious. And even out of the practical
consideration provoked by the new social tide that emphasizes social status,
she regrets that she loses all social standing after she cohabits with the
writer. In the new social setting in which the radical May Fourth idea of free
love became outdated, the "many classical and romantic novels" appear
hollow. Instead, "she had to have more!" Accordingly, the reason that she
has a sudden interest to dabble in revolutionary work is only because society does
not provide an appropriate space for her, as a mistress, to stand up and address
her needs.

## 四、A Cultural Worker Enlightening Oppressed Masses

In November 1930, Hu Yepin was elected as a representative to attend
an important conference to be held in the Communist Party base—Jiangxi
province; in January 1931, he was arrested. Without a proper trial, he was
secretly executed only three weeks later with twenty other Communist
sympathizers. Ding Ling, though often a sentimental woman, showed her
fortitude in face of this incident. She sent her child to her mother in Hunan
and decided to join the revolution more actively in support of her husband's
sacrifice. She accepted the League's assignment, becoming the editor of its
literary journal, *Beidou* (《北斗》), and joining the Party in 1932. The period
from 1931 to 1936 was a crucial one in Ding Ling's transition from social
critic to cultural worker (for the masses): in the wake of Hu Yepin's
martyrdom, she acknowledged her new identity as "a small but diligent and
faithful worker in literature, willing to belong to you" ("you" here referring

---

[1]   Feuerwerker, Y. M., *Ding Ling's Fiction: Ideology and Narrative in Modern
Chinese Literature*, Cambridge, Mass, and London: Harvard University Press, 1982:56.

to the masses).[①] She determined to work for the oppressed lower class by giving up her privileges as a lower middle-class intellectual and all differences as a feminine middle-class woman; for her, to be a cultural worker was to sacrifice the individual autonomy of an atomized writer in her secluded study in order to whole-heartedly devote herself to the collective interests of a mass revolution.

If we distinguish critical realism and revolutionary realism not by the period of events narrated in a story (the former pre-revolutionary, and the latter during revolution), but by the message sent forth—whether it exposes the darkness reality to only a certain degree, or contains a radical message that society is fundamentally corrupt and redeemable only by a violent, radical revolution—then *The Net of the Law* (《法网》)(1932), in terms of the inexorable, inescapable power structure it exposes, is a representative work of revolutionary realism.

Gu Meiquan, a blacksmith in a cigarette factory, loses his job after missing a day's work when he has to take care of his pregnant wife A Cui. Losing the only way to support his family, he falls into despair and turns to destructive behavior, abusing his wife and, worse, inadvertently killing the workmate's wife, his wife's best friend. He flees, but his wife is held hostage and dies in jail. Finally, he is arrested and executed. Although his workmate has accepted his apology, those who hold power nonetheless devour all these suffering people. The story is a staple of leftist literature, in which a poor criminal turns out to be merely a helpless victim of social injustice, perpetuated by its system as a "totality." The writer stands in the shoes of the masses to show their behavior in social relations; their conscious actions, themselves a result of this network, are in line with their class status and also convey the psychological state proper to their subaltern identity.

If the apt usage of imagery as political metaphor in *Flight* (《奔》) has been widely acknowledged, then *Flood* (《水》)(1931) is a further development in the writer's skill in describing the crowd. In 1931, a massive flood swept over sixteen Chinese provinces; this story takes the flood as its

---

① 丁玲:《丁玲选集》,万象书店 1936 年版,第 151-152 页.

subject, reflecting the writer's elevated political concerns over real social incident. The elaborate presentation of the masses' gradual falling into the slough of despond, because of repeated aborted illusions and their ensuing ascendance of inflammation as a result of being bullied and cheated, naturally and logically lead to the final eruption of riot—a precursor to and a primordial prototype of mass revolution. The psychological portraiture of atomized characters in anxiety is substituted by the agony and despair expressed by members of a family and some other minor figures, offering a vivid picture of the suffering community.

The writer brilliantly builds a portentous atmosphere by ushering in the discussion of a family about the incoming water. She also learns to apply animistic and naturalistic metaphors. The former is to drive home the fierceness of the torrents, which simultaneously refers to both the mercilessness of the corrupt regime and the unstinted power of the infuriated masses. The animistic and naturalistic metaphors are later combined to portray the emotional explosions and wild behavior of the repressed and exhausted masses. This literary technique graphically delivers the message that their overwhelming suffering is turning into an overpowering revolutionary power to bombard dark reality, like the unstoppable flood.

The fatalistic, cyclical view of history expressed by the senescent old who recall the rampant plagues and famines of the past is subtly subverted by the refutation of the young, which implies that the suffering that has been experienced for generations and taken for granted will be turned upside down. Some of them have articulated such messages as "standing up" (翻身) and "it is an action of taking back what we owned rather than a robbery"; which would be developed upon thereafter by revolutionary writers. All of these foretell, if not directly shown, the development of revolutionary consciousness in the writer's works. Indeed, the choice of the collective peasants as her subject and the improvement of her creative method both reflect the great change of the writer, something regarded as a landmark for both the writer herself and the proletariat literature in general. However, the problem lies in the fact that the subjectivity of the masses, as a revolutionary community, is not clearly presented. In fact, this dilemma persists in the writer's works before 1949—a historically-conditioned predicament，as I will soon discuss.

## 五、The People's Critic or a Party Intellectual?

Ding Ling was kidnapped by nationalist agents on May 4，1933. Confined for three years in various places，the KMT tried but failed to convert her. To avert public opinion，the authorities did not kill her，and she finally managed to flee to territory controlled by the Communist Party. She enthusiastically threw herself into the various activities of the Border Regions. With the outbreak of the War，she was assigned the task of leading the Northwest Front Service Corps from Yan'an to Taiyuan. For several months on the road，they maintained a military discipline and performed propagandistic plays and songs to the masses. In September 1941，she assumed the editorship of the literary page of the party's newspaper，*Liberation Daily*（《解放日报》）.

For a long period，Ding Ling took the same attitude—the stance of a social critic—as before on the "women's problem" she witnessed in the new area. This concern particularly manifested itself in her stories from 1939 to 1942. Written in 1941，*When I was in Xia Village*（《我在霞村的日子》）is a story about the deformation of a woman's femininity due to the war experience. Zhenzhen，a village girl，is captured by the Japanese and forced to serve as a sex slave；because of this，the party assigns her to work behind enemy lines as a spy，until she contracts a serious venereal disease and returns home for a cure. A superficial reading interprets her situation as a moral dilemma caused by the contradiction between nationalism and feminism，but this reading misses key evidence. What is her motivation for accepting the mission? Does she have the freedom to reject the seemingly inhuman request? We receive no information from the narrator，who is also a female party cadre visiting the village.

To the same critics，among others，the story is also a conflict between modern and traditional concepts of chastity，and thus the staple theme of May Fourth Literature on the modern versus the tradition. This reading is

justified partially by the first half of the text: her returning to the home
village brings her various responses from the villagers. While she herself
remains unperturbed on her experience, and some youths admire her
courageous, patriotic deeds, the love of her boyfriend unabated, the elder
generation of the village, including her parents and even a female party
cadre, see her experience as a great shame for a woman, feeling either pity
for her or regarding her as something subhuman. This focus on the response
of the ordinary people, combined with the cause of her capture by the
Japanese,① is typical of the May Fourth theme of free love, serving to
strengthen the argument that the writer is preaching a feminist message
against a feudalist consciousness.

But this explanation cannot account for the whole text, as the youth had
been used to the new ideas on chastity and repudiating the traditional. For
them, the ideas of the elder generation matter little. Moreover, the story is
not a story about the party's enlightenment of ignorant peasants; the
narrator is merely playing the role of spectator, often showing her doubts
and incertitude on what Zhenzhen thinks and behaves. Unresolvable by each
of these explanations, the theme of the work presents a puzzle.

I will suggest that this story, under the facade of being a story about
the "women's problem," shows the psychologically transformative condition
of the narrator as an intellectual figure. She is the real and only protagonist
of the story. When she sees the new outlook of the young peasants, she
observes with curious eyes and a skeptical mind. Apparently a newly joined
intellectual with her distinct habitus, she finds that their behavior has gone
beyond what enlightenment intellectuals had preached, and she feels
bewildered. But they still need her representation, and she still feels her
political correctness of being so. And thus she goes beyond her intellectual
parameter to represent Zhenzhen's psychology.

...I cannot find that she has many sentimental feelings and resentment; she never

---

① In love with a poor man, she is instead forced by her parents to marry to a
businessman. She escapes to the nearby church intending to become a nun when Japanese
soldiers come by.

shows a want that she hopes a man to ask for her, or even solace. But I still believe that since she was injured, precisely because she was so heavily harmed, it brought about her stubbornness as it is, so she looks as if nonchalant. But if there is some tender care, some pities beyond general sympathy to warm her soul, it is necessary. I would like that she can cry for a time, to find a place where she can cry for a time. I hope I'll have an opportunity to drink wine at the wedding feast of this family—at least, I'm also willing to hear good news before I leave.

"But what is Zhenzhen thinking? This [question] will not be put off, and it should not be a question at all!" I think on in this way, then I do not think it anymore.①

Here, Zhenzhen needs the pacification of a man with a physical touch; one finds it hard to fathom that she does not cry under this circumstance. For her, she should not appear so untouchable, so enigmatic, so strong-willed. "We" must warm her soul. She should get married. The narrator does not sense her epistemological violence at all. The subaltern cannot speak; they need her representation.

Indeed, Zhenzhen always appears asphinx to the intellectual audience. In the end, she informs the narrator that she is to be sent to an unspecified place (probably referring to Yan'an), and that she wants to stay there studying. Her statement, that "I make this plan for myself, but also for others, so I do not feel that I have something begging for others' pardon," again shocks the narrator, who acknowledges that "I was feeling greatly startled, new elements displayed in her again. I felt that she was indeed worthy of my study." Ultimately, the story is about a failed romance—an intellectual (and political) integration—between the intellectuals and the (new) peasants as "other".

Maintaining the habitus of a social critic, the writer now further exposes the seamy side of the party's work. In the Hospital (《在医院中》), written in 1941, is also led by an intellectual figure, now a third-person narrator, Lu Ping, a twenty-year old girl from Shanghai who comes to Yan'an out of idealism. Through her perspective, the reflection upon reality

---

① 丁玲：《丁玲选集》，四川人民出版社 1984 年版，第 448 页.

begins. Nevertheless ambitious to be a political supervisor, her dream is
hopelessly frustrated by the party's arrangement. Because of her educational
background, she is assigned to be a midwife nurse in an ill-equipped, remote
border hospital. She argues with her superiors and only reluctantly agrees to
go, under the condition of working for merely a year. This foretells her
unhappy experience thereafter. The "inhospitable reception" she receives,
the primitive conditions of the newly opened hospital, and "above all...the
incompetence and irresponsibility of the staff," are cast in contrast to her
dedication to her duties.[1] She feels alienated from her circumstance: she
passes judgment on everyone she meets and regards most of them as
disgusting; she finds the unsanitary habits of those hospitalized unbearable.
She argues for improving conditions, but little improves. She tries to adapt
herself into the community, but nothing avails. Ultimately, she finds that
she cannot fit into the community and quits her job, shifting to another
place.

   These events are all witnessed and narrated from her perspective. Even
so, we find a number of conflicting messages from the narrator that serve to
counteract this perspective. We notice that other members of the hospital,
including the directors, her two friends, though not self-willingly assigned
to their present jobs, adapt them well for the needs of revolutionary work.
Her two friends (one of which, a male surgeon, even often writes short
stories and skits), with their full-spirited dedication to their work, educate
Lu Ping and cast upon them an air of maturity.

   From the perspective of the party's critics, Lu Ping does not reform
herself to be a revolutionary intellectual; but the apparent neutrality of the
narrative voice provides the most difficult obstacle to our evaluation. On the
one hand, the narration shows her willfulness and immaturity, as one who
always believes that the truth is in her side. But because it tends to identify
with the vision of the heroine, this disclosure appears so objective and
nuanced that the readers hardly notice its critical effect.

---

   [1]   Feuerwerker, Y. M., *Ding Ling's Fiction: Ideology and Narrative in Modern
Chinese Literature*, Cambridge, Mass, and London: Harvard University Press, 1982:109.

To examine this paradox, we must juxtapose the text with the two previous stories. The narrator does not understand the new masses, nor is she used to their behavior. This does not mean Lu Ping's critique is unreasonable—in fact, the negative "dark" side that she witnesses often does exist. The problem is simply that she cannot balance her perspective with that of the others; lacking necessary working skills, her intellectual habitus, a fundamentally individual heroism, can only isolate herself from the community and helps little in real work. That she sees almost everyone as her "other" promises no hope for her ideals; with this mindset her accusation that all others lack love, or genuine revolutionary camaraderie, is not so reliable, and she herself is partially responsible. Meanwhile, in view of the generally harsh conditions of the environment, the lack of rationalization indeed requires time to be redressed. In addition, like *Thoughts on March 8* (《三八节有感》), this piece also shows a divisive tendency: she forms a clique that sees itself as the only innocent party in the community. Looking for evidence, she intends to incriminate her superiors.

Just at this time, a patient in the hospital calls on her and gives her a lecture. His words are meant to teach Lu Ping a lesson about how to behave properly, and he is a prototype of the revolutionary mentor figure. Even so, his teaching does not settle LuPing's doubts, and she inexorably leaves the hospital. For her, there remains ambiguity and contradiction in his lecture.

In their discussion, he tells Lu Ping that no matter who replaces the director, the situation will not improve. Like Lu Ping, he maintains the superiority of specialist intellectuals over the non-specialist political leadership. Referring to the latter contemptuously as either "illiterate cropper" or "cowboy" (we can read this sort of derogative label throughout the text), they do not trust them and are unfaithful to their supervision, believing they themselves should replace them as the leaders. This is a challenge to the party's political line, which aims to transform the "(petty) bourgeois" intellectuals into members of the proletariat by fundamentally transforming their political consciousness, rather than elevating the knowledge of the masses with the leadership of the bourgeois. The intellectual has no role outside of society; rather, he is expected to be integrated seamlessly with the people. In theory, he thus becomes the people's intellectual. But forced to follow the Party's political line and obey its policies, in practice he becomes the party's intellectual.

Ding Ling was not used to this role. Transferred from the editorship in March 1942, she had been persuaded to accept Maoist ideology, thereby conquering her sense of alienation in her full identification with the "people's stand," namely, the party's position. After Mao's Yan'an Talks, partially a response to the criticism offered by intellectuals like Ding Ling, she spent two years studying and participating in the movement of thought reform in the Party school. When she again started writing in 1944, she chose to write more on a positive note, on the "brighter aspects of life." Increasingly, she wrote impressions(印象记), communications（通信）, records of life（生活实录）, and reportage（报道）about model workers and soldiers, as well as heroic deeds. These heroic figures are not individualist heroes; rather, they are products of society, everyone "[incorporating] the ideals and institutions of his community into his own personal behavior."[1] At the same time, the characters often appear to be standing alone, aloof to the masses around them; the collective seem almost abstract, as if not a real entity, playing the minor role of cheering for the heroes' achievements.[2] Beyond the immature skills of the writer herself, these inconsistencies were also the result of existing social contradictions,[3] which serve as the framework for our

---

[1]    Feuerwerker, Y. M., *Ding Ling's Fiction : Ideology and Narrative in Modern Chinese Literature*, Cambridge, Mass, and London: Harvard University Press, 1982:111.

[2]    Feuerwerker, Y. M., *Ding Ling's Fiction : Ideology and Narrative in Modern Chinese Literature*, Cambridge, Mass, and London: Harvard University Press, 1982:111.

[3]    According to Jameson, the "adequation of content to form there realized, or not realized, or realized according to determinate proportions, is in the long run one of the most precious indices to its realization in the historical moment itself, and indeed form is itself but the working out of content in the realm of the superstructure…The insufficiency of a work of art is not at all to be seen as the result of individual clumsiness, Hegel tells us in the Aesthetics, 'rather, the insufficiency of the form derives from the insufficiency of the content.'" Jameson F., *Marxism and Form*, Princeton, NJ: Princeton University Press, 1974:329.

following discussion of Ding Ling's magnum opus from this period.

## 六、A "Proletarian Novel" without Class Subjectivity

In the last stage of Ding Ling's identity transformation (or rather, formation), endeavoring to change her style of writing from speaking for the people to speaking by the people, she sought to become a party intellectual, which for her simultaneously meant becoming a part of the masses. Such is her ultimate identification with society, dispelling her sense of alienation from the "new society" of the liberated region and the party's bureaucrats. Nonetheless, this identification could hardly be seen as complete.

Ding Ling participated energetically in the party's land reform movement in July 1946. *The Sun Shines over the Sanggan River* published two years later, narrates the process of land reform in a northern village and is the incarnation of this experience. As the writer's first experiment with the genre of the novel in depicting the revolutionary movement, the work represents Ding Ling's determination to correct her prior "false stance," presenting heroic party cadres to educate the masses.

The purpose of the land reform was as much to distribute the land of the landlords as it was to mobilize and awaken the peasants' class consciousness. Therefore, on the one hand, the characterization of the change of the characters' inner world, especially for the most conservative ones, represents the concept of "standing up" for the subaltern class; nevertheless, on the other hand, the significance of liberation is ostensibly challenged by obscure figures within the story. The misgivings towards the political act of land reform are articulated by Gu Yong, a well-to-do middle peasant. The narrator informs us that he achieves his economic success solely through forty-eight years of hard work. But he is labeled by the party's work team as a rich peasant, and out of pressure he is persuaded by neighborhood friend Hu Tai to submit his land to the team for redistribution.

Why does the writer include this plot, which seems to counter the message of "standing up"? Ding Ling certainly tries to expose the problems

in the Party's work, but different from the exposure literature created
earlier in her career, "The Sun Shines over the Sanggan River" is a problem
story, meant to invite the attention of the Party and to rectify the situation.
Since Ding Ling could not fully know the political import of land reform, the
traditional concept of "fairness" here still poses a great challenge to the
social leveling process that she aimed to extol and present [though, to a
certain extent, this "unfairness" could potentially also be explained away by
the traditional Chinese concept of "robbing the rich to help the poor" (劫富
济贫)].

Out of her consistent concern for the fate of women during this reform,
the author also describes the piteous situation of women from the landlord
families during the movement. There is also some ambiguity here: the
narrator indeed presents them as harboring resentment towards the
redistribution of their property—a sort of class hatred—but their emotive
performances not only invite the sympathy of the peasants who consequently
halt their actions in face of their tears, but also subtly trigger complex
feelings for the readers. Again, in order to counterbalance this uneasy
feeling, we are introduced to Heini, a girl originally cast as a close relative
of the landlord. Her identity is later revised to be ambiguous, perhaps a
niece of the landlord. Her upbringing further distances her from the landlord
family; because of the oppressive life she endures, she takes on a role as a
semi-proletariat figure. Her standing up, with her love affair with a party
cadre, further confirms her "real" class identity. Another woman worthy of
note is the wife of the assistant head of the village. Without even a jacket in
winter, she leads a difficult life. She thus receives the favor of a landlord's
wife, but because of this, she is beaten bitterly by her husband, a local
cadre. This embarrassing abuse of woman by a revolutionary cadre is
redressed in the end, in which she receives an exquisite set of attire and cloth
and proudly displays them to the passersby, when the villagers distribute
the property of the landlords. The message seems to be that revolution
would correct all the problems it engenders during its turbulent process.

But tensions still exist, as shown in the party cadres who lack proper
political consciousness. None are qualified to be called revolutionary

paragons，unlike the figures found in the writer's literary sketches. Again，these "non-typical phenomena" appear as discordant messages in the text，but they serve less as deconstructive elements than as elements showing the legitimacy of the reform itself. This is so not only because these "fissures" are oftentimes counterbalanced by other incidents within the text，[①] but also because when the revolutionary jobs are performed by these imperfect persons，it shows that the movement galvanizes a universal participation and effectively lifts everyone in the process.

Nevertheless，why does Ding Ling choose those "non-typical" landlords，upper middle-class peasants，and poor peasants without class consciousness，or at least without salient outer manifestations of class distinctions，as the protagonists of her novel? This question is closely related to her ideas about class consciousness and subjectivity，which show the distance of her viewpoints from that of the party. She acknowledges that the novel is "an 'interweaving' of actual personal experience and ideas absorbed from various party documents."[②] Though not exactly what she saw in reality，she nevertheless insists on an empirical approach to reality. Yet the socialist realism novel intends not only to dissect the existing world，but also to detail the process of creating a new world by constructing "a working model of historical forces in operation."[③] Literary works are thus more than presenting reality as it is. But the discrepancies between empirical reality and theoretical building seem to have made Ding Ling uneasy，analyzable through comparing the fissures in her novel and party discourse.

In Marxist theory，proper class consciousness is not a spontaneous

---

① For instance，despite the ill treatment of Dong Guihua，a party cadre，by her husband，he also confirms the strength of her work；and although Zhou Yueying，another cadre，suffered beatings by her shepherd husband，the narrator also informs us that "once her temper was up she feared neither man nor devil，and at such times people would gather round her and unite under her passionate leadership." See Feuerwerker，Y. M.，*Ding Ling's Fiction*，Cambridge：Harvard University Press，1982：172.

② 丁玲：《一点经验》，《作家谈创作》，中国青年出版社 1955 年版，第 4 页.

③ Feuerwerker，Y. M.，*Ding Ling's Fiction：Ideology and Narrative in Modern Chinese Literature*，Cambridge，Mass，and London：Harvard University Press，1982：142.

reaction that merely articulates the social beings encompassed within classes, encapsulating the complexities of social existence. Rather, it is a revolutionary class consciousness, aware of where the true interests and stakes of the class lie. But the subjectivity of the peasant class in the novel is merely taken to be their desire to acquire land. It is for this reason that we witness the ambiguous masses and the uneasy sentiments stemming from the loss of land acquired by personal toil. By contrast, the more important aspect of the Party's work—the fundamental transformation of the peasants' traditional ethical-moral concepts, including their idea of property ownership, in order to reach a true revolutionary consciousness to build a new society, with new social relations—is not seen in the novel.

The incapacity to describe this proletariat consciousness as the class subjectivity of the peasant masses is therefore not a result of the writer's own shortsightedness, but rather fundamentally conditioned by Chinese historical reality: the revolutionary consciousness of the "semi-proletarian"— the peasants, as theorized by Mao—was not existed in the class consciousness of acquiring land. Instead, it needed to be awakened, bettered, to be formed out of revolutionary theory promoted by revolutionaries. It did not exist as in the case of certain industrialized Western countries, in which the "proletarian"—the industrial workers—had for a long time cultivated a class consciousness supposedly identical to the revolutionary consciousness. If the first enlightenment movement of the New Culture Movement, which focused on the promotion of individual rights, freedom, and liberal democracy among urban citizens by the intellectuals of the May Fourth generation, did not succeed due to China's social contradiction, then this alleged new enlightenment, which centered around awakening the political awareness of the subaltern and establishing the "people's democracy," also failed to fulfill its potential. Nonetheless, though the masses were largely "liberated" by the party, they did not acquire the consciousness and the capability to be the masters of their own fate.

Consequently, the failure to present a collective subjectivity works side by side with a weak representation of a new individual subjectivity. This dilemma of forming class subjectivity, on both of the two levels, is also associated with the predicament of establishing a new culture—both of its premise and its outcome.

This "new culture" calls forth the assertion of a salient class consciousness, but it is a difficult job. The masses, as a new historical subject, as well as their own literary skills, cultural sophistication, and political distinction, still have to be fostered and cultivated. And since there was not a stage of fully-developed bourgeois culture in modern China, apart from traditional culture and a less than fully-developed May Fourth culture (more often than not despised by this new revolutionary culture), a culture needed to be formed from the void. Thus with rural peasants as the proletarian, this new revolutionary culture involved an urban life, a lifestyle that many Chinese revolutionaries had rarely experienced before.

In short, for this "new culture" as envisioned and tested by Ding Ling, the allegedly historically new subject, the peasant "proletarian," had to be represented—but they could not represent themselves, and the intellectuals who were to represent them themselves needed to be educated in revolutionary theory. In the final analysis, because of the lack of an existing proletarian consciousness, it is the Party, vanguard of the proletarian, that says the last word. Indeed, as Tani Barlow points out, the writer "achieves self-definition in the end through service to the Party,"[1] and she takes this simultaneously to be a service to the people.

From this point of view, the change of Ding Ling from a veteran May Fourth-styled writer to a staunch Communist writer can be appreciated from a new angle. And the fissures, cracks, and discordant voices/discourses in her novel can be put into a new framework, to be seen as a stage in a dialectical development in a transitional period, in an experiment with an "alternative modernity." The conflicting discourses in her novels, as well as in her articles, can be seen as a result of the social contradiction that was (and still is) far from being resolved.

---

[1]  Barlow, T., *I Myself Am a Woman: Selected Writings of Ding Ling*, Boston: Beacon Press, 1989:45.

## 七、Conclusion

This chapter suggests that the four-stage change of Ding Ling's intellectual position is simultaneously a gradual adjustment of her perspectives and a revision of her opinions of the "women's problem"; there was a shift of focus from the women themselves to society and its power of structure as the cause of the problem, and correspondingly, the modification of her cultural and political strategy.

In accordance with this change, her differing identities not only show her drastically shifted subjectivities in her efforts to conquer her sense of alienation, but also correspond to four shifting notions of literature as a socio-cultural institution. The ambiguities and tensions in her treatment of the "women's problem" throughout the period reveal irresolvable historical contradictions, making her efforts an unfinished revolution.

# Part Ⅱ.

Romanticism, Modernism,
or Modern Literati's Novel?

# Chapter Three    An Alienated Mind Dreaming for Integration:Constrained Cosmopolitanism in Wumingshi's "Modern Literati Novel"

## 一、Introduction

Wumingshi (Bu Naifu, 1917-2002) was one of the most popular writers in the 1940s' China. In 1944, he published two extremely popular novels consecutively, *Romance in the Arctic Region*(《北极风情画》), and *Woman in the Pagoda*(《塔里的女人》). They immediately became best-sellers, and the writer became a celebrity. After he returned to Chongqing, the wartime capital, his more serious literary efforts were devoted to the writing of a multi-volume *Book without a Name*(《无名书》), the project of which started in 1946 and spanned 13 years. Before 1949, three volumes were completed and published. The whole project was completed in 1960 and it amounts to two million words.

His stories, apparently located at the intersection of popular literature and "vernacular modernism,"① focus on legendary subject matters of

---

①    The concept of "vernacular modernism" was created by Miriam Bratu Hansen in her comparative study of early Chinese silent films and classical Hollywood cinema. In her view, "classical Hollywood cinema could be imagined as a cultural practice on a par with the experience of modernity, as an industrially-produced, mass-based, vernacular modernism," and the Chinese silent films of early twentieth century shared similar features. See Hansen, M. B., The Mass Production of the Senses:Classical Cinema as Vernacular Modernism, *Modernism/Modernity*, 1999,6(2):59-77. Zhang Zhen accepts this concept and takes it to study early Chinese films produced in Shanghai. See Zhang, Z., *An Amorous History of the Silver Screen:Shanghai Cinema*, 1896-1937, Chicago: University of Chicago Press, 2006.

contemporary society in the turmoil of modern world. They are fond of surrealist description and "unnatural" languages, having idiosyncratic styles reminiscent of some traditional and modern literary schools: the "Mandarin Ducks and Butterflies,"[①] Shanghai's "Neo-Perceptionalist,"[②] and even the late Qing "Literati Novel."[③] The writer himself says that his fundamental style is to "stubbornly reject realism, and perennially embrace futurism."[④] Some of his works are regarded as a sort of "philosophical fiction." Interestingly, what Yvonne Chang has characterized the modernist literary movement in post-1949 Taiwan can be applied to him as well: "The appeal to some forms of 'eternal myth' seems to inform" its "herculean enterprise of constructing a verbal edifice as a material vehicle for some idiosyncratic aesthetic visions."[⑤] Because of this feature, some scholars contend that he, together with another writer Xu Xu (1908-1980), constitutes a modernist

---

① The school of "Mandarin Ducks and Butterflies" was a disparaging term referring to a form of popular literature dominating the Chinese literary scene during the 1910s. In the beginning it just meant classical-style love stories, usually a troubled romance between a poor scholar and a beauty. But starting from the early 1920s, the term was used by young critics to refer to all forms of popular old-style fiction, including knight-errant novels, scandal novels, detective novels, etc. that were popular in the 1920s and 1930s.

② The "Neo-Perceptionalists" was a group of writers in Shanghai in the 1930s who were influenced by Western and Japanese modernism. They wrote fiction (mostly short stories) that was concerned with the unconscious or psychological reactions to the metropolitan settings. For more discussions, see Lee, L. O., *Shanghai Modern: The Flowering of a New Urban Culture in China*, 1930-1945, Boston: Harvard University Press, 1999; and Shih, Sh., *The Lure of the Modern: Writing Modernism in Semicolonial China*, 1917-1937, Berkeley: University of California Press, 2001.

③ The "Literati Novel" in late Qing refers to a kind of writing that was conditioned by the historically overdetermined formulation of the relationship between literati scholars and the society. Their identities rendered their literary reworkings of the perceived social realities. For more details, see Roddy S. J., *Literati Identity and Its Fictional Representations in Late Imperial China*, Stanford: Stanford University Press, 1998.

④ 无名氏:《绿色的回声》,花城出版社 1995 年版,第 8 页.

⑤ Chang, Y. S., "Revisiting the Modernist Literary Movement in Post-1949 Taiwan," http://www.soas.ac.uk/taiwanstudies/eats/eats2008/file43157.pdf. Accessed June 23, 2012.

school, or develops a "popular modernism." Yet because most of their
stories deal with romantic subjects and engage in passionate reveries, their
literary oeuvres are also named "post-romantic literature," or a kind of "neo-
romanticist writing."①

Against the grain of these interpretations which are based on a
superficial reading of the texts, this study, through a practice of political
hermeneutics, contends that Wumingshi's works are a brand of "modern
literati fiction," or a genre of "fiction of idea," a sort of middle-brow fiction
in the market of popular culture in modern China. I will firstly explore two
famed stories of his early years by analyzing their narrative strategy; then
meticulously examine his magnificent novel-cycle. My study finds that he
places himself outside of the mainstream realistic writing to construct an
individualistic narrative aiming to transcend the dominant discourse of the
time. Nevertheless, the cosmopolitanism that he tried to express in his
fictional works was constrained by the social-political momentum of the
time, resulting in many fissures and gaps. Only through this analytical
procedure, the true significance, import, and the inexorable dilemma of his
"modern literati fiction" could be fully appreciated.

## 二、The Maturation of "Middle-Class Romance" and Its Narrative Strategy

The early two novels that contributed to Wumingshi's fame in the
market of popular culture in the the 1940s' China have the same narrative
framework, in which the first-person narrator (the same one) comes to Mt.
Hua, a Taoist sacred mountain and a famed tourist resort in north China,
for convalescence from his meningitis. In the first novel, he meets a
strange visitor, who upon his unswerving, earnest request recounts his

---

① Yan Jiayan calls their works "post-Romantic literature" because their stories are
"imbued with the hue of romanticism," see 严家炎:《中国现代各流派小说选》,北京大学出
版社 1986 年版. For the naming of "neo-romanticism," see 耿传明:《轻逸与沉重之间:现
代性问题视野中的新浪漫派文学》,南开大学出版社 2004 年版.

love story; formally a sequel, the second story has a minor variation, where the maverick is a Taoist, who gives the narrator a manuscript recording his experience. This kind of legendary opening, usually couched in a first-person narration, was a much-used pattern in Chinese popular novels ever since the late Qing.

The first novel, *Romance in the Arctic Region*, itself appears hackneyed, which is reminiscent of the much-maligned, over-sentimentalized style and language of the traditional Mandarin Ducks and Butterflies School. A Korean captain is in exile in Siberia, where he temporarily stages to avoid the persecution of Japanese troops after the failure of the Anti-Japanese resistance by the local Chinese military force which he joins. He has an affair with a Polish woman. Tragedy is inevitable for this brand of sensational romance: because he would soon be dispatched back to China, the passionate woman commits suicide.

But why did a rarely fresh platitude attract the readers' minds and strike their hearts? There is little doubt that the happenings of this sort of affairs was a commonplace at the time, due to the much broadened social life as a result of wartime diaspora; but the teasing out of its essential ideologemes is the key procedure to find its mythical enchantment. The man is a new style of hero in the romantic stories of the time. He is, at least initially, playful and cynical, rather a man with unswerving faith in love. The girl early on mistakes him for her boyfriend in the snow field, and he takes this as an opportunity to have a taste of her beauty. But for a "romance" to be appealing, this image of playboy has to be replaced the sooner the better, so we witness his conflicting mind: on the one hand, he seemingly cautions himself of the unpropitious outcome of this doomed game; on the other hard, he is not willing to give up the relation and yields himself to be a "slave of passion." What ultimately props up his will to continue the dangerous play, however, is his desire to acquire psychosomatic pleasure, no matter how short-term it would be, and with little psychological burden of responsibility.

Although this middle-class attitude towards love affair is not unusual in the modern world, it was still at odds with the contemporary Chinese

ethical-moral convention. There should be a rhetorical explanation to be
offered for this "bourgeois hedonism," and here it is the wartime exigency
that plays the function:"The future prospect of the whole nation is invisible,
where is the perennial happiness for the individual? But this would not
hinder my pursuit of ephemeral spark of happiness." In view of this
predetermined rationale that aims to preclude and gloss over any sense of
guiltiness, his heart-broken pain after the death of his lover, while being a
natural response, has to be seen as a prearranged narrative setup. Whereas
some of Eileen Chang's (1920-1995) stories have begun to touch upon this
kind of relation, namely this middle -class romance, they have not reached
the degree of maturation, because the protagonists in her stories are still in
the half way towards this new identity—this self-willed middle-class
subjectivity which meant to satisfy its desires with much less sense of
imposed social and familial burden—and thus their psychosomatic conditions
are semi-traditional.

In these two novels, the apparent conflict between "love" and
"revolution" is very different from the pattern of "revolution plus love" that
was popular since the late 1920s. Here, it is not for any revolutionary
responsibility that love is sacrificed; rather, the woman's death, or at least
her disappearance, thus her symbolic death, is predetermined from the very
beginning to complete the narrative cycle:she is only a training ground and
the medium of sacrifice (as a necessary practice of ritual) for the will-power
of the man. She needs to be ousted from the man after she is consumed and
her role is over. But to undo anxiety resulted from moral qualms, the man
now has to be emasculate (symbolically castrated), to show his pains over
the loss of his lover, to compensate for his own wrongdoing, as a prop to
skirt the social-moral censorship. Meanwhile, for the melodrama to
continue, the woman is necessary to be always infatuated with love.

This is so partially because, even without the plot of dispatch as the
excuse, the woman would still never have an opportunity to live with the
man peacefully and happily, out of their incompatible identities:she is a
social outcast, a symbolically subaltern. Here, the girl is a Polish émigré, a
politically untouchable and abject person. Her father died as a result of the

Revolution; and for "political reasons," the narrator informs us, that she, and her mother, are detained there. Therefore, this apparent model of genuine love is merely a facade, a smokescreen to cover up the forbidden gap and the class divide that are not crossable. (In this case, this "class divide" is less about the empirical class structure than about the symbolic division between the superior and the inferior.) Furthermore, revolution here becomes the culprit responsible for the romantic tragedy, but this ostensible conflict between love and revolution bypasses the poignant social contradiction of the hypocrisy of middle class: women, always women, are the real victim of both the patriarchal gender relation and the symbolic class division. (The class division is not caused by revolution itself—the latter theoretically, if not always in real political praxis, repudiates any class hierarchy—but by conventional moral taboo. In the story, it is merely the real life burden—the girl has to stay there to take care of her mother, and the man has to leave—that is offered as the "inexorable contradiction.") On the surface, the text shows "love" (a "universal emotion and natural humanity") as the paramount power-force prevailing over the difference among classes, nations, and political persuasions, yet this apparent cosmopolitanism, if not internationalism, shown in a hackneyed romantic pattern, is thwarted by an invisible yet inalienable obstacle.

However, the (implied) author is honest enough to confess the hypocrisy of the middle class world; if not very clear here, then at the end of his second novel. There, he rhetorically poses the readers a question: in the first novel, the woman is dead, and Lin (the man) disappears; "if the former was not dead, and the latter did not leave, what would happen to them? The answer is 'a Woman in Pagoda.' In other words, if their story develops further, the result would be like that of 'Woman in Pagoda.'"[①]

In many aspects, the second novel is reminiscent of the pattern of the first one, though the protagonists are Chinese now, and the male protagonist here intends to transfer his beloved girl to another man. The model to unearth the "buried romance" in it is the same as the first one.

---

① 无名氏：《塔里的女人》，新闻天地社 1976 年版，第 176 页.

Meeting a Taoist in Mt. Hua, the narrator is astonished over his queer
behavior and pursues his secrets, finally the Taoist is "moved" by "my"
earnestness to entrust his monograph to "me," for he knows that "I" am a
writer. The following is again the same pattern: a first-person narrative from
the perspective of the male protagonist, who narrates his "tragic experience"
of a lamentable love with a girl. The girl now, as I just suggest, is
symbolically dead; and the man is always in deep grief. If an "aborted" love
intervened by the Japanese imperialism (which, as said, nevertheless is
merely a narrative setup) is what contributed to the sympathetic reception of
the first story in the minds of readers; then, what new elements in this
novel that led to its popular success?

   The story now is more saliently in the track of "Mandarin Ducks and
Butterflies Fiction," reminiscent of the traditional formulaic pattern of
"Love between the Talent and the Beauty" (才子佳人). The Taoist, with
his secular name Luo Shengti, was an entrepreneur, a doctor, and
simultaneously a musician (in particular, a violinist playing musical
masterpieces from the West). As a typical middle-class new rich, he is
engaging in passionate love with a female student after playing a long-term
game of love with the latter (a necessary formulaic element of the middle-
class romance), who also has an enviable background, delicate manner, and
similar mindset. In short, they are a superb match in terms of their class
distinction and tastes. Yet since he has an old-styled wife and children
owning to the traditional practice of prearranged marriage, he has to
sacrifice his love by recommending a handsome captain to his lover.
Mistaking the move as a gesture to repudiate her, the girl accepts the
arrangement, intending to revenge his betrayal. This leads to the unexpected
development and the miserable ending.

   On the surface, this "tragedy" is merely a result out of the conflict
between the old and the new, or tradition versus modernity. In other words,
the lack of social rationalization brings about the tragedy. Indeed, at the first
time when Luo Shengti plays violin in the school where the girl attends, he
deliberately dresses himself in an old-styled robe, the plot of which implies
that he has some self-imposed traditional concepts if not idiosyncrasies. But

if this is all that is conveyed by the text，did not this kind of story have been rendered numerous times ever since the late Qing period? The fact that the formulaic plots of the two novels—the two handsome men both gradually yet decisively conquer a pretty girl's heart，to the effect that both girls lose their pride falling desperately into their arms—are the set pattern of the middle-class melodrama has reminded us that this is not simply an old story being retold in new way. There must be new elements that made them stand out. To be sure，that the tragic tone of the two stories invited sympathetic reception in the tumultuous time，when a great portion of the nation experienced diasporic life，is easy to understand. The psychological complex of feeling always being late to achieve happiness，that their "golden age" of ten years are irrevocably lost，that both the desired and the desiring have passed their prime years，surely also has its social-phenomenological correlation. But more textual analysis is warranted to solve the enigma.

We need to note that Luo Shengti's hesitation is out of his self-consciousness to protect his social status (numerously he reminds himself，"Even if I live together with Wei，what would the society see it? Do I still want to accomplish something in the society?"). Nevertheless，this essential stake is glossed over by a magnificent rhetoric，"How do I have rights to accept Wei's sacrifice? Why couldn't I sacrifice myself for (my) family，for the society，for the tradition，and for the future of Wei?"[①] But shortly later，he easily turns down all these excuses when he finds the man he recommends does not fit in with his superficial appearance，and believes that the society would without much difficulty accept their relationship once he discloses publicly their affair. What this dramatic change discloses is that，this is not a traditional story about the oppression of conventional moral custom；rather，the society is now enlightened enough to take in the new practice. It is only because his courage is a little lagging behind the time out of his ingrained self-consciousness. But the other consciousness of this class—ever pursuing the happiness without the hindrance of conventional concept—is also developed enough now to surge up and prevail over the former one—

---

① 无名氏：《塔里的女人》，新闻天地社 1976 年版，第 106 页.

anyway, he has enough social capital to protect himself even if he takes the
bold action.[①] His failure to achieve this "happy consciousness" has its
particular reason:what he pursues is not pure emotion, but a passion based
on the beauty of women.

This disposition of indulgence in physical, carnal pleasure appears
ostensibly as a belief in beauty, or a sort of aestheticism, which is taken as a
life philosophy. So, for the sake of the rhetoric of "pure pleasure," even
though the text is filled with descriptions of the physical attraction of woman
( the girl ) with enticing sexual overtones and implications which are
reminiscent of both the style of the neo-perceptionalists and the sensual,
sexual descriptions in the works of the "expert of triangle affairs" Zhang
Ziping (1893-1959),[②] it decisively evades any possible charge of this sort,
and aims to show it as "pure art," thus we also see some seemingly classical-
style portraits of the beauty of a woman's body.[③] What needs to note here is
that the descriptions should not be seen as merely for literary effects,
although this does contribute to its sensational, popular success (thus its
"middle-brow" nature). Aside from the fact that the protagonist disclaims
his interests in carnal pleasure, and proclaims that his love is "the purest
sympathy, the cleanest fantasy, with some elements of religious import,"
he also tries his best to appear "innocent, natural, and sincere." However,

---

① For the description of this consciousness, see 无名氏:《塔里的女人》,新闻天地社
1976 年版,第 158 页. "For our happiness, I can sacrifice everything:my honor, social
status, personality, and any others. I only want one thing:happiness." 158. The "four
principles" that Luo Shengti finally generalizes out of his life experience also substantiate
this point:in his views, man should cherish the opportunity of acquiring happiness;
happiness is ephemeral, a man should not sacrifice too much for others as which will even
spoil the happiness of the other; meanwhile, he aptly sees his "self-consciousness" as the
main cause for the tragedy, yet he doesn't take it as his self-interested class consciousness,
but as his "self-respect." 174.

② For instance, for the description of Wei's beauty, see 无名氏:《塔里的女人》,新闻
天地社 1976 年版,第 25-26 页; the effects of his violin performance are like "caressing a
girl's fragrant body, a girl's fragrant bust," 32; and the psychosomatic feelings when he
embraces her, 60.

③ 无名氏:《塔里的女人》,新闻天地社 1976 年版,第 136 页.

once the romance is aborted, he finds carnal fulfillment by visiting prostitutes; and once he finds Wei has been too old to meet his dreams for beauty (in his eyes, now she is "the symbol of the end of the universe, too horrified"), he immediately leaves her without a second thought. But this egocentric indulgence in aestheticism, a typical life philosophy in the middle-class world, which now gradually emerges in the Chinese society, is in conflict with marriage as a social institution. This conflict between "aesthetic hedonism" and social rationality—both being the "bourgeois" dispositions, which then become irresolvable, immanent contradiction—is the ultimate cause of the tragedy, the tragedy being less the aborted romance between the youths than the final repudiation of love as selfless emotion: for hedonistic concerns, Luo Shengti engages in love without consideration of his social responsibility—the latter a form of the social rationality; and for the same aestheticism, he leaves Wei because she has been too old to arouse his interests—the action itself is also out of his "reason". Ultimately, then, what prevails in the last is his "self-consciousness," the bourgeois "self-respect," a class consciousness that aims to pursue individual happiness relentlessly without any hindrance in mind, no matter whether the hindrance is social customs or the interests of the other. This reading behind the facade of sentimentalism is contrary to what we understand superficially from the text.

To solve this conflict (or dilemma) between aestheticism and rationality, which is predicated on a social contradiction, the author has tried to resort to some "universal" ideas, in particular love, to bridge the gap and gloss over the fissure. That Luo Shengti apparently converts to religion is one kind of this effort. But there is another one. We need to note that what has been told by Luo Shengti's writing is not the whole story—the framework of the story informs us more. The narrator in the very beginning believes that "everyone is selfish, this is the truth of the universe. The difference is only that, some people understand that they are selfish, the others even do not understand the fact"; "I admit that I'm selfish, I understand that I'm selfish. To avoid the damage of others out of my selfishness, I can only seek for solitude." This idea is apparently identical

with Luo Shengti's，thus the narrator meets the latter in Mt. Hua，who has
been there for the same philosophy though for different reasons（it is also
due to this same life attitude that Luo Shengti sees the narrator as his peer
and has entrusted his manuscript）. But what is paradoxical is that，with the
rendition of Luo Shengti's tragic story，the text ostensibly eulogizes a
sublime spirit of self-sacrifice；which，ironically，is also attributed to be the
culprit of the tragedy. But this is merely a superficial smokescreen that
protects the inner cause of the tragedy.

The acknowledgement of ingrained selfishness of the human being in
the very beginning has laid out the internal contour of this new middle-class
world，which is confirmed again in the end by the narrator with another
story that explains the title of the novel. This story also links the two
novels—which the narrator has interpreted as of consecutive nature—
together. "Why the story is called 'Woman in the Pagoda,' whereas there is
none in the text that mentions a pagoda？My answer is：although on the
surface there's no mentioning of it，actually there are many places where I
have referred to it." The narrator says.[1] Then，he tells us the following
short story allegedly written by his friend. A woman was incarcerated in a
stone pagoda by his lover who is an aristocrat and who now does not love her
any more. She still remembers their love of the past decades，and does
everything she could do to commemorate her memory. When she is too old，
she is informed one day that her lover is dead；heartbroken，she dies
immediately. Whereas the true fact is：he is not dead，he is constructing
another pagoda for another woman. However，the narrator suggests
modifying the ending a little bit by making the "girl" resurrect herself and
smilingly enter the numerous pagodas the man constructs for her.

This serious exposure of the hypocrisy of the fundamentally patriarchal，
middle-class mentality—what needs to be stressed is that this mentality or
consciousness bears a particular Chinese characteristic；because with the
dominance of Chinese traditional gender concept in society，woman does not
hold an equal social status with man—as represented by the apparent

---

[1]　无名氏：《塔里的女人》，新闻天地社 1976 年版，第 176 页.

passionate yet merciless male lovers in the two novels who are the real protagonists, is neglected by almost all critics. Although the narrator here goes a step further to pinpoint the builder of the "pagoda" to be "some power-force that is not knowledgeable,"[1] his direct target is surely the freakish, capricious man. This is substantiated by the disclosure of the whole illusionary framework: it is nothing but a dream—the (implied) author—narrator does not go to Mt Hua the second time for recuperation. This set-up is typical of traditional Chinese narrative convention, which has a Buddhist connotation that implies everything in real life is nothing but illusionary (this also adds to its popular, "middle-brow" flavor). But what is important here is that what "awakens" the first-person narrator is Luo Shengti's hysteric reproach, berating "me" for publishing his story which exposes his mercilessness.

This analysis then turns the two apparent moving love stories upside down, revealing them as nothing but a critique of patriarchal hypocrisy and middle-class mentality; in particular, women become the testing ground for men's "self-consciousness" of class-bound "aesthetic" hedonism. But this is still not the whole picture. What immediately follow the acknowledgement of the middle-class selfishness at the beginning of this text, curiously, are some seemingly irrelevant anecdotes; which, however, after analysis will be found to be the core of the essential theme. A priest from Norway has published an English book *The Philosophy of Mozi and His Concept of Religion* in the Commercial Press, the top company publishing academic and teaching material which receives high acclaim in Chinese academy. This, together with his excellent language skill in Chinese, indicates that he is an authority of Chinese philosophy. The narrator believes in one of his "bold and fresh ideas," which holds that "the God has only symbolic value, the spiritual significance; it has no scientific import, and he doesn't need this, either."[2] But the narrator nevertheless sighs for his agony over the loss (the symbolic death) of the God. What this episode conveys is that, the outcome

---

① 无名氏:《塔里的女人》,新闻天地社 1976 年版,第 179 页.
② 无名氏:《塔里的女人》,新闻天地社 1976 年版,第 2 页.

of secularization, or the Weberian rationalization with the severance of art
and religion from politics, as the necessary procedure to develop modernity,
has resulted in a loss of the spiritual integrity. The disintegration of the
modern world has made the problem more poignantly stand out. With the
outbreak of the World War Ⅰ, the serious problems of the modern world
showed themselves more clearly. This social-historical context is the subtext
of the text. However, without probing the social-economic contradiction,
the intellectuals tend to attribute the problem to be a cultural one—with the
death of God, the loss of faith in any ethical-moral standard and system.

Besides the priest, the other one who talks to the narrator often was a
professor of philosophy. He now runs a mill, and his tenet is that the face of
donkey is cuter than a man's face, as it is more faithful. The breakdown of
the Western ethical-moral world which had been regarded as the most
advanced by the Chinese, led to a moral anarchism that is shown in the third
person that the narrator briefly introduces following the philosopher and the
priest:a playful girl who does not believe in love and trust man.

Therefore,taken together, the two texts both expose a paradox that is
seemingly insolvable:apparently, love is the paramount power-force that
holds people and conquers any barriers to the union of the humanity
regardless of race, religion, class, and political belief, yet this love itself is
greatly    impaired    by    ingrained    patriarchal    value    and    middle-class
consciousness. Cosmopolitanism is in vain or is greatly restrained, religion is
also useless to unite the disintegrated human psyche—although Luo Shengti
is a Taoist bearing a Buddhist name of "awakening to the void" (觉空), he
still indulges in his memory while playing violin! This dilemma, as a
predicament of the modern society, however, is ostensibly solved by the
author in his next work:the magnificent novel-cycle.

### 三、*Book without a Name*:A Bildungsroman or a "Philosophical Novel"?

*Book without a Name* was purported to explore, through the life
adventures of the hero Yin Di (which can be read as abbreviation of the

Chinese words "印证真谛", to prove the truth), the meaning of life and the cultural difference between the East and the West. The first three volumes: *Beasts*(《野兽、野兽、野兽》), *The Siren of the Sea*(《海艳》), *Golden Nights of the Snake*(《金色的蛇夜》) were published in Shanghai from 1946 to 1949 (volume three was only partially finished when Shanghai was liberated). Wumingshi calls this novel-series a kind of roman-fleuve(江河小说). Under its realistic plots, this novel-cycle is apparently "a summa in fictional guise" of Wumingshi's "understanding and appreciation of the earth, sun, and moon, of human history, and art, and of religion, philosophy, and all varieties of human love,"[①] but I will pinpoint the specific nature of this rumination in the context (as the subtext) of the historical dynamic and momentum.

## 四、Violent Revolution and Its Discontent

The first volume narrates the hero's passionate engagement with revolution. Brought up in a well-to-do family, like many idealistic youths at the time, he quits high school in Nanjing just before graduation and goes to Beijing to pursue knowledge and truth. He becomes a leftist after engaging in self-study and experiencing many menial jobs. When he returns to the hometown five years later, he has become an underground communist member. Soon he leaves home again to join the Northern Expedition Army and sets off for the First National Revolution against warlords. But the right-wing KMT's purge of the CCP and the subsequent massacre and white-terror strike a gigantic blow on his mind, leading him to suspect the meaning of revolution. He is arrested by the political enemy nevertheless. Although he refuses to betray his comrades, his release one year later out of his father's negotiation with the authority makes him dubious in the eyes of his comrades. He could not bear their coldness, and leaves the revolutionary rank. At the end of the novel, at the invitation of a friend, he goes to

---

① Hsia, C. T., Forward, In: *Red in Touch and Claw: Twenty-six Years in Communist Chinese Prisons*, Pu N. ed., New York: Grove Press, 1994: xvii.

Singapore to help run an overseas Chinese newspaper. If Yin Di's
revolutionary experience is typical among the idealistic youths of the time,
his gradually ascending suspicion and final resignation of the revolutionary
cause are rarely seen in the literature of the time. This entails a more
detailed textual analysis with the assistance of the historical subtext.

By close scrutiny, the seeds of the "betrayal" have long been planted
into the mind of this aristocratic youth. His "idea of reform," according to
him, is "very simple, in other words, my belief is very simple": "In the
screen of this epoch, every color is dark, only one color is spectacular, it is
called 'bloodiness.'"[①] This naive belief in violence is less based on any solid
revolutionary class theory than on some sort of blind anarchism; its origin is
derived from other sources, in particular, from his youthful rebellious spirit
which has a class nature. He confesses to his father that his abortion of
school and leave of family are out of a sort of "blind impulse," out of his
fatigue with the ordinary discipline of the conventional life, especially the
strict and repressive school life. For the "awakened soul" of Yin Di, he sees
all the outside darkness and dirtiness; he thus, like his erstwhile father,
decides to reform it. The buddy of an emergent self-consciousness of this
new aristocratic class requests its own development and growth, just like his
obscured pursuit for fresh atmosphere out of the constrained, oppressive
social circumstance and a naturally-born sense of justice asking for social
equality demands its own fulfillment.

But just like his rebellion of the family is merely springing forth from a
youthful impulse of an aristocrat, his fight with the dark society is also more
for the individual urge of this oppressed, elite intellectual class, than for the
interests of the suffering masses. Later on he confesses that from the very
beginning, he is an individualist with an aristocratic consciousness, a person
with the Nietzschean concept of "superman."[②] Nevertheless, if his belief is
so easily set up, it is also easily to be shaken and torn apart. This happens
when he sees numerous deaths and overwhelming bloodiness in the anti-

①　无名氏：《野兽、野兽、野兽》，黎明文化事业股份有限公司 1995 年版，第 36 页.
②　无名氏：《金色的蛇夜》，新闻天地 1977 年版，第 123 页.

revolutionary massacre, and after he feels greatly wronged when he is tested by his comrades. He does not know why the counter-revolutionary split happens and attributes the cruel massacre to the bloody revolution itself, feeling complete disillusionment.

This picture is more or less faithful to the historical reality and had been depicted by the Communist writers themselves, such as Mao Dun's "Trilogy of Hesitation." Yet what makes the author's portrayal depart from the latter is not his seemingly careful anatomy of the psychology of this group, but his description of the process of resignation.

Even during the high-tide of revolutionary zeal, the seeds of distrust and discontent have been implanted. The oftentimes caricatured portrayal of the zealous radicals serves as a counter-point to the always "reasonable," cold attitude of the hero. Although Yin Di acknowledges they always do excellent job in revolution, their "pragmatism," "opportunism" are directly in contrast with the protagonist's idealism and political correctness. Under this conscious contrast, even Yin Di's obvious venturesome plan of organizing gigantic worker strikes is shown as better than his colleagues' inexorable terroristic strategy. If this has thrown the hidden line for the later plot development, then after the purge, the refutation of the revolution per se becomes more clearly presented through the narrative voice: to examine "what on earth the authentic countenance of this so-called 'revolutionary war' is? What on earth of this so-called "sacred bloodiness' is!"[1]

While most times ahistorically attributing the failure of revolution to the bloody revolution itself,[2] the narrative voice also sometimes shows its indignation over the betrayal of revolution by the reactionary: "History can be betrayed by careerists, but will not serve as their prostitute for a long time. Revolution can be betrayed by kidnappers, but the truth would not be

---

① 　无名氏:《野兽、野兽、野兽》,黎明文化事业股份有限公司 1995 年版,第 233 页.

② 　For instance, it says, "history requests peace, blood demands craziness; history asks for life, blood orders death." 无名氏:《野兽、野兽、野兽》,黎明文化事业股份有限公司 1995 年版,第 247 页.

betrayed! The justice would not be betrayed."[1] This ambivalence itself
needs to be analyzed with the paradoxical mentality of some intellectuals.
Incapable to see the future of the mass revolution, thus tired of and appalled
at the bloody violence, though still repulsive of the "counter-revolutionary"
policies of the ruling regime, some of the intellectuals then intended to seek
for an alternative way to the national salvation, which would be more
"natural," peaceful, and in no need of violence.[2] Because of this way of
thinking, even the recourse to history itself appears a hollow rhetoric,
because there is a realm that is transcendent of history, that is, the nature.
This message is especially conveyed by the imagery of the peaceful and
beautiful ocean, which repeatedly shows up. This then sets the tone and the
thematic focus for the second volume, which is about a pursuit of romantic
love.

## 五、Romantic Love and Its Ennui

*The Siren of the Sea* is about a romance and its unexpected disillusion.
Yin Di's overseas adventure in journalism is aborted due to the intervention
of the domestic authority who keeps an eye on him, and he returns back to
China. He meets in the returning steamship an elegant yet phlegmatic girl.
They spend seven nights in the ship and have mutual feelings after a few
exchanges. At the destination the girl disappears without notice, only to be
met surprisingly in Hangzhou when Yin Di goes to visit his aunt, and he
knows that she is his cousin, Qu Ying, who he befriended intimately in his
childhood. After four months of pursuit, he wins her heart and they
consummate their love. Experiencing extreme happiness, Yin Di falls into
fatigue. Having an agonistic feeling and an existential anxiety, he leaves for

---

① 无名氏:《野兽、野兽、野兽》,黎明文化事业股份有限公司 1995 年版,第 246 页.

② "In one epoch, oftentimes it only allows the existence of two forces. If a third one
exists, either it is too small to invite attention, or is forced to side with one of the two
forces, or is hung to death by the coalition of the two." 无名氏:《野兽、野兽、野兽》,黎明文
化事业股份有限公司 1995 年版,第 477-478 页.

the Northeast China to join the Anti-Japanese Voluntary Army in the wake of the "September Eighteen Incident."

When the volume opens，Yin Di is searching for peaceful "beauty and dream" after being tired of politics. Allegedly the "absoluteness" that he pursues in vain in the past years in political struggle is now effortlessly acquired "in an instant."[①] Like Qu Ying，he treats the ocean as a certain set of metaphysics，and he believes the nature is "wiser" than the philosophy of Kant and Hegel.[②] But just like Qu Ying has aptly commented，"to walk under the moonlight，one is easily to have a wrong impression that believes himself as not living in the secular world,"[③] this dream to bring the peace and beauty of the nature to the world via transforming the minds of the populace is an idealistic reverie. (Yin Di admits that what he pursues is merely "something that is super-real. The further it distances itself from the reality，the better. Now I only love a little illusion，a certain relaxation.")[④] He now puts his hopes on the "metaphysical" or "idealistic" level："Ugliness and foulness not only live themselves on the system，but also live in the human mind. To change the system，firstly it has to change the (mind of) people."[⑤] Apparently，this is a mentality that was promoted since the late Qing period which tried to reform the "backward mentality" of the nation，what is different is that what Yin Di intends to preach to people now is not any progressive political idea，but "poem" and "beauty"："If everyone can admire and believe in it，the ugliness will not come out."[⑥]

This search for the "absoluteness," for the "eternality," has its own raison d'etre. Ever since the disintegration of the traditional world of life with the enforcement of modernity，the disenchantment of traditional culture first and foremost means the dispersal of the traditional Chinese

---

① 无名氏：《海艳》，花城出版社 1977 年版，第 4 页.
② 无名氏：《海艳》，花城出版社 1977 年版，第 28 页.
③ 无名氏：《海艳》，花城出版社 1977 年版，第 29 页.
④ 无名氏：《海艳》，花城出版社 1977 年版，第 47 页.
⑤ 无名氏：《海艳》，花城出版社 1977 年版，第 79 页.
⑥ 无名氏：《海艳》，花城出版社 1977 年版，第 79 页.

worldview of "天理"(Heaven's mandate, or principle of nature). With the
introduction and indoctrination of "公理"(universal principle or axiom), the
Western bourgeois (as a new world class) world view of struggle, evolution
(a linear, teleological historicism often in the form of social Darwinism) has
become the new world picture. Yet the great disaster of the World War I,
with all its inhuman casualties and destruction of human culture, made this
picture again blurry and the value system dubious. A search for a new
ontological foundation for the humanity was regarded as a necessity. And,
since for modern Chinese intellectuals, the Marxist internationalism is
premised on a theory of class struggle as the propelling force of history that
they could not wholeheartedly embrace, their revamped "cosmopolitanism,"
which now was against "wholesale westernization" and encouraged by the
wartime cultural nationalistic sentiment, could not but find one channel out:
the allegedly Caesaristic, materialistic Western culture needs to be
synthesized with the peaceful Eastern (Chinese and Indian, but usually
implicitly referring to the Chinese only), spiritually-oriented culture.

　　This searching for a new ontological "beingness in the world" was a
development of the Chinese New Culture Movement. But it had trekked a
path that departed the material ground of contemporary history and became
a metaphysical deliberation. For Wumingshi, following the suit of the
wartime intellectual trend of cultural nationalism, this effort was not "to
reconstitute the mutual relevance between the form and the content of a
society and its culture by means of breaking the formal reification of
'tradition' so as to have a re-encounter with the changing daily reality of the
modern,"[1] but it departed from the social reality and aimed to
fundamentally change the minds of the humanity to be peace-loving, in order
to bring harmony to the world. As its goal and its means are nothing but the
same one, this culturalist, "philosophical" contemplation short-circuits
itself. However, the emergence of this mentality which led to this genre of
writing is also not merely a fantasy of the "modern literati," but this

---

　　① 　Zhang, X., *The Politics of Aestheticization: Zhou Zuoren and the Crisis of
Chinese New Culture* (1927-1937), Ph Dissertation. Duke University, 1995:17-18.

intellectual habitus or disposition has the social-historical overdetermination: the New Culture Movement of the previous periods, in its urge to "catch up with the (Western) world," had barely considered the Chinese life-world as a self-sustained cultural world itself that has its own particular cultural tradition, which was compounded by the fact that the tradition was wholly disenchanted with the holistic change of mode of production and the ensuing sea change of relations of production, and this tradition was hard to be revived without a holistic overhaul under the perspective of the modern.

Yin Di the protagonist serves as a tool for the expression of this intellectual thought. But, contrary to what we might expect, the narrator does not tell how the hero propagates the sermon and preaches the gospel of love and beauty to the people, but instead shows how he has his individual happiness in his secluded life in the famed resort—West Lake of Hangzhou. Perhaps this serves as an example of how happy a person could be if one chooses to leave social revolution. To be sure, however, not everyone can afford the privilege that he enjoys: to prepare for such a life, his mother has pointed out that he intends to use his father's fortune; whereas while Yin Di protests a bit by arguing that he can earn some money by writing column articles and by acquiring a nominal job (without working) by nepotism, he acknowledges that to have the way of life he desires, he has to "plunder money" from his father.[1] The supposed hostess, Yin Di's aunt, is also a rich widow whose stock share inherited from her late husband (who was a tycoon) is magnificent.

This hedonistic thinking is premised on a nihilistic mentality. To live without any desire, or with the minimum desire, is regarded as the core of acquiring happiness. This philosophy in its turn contributes its share to the mentality of hedonism. "To pursue a meaning in life? Then it is only through happiness, especially through the happiness derived from beauty."[2] He admits this is a fantasy, yet he believes that "fantasy is as inexorable as reality. ...Phantasmagoria is also a sort of reality...the reality is also a sort of

---

① 无名氏：《海艳》，花城出版社 1977 年版，第 105 页．
② 无名氏：《海艳》，花城出版社 1977 年版，第 186 页．

fantasy."[1] Moreover, this mentality is premised on a discourse of universal
humanity regardless of class distinction: it is believed that anyone who has
sensory organs can enjoy the beauty.[2]

Qu Ying, the girl that Yin Di meets in the steamboat, now appears in
the stage. Traveling around the country and even to some overseas nations,
she shows a robust spirit full of curiosity. Yet her listless lifestyle is merely
for her self-interests and is largely depended on the money supply that her
middle-class family offers her all the time, though she allegedly has done
several jobs (just like earlier Yin Di). The two are indeed an excellent
match, given their highly coherent individualistic tendency, their hedonistic
fantasy, their elite consciousness, and their comparable family backgrounds.

Although Qu Ying shares his philosophy,[3] she pays a great price for
her blind love. Having fully enjoyed and consumed her, Yin Di still feels
that his sensual indulgence is not enough, and he leaves her for further
adventure; consequently, Qu Ying falls into a maniac status.

So far, this version of narrative on "revolution and love" is a far cry and
a gigantic departure from the "revolution plus love" formula popular in the
last two decades. But this disenchantment of revolution and love is merely a
symptom of a specific intellectual stratum in this particular era. It narrates
the experience of an intellectual who is disillusioned with the prospectus of
revolution and cynical with the hopeless social reality. With his kind of
"spiritual anarchism," he is doomed to descend into a more thoroughly
moralistic nihilism.

## 六、Morbid Metropolitanism and Its Disenchantment

The third volume *Golden Nights of the Snake* omits Yin Di's one-year
failed military experience in Manchuria. When the curtain unfolds, he has

---

① 无名氏:《海艳》,花城出版社 1977 年版,第 187 页.

② 无名氏:《海艳》,花城出版社 1977 年版,第 189 页.

③ She says that "politics harms one's soul." 无名氏:《海艳》,花城出版社 1977 年版,
第 367 页.

joined a smuggling gang peopled by his former comrades. He leads a debauched life in this new circle：they gamble, visit prostitutes, take drugs, etc. He also takes a mistress—the former government's agent who earlier has tried to seduce and convert him in the prison. He is furthermore enamored of a "dance party queen" named Sha Kaluo. Indulging in such a fin-de-siecle sensuous and corrupted life, Yin Di finds his bed of flowers. Apparently, decadence and desire are the theme of this volume. This unusual plot development should not be simply understood via the realistic framework, but needs to be taken in an interpretive scheme in which it is read as a rendition of certain conception, because the dissipated form of life harbors a profound disenchantment with a morbid metropolitanism.

This disenchantment is first and foremost brought about by the hopeless social-political circumstance of the era. From the very beginning of the volume, through a discussion held in an artistic salon, the epochal feature is laid out：a picture portraying a fin-de-siecle carnival beside a volcanic eruption, an ostensible illustration of Pompey's historical destruction, is graphically presented, which is suggested to be named neither as "Doomsday," nor "The Destruction of Pompey," but as "Our Era."[1] This is because, as the artist explains himself, what he portrays is a China that faces the analogous last moment of Pompey, a world that is repeating the destiny of the ancient city, when the upper-class gentlemen and ladies are still immersed in shameless indulgence.[2] "Our Era：Corruption and Death." He concludes.[3]

If for the earlier neo-perceptionalists, the bourgeois salon and party appear exotic and appealing for they provide the occasion for "high-brow" intellectual exchange; then here, they play an essential role in Yin Di's dissolute life, where he meets friends, prostitutes, and psychotics who are wrecked by the war experience. Here, Yin Di also happens to see the woman who has induced him to capitulation. The description of their association and

---

① 无名氏：《金色的蛇夜》，新闻天地 1977 年版，第 3 页.
② 无名氏：《金色的蛇夜》，新闻天地 1977 年版，第 4-6 页.
③ 无名氏：《金色的蛇夜》，新闻天地 1977 年版，第 8 页.

her life experience reminds us Mao Dun's novel *Corruption*(《蚀》), written
in 1942, which is, in a diary form, about a degenerate female agent of the
corrupted regime. But if the theme of the latter is quite prominent—a
critique of the dark, "reactionary" authority, here the role of a former
femme fatale is ambivalent. Since Yin Di now has repudiated his
revolutionary ideas, he finds her much-used and abused body attractive.

But his enchantment with the mysterious Sha Kaluo is more profound.
"She is the doomsday of the upper-class in this metropolitan city. Where she
goes, there is an end there... This strange woman then becomes the core of
the pathetic culture of this metropolis."[①] Watching this demon-like yet
plump and attractive female figure, there is a strong desire that arises in Yin
Di's mind, and he shamelessly pursues her in many ways. Curiously, Yin
Di's decadence is seen as a training ground leading to the eternity. To be
sure, the narration of his pervert life recalls the doctrine of Western
demonism, a popular trend of modernism of the nineteenth century,
according to which "a demon is a fallen angel who, of his own free will,
chose Satan's side during the angelic revolt," and "one third of all angelic
creatures are demons." Meanwhile, "demonism is characteristic of evil
rule."[②] Whereas Yin Di's experience of demonism is correlated to his "great
tribulation" in this period, this narration has more to do with a Buddhist
conception which holds that human desire, or his self-consciousness, is the
ultimate evil responsible to all the evildoings waiting for the ultimate nirvana or
enlightenment.

Nevertheless, this ostensible transcendentalist idea expressed by the
story's narrative has its realistic premise which is yet founded on an un-
dialectic rationale: he "repudiates the time, just like a fighter that throws
away his gauntlet." Though he believes that he is "now swimming in the
river of eternity," when he betrays the mission of the time, he is only

---

① 无名氏:《金色的蛇夜》,新闻天地 1977 年版,第 18 页.

② See "Doctrine of Demonism." http://www.versebyverse.org/doctrine/demonism.
html. Accessed Dec. 29, 2009.

thrown to the dark world, leading an eternal life of darkness.[1] Unable to subscribe to any political doctrine, the rapidly-changed political map makes Yin Di feel that "the truth of politics is merely an ephemeral truth."[2] Therefore, he believes that "the truth of a demon is more authentic than the hypocrisy of an angel."[3] He submits to the demonist belief which claims that "a sinless soul does not enjoy the authentic freedom; a man without experience in crime is not a real superman."[4]All these beliefs, however, are paradoxically revealed by the narrator as pretexts that "cover up the individualistic nudity hidden deeply in his mind."[5] Yet, still, the protagonist takes this degenerate life as more genuine than the sublime spirit that he has devoted to the revolution. To him, now demonism is more profound and eternal than divinity. But this self-defense based on a discourse of natural humanity is in conflict with his self-reflections when they visit upon him, during which he feels regretful over his betrayal; he realizes that his "own self" is sinking and corrupted. It is in this loss of hope in reality that the novel brings out a feeling of resentment over Caesarism and the disenchantment over metropolitanism. The city is a den of evil. The disenchantment of metropolitanism is fully displayed in Yin Di's relationship with Sha Kaluo that is unfolded fully from then on.

Yin Di's will to pawn his soul to the demon, on the surface, is comparable to that of Frost's action, as the narrator sometimes informs us.[6] Yet Frost's experience is a sort of adventure in the world of modernity to seek the full realization of one's potential, while Yin Di's degeneration is out of the social-political predicament. If Frost fully appreciates the enchantment of the modernity shown in the metropolitan culture (including its materialistic, mercenary culture), then Yin Di's adventure is an experience

---

① 无名氏：《金色的蛇夜》，新闻天地 1977 年版，第 45 页.

② 无名氏：《金色的蛇夜》，新闻天地 1977 年版，第 120 页.

③ 无名氏：《金色的蛇夜》，新闻天地 1977 年版，第 118 页.

④ 无名氏：《金色的蛇夜》，新闻天地 1977 年版，第 122 页.

⑤ 无名氏：《金色的蛇夜》，新闻天地 1977 年版，第 123 页.

⑥ 无名氏：《金色的蛇夜》，新闻天地 1977 年版，第 344 页.

of a social outcast that aims to release his resentment against the society; it
is the onslaught of the evil on the semi-colonial, semi-traditional China that
to him is bereft of any hope and salvation. The metropolitanism of the
modern world that is praised by Frost is now cursed by Yin Di—he is now
not a Frost-like constructor of the modernity, but a builder of the hell and
the grave-digger of the perverted upper-class, as he himself acknowledges.

In this perspective, Sha Kaluo is "the core of the pathetic culture of this
city." She admits that "a woman like me symbolizes an era, a season, and
the plague. Before the era dies out, I will not die. Before an era fully
corrupts, I will not rot away."① When she finally confesses her experience to
Yin Di, it shows that her life corresponds with every major historical
catastrophe in modern Chinese history.② As she is the symbol of desperation
itself, Yin Di's consummation of his desire means to be an allegorical
rendition of the last bound into the heart of darkness. Therefore, the
legendary experience of this couple (they happen to meet one time in the cliff
of a mountain) which apparently contributes to the popular tastes and the
middle-brow nature of this volume, is ultimately a literary rendition of a
concept of a specific stratum of the "modern literati."

This degenerate world, as well as its residents, is sinking, but it is also
urgently looking for its own salvation. This central thematic concern is
realized in the following volumes, which were completed after 1949. After
many more tribulations—Yin Di has converted sequentially to Catholicism
and Buddhism, but disillusioned with both of them. After meditation,
eventually he feels that he acquires the ultimate enlightenment, or nirvana.
The conclusion that he derives is that because the people, especially the
rulers, fall short of a universal wisdom, thus they commit mistakes.
Consequently, it is necessary to create a universal culture synthesizing
essences of the East and the West based on a "philosophy of the universe,"
which not only would resolve all sorts of social unrests, settle all the
problems in the world, but would also bring the perennial peace to the

---

① 无名氏:《金色的蛇夜》,新闻天地 1977 年版,第 396-397 页.
② 无名氏:《金色的蛇夜》,新闻天地 1977 年版,第 464 页.

humanity. This fantastic reverie reaches its epitome in the last volume. At the end of the Sino-Japanese War, Yin Di returns to Qu Ying, and lives with her and their newly born son happily on an idyllic farm. Having completed his philosophical quest, he is inventing a new culture for contemporary China. The utopian connotation is displayed ultimately in his political project of establishing a "Global Farm." This fascination with a new human existence and a more perfect interpersonal relation is reminiscent of the late Qing literati's similar effort at envisioning a utopian future for a China in a gigantic crisis, thus accomplishing its ultimate mission of composing conceptual fiction.

## 七、Conclusion

Wumingshi's "romantic" writings, which make inquiry into the "ultimate meaning" of life with a hue of aestheticism, are a response (in the sense of being a symbolic reaction) to the political and cultural crisis of the era, where there was little condition and space for the existence of such illusionary reveries. Whereas his voluminous *Book without a Name* intends to present a "bildungsroman" of a restless youth, the novel is revealed to be a pseudo-bildungsroman or reverse bildungsroman. The "spiritual quest" that is shared by various characters and the first person "I," the alter ego of Wumingshi, finally becomes the subject matter of a middle-brow literature—a modern literati's conceptual fiction, an idiosyncratic genre unique in modern Chinese history.

It is a sort of "'modern' literati novel" because the intellectuals held the modern concept of cosmopolitanism against the earlier scholars' traditional ideas (such as filial piety, chastity, etc.), yet it is still a brand of "literati novel" because the writer did not delve into social-economic milieu to explore the overdetermination of political predicament yet was merely engaged in cultural reveries and ethical-moral dilemma, the usual practice done by traditional literati. When we correlate the literary texts and the social-historical subtexts, this interpretation will also shed a new light on the intricate relationship between modernism and modernity in a different

national setting:The dearth of modernity in modern China makes a full-
scaled modernist writing impossible, but brings about a sort of middle-brow
fiction in the market of popular culture which is a hybrid of various styles
and genres.

# Chapter Four　Illusionary Cosmopolitanism and Flawed Humanity: A New Interpretation of Xu Xu's "Modern Tales of the Strange"

## 一、Introduction

For our general understanding, cosmopolitanism is an ideology that holds that all human ethnic groups belong to a single community premised on a commonly-shared morality; whereas a cosmopolitan community is one in which individuals from varying locations form a relationship of mutual respect regardless of their differing races as well as religious and political beliefs.[①] Being one of the most cherished values or concepts in modern China (roughly between the May Fourth period of the 1910s and the establishment of the People's Republic of china in our context), cosmopolitanism was taken seriously by the liberalist-oriented writers, who expressed through their fictional narrative their yearnings for universal brotherhood and unconditional love in the tumultuous age. Xu Xu (1908-1980), for one, is among the most famed intellectuals in the turbulent era. His "modern tales of the strange," written during the exigency wartime of the 1940s, were his "trademark" and very popular when and after they were published, which specially articulate the sense and sensibility of cosmopolitanism. Up to now, these writings are generally read against the framework of "romanticism" or "modernism," as literary movement/genre imported from the West. In the wake of the pitfall of literary comparison between two cultures with distinctly diversified traditions and social-historical trajectories out of the

---

① Appiah, K. A., Cosmopolitan patriots, *Critical Inquiry*, 1997, 23(3):617-639.

recent development of scholarship in the field of comparative literature, it is time for us to take a new perspective looking into these works by including the particular social-political context as their subtexts.

A brief introduction of Xu Xu's (real name Xu Boyu) biography would help us understand the nature of his conviction of cosmopolitanism, which was a result of his disgust of the merciless power struggle within the international Communist movement (in particular in the former Soviet Union under Stalin's ironclad rule) and thus his turning away from the leftist camp, a case shared by not a few Chinese intellectuals at the time. He was born in 1908 in a rural household of Cixi, Zhejiang province, which had fallen into poverty in his father's generation. His parents separated and when he was five, consequently he was sent to a missionary school as a boarder. The life of solitude contributed to his longing for parental love. Graduated from the Philosophy Department of Peking University in 1931, for two years he continued to study in the Psychological Department out of personal interest. Around this time, he began his literary endeavor. After that he went to Shanghai to assume the editorship of the popular liberalist-oriented magazines such as *Analects*(《论语》), *The Human World*(《人间世》), etc., which were led by Lin Yutang (1895-1976), the famed promoter and leader of "humorous literature." In 1936, he went to Paris to study philosophy, but soon returned to Shanghai when the Anti-Japanese War broke out one year later. Five years later, he went to the wartime capital Chongqing in 1942 and worked in a bank, while simultaneously holding academic positions in some universities. He was sent to the United States as a special correspondent for a domestic newspaper in the year of 1944, and returned back to China after the Anti-Japanese War ended the next year.

Like many intellectuals in his time, Xu Xu had undergone a left-leaning period. He read many Marxist canons in his college years, and his earlier writings bear the imprints of the leftist thoughts. They express compassionate feelings towards the repressed and the dispossessed. Yet elements of class struggle aside, his works also show sympathy towards degenerate people, displaying his ingrained belief in the bourgeois ideology of "universal humanity." His overseas study in France consolidated his turning away from radical politics. The reading of the trial records of Trotsky facilitated his disillusion with the merciless power struggles within the revolutionaries，and thus the communist doctrine. Meanwhile，the advanced capitalist society of France with its "free way of life" greatly attracted him. From then on，he regarded himself as an individualist，and abjured revolution and mass movement.

The writer's subscription to the discourses of "human nature," love and beauty and his curiosity in romantic adventures characterizes his creative direction. But the "universal" and the "common" can only be understood through the analysis of the concrete and the particular，namely the ideologemes within the texts.

## 二、Aborted Romance and Illusionary Cosmopolitanism

Xu Xu's stories often focus on such thematic concerns as cosmopolitanism and "universal humanity," and are also often couched in aborted romances，filled with shadow and tension.

During his study in Paris，he wrote his first masterpiece，the novelette *Love with a Ghost Girl* (《鬼恋》). The story was well received and went through nineteen printings in seven years. The first-person male narrator，with an ambiguous identity but almost can be identified with the author-like figure in many of his stories，happens to meet the heroine in the street in a night. She addresses the narrator as "man," which triggers the narrator's curiosity，but she soon reveals herself as a "ghost." Being enchanted with her mysterious beauty，the narrator is struggling between his sense of modern "rationality" and the credulity of this unbelievable captivation. Nevertheless，she insists that love is futile between a man and a ghost. Finally he gets her story，though he still could not get into her heart. It turns out that she was once an underground revolutionary. Having assassinated more than a dozen political enemies，she was imprisoned and had lost her lover. When the revolution is betrayed，she declines the daylight world. Though the narrator wishes a normal union with her，she leaves him without notice. The phantasmagoric plot as well as the fantastic atmosphere envelopes the story in a surrealistic ambience.

Ostensibly a realistic work about an aborted romance between the narrator—an alter ego of the author—and an erstwhile revolutionary, the story is better to be read as an allegory: from the very beginning, this chance encounter is, if not a daydream, then a night-dream that barely can be seen as realistic. But more incredible is the "love" between the two. In all aspects, both the female revolutionary's legendary career and her mercurial character appear mystical to the narrator. He admires her courage, and is attracted to her revolutionary ideal, to be sure; yet unearthly as she is, she is always an alien to him, refusing his intellectual understanding. She is "unreasonable"; whereas reason, or modern rationality, is what is cherished by the sober intellectual. With a seemingly sacred aura, she is nevertheless a "ghost" that cannot appear in daylight world. She is less plausible, hard to be approached. Though she still sends flowers to the narrator when he is ill, he never sees her any more—the spiritual relations still continue, he is still sympathetic to revolution and his erstwhile leftist ideal, yet there is no possibility for him to return to the historical site, to join with the ghost-like, mysterious, attractive yet dangerous alien, although he is "blessed" by the latter. The aborted romance is a fable of a failed integration. That this episode is narrated in the present time-space when it has passed ten-more years reveals that this is a memoire about a phantom, or a romantic reverie. To be more specific, the story, in its renewed, modern version of "the traditional Chinese tale of mortal man enthralled by predatory female ghost,"[1] narrates in a historical fable symbolically the author's severance with his erstwhile leftist passion with the revolutionary ideal.

What makes the "romance" possible from the very beginning, however, is that this "revolutionary" has died to the world; (she insists that she is a ghost. Dressed as a Buddhist nun, she wishes to escape from reality); in other words, she does not hold her erstwhile passion any more, and loses

①   Polland, D., Entry of *Guilian* (*Love with a Ghost Girl*), In: *Selective Guide to Chinese Literature* 1900-1949 (Vol. 1), Milena Doleželová-Velingerová Ed., New York: Brill Publishers, 1988:188.

her faith in the cause. This makes her more compatible with the narrator. Still, she is a mysterious alien. Apparently she refuses the narrator's proposal because she regards love an absurdity in the human world; but it is not difficult for us to recognize that it is because she harbors deeply, genuine emotion towards her late lover, a martyr, that she could not accept any other man any more. Revolution is subtly conveyed as uncanny; but since she has negated the political cause, there is barely reasonable that she still refuses to enter the secular world—if it is because her heart has been dead, it is paradoxical that she still cares for, if not falls in love with, the narrator. The latter's crossing of the boundary between the real and the unreal to deliver his intended message, in this light, has many fissures waiting for patch-up.

*Goddess of the Arabian Sea* (《阿拉伯海的女神》) is another story that the writer produced when he studied in Paris. The first-person narrator meets a woman in a steamship when he travels to Europe. Her unusual mannerism and unbelievable youthfulness indicate she is a surrealistic character. She informs him that she is a nomadic sorceress traveling around the world. And her cosmopolitanism is shown in her erudition of world cultures and her capability to speak fluent Chinese. But what is significant in their discussions of all supernatural tales is the story about the legendary Goddess of the Arabian Sea, who was a beautiful Arabic girl. She is looking for the truth from various sacred doctrines, such as Confucianism, Christianity, Buddhism, and Islamism, yet could not decide which one she should take in as her religious faith. After many overseas trips looking for the ultimate enlightenment, she avails nothing so she drowns herself. The sorceress' question for the narrator is: what he can answer if the Goddess seeks from him the answer to her query. What he replies indicates that he takes love to be the highest truth: as he says, "religious commandments are nothing but the sublimation of sexual desire...while love is the God for the youth." Unquestionably, for him, the "universal humanity" of love prevails over any religious teachings.

In another evening, she tells the man a modified story that the story she has told changes to be her personal encounter with the Goddess some twenty

years earlier. This makes her words less credible to him. In the second day,
he meets a girl with a black veil over her face. He suspects her to be the
Goddess, and tells her that for the Chinese, there are three phrases of
religious belief. "When he is a child, his parents are his religion; in his
youth, lover; and in his old age, his scions." He explains his words:
"Religion is love, is a belief, is (the will to) sacrifice;" for the Chinese,
secular concerns are their religion. However, this self-supported, secular
belief is challenged by the following happenings.

He gives her his ring as a gift because she likes it. The next day he finds
that she wears a gigantic silver ring with some pictorial inscription on it.
Upon his request, she informs him that there was a custom that was
practiced in a certain place, where lovers of different religious beliefs, for
the sake of living forever together without the intervention of religious
taboo, would kill themselves. She gives him the ring, and accepts his
request to let her mask be unveiled. The blessed moment of this symbolic
exchange of token of love is sabotaged by his careless missing of the girl's
veil to the sea, which leads to the final episode, when the sorceress appears,
he is informed that the girl is her daughter. As the latter's heart has been
taken by a man (the mask symbolizes the chastity of an Arabic woman), she
could not take her mother's occupation anymore but has to marry him. Yet
like Luo Shengti in *Woman in Pagoda*, only at this moment the narrator
"remembers" that he has a wife and three children. He has to throw himself
into the sea; the girl follows. Immediately, all of these are revealed to be a
"romantic" dream.

Again, apparently "love" surmounts all the divides among religions,
races, morality, and even any ultimate concerns—if we remember that the
secular persona of the "Goddess" has committed suicide because she could
not find the ultimate belief, then now she does it a second time just for love.
In this way, she gets what she desires—the eternality, because love in this
moment is seen as leading to the eternality (she says to "me" when she
jumps to the sea: "My lover, this is our life in the secular world.") Love,
even it is merely a moment, prevails over any secular concern, and defeats
mortality.

Yet from another perspective, we can also see love simultaneously loses its battle with the religious taboo, and with the secular morality: the narrator can excuse his emotional impulse by arguing that his heart has a correspondence with the girl, yet he implicitly refuses her mother's request to marry the girl for the ethical-moral convention of his mother country; meanwhile, they have to die in order to get love. Cosmopolitanism—love as a medium to tie in people around the world regardless of their religions—is a dream that is in no way to be realized in the real world. Indeed, as the narrator admits his life philosophy to the sorceress, "other people are seeking for true dream in life, whereas I'm seeking for a real life in my dream." We can rephrase this sentence a little bit to make its import clearer: there are some who seek to realize the utopian project in the secular world, whereas I construct a utopian world in my daydream. "Abandoning the present" is seen as the inevitable road leading to the utopian "seeking for the eternity." But whereas he sees this as "a possibility that at least offers the freedom [to choose by oneself]," by taking the false for the real, this fantasy merely becomes a modern literati fiction.

This tendency is more explicit in a later story *Absurd Dover Channel* (《荒谬的英法海峡》). Under the same framework of the narrator's daydream, it recounts his experience in a utopian world, a place reminiscent of the Peach Blossom Shangri-la (桃花源) offered by the ancient Chinese poet Tao Yuanming (367-427), but the social-political structure of the society and the spiritual world of the populace are more bearing the imprints of the political utopia described by Thomas More (1478-1535), the famed pioneer of the "Utopian socialism." Being "kidnapped" by pirates in a steamship, "I" am invited by the pirates' leader, a captain who loves Chinese culture, to live in a paradise which has no hierarchy of classes, no discrimination of races, no commodities and currencies, and has goods allotted by needs. This implicit, yet also more-than-clear reflection and critique of modern civilization are aided by the repetition of a complaint articulated by the passengers and the narrator himself at the beginning and the end of the text respectively: while the distance of the strait that divides the two states is short, there is no possibility to build a bridge or undersea tunnel to facilitate communication.

This is a man-made obstacle that separates people, making cosmopolitanism merely a daydream. The critique of capitalism, and in particular imperialism, which hampers the realization of this "great union"（大同）is conveyed by the narrator's reference of the forefather of the British as the originators of the pirates, and the denunciation by the leader of this socialist fantasyland, who accuses the imperialists for their plunder in their colonized areas.

Free-willed reveries aside, here the author shows a strong tendency of anarchism, a cultural-political radicalism that repudiates any collective organization in a community; instead, in the fantastic dreamworld there is no class, no bureaucracy, because "everyone is governing himself and the others" and there are simply no fights out of differing interests; the leader is merely the servant of the people and he has no authority; there is no college there because everyone is simultaneously engaged in work and study. To be sure, the author probably intends the piece to be a mirror reflecting back the contemporary dirty reality. ① And this critique was supported by the intellectual trend of the time interrogating the validity of modernity for the realization of happiness, or the debatable value of modernization (there is no mobile bicycle in the "state"). Yet the author has no way to evade the social-historical institution that casts a shadow over the dream, which is in particular shown in the formulaic entanglement of various forms of "love triangles." He stresses that marriage as an institution is well observed there, for which he nevertheless faces a dilemma: falling in love with a girl—the sister of the captain that he befriends—he has his wife and children in his homeland; meanwhile, a local youth is also enamored of the beauty and envying the love that his sweetheart bestows upon the narrator. This predicament also besieges the captain and the Chinese girl that he loves who has been detained there for three years and who has her own fiancé back home. The solution for all these entanglements is debatable: because there is

---

① Apart from a critique of Western and Japanese imperialism and Soviet-styled Communism, China is not absent from this picture, as the narrator numerously attacks the ugly world of the contemporary Chinese society.

a local carnival festival in which the order of women is irrefutable, so everyone implicated finally seemingly gets his/her desired outcome: the Chinese girl proclaims the leader as her lover, the leader's sister accepts the advance of the local youth, and the narrator gets what he does not expect and might not be very pleased: another girl that he socializes in those days. This picture is made possible by the change of mind of the Chinese girl (which is unexplained) towards the proposal of the leader; to further the settlement of the difficulties, the two set the arrangements for all the others. But we might ask: is the girl who is going to marry the local man really happy, given her passion on the narrator? Will the "marriage" between "I" and the other girl be happy, given that "I" never has romantic feelings to her? How should the girl being engaged to the leader deal with her fiancé at home, and "I" with "my wife and children in my home country"? Cosmopolitanism (or rather, here a form of internationalism) is impossible here, not merely because of the separation of states, not even by the imperialists' colonial advance, but it is by something invisible. As a "story of conception," it has entertainment value (thus entitling it to be a "middle-brow" literature, namely a work for the distraction of middle-class readers), whereas its social concern and critical message are undercut by its "unrealistic" reveries and easy-and-cheap ending. While in the text social democracy and internationalism are idealized, it only betrays the real shortage of these in reality; thus the utopian picture offered there in terms of a new political world has much more entertainment value than any realistic significance.

### 三、Shadow and Tension in "Universal Human Nature"

As said, the cosmopolitanism expressed here is premised on the belief in a universal humanity regardless of social-historical limitation. Yet the series of "romance stories" that the writer created thereafter, while still preaching this "religion of love," again show the fissures therein.

Secluded in Shanghai, Xu Xu continued to write stories, which established his artistic parameters and brought about such stories as *Gypsy*

*Enticement* (《吉普赛的诱惑》), *Elegy of Psychotics* (《精神病患者的悲
歌》), and the one we just discussed. On the surface, the first story eulogizes
a free-willed life unconstrained by social customs; the second exemplifies a
selfless love and self-sacrifice. A careful textual analysis will reveal multiple
tensions underneath the euphonious, and numerous gaps within the narrative
texture, to the extent that they deconstruct the superficial message,
showing desolate ruins out of the relentless demolishing force of the
inequality of class hierarchy.

Ostensibly, *Gypsy Enticement* presents a romance between a first-
person narrator, a Chinese intellectual who is returning from Paris to China,
and a French model, who is a socializing celebrity. A romance between a pair of
couple who own vastly differing identities apparently displays a cosmopolitan
flavor.

With the help of a Gypsy vagrant Laura, I meet the beauty named
Pauline (Pan Lei as her Chinese pronunciation) who works in a fashion
boutique, taking her to be an innocent fairy. Yet she tells me that she only
leads a misshapen, chaotic, and contradictory life everyday, because she has
to support her family. I spend large sum of money to please her, taking it to
be a spiritual love, which invites mockery from Laura, who scoffs at it as a
"middle class bookish romance" and informs me that Pauline can be easily
prostituted if I pay money. Infuriated, I reluctantly agree to test Pauline for
what Laura says, and I am appalled to find that it is true. Out of indignation
and disappointment, I scold Pauline mercilessly. But shortly later, I have to
accept Laura's advice to sell myself to a rich bitch because I'm penniless,
only to find the guest is Pauline. Having reconciled with her, I bring Pauline
back to home country for marriage, irrespective of Laura's warning that she
is a "bourgeois" woman who is used to an extravagant life and would not be
used to a simple life. Again, Laura's premonition comes true, and I have to
take her back to France. Pauline works in her previous profession, having
much commodity value for the products she helps to promote. But I feel
sloppy, and follow Laura to travel to the United States and South America.
After several months, being afraid that I'm falling in love with a Gypsy girl,
Pauline resigns her job and follows me. "We" follow the Gypsies to travel

everywhere as they please. Taking mendicancy and legerdemain as a profession，from now on we live a happy life！

The adventure itself is a middle-class romantic fantasy. From the precondition for the acquaintance (even though the narrator is a middle-class intellectual，Laura tells him that only when he dresses in handsome coat could there be the possibility for him to attract the woman) to the process of acquiring her heart ("I" spend lost of money，even by borrowing debts，to win her favor)，all of which indicate that this romance itself has its particular class nature. Pauline can lead a decent life by her legitimate profession，but she works as a prostitute for more luxurious life.[①] Laura has aptly remarked on the true nature of this romance："In all honesty，what is your love towards her？ It is nothing but her pretty outlook and pleasant manner."

Exotic orientalism is everywhere，which is taken to be a form of cosmopolitanism. "To be natural，always in exile，and free—this is the soul of our nation." Laura，the Gypsy girl says. I admire this "spirit，" and recommend this to the readers. What is easily neglected，however，is the price this "romantic" life pays：Laura has to engage in a career that "professionally" hoodwinks money from the rich (and ironically "I" even recommend this as one asset of the ethnic group for emulation)，and her repetitive insistence on getting exorbitant pay from me for any "service" she provides has also invited my antipathy. She also has complained that the children of the race have to travel everywhere to beg for food and clothes，living a miserable life. Therefore，although they see themselves as a group and help each other when needed，they are none other than the class of "lumpen-proletariat" without a salient class consciousness. They are the subaltern，the outcast，rather than a free nation that this legendary tale holds. Yet，out of the mouth of Laura the author shows the seemingly

---

① Laura aptly comments on her life，"She is a genuine bourgeois woman in a capitalist society...Life to her is fire；she is used to a romantic，sumptuous life-style，in need of meaningless party；fresh stimulations give her excitement." 徐訏：《吉普赛的诱惑》，安徽文艺出版社 1996 年版，第 151 页.

enviable free lifestyle and "philosophy of love and beauty" of Gypsy—they engage in "free romance" anytime they please; yet for the Gypsy, this is a custom that is brought about by their destitute and insecure life; while for the author, or narrator, it is another middle-class fantasy about "free love."

When Laura preaches this "carefree and natural" "Gypsy soul," the "happiness" of the group is attributed to their "free will" that obeys the order of the supernatural, while they fight nothing for the betterment of their life. The narrator expresses his admiration of this philosophy, "I love the attitude of your race: your generosity, innocence; you are not engaged in overdue study, not immersed in the interests of social affairs, having no curiosity over anything, not making deliberate efforts, not determined to devote to anything, not pursuing knowledge perfunctorily, not fighting for success, having no ideal and desire... You are only believing in the blue sky and the bright moon, living peacefully and leisurely underneath." This exoticization of the oppressed race is not merely out of the influence of a Buddhist philosophy, not even from the ideal of Christianity, but it is for the spiritual needs of the Chinese intellectuals seeking for a utopian life outside the constraint of the harsh reality. It is believed that if an individual has no power to change the world, he can at least follow the "nature," the order of the God, to acquire happiness. "I prefer to seek a true life in daydream." The narrator says.

*Elegy of Psychotics* is about a healing process for the "convalescence" of a "psychotic." "I" am a Chinese student studying psychology in Paris, and hired to be an assistant of a psychiatrist for the treatment of a madam named Betty (Bai Di), who lives a debauched life ever since she was forced by her father to marry his business partner (which she declines). To prepare for this mission, I'm asked to receive some special trainings, such as boxing, shooting, horse riding, etc., which is reminiscent of the special training that some employed agents have received from their employers for tough mission—and indeed, some of the trainings play their role when I deal with the subaltern world where Betty is socializing. After observation, "I" believe the cause for her abnormal behavior and psychological disarray is her distrust of any person around her, who in her mind only uses her whereas harbors no love for her. To remove this mentality，"I" set up a scheme，firstly by persuading her that her maid Helen（Hailan）and "I" are truly caring for her；then by pretending that I'm in love with Helen in order to arouse her envy and passion. Betty is almost "cured，" yet unexpectedly Helen and "I" are really falling in love with each other in the process. The maid commits suicide to fulfill the will of her master. Moved by this "self-sacrificing" behavior，Betty devotes herself to the God by becoming a nun and "I" decide to work in the psychotic hospital for my remaining time.

The latter half of the story is a moving，if somewhat sentimental and stereotyped，melodrama. Nevertheless，when the "romance" is undergoing a social-psychoanalytic procedure，everything apparent that has been narrated would be turned upside down. To begin with，"I" am merely a hired employee，as Betty accuses me incisively when Helen commits suicide，that I "devote life，time，love and passion to be a slave of several thousand Francs." Although "I" try to explain away this apt charge by arguing that "I am only a slave of my job. I love my job，and I'm willing to devote everything for my job." We should remember that "I" have tried to quit my job quite several times，but "I" am rejected by the threat that "I" have signed a contract so "I" should be "willing" to do everything that is requested. And this requirement obviously compromises "my" integrity. When Betty continues her perceptive interrogation，"You dare to use your base scheme to beguile two vulnerable girls" by using innocent Helen to manipulate her emotion，"I" try hard to gloss over the ulterior motive of my intension to accomplish my assigned mission；in particular，"I" use the rhetoric of love. In counteracting her accusation that "your job is being hired（by my parents）to cheat me，" "I" protest："But I know their intension is love." Obviously this is a（at least partially）false excuse，as Betty had been forced to marry a business partner for business interests.

The following self-conflicting excuse furthermore betrays my innate scheme and my guilty conscience. Betty cynically yet perceptively points out my hypocrisy，"Your 'love' is your job." "'No，' I protest，I can swear that only during my work love emerged in my heart." "What is your job anyway apart from 'love'?" Betty ingeniously fights back. Besides，granted what

"I" said is true, this "love" is in conflict with the professional ethics, so "I"
haste to gloss it over, but in this way "I" have refuted what "I" just said,
"Supposed my job is merely love, and this 'love' is real, what is the
disgrace anyhow?" This "supposition," however, is a completely fake
hypothesis. Earlier "I" have confessed that I do not love Betty at all; but to
achieve the goal (of letting Betty become a "normal," "decent," middle-
class aristocrat woman), "I" have pretended to love Betty, arousing her
passion by manipulating Helen. Betty eventually sees through the scheme,
and reproaches convincingly my scurvy motive and behavior. "I" have no
way to refute her accusation, but try to evade her incisive interrogation with
the rhetoric of love.

This does not mean Betty has no her problem. Though she earnestly
looks for genuine love that her highly oppressive family declines to her, she
also tries to selfishly manipulate and monopolize "my" love; when she sees
the manifestation of "love" between Helen and "me," she indeed falls into
the pitfall that "I" set up for her. Having been aroused of her sense of envy,
and with the death of her maid, thus the removal of her rival in love, she
returns to be a "normal" woman. That she finally decides to join a convent is
due to her realization that she has vicariously deprived the love of her maid,
and forced her to commit suicide (Helen has no way to compete with her
master for love). But the cardinal culprit of the tragedy is "me,"
nevertheless. Alienated by the capitalist money economy, "I" sacrifice my
integrity and use foul means. That "I" eventually decide to work in the
psychological hospital, in this light, is a sign of atonement; but judged with
what "I" have done, this action appears dubious, if not ridiculous.

Like the last story, this tale tries to displace the difference between
classes, and the concomitant problems it brings about (the inhuman work
ethics, the inequality between the master and the maid, and the mercenary
nature of money economy) with a discourse of natural humanity. But this
story of apparent euphoria of love displaces and covers up a merciless, cruel
tragedy perpetuated not merely by individuals, but by the whole social-
economic system in general. The author has tried to smooth over the edges
with a beautiful veil, yet the tensions and fissures exist in all those rhetorical

exchanges betray the ulterior secret.

In *The Jewish Comet* (《犹太的彗星》), again the discourse of universal humanity is superficially eulogized, now with a tone of patriotism, while in actuality it exposes the cruelty of the war that wreaks havoc on the human mind. The first-person narrator Xu is on a ship journey to Italy with a Jewish girl Katherine, nominally his wife. Then in a long flashback we are informed that he is introduced by his friend, a Norwegian Jew named Sherkels, to this girl because she needs a sham marriage to claim an inheritance home, and he agrees to do so for curiosity and for the discounted steamer ticket. On board, while they gradually fall in love with each other, Katherine is socializing frequently with an Italian sailor, which causes the narrator's discomfort. When they arrive in Naples, he is informed by Katherine that they have to wait for five days for a lawyer, yet she is out everyday, seemingly for hedonistic activities. While she asks him to consummate their love, he discovers that she intimately hangs out with the Italian sailor. But ultimately she reveals the mysteries to him: Katherine's mother is fighting the fascists now in the Spanish civil war (to which historically many international socialists voluntarily joined). She is offering her hands by sabotaging the weapon supplies that Italian fascists provide to Franco. What makes us feel less comfortable, however, is that while she needs Xu's assistance to enter the country, she has schemed to trap him because the task this time risks a person's life. The real victim for this mission, however, turns out to be the Italian sailor, who loves Katherine and is hoodwinked to help her. He becomes the scapegoat for Xu, in other words. But Xu and Katherine consummate their love after they arrive in France. Shortly later Katherine departs for Germany again and sacrifices her life in another anti-war mission.

For love, Katherine can spare Xu's life; yet also she inhumanly manipulates the love of the Italian sailor. Xu's friend Sherkels has joined to the scheme which almost claims his life. Love and friendship are unreliable during the wartime. In the story, for the war efforts, any foul means are appropriate for the success of the war. In short, the war profoundly changes the "natural humanity" of the mankind. Although the story extols Katherine's "love and beauty, her spirit and her body," the cruel aspects of the war are subtly conveyed.

This nuanced indictment becomes clearer in the writer's major novel, his most celebrated *The Blowing Wind*(《风萧萧》), which was a big stir at the time. It treats the subject of resistance and mergers elements of love stories and spy fiction, and is engrossed in a thrilling atmosphere. Again this is in a first-person narrative, which narrates the experience of a "modern scholar" (who studies philosophy) in the spy world. Like the author's other stories, its popular reception and enticing subject matter endow it a "middle-brow" quality, what is often neglected is that it is also a "fiction of conception" or a "modern literati novel." Interestingly, this novel shares many features of Wumingshi's *Book without a Name*, as its essential stake lies in a narration of an intellectual's "spiritual quest," though now it tells a more intriguing story with absorbing plots.

The story takes place in Shanghai, the place of which served as a locale for many espionage stories both in fiction and in reality at the time. By chance "I" rescue a wounded American military doctor named Steven and we become friends. Through him "I" meet Bai Ping, a beautiful nightclub hostess, and Mei Yingzi, a dazzling lass. After the outbreak of the Pacific War, Steven is captured by the Japanese and dies in the concentration camp. "I" am informed by Mei Yingzi that they both are agents working for the Americans, and "I" become her assistant. Mei Yingzi mistakes Bai Ping for a Japanese spy for her close association with the Japanese; yet Bai Ping actually is an agent for the government. "I" am assigned to steal letters from Bai Ping, but the action is discovered and I'm badly wounded. The miscommunication is reconciled shortly later, but the arrival of a Japanese female spy costs Bai Ping's life. Mei Yingzi revenges her by poisoning the enemy. When the story comes to its end, Mei Yingzi resumes her duty in Shanghai (her identity is still uncovered), and "I" leave for the interior engaged in "philosophical contemplation." Throughout most of the narrative space there is also a minor role, an American girl named Helen.

If the novel is read as a spy story, there are many technical problems. But the sort of discussion bypasses the real nature of the novel. As a "story of conception," like the author's other stories of this kind, again here political issues are treated from the perspective of cultural difference (although it is less distinct here, there is little political context that is described). Mei Yingzi was raised in Japan, with an American mother and a Chinese father (and implicitly trained by American military weapons); her "hybrid" nature might have something to do with her unusual, merciless personality that spares no mercy on any innocent people with stakes in her political machination. This constitutes a sharp contrast to Helen, whose character more resembles the classical, allegedly peaceful Greek ideal; and it is also a contrast to Bai Ping, who, holding many traditional Chinese feminine features, is the embodiment of "a general harmony" or a "glittering conglomeration of all the graces of Nature."[①] For this, "I" have preferred to have her as my social mate (in fact "I" have stayed in one room with her for a sort of "spiritual love"). To be sure, here the author has no way to evade political issues. But politics, even the cause of national resistance, appears in the novel (to "me") as nothing but conspiracy that is repulsive. "My" idealism of the universal humanity, in particular shown in beautiful girls, is sabotaged by these female spies with political missions. "I" feel repulsive over Mei Yingzi's merciless manipulation of Helen as a pawn for fulfilling her duty. In this regard, Bai Ping appears more human. Although she suspects "I" am a Japanese spy, she does not kill me and allows me to be taken to hospital. The Japanese spy is simply evil that is hard to be understood. Only Helen, a girl with no political consciousness, appears to me as the most ideal and becomes my true lover. "My" unhappiness with the utilization of innocent people as the political instrument is unquestionable, but the problem is that "I" take the specific action, which itself is a form of class politics, to be the politics per se.

On the other hand, here cosmopolitanism is also broken apart under the war circumstance. All these destructions of the intellectuals' ideal are a result of dirty politics. The "inhuman" side of the spy serves to be a metaphor for the politics per se. Yet this apathy and repulsiveness towards

---

① 吴义勤：《徐訏与中外文学渊源》，《中国现代文学研究丛刊》，1933（3）：146-61，151-152.

politics can only be examined at the particular social-historical moment and
under the vulnerable identity that "I" assume in mind. The male narrator's
participation into the patriotic resistance is only of a temporary nature, less
for the sake of patriotism itself than for conquering his sense of
existentialistic angst and cultural-political anxiety (the loss of belief in the
meaning of life). It functions as a medium for the narrator to look for an
"ultimate," "transcendental" life philosophy, for an identity that he is
missing. Once he seemingly finds the latter out of a short-term adventure,
he quits the dirty political world and packs off to the interior, returning to
his life of "metaphysical thinking." The political world of resistance is still
an alien to him. He always "refuses to become entangled with reality"; he
seemingly "can still transcend reality by embracing something deeper than
patriotism—the quest for the meaning of life."[1] Yet without the patriotic
activities he temporarily joins, how can he settle his anxiety over his
(national, and cultural-political) identity? After he ostensibly has
established his identity and goes away, where does he embrace "the meaning
of life"?

But just as a feminist critic has pointed out, although here to him "the
professional female spies... do not seem to have the same ability to be
introspective about their situations," and they have "always erotic bodies
with no access to this purified world," [2] it seems that these female
professionals devoted to the patriotic mission have more solid subjectivity
than this somewhat arrogant, and somewhat bookish man that often appears
clumsy and wavering in the actions that he takes. His philosophy of
celibacy—as he brags that "the love of a celibate belongs to the spirit...it is
abstract and empty; it is perpetually giving instead of receiving; it belongs

---

① Liu, J., Gender Geopolitics: Social Space and Volatile Bodies, 1937-1945,
*Journal of Modern Literature in Chinese*, 1998,2(1):68.

② Liu, J., Gender Geopolitics: Social Space and Volatile Bodies, 1937-1945,
*Journal of Modern Literature in Chinese*, 1998,2(1):68.

*to all men and to history,*"①—appears hollow and empty. But I would suggest that the philosophy itself serves as a metaphor for a fruitless life-attitude of a certain class stratum when it is hopelessly being sandwiched among various political forces and propelled by the historical wind towards the future. But he is not the Benjaminian "angel of history," as his life is saved and spared by those female political workers that seemingly do not own his intellectual power. The distance that he tries to keep from the political world is illusory, this is not merely because he could not help but be embroiled in the political world by his secular concerns, but it is also because apparently only from the politics his "existentialistic angst" can be eliminated.

## 四、Conlcusion

Xu Xu's "romantic" writings in the 1940s' China are a symbolic reaction to the political and cultural crisis of the era, where there was little condition and space to realize the idea of cosmopolitanism. Consequently, aborted romance and shadow and tension in a "universal humanity" are the most often witnessed subject concerns in the author's works, which appear as illusionary reveries. Being essentially a sort of "story of conception," this kind of fictional narrative has much entertainment value (thus entitling it to be a "middle-brow" literature, namely a work for the distraction of middle-class readers); whereas its social concern and critical message are oftentimes undercut by its "unrealistic" reveries and easy-and-cheap ending.

Put in other words, Xu Xu's "modern tales of the strange," being a genre of "modern literati fiction," aims to articulate the writer's political anxieties in a seemingly hopeless social-historical situation, in which ruthless class hierarchy, mercenary commodity economy, as well as turbulent wars and revolutions bring about a world filled with material

---

① 徐訏:《风萧萧》,花城出版社 1990 年版,第 488 页. Quoted from Liu, J., Gender Geopolitics: Social Space and Volatile Bodies, 1937-1945, *Journal of Modern Literature in Chinese*, 1998,2(1):68.

wastelands and spiritual ruins. It shows the predicament the bourgeois intellectuals faced in the 1940s' China where there were scarcely material conditions to actualize their ideal of cosmopolitanism and universal love. Cosmopolitanism was in ordeal at the time, and Chinese intellectuals eagerly pursued it yet their dreams turned out in vain.

# Part Ⅲ.

## Cross-Cultural Transaction in "Boudoir Stories"

# Chapter Five    Eileen Chang's Cross-Cultural Writing and Rewriting in *Love in a Fallen City*

Witnessing in her formative years the irrevocable decline of the class of Chinese mandarin and gentry, the much-acclaimed literary genius in modern China, Zhang Ailing ( Eileen Chang, 1920-1995 ) held unapologetic individualism. Located at the cracks and gaps of history, situating her in a besieged society, as fragments and residues of a previous world congealed, she appropriated her writing as a means to enter the soul of a particular class that she belongs, to "dream its dreams and roam inside its unconscious." [1] This effort brings out the interior life-being of Chinese urbanites, the middle-class Shanghainese in particular, of their anxiety on love, marriage, and personal identity, which then "becomes an allegorical stand-in for the world of things and commodities through which a narrative totality of a historical experience can be held"[2], particularly the ambiguity and dilemma of this precarious class situated within the unsettled contradiction of history.

To be more specific, from the perspective of her cross-cultural writing and rewriting (or appropriation) of Eugene O'Neill's (1888-1953) imagery of the Magna Mater, or the Maternal Goddess in her famed novelette *Love in a Fallen City*(《倾城之念》), this chapter analyzes the writer's archetypal, paramount thematic concern of her oeuvre—a profound matrimonial anxiety in a besieged city, by which it delves into the identity politics of her ostensible apolitical stories. It shows the predicament of marriage and love as

---

[1]    Zhang, X., Shanghai Nostalgia: Postrevolutionary Allegories in Wang Anyi's Literary Production in the 1990s, *Positions:East Asia Cultures Critique*, 2000,8(2):382.

[2]    Zhang, X., Shanghai Nostalgia: Postrevolutionary Allegories in Wang Anyi's Literary Production in the 1990s, *Positions:East Asia Cultures Critique*, 2000,8(2):382.

social institutions in a semi-colonial, semi-traditional society. This study suggests that her stories demonstrate individualism—the cardinal principle of the middle-class world—was in a deep crisis, which brings about a profound cultural nihilism in her fictional world; and this is because the social-historical reality—the semi-traditional, semi-colonial situation— restricted and constrained the process of a cultural embourgeoisement.

## 一、Love as Social Institution and Individualism in Crisis

*Love in a Fallen City* seems to be a melodramatic romance that finally comes to fruition. Typical of the writer's story about social mannerism, the story is "filled with witty conversations and relentless gossip; intricate codes of dress, dining, and socializing…; and arabesque patterns and mannerisms in both private and public domains that are taken as matters of life and death for those leisurely regulars."① But the heroine Liusu, though a "typical" semi-traditional Chinese woman who has received little education, is a rare figure in Chang's stories, as she takes the initiative to divorce his husband because of the unbearable abuse she has suffered. This plot itself shows the society has been more enlightened to accept this bold action. Having returned to her own extended family for more than seven years, now she is at the age of twenty-eight. She is discriminated and expelled by brothers and sisters-in-law, who apparently still hold the old mindset and follow traditional ways of life. She has to look for a second marriage to avoid further humiliation.

From this urge to rise above her situation, an impulse to ascend into a higher class to ensure her security and dignity, comes a "narrative experiment" that develops the whole story, which "opened up a space unrealizable in the asphyxiating conditions of a reified existence and of an

---

① These descriptions are originally for a novel written by a contemporary writer Wang Anyi, but they are also valid for this story in particular, and for many of Eileen Chang's stories in general. See Zhang, X., Shanghai Nostalgia: Postrevolutionary Allegories in Wang Anyi's Literary Production in the 1990s, *Positions: East Asia Cultures Critique*, 2000,8(2):359.

empirically unchangeable destiny."① A relative offers her a prospect of finding a man for her. Returning upstairs, she appreciates herself in front of a mirror. A cinematic "close-up" in a subtle way conveys her psychological nuance:

> Following the undulating tune (of huqin, a traditional Chinese music equipment), Liusu's head tilted to one side, and her eyes and hands started to gesture subtly. As she performed in the mirror, the huqin no longer sounded like a huqin, but like strings and flutes intoning a solemn court dance…Her steps seemed to trace the lost rhythms of an ancient melody.②

Her performance is a rehearsal, a tryout of seduction to be performed in reality. Her behavior is like "a solemn court dance," to trace the trajectory of ancient beauty represented in classical Chinese romance. This narration implies the feature of her adventure: a modern rehearsal of the traditional motif of a woman seeking her master's favor. Yet precisely due to this, it also casts a shadow over her fate, because legendary ancient beauties mostly ended tragically.

Her self-appreciation does not end up in this: "Suddenly, she smiled—a private, malevolent smile—and the music came to a discordant halt. The huqin (胡琴) outside continues, yet the tales of fealty and filial piety, chastity and righteousness the huqin tells of had nothing to do with her." The melody in her mind is her own internal movement, which aims to break out the old world and its moralistic straitjacket to make adventure into a new world. Hypocritical or not, this role-play would define her new identity, individual as well as national, insofar as her current identity of being a Chinese woman is specified by the traditional code, which now is "nothing to do with her." This repudiation of traditional Chinese ethical-moral code is simultaneously a process of formation of a new subjectivity, which is also a new class identity. Before this process is completed, she is still a woman torn between two incompatible worlds.

---

① Jameson, F., *Political Unconscious: Narrative as a Socially Symbolic Act*, Ithaca, N.Y.: Cornell University Press, 1981:20.

② Chang, E., *Love in a Fallen City*, Kingsbury S. Trans, New York: New York Review of Books, 2007:121, with slight modification of mine.

## 二、A（Non-）Romanic Adventure

In a party, she accidentally meets Liuyuan, a Hong Kong based, British educated dandy and an over-thirty overseas Chinese who just returns from England. He is the mirror image as well as the "other" of the devastated Shanghai middle class, who seemingly owns some refined tastes in this vulgar age, as he harbors a sort of nostalgia towards sophisticated Chinese traditional high culture. But Wylie Sypher has pointed out that a dandy is only "a substitute for the aristocratic who has lost its castle...a middle-class aristocrat, a figure who could make its entrance only in the cities that were becoming the milieu for the bourgeois." [1] In contrast to its image in its original Western context, where the poet as a dandy "distances himself from the bourgeois values that brought his cultures into being," [2] Liuyuan's dandyism is much less a mockery than a by-product of Shanghai's proto-bourgeois middle-class values. Yet also analogous to Baudelaire's dandyism, he has a "nostalgia for a spiritual homeland or city that existed beyond the visible world," with an internalized "sense of decay and decline" of the culture. [3]

Seeing this as a rare opportunity, when Liuyuan returns to Hong Kong, Liusu puts aside her female dignity as well as traditional ethical-moral code, going there fantastically to pursue her dream. A series of flirtations take place at dance halls, restaurants, the hotel's lobby, on the beach, and in the heroine's room, all of which are the living rooms of leisurely middle class, though now it is in the overseas colonial land. Leo Lee has subtly insinuated that this is not a realistic scenario, because Liusu, being "a traditional, nearly illiterate woman," seems unable to conduct these "sophisticated

---

[1]  Sypher, W., *Loss of the Self in Modern Literature*, Westport, Conn.: GreenWood Press, 1979:36.

[2]  Sypher, W., *Loss of the Self in Modern Literature*, Westport, Conn.: GreenWood Press, 1979:382.

[3]  Lehan, R., *The City in Literature*, Berkeley:University of California Press, 1998:75.

flirtation and witty repartee" (it seems "almost out of character").[1] However, the loosening of rigid caste system in a turbulent time, as well as the particular taste of Liuyuan thanks to his peculiar experience (and the anachronistic facade of a performed "authentic" Chinese femininity represented in Liusu), might help to explain his interests in Liusu. Moreover, Liusu's will to remarriage is necessitated by her hardship in the life of the extended family, and Liuyuan only wants to court her to be his mistress. For both, love as a passionate emotion and will of self-sacrifice is only a luxury.

Since Liuyuan apparently knows her intention, he only "treats her as an exotic oriental woman under his 'colonial' gaze."[2] This in fact is also a humiliated experience for her. Realizing that Liuyuan not only does not want to marry her, but also publicly maintains an ambivalent facade to let her shoulder the burden of public opinion (in order to subdue her pride and make her willing to be his mistress), Liusu returns to her home in Shanghai. Yet she still harbors a deep hope that Liuyuan might still call her back, as he still has not owned her body.

A fall passes, and Liuyuan indeed sends her a telegraph. Yet Liusu feels she failed: because she is older and could not afford any procrastination. But she does not fail completely; at least what happens in the night when she arrives in Hong Kong is exactly what she expected in the beginning when she practiced her seduction in front of the mirror. In this mutually willing consummation, he quietly walks behind her, twists back his face and kisses her, then "he pushed her into the mirror, they seemed to fall down into it, into another shadowy world—freezing cold, searing hot, the flames of the forest burning all over their bodies." In this consummate scene, the lust of desire finally prevails over any mundane calculation.

---

①    This is because their class hierarchy that makes their romance less credible: "In the scale of realism, it would be hard to imagine a more incompatible couple, given such diverse background." Lee, L. O., *Shanghai Modern: The Flowering of New Urban Culture in China*, 1930-1945, Cambridge: Harvard University Press, 1999:293.

②    Lee, L. O., *Shanghai Modern: The Flowering of New Urban Culture in China*, 1930-1945, Cambridge: Harvard University Press, 1999:295.

What this mirror scene—which reminds us of a famed scene in *The Story of the Stone*, the latter of which is a caution against lust—indicates is that this moment only reveals the ungrounded and vulnerable nature of their relations. Thus after this enjoyment, Liuyuan decides to depart for England again. Refusing to take Liusu together, he still just wants to keep her as his paramour. But the Japanese bombing of Hong Kong aborts his plan. Now the shadow that has casted over Liuyuan's mind finally comes true. Since both are struggling for their survival in a crowded and besieged city, for this they have to extend help to each other; to evade such an unhappy consciousness, they muddle through their days and get married. Do they love each other? The only indication of "love" is conveyed in this way, "She suddenly moved to Liuyuan's side in bed and embraced him through the quilt. He pulled out his hand to take hers, and they saw through each other. It was a mere instant of complete understanding, but the flash could enable them to live in harmony for the next eight to ten years." Their mutual understanding of each other's selfishness is started from the very beginning. In this passionate moment, they merely reach a mutual compromise and forgive each other. Yet it also signifies Liuyuan's concession of his idealism that yearns for an eternal happiness, but not the ephemeral pleasure.[1]

---

[1] If it is believed that love comes as a result of this sexual intercourse, it is another optical illusion. This "belief" has its particular social-historical overdetermination: as the enfeebled Chinese middle class lacked any sense of either financial security or political power, to engage in romantic love is a luxury for them, and thus temporary satisfaction of desire becomes a preferable choice. It is also worthy to note that while this image is reminiscent of Lu Xun's famed imagery of "dead fire," it is the complete reverse of its connotation: for Zhang, "when the 'searing hot' passion is burned out, its ashes...can only decorate the 'freezing cold' landscape of 'the aged earth, the world at its end.'"—In short, "in Chang's world of desolation, passion can only be... a 'dead fire'" (This is because their class hierarchy that makes their romance less credible: "In the scale of realism, it would be hard to imagine a more incompatible couple, given such diverse background." Lee, L. O., *Shanghai Modern: The Flowering of New Urban Culture in China*, 1930-1945, Cambridge: Harvard University Press, 1999: 301); whereas for Lu Xun, a dead fire is inclined to change itself to be a passionate devotion.

Nevertheless, here the narrative voice celebrates this success:

> In this world of turmoil and tumult, wealth, property and all other things that
> used to last forever are now all unreliable. All she could count on were the breath
> within her throat and this man sleeping beside her... They looked and saw each other,
> saw each other entirely. It was a mere moment of complete understanding, but it was
> enough to keep them happy together for a decade or so. He was just a selfish man, and she
> just a selfish woman. In this age of military turmoil, there was no room for individualists,
> but there was always a place for an ordinary couple. [1]

We cannot distinguish whether this is the narrator's voice or it is the
interior psychological movement of the heroine. In fact the two are now
inextricable, which is a rare case for the author, who mostly keeps an
ironical distance in the narrative voice (of her fictional texts). From the
perspective of Liusu, this is a consummate moment, which is also the
climax of her (non-)romantic adventure. To her, the man sleeping beside
her is really the only one she can count on at the critical moment, and the
vice versa for Liuyuan. But if this is a mutual "complete understanding,"
then they both would know that when the temporary war is over, how long will
they live together is hard to predict, as the narrative voice also acknowledges. As
critics, we have to refrain from falling into the same overt sentimentalism to
endorse this lyrical flight, and to be honest enough to question literally the
"literary" rhetoric; insofar as the narrator acknowledges that individualists have no
peaceful and safe place to stay in the war, then whereupon can this selfish couple
find a room to drag on their lives, no matter whether they are really "ordinary" or

---

[1]   Chang, E., *Love in a Fallen City*, New York: New York Review of Books,
2007:164.

not?[①]

Obviously, this illusion of an eternally still life not only belongs to the protagonists, but is also that of the narrator, who now becomes their alter-ego. To be sure, they realize the fragility of their existence amid chaos where they are helpless, yet such a realization could not guarantee that a dandy could change his character as the woman hopelessly wishes. Still, the narrator lets out a passionate exclamation:

> Hong Kong's defeat had fulfilled her dream. But in this irrational world, who knows what cause is and what effect is? Who knows? Perhaps it was for her fulfillment that a great metropolis was leveled. Countless thousands of people die, countless thousands of people suffer, and what follows is an earthshaking reform… Liusu didn't feel that her place in history is anything remarkable. She stood up, smiling, and kicked the pan of mosquito-repellant incense under the table.

> The legendary beauties who felled cities and kingdoms were probably all like this.[②]

---

[①] Chang, E., *Love in a Fallen City*, New York: New York Review of Books, 2007:167. When read side by side with the fact that in the war "numerous people die and numerous wounded," they are far more than "ordinary." In fact, compared with those without basic human condition to live, they should be regarded as belonging to a middle-class stratum owning certain level of privilege, though this is merely a precarious privilege. Edward Gunn also notes that, although "it is a sophisticated joke, the story also suggests the amoral ruthlessness" which she believes lies "at the heart of human desire, and in the world in which that desire exists." Gunn, E., *Unwelcome Muse: Chinese Literature in Shanghai and Peking* 1937-1945, New York: Columbia University Press, 1980:217. While Edward Gunn here emphasizes the universal character of the evil side of human nature, I wish to call attention to the peculiar nature of this particular set of humanity, as Edward Gunn also admits, "the details which comprise that (psychological) realism are ordered to embody a particular view of psychological reality." Gunn, E., *Unwelcome Muse: Chinese Literature in Shanghai and Peking* 1937-1945, New York: Columbia University Press, 1980:217.

[②] This exaggerated and alarming articulation of a private feeling is not merely a metaphorical expression conveyed by an obvious womanly narrative voice; but insofar as this repudiation of exploring the socio-economic contradiction as well as the political overdetermination of wars and conflicts (which are condemned in a breath to irrationality, not aware of this explanation itself is irrational) is not merely an individual choice, but a general practice owned by a certain social group, it is less a literary rhetoric than a manifestation of a particular cultural-political unconscious.

The expression of a privileged feeling notwithstanding, it also subtly produces an ironic twist that finally deconstructs what it meant to convey. As easily recognized by average Chinese, the last sentence echoes and brings out the theme of the title (and the story in general), because the original Chinese phrase for "love in a fallen city" can also be read as "love that topples cities," which, as a historical idiom, narrates a historical story in which a concubine enchants a king to such an extent that, to satisfy her idiosyncratic taste in order to please her, the king signifies false alarming signals to call back his forces; numerous turns of such a hoax lead to the loss of vigilance of his army and when the true enemy comes, nobody arrives for his order and as a result, the kingdom is toppled. From a feminist perspective, this traditional story can be read as a misogynic narrative (regardless of whether it is a real historical fact or not). Yet the narrative voice here (which goes beyond psychonarration, borders on narrated monologue, and even confuses itself with the female character's psyche) precisely articulates such a discourse to utter a wholly "irrational" feeling and "absurd" rationalization; it is the contemporary war that levels the city, bringing thousands of people to death to "fulfill" (a literal translation of the original Chinese word of "成全") her dream. This narration indeed subverts conventional ideas of male-dominated history, or patriarchal historiographical writing, yet this womanly indulgence in her "success" not only emits a strong pull of chilly air among readers (or at least some readers), but also falls into the same traditional pitfall of misogynic representation.

### 三、Two Value Systems and the (Im-)Possibility of Love

To be sure, this repudiation of civilization has its own rationale in the text, which is conveyed in the imagery of a dilapidated wall. When loitering around the ruins and observing the object, Liuyuan tells Liusu, "One day when our civilization is completely ruined and everything is destroyed— burnt, burst, utterly collapsed and ruined, maybe this wall will still be there. If, at that time, we can meet at this wall…then maybe, Liusu, you will hold a little sincerity towards me，and I will towards you." According to this confession，if their marriage indeed indicates that there is any sincerity between the two，then at least partly it is because in his eyes，the civilization has almost come to its end.

As Liusu immediately rebukes，this expression amounts to say that he would never have a sincere feeling towards her. It is a complete subversion (as a reverse) of the famed original Chinese classical verse line that Liuyuan's phrase is based upon:"地老天荒不了情，" which means "our love will never end until the moment when the earth ages and the heaven grows old." It signified the distrust of love as genuine，selfless emotion.

The conjuring up of "aged earth and deserted sky" has alluded to dynastic changes，the displacement of people，their exile，and their tragic death，which casts an ominous shadow. Even at the moment of climactic scene of courtship which leads to the consummation of their physical desire，this sentiment still prevails. This scene appears as a phone-call. This scene ostensibly looks like a formulaic scene of Hollywood romantic comedies. In a deep night，Liuyuan calls Liusu and quickly say"I love you" and immediately hangs up. After a moment he calls back again and asks "Do you love me?" Again，quite out of sync with his character，he quotes a classical Chinese verse to convey a profound anxiety "Life，death，separation—with thee there is happiness；thy hand in mine，we will grow old together，" and says "I think this is a very mournful poem which says that life and death and parting are all enormous things，far beyond human control."

This lamentation discloses Liuyuan's premonitory sense of doom and thus his cynicism whereupon his dandyism is nourished. Indeed，this sentiment saturates the atmosphere of the whole story. When we break the facade of private，fantastic flirtation and courtship and tie in the statement with the broad historical context as its subtext，this lamentation is not enigmatic and not hard to understand：his class，as an amorphous stratum straddling between the residual aristocratic gentry-class and the emergent bourgeois middle class，had missed its historical opportunity. Caught in the historical conjuncture of a slowly-progressed rationalization which was furthermore stymied by the imperialist invasion，it faced the blank wall of an "end" of history in its destiny as an immature yet precocious social group.

Here, Liuyuan's distrust of love and marriage should not merely be seen as his nature as a playboy, but it should be placed vis-a-vis the historical context. Although his vision that one day, "civilization is completely ruined and everything is destroyed," is still not a prospect closed by for eyes, it is already an imaginable vista in mind. This pessimistic view reflects a mood of despair towards the looming aggravated and protracted World War II, and the loss of hope on the consolidation of power and wealth of this defenseless middle-class stratum. Therefore, though Liuyuan's anxiety is a projection of the author's own point of view,[1] it is not out of sync with his character.

A veteran playboy as he is, Liuyuan also looks for genuine affection, and pleads for Liusu's understanding. So he even breaks out his cold facade to iterate the poem from the *Book of Songs* (《诗经》). This yearning for a genuine love can be seen as a longing for a spiritual love born of a desire for a long-term love—he is not satisfied with his alienated, debauched life either.

Both Liuyuan and Liusu have alienated feelings. That Liuyuan has an alienated feeling is partially because he straddles two worlds: the British life experience has endowed him a highly rationalized mind, so he even feels bored and longs for some orientalized flavor; yet the Chinese socio-economic situation is so hopeless that his plan of keeping a mistress is blown away by a by-no-means abrupt foreign invasion. Liusu is also torn apart between two worlds: the traditional household which she decides to break with, and a rationalized bourgeois life in which, due to her background, she can only serve as a mistress in normal situation.[2] While the seemingly "abnormal" temporarily leads to an unexpected alliance and transaction between the two

---

[1]   Eileen Chang herself has uttered similar points now and then in her preface to *Romance*.

[2]   Jameson has informed us "alienation here designates class alienation and the 'objective treason' of intellectuals perpetually suspended between two social worlds and two sets of class values and obligations." Jameson, F., *Political Unconscious*, Ithaca, NY: Cornell University Press, 1981:200.

worlds，what would we expect when the "normal" time again arrives? It is also against such a situation can we understand why desolation（苍凉），an aesthetic state that literally means "bleak and cold," defines the narrator's view upon the world in general，and love in particular.

Following Liuyuan's exclamation，Liusu immediately refuses his rationalization，seeing it merely as excuse for not marrying her. She changes the direction of the talk by assuming a misinterpretation of his words："A person so careless like you，if you cannot decide it，who would decide it?" Liusu might misunderstand his import due to her ignorance of the socio-political circumstance，as what fills her mind is to fasten a marriage；yet Liuyuan curiously follows her suit by changing the deliverance of premonition of doom to issue of private love. When she says coldly，"You do not love me…，" he reciprocates by saying that he cannot "waste money to marry a woman who has no emotion towards him," and he rebukes Liusu that "essentially you regard marriage as a long-term prostitution." What they are fighting about in this second stage of discussion is not about social-political issue which Liusu might not be interested in and has knowledge of，but a talk around the existence of genuine love between them and the marriage as a social institution. It conveys the message that genuine love is the moral basis of a marriage，rather than marriage is a way to secure economic safety.

Throughout her career，Liusu has a clear consciousness of her own precarious position—her class status—in the world. The preoccupation with perpetuating her mode of life as ritualistic mannerism of mundane enjoyment reveals the repressed unconscious of the precarious status of the petit-bourgeois middle class who always feels being threatened. In the story，the couple has intuition of the vulnerability and helplessness of this class. Liusu's misunderstanding is thus deliberately arranged：by this tactic，the author supplies a condition for a negotiation which supposedly leads to the final mutual understanding between the two. But more importantly for us，the process of negotiation itself contains heterogeneous voices，in which two value systems are colliding with each other：one is Liuyuan's about the modern concept of love as the basis of marriage，which he acquires when he studies in England; the other is Liusu's, which is based on the traditional practice and morality.

The coexistence of the two value systems is because there are two worlds there. This romance can only take place in Hong Kong because it, as Leo Lee has noticed, is "a thoroughly alien colony with none of the native sights and sounds of Shanghai." In this alienated world, the ingrained traditional values no longer hold sway (as there are not many middle class families there), and so in this unfamiliar setting without close relatives Liusu can disregard gossips that might arise from them (though only to a certain extent). She can perform any tricks and display any unconventional gestures that are pleased to her. In a word, they court each other in a borrowed time and space, or chronotope. Though, this colonial setting also sets up certain unpropitious conditions to her: since it is also a haven for those overseas refugees, Liuyuan can flirt with other oriental women, including an Indian princess in exile, to dispel the attraction of Liusu and to stimulate the latter's envy and desire.

## 四、Dilapidated Wall and Robust Coquette

If the existence of two worlds contributes to the (im-) possibility of love, then what kind of wall triggers Liuyuan's tinge of emotion and passionate lament at the moment they take a walk near the Shallow Water Bay? "This wall," Liuyuan says, "I don't know why, makes me think of the old sayings about the end of the world." It is "a gray brick wall…cool and rough, the color of death." The remains of historical catastrophe, it is a symbol of death.

However, this is only part of the story. It is easily neglected that the wall is also "so high that its upper edge could not be seen." As a residual ruin of history, we could hardly imagine it could still be so magnificent (just like we can barely believe a dandy with half-baked Chinese learning can express such a profound longing for eternal love). These might be read as formal incongruities. But as Fredric Jameson informs us, "The very formal contradictions are themselves the most precious indications as to how we stand with respect to the concrete reality of social life itself at the present moment of time." [1] Thus they should be explored with a consideration of the authorial intervention. This does not mean a residue in actual life can never happen to be so high, but what we need to inquiry into is why the "endless" height and the coldness of death are placed together: anyhow by evoking the Chinese idiom "断壁残垣" (crumbling walls and residual curbs), the wall is surely short in readers' mind.

Fredric Jameson's another saying might offer us cues: "The influence of class consciousness on thought is felt not so much in the perception of the individual details of reality as in the overall form or gestalt according to which those details are organized and interpreted." [2] The issue is not how the wall appears in reality, but how it appears in the viewers' mind. In this light, the wall, in its grand, sublime figure (besides of its "cold, rough" surface) disregarding time's erosion and alien invasion, also symbolizes the middle-class's consciousness of a timeless, natural present of a sustainable life, or the will to such a life. It is a reification into which the outside world was frozen. An ideology as it is, it is simultaneously a utopia. Or, submitting to "fate" notwithstanding, there is a hidden utopian sentiment that bears a strong will to live an eternally peaceful, comfortable life. It is utopian in the sense that this sentiment holds that "the ultimate ethical goal of human life is a world…a world in which meaning and life are once more indivisible, in which man and the world are at one." [3] Thus Liusu combines her existential meaning with her life; the world that she lives in and she herself are at one; and this is her ultimate ethical code. In this light, the wall here is a symbol for an ironclad will of power to drag on a difficult life, to keep a self-privileged world, against any historical vicissitude.

---

① Jameson, F., *Marxism and Form*, Princeton, N J: Princeton University Press, 1974: 57.

② Jameson, F., *Political Unconscious: Narrative as a Socially Symbolic Act*, Ithaca, N Y: Cornell University Press, 1981: 184.

③ Jameson, F., *Marxism and Form*, Princeton, N J: Princeton University Press, 1974: 173.

Along the same line of inquiry, we can understand another image
related to the wall, a female figure in a local folk genre called bengbeng
opera. In another place, Eileen Chang has described this image in the way
very much reminiscent of the rhetoric articulated by Liuyuan for the wall:
"In the wilderness of the future, amidst the ruins of buildings and walls,
only a woman like the heroine from a bengbeng opera can survive and live on
peacefully, because there is a home for her in any era, any society,
anywhere."[①] It is obvious that the "sublimity" of the wall is identical to the
"vitality" of the woman. Leo Lee thus has aptly noted that Liusu is "very
much modeled after such a heroine."[②] That Eileen Chang focuses on the
description of this figure in her short preface to the second edition of
*Romance* is noteworthy, as it implies that the spirit of the coquette is the
core of most of her robust, unabashed female characters. Therefore, more
detailed examination of the nature of this character is warranted.

Bengbeng Opera is a local opera for lower-class audiences. In Shanghai,
this earthy play had been "out of fashion" at the time. Although she
hesitates, Eileen Chang still wants to watch it: "I have so much interest on
this discarded, lower-tasted material that I'm even abashed to invite other
people (to see it together)." After she watched it, she gave a depiction of
two scenes with two noted figures: one is Li Sanniang, an empress in a
dynasty of Chinese history, but in the show she was still a laboring
countrywoman; the other is a wench who murders her husband and in the
play tries to explain the crime away before an interrogator.

By offering these two figures as the representative of the vivacious
young woman or coquette [huadan(花旦)], a fixed role in Chinese opera],
the intention of the author is rather very ambiguous. Although she refutes
the general impression that sees these "women who acquire power in the
primitive and barbarian world" with "sear and passionate big eyes, firmer
than men, holding a horsewhip in hand and whipping people now and then,"

---

①  张爱玲:《张爱玲短篇小说集》,皇冠出版社 1984 年版,第 3 页.

②  Lee, L. O., *Shanghai Modern : The Flowering of New Urban Culture in China*,
1930-1945, Cambridge: Harvard University Press, 1999:297.

as "wild rose in the fantasy of average people" (she says "that is merely fabricated by urban dwellers who need new stimulation"), she does not give any clear explanation. Yet based on the earthy language and the primitive energy shown by the two women, their spirit can be generally understood as so robust, audacious, and unabashed without any sense of shame brought about by any civilized culture.

A lady from an aristocratic high-class family with refined taste, Eileen Chang's identification with this vulgar image, just like her identification with the lower-class, folk culture, is apparently surprising. Yet I will read this as a variation of her ingrained sense of sophisticated and refined tastes, and a projection of her anxiety of being a vulnerable woman—now an unprofessional, semi-traditional middle class woman without practical skills and thus financial security in the "new" society. What Eileen Chang implies is that in harsh times, only primitive, "genuine" human instinct (both related with the feminine and the sexual) bereft of any hypocritical and masculine (patriarchal) traits can survive in the world. But since this matriarchal myth totally banishes the role of any male figure (or the latter as its sex servant?), it might be another myth which is metaphysical and historically ungrounded. In other words, while this statement can be read as "a reaction against modernity," to see it as "a return to native Chinese sources for intellectual nourishment and aesthetic pleasure"[1] is only a hallucination, or an optical illusion; because neither Li Sanniang nor the vicious wench who commits matricide can shoulder the burden of "fulfilling" the ideal of "living on peacefully … in any era, any society, anywhere." I will suggest that fundamentally, this is a projection of a different sensitivity nourished by traditional Chinese folk culture (which nevertheless derived its ideological inspiration from the imperial high-brown culture) and modern Western art (such as the image of the prostitute in Eugene O'Neill's drama

---

① Lee, L. O., *Shanghai Modern: The Flowering of New Urban Culture in China*, 1930-1945, Cambridge: Harvard University Press, 1999:288.

*The Great God Brown*)[1] which is thrown into the native folk culture, founded upon a cultural-political anarchism premised on primitivism. But why did this weird invocation of a rigorous dancing woman exist, which apparently appears to be an epiphany?

## 五、Mythology, Symbolism, and Cultural Nihilism

It is known that apocalypse oftentimes appears in wartime period, during which the whole collectivity is involved. Here, it seems that this sudden appearance of epiphany is from the resource of some popular novels and theaters, but we need to make a fine distinction between the "sense of vitality" on the one hand and "cliché" or "primitive thought" on the other. Mythology and folklore are engraved with superstitious mentality, ignorance and conformity; yet the fictional characters seem to be inspired by the soundness and optimism, the strength and imagination preserved among the ordinary people despite miseries perpetuated in their life. This entails more deliberation of the two figures that Eileen Chang has discussed.

Li Sanniang (913-954), an empress, is the wife of the Gaozu of Later Han or Liu Zhiyuan (895-948), the founder of later Han dynasty (947—951).[2] The historical legend holds that she came out of her poor background to become the empress thanks to her vitality and perseverance (the latter of which the drama has tried to present); and she was so wise that she peacefully died while her son, the succeeding emperor, was killed because he intended to subdue a powerful subordinate which Li Sanniang had vainly advised against. Obviously in this image the folks (as well as the author) have deposited their dream for a peaceful, comfortable life despite the hard

---

①　Eileen Chang has directly talked about this image in the same rhetoric as she discusses the dancing woman in her essay "On Women" (《谈女人》). See the following detailed discussion.

②　The dynasty lasted only three years and is the fourth of the five dynasties in the Five Dynasties and Ten Kingdoms Period of Chinese history. See Mote, F. W., *Imperial China*；900-1800, Boston：Harvard University Press, 1999.

life conditions (including wartime chaos) that they had to endure at the moment. But if Eileen Chang did not make it clear when she introduced this character, the import is abundantly explicit in the vamp (who commits a matricide) and the dancing girl, the latter of which, as I just suggested, is correlated closely with the imagery of the Magna Mater, or the Maternal Goddess in Eugene O'Neill's drama *The Great God Brown*.

In O'Neill's drama, the incarnated character is a prostitute named Cybel. Eileen Chang had translated several key sentences from the drama characterizing her："full breasted and wide-hipped, her movements are slow and solidly languorous like an animal's…She chews gum like a sacred cow forgetting time with an eternal [cud]." While these features surely remind us what Eileen Chang had described the dancing girl, the stake to disclose the secret of this correlation lies in another place, namely a deeply-seated impulse to establish the Magna Mater, or the Maternal Goddess as the Messiah, which is apparently shared by O'Neill and Eileen Chang.

O'Neill (1888-1953) has fought a complex of the Magna Mater, or the Maternal Goddess throughout his creative life, which is witnessed in several of his plays. According to the study of Thomas E. Porter, Cybel of *The Great God Brown* is but "one of the 'many faces' of the Magna mater." In another play *Dynamo*, the writer "attempts to fuse the divine and the maternal" by presenting "the figure and features of the Magna Mater, the primitive goddess of Oriental-Helleistic mystery religions." In *Strange Interlude*, the heroine Nina Leeds advocates "replacing a stern and indifferent Father/God with God the Mother." As Thomas E. Porter aptly notes, "This development of Mother-God images in the plays is a valiant attempt by the playwright to fashion a faith he could live with."[1]

Eileen Chang apparently shares a similar faith. But if O'Neill's belief derived from the source of Irish Catholicism and was out of his feeling that

---

① Porter, T. E., The Magna Mater: the Maternal Goddess in O'Neill's Plays, *Eugene O'Neill Review*, 2005,(27):42.

he had been *"abandoned by those he longed for most 'Mother and God,'"*[1]
then Eileen Chang's conviction lies in her feminine consciousness and her
sense of being abandoned by the State and the time (in addition to the sense
of being abandoned by her parents who did not provide much parental love,
especially her father), the sense of vulnerability. Thus her imagination of
the character (the dancing girl) bears many features that C. G. Jung has
aptly described pertaining to the Magna Mater archetype.

> The qualities associated with [the Magna Mater archetype] are maternal solicitude
> and sympathy; the magic authority of the female; the wisdom and spiritual exaltation
> that transcend reason; any helpful instinct or impulse; all that is benign, all that
> cherishes and sustains, that fosters growth and fertility...[2]

Eileen Chang's sense of maternal divinity, coming from the "Magna
Mater" icon of the mystery religions, aims to dispel any inhuman onslaught
(from the patriarchal society) on women, which is seen as on the human
race in general, as well as the civilizationper se. In its image of a rouged
temptress, it is symbolized as the spirit of vital renewal, with an
unimaginable political power that offers new life and immortality.

Nevertheless, since "myth, insofar as it's rooted in a collective
superstition or a false consciousness, is reflexive of something that's equally
accessible from political perspective."[3] As the "intimation of death is already
written on the wall," how and where can this female figure always find a

---

①   Porter, T. E., The Magna Mater: the Maternal Goddess in O'Neill's Plays,
*Eugene O'Neill Review*, 2005,(27):41.

②   Jung, C. G., *The Archetypes and the Collective Unconscious*, Hull, R. F. C.
Trans, 2nd ed, Princeton, N J:Princeton University Press, 1980. It is worthy to note that
C. G. Jung also points out the negative side of the Magna Mater: "[It] may connote
anything secret, hidden and dark; the abyss, the world of 'The Dead,' anything that
devours, seduces, and poisons, that is terrifying and inescapable like fate." Jung, C. G.,
*The Archetypes and the Collective Unconscious*. Hull, R.F.C., Trans, 2nd ed, Princeton,
N J:Princeton University Press, 1980. O'Neill also stresses this dichotomy which Eileen
Chang obviously neglects.

③   Zhang, X., *Chinese Modernism in the Era of Reforms*, Durham:Duke University
Press, 1997:311.

place for herself? Leo Lee has perceived that there is no place for man (Liuyuan) here, thus he ponders:"It seems that in this larger allegory of life, Chang has reserved a special place for her half-traditional heroine, not necessarily for reasons of her gender but for what her gender represents in Chinese culture in this transitional era."[①] Disillusioned with the grand narrative of progress and enlightenment held by the May Fourth styled intellectuals and propagated by various political forces, Eileen Chang's skepticism of modernity reveals the painful, checked, and diversified road to a modernity that seems to be of little hope of reaching full rationalization.

Still, how can a feminine Chinese culture, and even the unabashed dancing girl, survive "peacefully" under the shadow of intimation of death and doom, if not dragging itself on ignobly? It has been noted that "the 'rebirth' the goddess holds out and the ecstasy she affords are rooted in a 'primitive naturalism,' in the energy of the sexual drive;" and "this atavistic, amoral aspect of the Great Mother…dashes…(the hope) for achieving the transforming ecstasy."[②] Meanwhile, "O'Neill's valiant attempts to rehabilitate the Magna Mater myth fail because he cannot honestly discover in Nature a benevolent alliance of power and love."[③] If O'Neill fails, did Eileen Chang succeed? Against Leo Lee's interpretation, I would read Eileen Chang's figures differently, by arguing that rather than a cultural issue, this seemingly salvific and messianic image, premised on a gender difference, is a displacement of a political issue, as the class conflict is rewritten in terms of sexual differentiation and the "women's question." Jameson's argument again is helpful here: by doing this, it allows the "experimental situation"—what we have mentioned at the beginning—"to be staged within the more conventional novelistic framework of marriage,

---

① Lee, L. O., *Shanghai Modern: The Flowering of New Urban Culture in China*, 1930-1945, Cambridge:Harvard University Press, 1999:297.

② Porter, T. E., The Magna Mater:The Maternal Goddess in O'Neill's Plays, *Eugene O'Neill Review*, 2005,(27):48.

③ Porter, T. E., The Magna Mater:The Maternal Goddess in O'Neill's Plays, *Eugene O'Neill Review*, 2005,(27):49.

which thereby gains an unaccustomed class resonance." ① Here, in particular, the imagery is a token for the inexorable determination of the middle-class residents to struggle to live on against all odds.

Accordingly, this imagery as a symbol has two levels of significance: it is both a reified ideology and an unyieldingly utopian longing. We must unravel more the cultural significance of this sort of symbolism. Jameson has pointed out its ideologically illusionary nature:

> Symbolism is not just one literary technique among others, but represents a qualitatively different mode of apprehending the world from the realistic one… (It is) always a kind of admission of defeat on the part of the novelist, for by having recourse to it the writer implies that some original, objective meaning in objects is henceforth inaccessible to him, that he must invent a new and fictive one to conceal this basic absence, this basic silence of things. ②

For him, the coming-into-being of the symbol "results not from the properties of the things themselves but from the will of the creator, who imposes a meaning on them by fiat: it represents the vain attempt of subjectivity to evolve a human world completely out of itself." And so,

> In symbolic works of art, we strive for some meaningful relationship to the outside world, to objective reality, only to return empty-handed, having lived our life among shadows, having touched nothing but ourselves in the world around us. ③

How is symbolism produced? What is the origin of it? Jameson cites Plekhanov's discussion of symbolism to reveal the secret: one employs symbols "when he's unable to grasp the meaning of that particular reality, or when he cannot accept the conclusion to which the development of that reality leads." Thus, "He resorts to symbols when he cannot solve difficult, sometimes insoluble problems… And so in art, when artist leans towards

---

① Jameson, F., *Political Unconscious: Narrative as a Socially Symbolic Act*, Ithaca, NY: Cornell University Press, 1981: 204.

② Jameson, F., *Marxism and Form*, Princeton, NJ: Princeton University Press, 1974: 197.

③ Jameson, F., *Marxism and Form*, Princeton, NJ: Princeton University Press, 1974: 198.

symbolism, it's an infallible sign that his thinking—or the thinking of the class which he represents, in the sense of its social development—does not dare penetrate the reality which lie before his eyes."[①]

This incapability to "grasp the meaning" of particular reality by way of symbolism shows simultaneously a process of building a new totality in mind to interpret the totality of the world and the society:

> …in spite of their depersonalized and well-nigh inhuman surface, they represent an attempt to construct a new and intelligible totality upon the ruins of the older individualistic one; they reflect psychic disintegration, to be sure, but at the same time they mark an effort at overcoming that state by the very fact of making it present to us as a complete process.[②]

To be sure, this particular story does not aspire to merge with the society into a unity, but the individual fate still becomes part of a communal destiny. To the extent that this historical imagination finally points to a deferred union of society and individual (the declined society precipitates the fulfillment of the wish of the individual), this pseudo-allegory (of "love in a fallen city") turns out to be a work of symbolism, an imaginary and formal solution to social problems, which conceals itself immanently behind the fictional narrative.

While this symbolism has an ahistorical inclination, this metaphysical choice itself is a human response to a historical situation, yet it is ahistorical, metaphysical way of viewing human life in the world. The image of the dilapidated wall and the image of the robust dancing woman entangle and intertwine together. Both are naturalized historical objects, which appear to be unhistorical and eternal. It is against the socio-political vicissitudes and against the precarious and ephemeral marriage prospectus that the dilapidated wall is employed as a natural-historical object to convey a bourgeois utopia of a perennial, "aestheticized world of unmediated nature

---

① Jameson, F., *Marxism and Form*, Princeton, NJ: Princeton University Press, 1974:337.

② Jameson, F., *Marxism and Form*, Princeton, NJ: Princeton University Press, 1974:129.

by means of which an alienated way of life is perpetuated."[1] The wall is a monument of symbol of death, but it is also a vehicle to express the idea of universal love. Insofar as it is the inextricable object and tool of this expression, through a metonymic displacement, it becomes a substitutive symbol of love (just as Liuyuan takes it to be). Such a political (un) conscious correlating death and eternal love is really ironic. What links them together is a historical consciousness towards the ruthless world that they live, which destroys any prospect of genuine and eternal love. It is an alienated world that makes inhuman the human world, to the extent that only death equals everyone. Facing this "irrational world," they feel hopeless.

We need to go a step further into this "natural-historical image," which apparently bestows certain epiphany upon Liuyuan, by dwelling for a moment on the concept of "natural history." While in Benjamin, "it is the fallen nature which bears the imprint of the progression of history;" in Eileen Chang here, it is the piles of ruins which attest to the imprints of historical catastrophe, that become the symbol of unchanged authenticity of love as nature. In other words, if Max Pensky has explained Benjamin's dialectic of natural history as this: "petrified, transformed into the specter of repetition, history is transfigured into dead nature; mortified, nature becomes the elements of historical ruin and the universality of death;"[2] then here, it is the wall, as the ruin of history, taken to be nature, that becomes the symbol of the universality of life and love. In short, this ostensible picture of natural history in its essence is but the diametrically reverse of "natural history" in its original sense, as a profound nihilism. This elevated and sublimated image of the wall is a metonymic displacement of a historical

---

① Zhang, X., Shanghai Nostalgia: Postrevolutionary Allegories in Wang Anyi's Literary Production in the 1990s, The intensity of Liusu's love-affair with her own image in front of the mirror is also an effort to seize a fleeting moment of beauty and enchantment to turn it into a bait for something eternal and dependable.

② Zhang, X., Shanghai Nostalgia: Postrevolutionary Allegories in Wang Anyi's Literary Production in the 1990s, *Positions: East Asia Cultures Critique*, 2000, 8(2): 382.

account of socio-political changes. In a nutshell, what it conveys is nothing but a resignation of self-will and self-determination in front of the gigantic, inhuman, naturalized historical force. The atomized Liuyuan and Liusu have no power to combat it, no matter how strong an individualism they elevate to protect their maximum individual interests. The ostensible symbolism of (a will to) love represented by the sublime wall (together with the symbol of life—vitality incarnated in the metaphysical puppet-icon of a robust, unabashed and amoral dancing woman upon which Liusu is modeled), in this light, turns on its allegorical counterpart: it is none other than an egotistic individualism in a historical crisis, which then is bordered on a cultural—as well as historical—nihilism. Caught between the rebellious masses and the invading imperialists, between the highly oppressive state and the semi-traditional society, when the last line between barbarism and civilization crumbled even before a New Culture was established, the author found herself facing the abyss of a doomed civilization.

In short, if the concept of "natural history" that Benjamin and Theodor Adorno hold it, as Xudong Zhang aptly summarizes, "signals liberation from the anthropocentric icon cage of rationality, historicism, and subjectivism in order to envision a concrete history;"[1] then these two images, while they appear ostensibly to be a critique of rationality and historicism, do not escape from the pitfall of a subjectivism that fantasizes an everlasting, primitive, yet historically ungrounded "life vitality" which repudiates socio-political intervention.

## 六、(Non-)Romantic Melodrama and Historical Contradiction

In this fictional narrative, Eileen Chang uses the narrative paradigm of (Hollywood-styled) melodrama (as "one of the principal devices by which

---

① Zhang, X., Shanghai Nostalgia: Postrevolutionary Allegories in Wang Anyi's Literary Production in the 1990s, *Positions: East Asia Cultures Critique*, 2000,8(2):271.

modern literature has sought to conceal its contradictions")[1] to organize
middle-class fantasies about "solutions" that "might resolve, manage, or
repress the evident class anxieties" aroused by the existence of outside
suffocating pressures.[2] But as critics, we cannot fail to see that what the
story finally celebrates is the fortunate attainment of a tricky scheme; it is
unaware of, or refuses to consider, the ultimate ending of the "romance,"
partly because wherewith the history will go is blind to it.

Above all, they live in a "borrowed time and space" which is not owned
by them. This is not only literally true in the story, as Hong Kong was for
the two a temporary living place; but also metaphorically authentic, as the
whole China at the time was a time and space which they could not master
their own fate. This predicament did not just exist for them, but for the
whole class they belong to. Cast in this perspective, the story ultimately is a
relentless show of the inexorable fragility of a precarious proto-bourgeois
class, together with its (love and hate with its) ephemeral life form.

This crisis is a crisis of the formation of a class identity/subjectivity. As
Leo Lee notices, Eileen Chang's heroine "is not bemoaning the passing of an
era but rather wishes to liberate herself from it."[3] This liberation is a flight
from the traditional to the modern, but a modern with its own peculiar
identity. She aims to elevate herself from a half-traditional woman in the
gentry family to be a bourgeois middle-class lady, yet this transformation or
metamorphosis is precarious: since she has no practical skills, she has to rely

---

①    Jameson, F., *Political Unconscious: Narrative as a Socially Symbolic Act*,
Ithaca, N.Y.: Cornell University Press, 1981:186.

②    Jameson, F., *Political Unconscious: Narrative as a Socially Symbolic Act*,
Ithaca, N.Y.: Cornell University Press, 1981:200. Although Eileen Chang's stories do not
have "violent clash between larger-than-life collective units" or "between absolute good and
evil," which was the characteristics of archetypal melodrama, they nonetheless still conceal
"the absence of any genuine human interrelationship on the individual level, in individual
lived experience." Jameson, F., *Political Unconscious: Narrative as a Socially Symbolic
Act*. Ithaca, N.Y.: Cornell University Press, 1981:186.

③    Lee, L. O., *Shanghai Modern: The Flowering of New Urban Culture in China*,
1930-1945, Cambridge: Harvard University Press, 1999:298.

on her fading beauty to seduce a playboy in a similar precarious financial status.[①] Her identity is far from being consolidated: she could lose this new identity at any time, due to both the unexpected outside social-political vicissitude and her bereavement of physical attraction.

## 七、Conclusion

With a meticulous examination of the writer's cross-cultural writing and rewriting (or appropriation) of O'Neill's imagery of the Magna Mater, or the Maternal Goddess, in this novelette, this chapter suggests that the archetypal motif of Eileen Chang's stories is individualism in crisis, which leads to, and is also part of the reason for, an anxiety of self-identity. Due to the lack of rationalization of the society, and various domestic and international conflicts that were epitomized as the rhetoric of "war" under the writer's pen, a bourgeois subjectivity is difficult to establish. The predominant thematic focus of the writer is a matrimonial anxiety, which aims to cash in on any opportunity unabashedly to transcend its class status to secure financial security and boost social status. In its response to the crisis of marriage and love as social institution, it articulates, crystallizes, and projects the social-political dilemma and predicament of this class. Yet more often than not this effect results in utter failure or illusionary success.[②] The feeling that "we have been deserted" articulated by the writer echoes this sentiment of a fundamental crisis. Together with the pessimism towards the social turmoil and human costs of the "war," a sense of resignation appears, which, while sometimes personates itself as a robust womanhood, in its core harbors a profound cultural and historical nihilism. To fully

---

① Liuyuan has fought for a long time with his relatives to earn the inheritance from his father. In "Aloeswood Ashes: The First Burning," the hero George Qiao that the heroine Weilong pursues is also a penniless gigolo dreaming for his father's property.

② When this feminine concern is projected back to the broader social arena, from which to observe the middle-class women's vain struggles to acquire a "normal" bourgeois respectivity, an esteemed class identity, the story is often narrated from this peculiar perspective; for instance, *Red Rose and White Rose* (《红玫瑰与白玫瑰》).

understand this, it requires us to dissolute the reified artwork which crystallizes fantasies and utopias into its historical on-site. This will give us a fair and sympathetic evaluation of the artistic achievement as well as the dilemma of the subjectivized narrator/writer in a tumultuous and confusing society.

# Chapter Six　Matrimonial Complex and Identity Anxiety：Eileen Chang's "Boudoir Stories" and the（Im-）Possibility of Modern Chinese Bourgeoisie

The conventional interpretation of the works of the famed modern Chinese female writer，Eileen Chang（Zhang Ailing，1920-1995），is generally couched in the Freudian psychoanalysis. This chapter reads her stories through the perspective of identity politics. In analyzing the paramount thematic concern of the writer's stories，which shows a profound matrimonial anxiety in a besieged society，it further more delves into the identity politics of her ostensible apolitical stories. It shows that the institutions of marriage and love entrapped in predicament is closely related to the intense anxiety of self-identity，which is pertaining not only to the individual status，but also to a collective，class/national identity.

Methodologically，this chapter takes a psychoanalytical procedure to understand her architectonics of signs and parables. This "psychoanalysis" is not necessarily founded upon a Freudian system of pathology，but bases itself on an understanding of the characters' mental-physical responses to the outside social-political onslaught. Once this procedure is turned into its allegorical counterpart in social space，her fictional style，a hybrid of traditional taste and western techniques，becomes a labyrinth of symbols and images and an elaborate mechanism to absorb the frustration and shock she experienced，which aimed to resist assaults on vulnerable individuals from a hostile environment. Consequently，her narrative is embroiled with a profound ambiguity：although there was no sentimentalism and nostalgia towards the past，the emotional atmosphere of a sense of regret and pity over the mundane concerns and strivings of her characters oftentimes permeates the narrative space, with a sarcastic reservation sometimes, which underscores the sense of historicity of the narrative voice.

## 一、Marriage and Love in Predicament

It is worthy to note that most of the writer's "love stories" in her collection of stories *Romance*[①] are not about love as a romantic feeling and emotion, but are about desire. The various episodes of flirtation, courtship, or affair have physical instincts as well as economic consideration. C.T.Hsia has perceived this dimension in his comment on the non-tragic nature of the apparent tragic and desolate romances: "Miss Chang professes not to abide by the classical formula of tragedy because it is her belief that the sheer weight of habit and animalism precludes the possibility of any prolonged flights of sublimity or passion."[②] Indeed, love as a romantic emotion oftentimes demands willing self-sacrifice, a passionate feeling of sublimity; yet more often than not what the frustrated physical and social desires in Eileen Chang's stories bring about are nothing but many perverse pursuits and cruel calculations. However, these various apparent "inhuman" tricks do not indicate that the characters are less human, but they point to love and marriage as social institutions; and in modern China, these institutions have peculiar features and functions, which show the morbidity of the culture in an "abnormal" society. Four stories here are analyzed as case studies.

The real nature of marriage, being a social institution to ensure social security, as a sort of "long-term prostitution" for some women at the time is unveiled numerous times in writer's essays as well as stories, which is more relentlessly expressed in *Aloeswood Ashes: The First Burning* (《沉香屑:第一炉香》). It is a story about a woman who becomes spiritually debilitated in Hong Kong.

Weilong, a Shanghainese middle-school girl who immigrates there, in

---

① 张爱玲:《传奇》,杂志社 1944 年版.

② Hsia, C. T., *A History of Modern Chinese Fiction*, Bloomington: Indiana University Press, 1999:398.

order to complete her study, seeks help from her well-off aunt, erstwhile a concubine of a wealthy merchant and now widowed. Yet her aunt is indulgent in seducing gigolos and playboys, so her consent of offering financial assistance to Weilong harbors a concealed intention of exploiting the latter as bait for her to lure young men (later on she indeed snatches away one Weilong's admirer). Weilong tries to keep herself away from the nasty affair, yet she is soon submitting to the overwhelming material luxury her aunt offers, and then the physical attraction of George Qiao, a mixed-blood gigolo.

A notorious playboy, George Qiao is the thirteenth son in his big family. His mother is a Portuguese prostitute from Macau, while his father has acquired an English title. Yet he has stopped receiving financial assistance from his father because of his dissolute life and bad repute, he is by no means rich. As a young girl, Weilong soon falls to the prey of her desire by accepting the sexual advance of this good-for-nothing boy. Yet, immediately she finds that he also plays around with one maid in the house. Her hysterical disruption exposes her affair. To gloss over the scandal, Weilong's aunt arranges their marriage by persuading George Qiao that he can find an easy excuse to divorce Weilong when he has no interests any longer on her. Apparently a comfortable life is proffered as George Qiao's father renews his funding for his son because of this marriage.

Compared with Qiqiao (to be discussed soon), Weilong's marriage would be what the former has dreamed of. The difference between them lies in her particular social status. Though the women both need social-economic security, for Qiqiao, who comes from declining households and without much education, material independence is the only concern; yet for Weilong, a student with a middle-level learning and being more open to modern ideas, she knows her own degradation: coming from a self-supported middle-class family, she can expect a more handsome husband with a higher social standing and reputation. She knows the true nature of his husband, the nature of the marriage, and the final unpropitious prospect.

So when George Qiao teases her by insinuating that the European marines have mistaken her to be a prostitute, she admits that the only

difference is that "they have no choice. I've done it of my own free will."
She recognizes unambiguously the ruin of her youth innocence and the dire
prospect of her future:

> Beyond these lamps, people and goods there are sadly limpid sea and sky-
> boundless desolation and boundless terror. Her future is just like that-she could not
> bear to think of it, for these thoughts could only give rise to endless fears. She had no
> long-term plans. Only in these trivial matters could her fearful and agitated heart find
> some momentary rest.[1]

To find solace in forgetfulness by immersing in trivial goods and curios
is the last resort for a helpless woman to dawdle away her decadent life in a
colonial society. She has no way to extricate herself. This indeed is a
desolation that wants salvation.

This degradation is brought out as much by the society and its culture
as by Weilong's mind of calculation. For the former, Leo Lee has aptly
commented, "Mrs Liang... embodies a culture in Hong Kong which is
stagnant and materialistic. George Ch'iao and his sister, both Eurasians,
represent the plight of those doomed to entrapment in this culture, rejected
by both Chinese and Europeans, save in a purely commercial setting. Thus,
Weilung's marriage to George is the final burial within such a culture."[2]
Edward Gunn also perceptively points out that "ultimately, such a society is
portrayed not for itself, but as a representation of the failure of the human
condition in which the protagonist must either destroy herself or submit her
vain longings to the destruction that life inevitably carries out."[3] It is of
little doubt that the fundamental motive behind Weilong's series of decisions
(to stay in Hong Kong, rely on her decadent aunt, and finally resign to

---

[1]    Chang, E., *Aloeswood Ashes: The First Burning*, Cheng S., Trans, with a few
of my modifications; Cheng S., Themes and Techniques in Eileen Chang's stories,
*Tamkang Review*, 1977,8(2):178.

[2]    Lee, L. O., *Shanghai Modern: The Flowering of New Urban Culture in China*,
1930-1945, Cambridge: Harvard University Press, 1999:310.

[3]    Gunn, E., *Unwelcome Muse: Chinese Literature in Shanghai and Peking 1937-
1945*, New York: Columbia University Press, 1980:224.

marry George Qiao) is a desire to earn her social-economic security and, if possible, to further her social advancement.

Similar consideration was taken by Cao Qiqiao, the cardinal protagonist in *Golden Cangue* (《金锁记》), with a result more than a tragedy for the heroine alone. As the most acclaimed literary piece of the author, the story has received many perceptive analyses, I will only propose a different perspective: differing from the interpretations thus far which focus on the vulnerability of human nature (vanity, mammonism, and sometimes even sexual desire as the "golden cangue"), I will argue that her perversity is a result of the social system (in particular to the system, or the social institution of love and marriage), as her tragic fate is preconditioned—if not predetermined—once she is married into the family.

The endless series of formalities and rituals introduced throughout do not invite blissful feelings in the readers, but they bring about a claustrophobic atmosphere. This is an aristocratic family household in decline and its fortunes going down: they immigrate to Shanghai as refugees due to chaotic dynastic changes. The physical web and cultural institutions of the traditional-styled family household remain almost intact, appearing as ancient as an archeological site.

When Qiqiao is firstly introduced, she appears as the object of maids' gossips, which not only reveals her original family background—located in the lowest social stratum selling sesame oil, but also exposes the cause for her marrying to this gentry family: she at best can be a concubine in this upper-class family due to her humble origin, yet since her husband is crippled and so could not find a woman of comparable fortune and social status, she becomes his official wife. The chitchat of the maids also reveals the reason that she is held in contempt by others, even by these maids whose status is lower than her. This is as much to do with her humble origin as the class habitus internalized in her unconscious, inscribed in her psychology, and shown in her behavior: the slang comes out of her mouth is so improper that it shames even these maid servants. Worse, she is indulged in opium-smoking.

That she is so entrenched in her own class habitus also appears in the

fact that, although she knows that she is despised by everyone, she is still
actively urging the matriarch to marry one of her daughters out, implying
that this can forestall improper affairs. Since she moves to an upper class she
does not belong to, she is not used to its mores and conventions, but still
holds ideas and habitus of the lower class and projects them onto her
contemporary living circumstance. She wants to behave like an upper-class
woman, yet she doesn't fit in the family. A tangential remark articulated by
her niece affirming her superstition of the medical function of opium
substantiates the fact that the tragedy of her degradation is partly a result of
her poor and ignorant upbringing which does not match the life style of the
high class she lives in.

Qiqiao's frustration and her own impetuous temper are attributable to
her cripple husband, who because of his tuberculosis becomes a puny
invalid. She has to repress her sexual desire in order to get the inheritance
she is expecting for. When ten years later, the time finally arrives for her
relief from her boredom and endless anticipation, it only turns out that her
life of humiliation does not pay off. She does not get as much as she expected
in the property-division; moreover, her dream for a better private life is
thwarted. During these years, she has contained a desire for her brother-in-
law—a good-for-nothing    in    his    nature    who    plays    around    outside
notwithstanding. This man dares not engage in affairs with her. Only when
the time now comes and Qiqiao wishes to realize her dream, he arrives with
an ulterior motive. Yet Qiqiao's feeling of sweetness swiftly changes to be a
rampant rage when she suspects his sweet words are just snares to swindle
her hardly-acquired money by catering to her fantasy of love. Her angry
expulsion,    however,    is    self-destructive    as    it    not    only    destroys    the
simulacrum    of    love,    but    also    her    spiritual    and    psychological    prop.
Immediately after he leaves, she falls into remorse. The narrator here is
completely    empathetic    with    her    feelings    in    an    ostensible    narrated
monologue: "Today it is completely her faults. He is not a good man, she
knows this. Yet if she wants him, she has to pretend ignorance, has to bear
his perversity. Why did she expose him? Isn't the fact of living in the world
just that case? In the final reasoning, what is true, and what is false?" This

feeling of incapability to differentiate between the real and the false extends to a visual confusion—in this moment of trance, when she sees the shadow of various characters (a policeman, a rickshaw, a boy, and a postman) in the window glass, the narrator again presents her feeling: "All ghosts, ghosts of many years ago or the unborn many years hence...What is real and what is false?" As her mind is enclosed by the golden cangue to secure material independence, her past, present, and future lives are leveled to be the same one and are sealed off. Yet the reason that genuine intention is equated with false perception, and veritable life with muddled living, can only be appreciated with the particular social conditions in mind: in this society at the time the demand of genuine emotion was more often than not compromised, surpassed by, and sacrificed for the imperative of survival; marriage as a social institution to a great extent is a necessity not of love, but of sustenance.

When this last sprout of love is pinched off by her, Qiqiao's life is a hopeless drift muddling along homogenous, empty time. Worse, her unsatisfied desire and yearning transform her to be a ruthless monster that destroys the lives of her own scions. She keeps an ambivalent relationship with her son Changbai (who has become a docile weakling, having little schooling, and indulged early in dissipated life), requiring him to accompany her all the nights chatting, urging him to tell her the secrets of his wife. Unable to suffer the humiliation, Changbai's wife commits suicide. As macabre as this is the way she passes her own tragedy to her daughter, Chang'an, by treacherously crushing the latter's love in her calculated calumnies, out of her perverse envy of their genuine emotions.

This unnamed, inhuman malevolence towards everyone around her is her metamorphic revenge on the inhuman society. Although she never fits in with the manners and mores of the upper mandarin class she lives in, she turns up to be its most poignant spokeswoman. The transgressing of class boundaries makes her pay much more than she has expected, her nature is distorted in this process and she is devoured by the system, which punishes any unblessed attempts at boundary-transgression in terms of class division and distinction.

In this light, the story is a narrative elaboration of the macabre silence of a petrified history. In her malevolent struggle against the nothingness of meaning behind the death mask of history, Qiqiao arouses sympathetic and disgusting feelings simultaneously for readers, and the suffocating density and intricacy of this world are exposed. The silent, ghostly appearance of Qiqiao is an allegorical figure of the shadowy existence of traditional form of life in the passage of time. The residual way of life and its ethical straitjacket, appearing not as concept but as image and material concreteness, shows its aging face and merciless code. Embroiled with the relentless social conditions of traditional family structure and class hierarchy, the tragedy is decidedly anti-romantic.

In this world, authentic passion is impossible, which is expressed by the question raised by the narrator again and again "in this world, what is real, what is false?" The misgiving itself shows the confusion of human emotion in a transitional society in which love and marriage, as "structures of feeling," or social-cultural institutions, are drastically shaken and shifting. The narrative voice, due to a perspective of universal human nature, attributes the tragedy to certain historical/ahistorical cyclicity,[1] as if this is an everlasting cycle with no hope of escape. Delivering the message of an *everlasting* cycle with no escape, it conveys the narrator's pessimism on the inevitable fate of sorrowful human condition, which is deeply rooted in a belief in ingrained human nature regardless of the permutation of history with its social-economic structure.

Yet this apparent distrust of love as a genuine emotion that requires self-willed sacrifice met a drastic turn in her third novel, *So Much Regret* (《多少恨》), written in 1947. Adapted from a movie script *Endless Love*

---

[1]    Thus the narrator in the framed structure of the story's narration subtly expresses her opinions on this sad story: in the beginning she informs us that it took place thirty years ago (which means the late Qing period), while in the ending she returns to this moon imagery, bringing about a melancholy atmosphere of tragic continuity: "The moon of thirty years ago has gone down long since and the people of thirty years ago are dead but the story of thirty years ago is not yet ended—can have no ending."

(《不了情》) produced earlier that year, this is a story in a light, popular style, in contrast to the previous novels and stories which have strong flavors of traditional novel.

The story itself is a conventional, yet for Eileen Chang an unusual, love story. Jiayin is a twenty-five years old girl, and Zongyu a factory manager ten years older. Two chance occurrences help them develop emotional attachment: they meet by chance in a movie theater (a modern institution) at the beginning of the story, and later encounter each other again when Jiayin happens to be introduced to work as a family tutor for Zongyu's daughter. Unfortunately, Zongyu has an uneducated and sick wife living in the rural area that he married earlier following the traditional practice of parents' order. In order not to harm the child, Jiayin sacrifices herself by pretending that she will return to her hometown to marry her cousin, while in reality she is leaving for a remote city to teach. Jiayin's father, a minor character in the story and an old, degraded philander, serves to accentuate Jiayin's selflessness: he tries to get his best from their relations, even by sacrificing his daughter's happiness with a promise to Zongyu that he could urge his daughter to become the latter's concubine.

If not put in the historical context, this story would appear merely as a mediocre middle-class melodrama. The cause of the unfruitful love of the couple now is not a result of some evil, powerful figures, as what we have seen in the Mandarin and Butterfly stories, nor the reactionary, traditional force as what had appeared in the May Fourth stories (Jiayin's father may look like such a candidate, yet he is not obstructing their romance). Living in a society in rapid transition, they cannot satisfy their wish only because of the hindrance of the residual social relations and traditional leftovers.

What is new that emerges from the story, however, is a new passion arising from this middle-class stratum. Jiayin sacrifices self-willingly her own romance to fulfill the prospectus of this new institution of love (and marriage). Because she is now financially independent (though her educational background is not introduced, she can work as a tutor now, and later will become a school teacher), she needn't rely on men nor her father

to support her life, so she can entertain her romantic feelings and envision a
promising prospect. A will to make self-sacrifice, a crucial element in
genuine, romantic love, thus rises up. The author was so enamored of this
feeling that she "felt a subtle attachment to this story." To this extent the
story indeed can be said as a sort of "wish fulfillment" which the writer
yearned for yet did not enjoy in her own life, at least until this moment.

Marriage as a social institution receives a different treatment in one of
Eileen Chang's early stories. Though *Aloeswood Ashes—The Second
Burning* (《沉香屑:第二炉香》) is appearing as a serial to *Aloeswood Ashes:
The First Burning* (they are the first two stories that the writer submitted
to journal editors as her maiden work), and its setting is also located in
Hong Kong, yet its content is vastly different from the other story. On the
surface, the story is nothing but an incident about an ignorance of sexual
knowledge by the colonial subjects that leads to a tragedy, with Freudian
undertone of abnormal psychology. In showing the distorted, "unnatural"
form of life under the strict colonial control and seamless blockade, the story
is a disclosure of the hypocritical manner of the dominant class in the
colonial society. But another dimension of the historical subtext must be
brought in, which is also closely related to its prose style. Leo Lee noticed
that the story is "framed in a third-person narratorial voice (presumably
Chinese) that has subtly humanized and 'sinicized' them." The result is that
"the characters' speech patterns are unmistakably Chinese."[1] How to
understand this narrational choice? Rather than echoing Leo Lee's view that
because of this arrangement "there is hardly an 'alienation' effect,"—the
feeling of reading this story, with all of its characters being British yet their
words and gestures "sinicized," is quite weird and awkward—I will suggest
that the author's stylistic choice has a close relationship with her intention to
conduct a subtle dialogue between Chinese and Western (secular) culture.

Edward Gunn has noticed that the author's descriptions of the female

---

[1]    Lee, L. O., *Shanghai Modern: The Flowering of New Urban Culture in China*,
1930-1945, Cambridge: Harvard University Press, 1999:311.

characters bear similar imageries in several places.[①] While I agree with Edward Gunn's perception that these skillfully employed imageries are probably used "to enhance the quality of the work and especially its central theme,"[②] I think she might neglect the subtle Chinese reference of these images. These descriptions such as "a row of tiny teeth," "so white they were blue," and that "they suddenly shot outwards, reaching out as two-inched sharp fangs," will immediately invoke in the mind of an average Chinese the image of ghost which is generally regarded as "ferocious in appearance; with a green face and jagged teeth like a saw," as the Chinese idiom "青面獠牙" indicates. If we remember that Chinese at the time often referred to foreign imperialist invaders as "foreign devils" (洋鬼子), such imageries in Eileen Chang's stories might invite more associations.

These repeatedly occurring imageries show the evil side under the facade of seemingly innocent figures. Susie appears to be angel-like, yet to show her innocence, she does not hesitate to implicate Roger. Is she a devil or an angel? To be sure, for a certain discourse of humanity, the two sides coexist in human's nature. But aside from the social cause for this ignorance which has been discussed, an allegorical reading is helpful here. This invites a subtle comparison between the Western culture and Chinese culture, in particular the mores of sex—we must notice that the story takes place in a colonial land, and the community (a Hong Kong university). If the

---

① For instance, Millicent is described in this way, "when she mentioned her former husband's name, Frank, her thin lips curled upward, revealing a row of tiny teeth which under the light were so white they seemed blue, small, blue teeth…Roger shuddered." Roger sees the similar image in Susie, "Laughing, she showed a row of small teeth, so white they were blue…small, white teeth, but how beautiful." And he sees this image again in his final moment of suicide when he is immersed in the gas: "…All that remained was a tidy ring of small, blue teeth, the teeth gradually fading. But, just before they vanished completely, they suddenly shot outwards, reaching out as two-inched sharp fangs…" Gunn, E., *Unwelcome Muse : Chinese Literature in Shanghai and Peking* 1937-1945, New York: Columbia University Press, 1980:206-207.

② Gunn, E., *Unwelcome Muse : Chinese Literature in Shanghai and Peking* 1937-1945, New York: Columbia University Press, 1980:206-207.

colonizers allegedly undertake the honorable mission of civilizing the
colonized, ignorant people, with their own treacherous life, their hypocrisy
is exposed. Then the bankruptcy of its ethics and morality falsifies the
grandiose narrative itself to a certain extent; and while the colonizers keep a
strict, Victorian-style formidable more regarding sex, Chinese sexual
conventions seem more "natural," pragmatic, and so "civilized." This
comparison of sexual mores (as institutions of marriage) surely subtly subverts
the hierarchy of cultural sophistication (modern versus tradition, new versus old)
between the colonizers and the colonized people.

But this underlying cultural comparison becomes more obvious only in
another story *Red Rose and White Rose* (《红玫瑰与白玫瑰》), which goes a
step further to explore the overlapping and blurred boundaries between what
is regarded as Chinese (but not modern) and what is modern (yet not
Chinese), through the narrative vehicle of the writer's staple theme:
unhappy love and marriage. Yet the subtle sense of superiority is now
apparently replaced by an anxiety, in the disguise of irony and mockery.

## 二、Anxiety of Self-Identity

The leading role of the story is Tong Zhenbao, an accomplished textile
engineer occupying a high-ranked position in a foreigner-controlled company
at his hometown Shanghai. He received advanced education in Edinburgh and
has recently returned to serve his country. Shouldering the high expectation
of the society towards Westernized social elites, he "is determined to create a
'correct world' that he can carry with him. In that pocket world, he will be
the absolute master." This "correct world" is also what the society expects
of him, who has enjoyed the then rare privilege of studying abroad. But his
unfailing conformity with social convention and order could also be seen as
what he learned from the Britain, where the social rationalization has
brought about a highly rationalized society, in which a British gentleman
would be expected to behave properly in an unconscious way. So when he
returns to China, he brings (and is expected by others to bring) this
rigorous mannerism to his homeland. Seen in this light, his apparent robust

will power is a manifestation of a promising subjectivity. Yet facing China's social reality, this subjectivity collapses even before it is solidly formed.

The central plotline is Tong Zhenbao's emotional experience, alongside with his comparison of various women. His first sexual tryst is conducted in Paris with a local prostitute, during which he sees her in mirror an image reminiscent of the writer's description of the physiognomy of Western women in *Aloeswood Ashes: The Second Burning*,

> Her eyes were blue, but for a moment these spots of blue sank into the green make-up under her eyes, and the eyes themselves turned into transparent glass balls. It was a severe, cold, and masculine face, the face of a warrior from distant ages. Zhenbao's nerves were jolted.

Apparently, he feels that he is threatened. At Paris, the "capital of romance," this experience is unusual. What it reveals to him is that Western girls, or Western culture in general, is cold rather than passionate, like "a warrior from distant ages." Facing this image, certainly the master is the woman who has subjected him to her manipulation. Hereafter his impression towards Western women is unsounded, which foretells his interests in and evaluation of various Chinese women. But before this is to be unfolded, he needs another (Western) woman to test his caliber. And this one is properly to be a semi-British, semi-Chinese girl. Though she loves him dearly, he controls himself not to consummate his desire. All the descriptions of his behavior and mentality meant to show that he is "fundamentally a (traditional-typed) Chinese" who has no concept of gender equality; on the contrary, patriarchal, male-chauvinistic mentality defines his beingness in the world.

These two incidents may look like a sort of Bildungsroman for him, as from the first incident he grows up as a "man", and from the second one he brings out a sort of "subjectivity" to control his desire. Yet according to Hegel's master-slave dialectic, a subject needs to be formed via a subject-object relationship, in which the "object" needs to be one having comparable subjective spirit, which he can challenge with his wisdom and strength. As the girl with a half-Chinese blood is so free to accept men's advancement, and too meek to spare him any stamina, Tong Zhengbao's "subjectivity" is not formed at this moment, not to mention that he always feels regretful for not taking her from then on.[1]

This girl bears blue eyes; "when her eyes opened wide, the whites show blue as though she were gazing into the deepest of the skies." Therefore, she is still too "Western" to satisfy his taste—her outgoing behavior and nonchalant manners make it impossible for him to accept her, as he fundamentally is a conservative man sticking to traditional Chinese morality. Thus when he returns to the motherland, he is a man equipped with both Western rationality and Chinese ethics; or, Chinese (morality) as his essence, Western (reason) his appearance. This is a dichotomized world, yet the tension is seemingly balanced very well in his split mind.

The story begins with a metaphorical description of two types of women—"There were two women: he says one is his white rose, one is red rose. One was a spotless wife, the other a passionate mistress. Average people are always speaking of '节烈' (chaste and passionate) separately. Maybe every man has had two such women—at least two." Just as the phrase refers to a particular Chinese moral standard, we also need to subject this pun into the particular moment of Chinese context: his differentiation between chaste wife and passionate mistress is less from what he learns from Western experience than from Chinese tradition, especially the one since the late Qing period, when many gentry-class men kept one wife and (at least) one concubine. In his time, this practice had been less popular, yet its residual influence was still prevalent: some allegedly enlightened "new youth" kept passionate mistress outside of the parameter of marriage. The New Culture Movement[2] did not institutionalize new morality regarding gender equality in society. Even in the realm of marriage, many Chinese still managed to

---

① Hegel says: "What now really confronts him is not an independent consciousness, but a dependent one. He is, therefore, not certain of being-for-itself as the truth of himself." Hegel, G. W. F., *Phenomenology of Spirit*, Miller, A. V. Trans, Oxford: Clarendon Press, 1977:117.

② Chinese intellectuals had long been engaged in various projects to rejuvenate the Chinese nation and its culture. From around 1915 to the 1920s, they launched a New Culture Movement. Iconoclasm and radical anti-traditionalism that vehemently attacked neo-Confucian values, superstitions, and classical Chinese language featured its dynamic momentum.

make the Western standard accommodate their customary ways of behavior.

It is in terms of this phenomenon that here the narrator makes ironical comments on Tong Zhenbao's personality, which would constitute a sharp contrast with what to be happened:"Zhenbao is not this kind of person. He is always carrying things through to the end and in an orderly way. He was, in this respect, the ideal modern Chinese man. If he did bump into something that was less than ideal, he bounced it around in his mind for a while and—poof! —it was idealized:then everything fell into place." What this "ideal modern Chinese man" learns from the West is that he can develop extra-marital relations to a certain extent; yet unlike in Western society, where such extra-marital relations can "naturally" lead to divorce and remarriage, the Chinese social custom requires him not to break up the formal marital institution, but to uphold an upright image at any cost. Because in Chinese tradition, if a scholar visits prostitute or keeps a concubine, he can be called "romantic" （风流） and is forgiven by the society so long as he keeps his official marriage unaffected. While if he divorces because of his passion with the woman having affairs with him, he would be regarded as dissolute and irresponsible and would be reproached and despised. It is due to this strong conceptual restriction, which is "half-modern and half-traditional", that Tong Zhenbao, as an "incomplete man" （不彻底的人, what the writer refers to Shanghai's "petty urbanite"）, tries his best to fit in with the social expectation.

Therefore, although he submits to the temptation of his friend's wife, Wang Jiaorui, an overseas (Singaporean) Chinese and once a party girl when she studied in London, no matter how she loves him, and how she is willing to divorce for him and reforms herself to be a "chaste" woman, he does not want to discard his social mask and ruin his long-term career plan. Therefore, he goes on carrying the image of being an upright man and a promising engineer as well as a filial son that Chinese morality requests of him, and abandons her and follows the social convention to marry an obedient bride named Meng Yanli who is from a proper family and also receives college education, which is rare at the time. She gives birth to a daughter for him. Everything goes the normal track, appearing idealistic as the society expects. When the story opens, her daughter is nine years old and "the fee for her college education is already prepared."

Yet Meng Yanli is not a woman with the modern feminist consciousness of "lady first" and appears too meek and bland. She is even sexually frigid. Zhenbao soon loses his interests in her and visits prostitutes outside. What happens the next falls out of Tong Zhenbao's expectation and control. Meng Yanli's blasé towards her tasteless family life and her disrespectable status at home (she is so often rebuked by her husband and her mother-in-law that she is despised by her maid) leads her to having an affair with her tailor. Tong Zhenbao, again, does not divorce her. But he falls into a more degenerate life in his private life. Several years later, when he meets Wang Jiaorui again in the car, after hearing that she has learned to control her desire, put down her vanity and led an honest and simple life, "suddenly his face begins to tremble. In the mirror he saw his tears streaming down. Why, he didn't know himself." Is he envy of her apparently "happy and genuine" (or rather, mediocre and vulgar, as she turns fat and less charming) life, the dream of middle class women? Or is he regretful over his earlier hesitation and his betrayal of his "genuine love"? Differing interpretations of this seemingly unusual move aside, for him, life is still a painful struggle, which demands the self-sacrifice of his own happiness. So, after many times of dissipation, he "makes self-reform and changes again to be a good man."

On the surface, with a subtle authorial intervention running throughout the text, this story shows the protagonist's resolution and willpower. Yet nobody will miss the barely concealed satiric tone and the ironic twist, which reveal his resignation and willingness to settle for an unhappy life. In contrast to the impression the narrative voice strongly imposes on us, Tong Zhenbao in fact never believes or views himself as a "good man," or has unperturbed confidence in his ability to control his destiny; for he surely understands that his dissipated life, which after he discovers his wife's adultery becomes more open and perverse, and his disregard of the welfare of the family (he refuses to provide spending money to his wife) would totally ruin his public image, and his incapability of controlling even his own behavior, and further more, his family life, only shows his incompetence in dealing with worldly affairs (according to the standard of the famed traditional Chinese saying which dictates the four stages of being a successful man: "to cultivate oneself and then put family in order, and then by which to administer state affairs and manage the world in harmony," he surely fails even in the first step). His rash and futile attempts, like his tears trickling down before Wang Jiaorui in the bus, expose his feeling of impotence, enfeeblement, and failure. Yet the crucial fact that is generally neglected by most readers and critics is that, what he does not want to ruin throughout his career is not his reputation or his marriage, but rather, his long-term professional scenario.

While the narrative voice seemingly holds an untouched, cold depiction, it now and then betrays a tone of ridicule, which belies its feminine overtone—this is a narration articulated by a feminine figure.[①] Even though this womanly voice cannot help but stand out numerous times commenting on the hero, what supports Tong Zhenbao and his unremitting efforts is rarely explained by it. It is not difficult for us to feel that it tries to impose us an impression that it is Tong Zhenbao's vanity of keeping his reputation that he acquires a dual personality and lives a double-sided life. To be sure, this voice also does not overtly show that he is only a hypocritical man, but we need to go by ourselves to find the ultimate motivation that keeps him working with his idiosyncratic behavior, which the narrator apparently shows no interests to explore.

The story as a whole is a story about some years in Tong Zhenbao's life. Although he is always perturbed and harassed by his own desire and outside enticement, and is always skeptical of himself, he has a strong will to maintain a "correct world." He could not, but neither does he desire to, break out of the social order. What helps him maintain a united ego is his long-term plan, for which the narrator has informed us as "boosting his

---

① For instance, she narrates that when Tong Zhenbao considers his social responsibilities, he feels that "not only one mother, but everywhere standing in the world are all his mothers, with tears full in their eyes, what they see is only himself alone." There is clearly an authoritative intervention here.

professional position, then after he has social status he would do some
things beneficial to the society, such as opening a technical professional
school for poor students, or building a model cloth factory in his
hometown." As a social elite, he consciously shoulders this burden to
contribute himself to the society, which is still highly bounded by traditional
moral conception and falling short of rationalization. His anxiety, disturbance,
dual personality and double life, and even both his hope and degeneration, can
only be understood with these social-historical conditions in mind.

Yet towards such a self-sacrifice, the narrator, from a feminine or
womanly perspective, keeps an ironic distance, and coldly observes his
struggles and his failure. From this perspective, Wang Jiaorui's later
marriage life is "authentic," whereas Tong Zhenbao's sacrifice is hypocritical
and unworthy. His self-reform, as self-discipline of a middle-class man to
fulfill his socially expected goal, is regarded as unreal and is subjected to
ridicule. But we can not afford to neglect the narrative irony: as a whole, this
description of the "incomplete" figures, both Tong Zhenbao and the two
female figures Wang Jiaorui and Meng Yanli included, shows the
incompleteness of Chinese "modern consciousness" promoted since the May
Fourth era (or the inefficiency of the New Culture Movement as a social-
cultural project), in which not only the concept of "new woman" did not,
and could not, accomplish its ideal, but the idea of "new man" in general
also could not lead to a fruitful direction of modernity. As a social
melodrama, the story reveals both the moral hypocrisy of the Chinese
middle-class stratum (its decadence) and its inexorable struggles, thus
finally speaking to the shaky condition of the semi-traditional Chinese society
itself, which was stranded on a dubious and doubtful hope of achieving full
rationalization, due to the intrinsic defects of the elite class carrying out the
mission (Tong Zhenbao, as noted, is incapable of "transcending his flawed
vision,"[1] and is engaged now and then in self-delusion and dissipation). To
put it in other way, Tong Zhenbao's failure to form his subjectivity is itself a

---

[1]   Gunn, E., *Unwelcome Muse : Chinese Literature in Shanghai and Peking* 1937-
1945, New York: Columbia University Press, 1980 : 212.

symptom and an allegory of the failure to forge a new, modern identity, with the "bourgeois" reason as its core.

Tong Zhenbao is a cardinal embodiment of modern urban business class from Shanghai. A product of the Treaty Port system and having received the baptism of Western technical as well as Enlightenment knowledge, this class distinguished itself from the older business class of the gentry-bureaucratic regime under the imperial order. Conscious of itself as an elite group, it committed to working on and building a modern business norm. Yet while this new class fought stoically against the harshness of the environment and its own limitations to create a new order, it nonetheless failed miserably. It is generally a consensus among historians today that the ultimate incapability of the Chinese bourgeois in modern China to claim its rights and privileges was (at least) partially the responsibility of the domestic regime, which "missed its vocation to assist and encourage, as States had done in the rise of Western capitalism, or because, by default, it allowed the country to slip into the sterile evils of militarism."[①] This research calls into attention the troublesome relationship between state and society in modern China, which is allegorically rendered as (inter-) personal psychological trauma in the writer's other stories.

*Jasmine Tea* (《茉莉香片》) is another story about quest for self-identity. This quest is through the identification of and seeking for a father figure. It is also a play crisscrossing the twin cities: the hero is moving with his family, an opium-addicted father and stepmother, from Shanghai to Hong Kong to seek refuge away from the Sino-Japanese War.

Nie Chuanqing is a twenty years old college student, who appears older than his real age yet is effeminate in his physique and spirit. He is nervous after he finds that his deceased mother, Feng Biluo and his professor, Yan Ziye, once loved each other. He becomes fantasizing that he would have been the professor's son if his mother (now deceased) was courageous enough to

---

① Bergere, M. C., *The Golden Age of the Chinese Bourgeoisie*, 1911-1937, Lloyd J. Trans, New York: Cambridge University Press and Maison des Sciences de l'Homme, Paris, 1989:5.

elope with Yan. He makes no efforts to improve himself but only blames his destiny.

This fantasy leads to his distorted view of Professor Yan's daughter Danzhu. Jealous of her identity of being the descendent of his mother's true lover, he displays various symptoms of paranoia: love, hate, jealousy, self-abhorrence, and even impulse to kill and self-destruction. Yet, as an egocentric adolescent, he does not love anybody, what he wants is to attain a weird love between him and Danzhu in order to empower himself and to jettison his visionary, inglorious past. In one instance, he says passionately to the girl, "to me, you are not only a lover, but also a creator, a father and a mother, a new environment, a new heaven and earth. You are the past and the future. You are god." A seemingly narrated monologue helps to strengthen his sense of doom:

> No escape! No escape! If there had been absolutely no alternative, it wouldn't have mattered. But now…he for the first time realized that over twenty years ago, before he had been born, he had had the chance for escape. There had been the possibility of his mother marring Yan Ziye. He could have been Yan Ziye's son, Yan Danzhu's brother. Probably he would have been Yan Danzhu. If there were he, there could not have been she.[1]

Given that this absurd rationalization is possible only from a state of delirium, it can only be an indirect deliverance of Nie Chuanqing's own hysterical thoughts. But is it really so? We further see that his paranoia metamorphoses to be an unreasonable impulse to revenge, which is enforced upon Danzhu:

> Chuanqing forced these words out of his clenched teeth:"I'll tell you. I want you to die. If there were you there wouldn't be me. As there is me here, there should not be you. Understand?" He clasped tightly both her shoulders with one arm, and with the other hand he pushed her head down so hard that it seemed as though he wanted to shove it back into her neck. She should have never been born into this world…He couldn't help kicking her savagely a few more times for fear that she might still be

---

[1]　Hsia, C. T., *A History of Modern Chinese Fiction*, Bloomington: Indiana University press, 1999:409.

alive…He ran as if he was in a nightmare…①

His resentment releases his anxiety, which is a projection of his envy of the "other." In his mind, this other also defines negatively his ignoble identity. Ashamed of his own family background (because he was born in this family, but not out of a crystallization of "love," as the new morality of the society mandates), he simultaneously fantasizes of creating a "new heaven and earth" with this "other," and shows a possessive mania: what I cannot get, you also should not possess it. The resentment is a transformation of this envy. Thus he tries to push Danzhu's head into the abdominal space, which vicariously shows his own anxiety of being an abnormal human growing out of a deformed fetus.

How to understand this unusual story with such an abnormal mind? He is an effeminate introvert because of the repression of his oppressive, decadent parents, to be sure. In his quest for his identity, he is shameful of their past and bemoaning his lost opportunity to be a crystallization of genuine love. Yet that he releases his anxiety by abusing the "other," the one that he cannot be, and his envy and abhorrence of the happiness that this "other" enjoys, expose the fact that he is still deeply entrenched in the epistemological world that sees no alternative or remedy. His wasted life and ruined youth without the vista of hope and salvation, as this abject soul is merely desperately trying to recover its own ego, its own self-importance, which is devoid of any social significance. His future seemed doomed: at the end of the story, he learns that his father and stepmother are arranging his future by assigning him a wife. Tears running down his face, "He couldn't escape."

Without correlating with the social-historical experience, critics mostly resort to the Freudian interpretation of abnormal psychology to explain the incident and all his uncanny phenomena. This shows a general tendency in interpreting this type of story, which sometimes also correlates the author's own experience. While these unhappy marriages, abnormal parent-child

---

① Hsia, C. T., *A History of Modern Chinese Fiction*, Bloomington: Indiana University Press, 1999:409.

relationship bear certain relations with the author's own family bonds, we need to go beyond these autobiographical elements to read it against the broader social-historical context. Insofar as the author has placed the hero against a peculiar Chinese decadence, this experience can only be examined from a class perspective in the particular historical moment.

Indeed, if we read this story allegorically by associating it with the social-historical subtext, we will witness more fruitful direction. It is due to the incongruence of family backgrounds—Yan Ziye is from a merchant family, the profession of which is traditionally despised in the society and located in the lowest rank of the professional hierarchy: "scholar, farmer, artisan and merchant;" while Feng Biluo is from a mandarin gentry-class household—that they were not allowed to be married. It was out of this stimulation that Yan Ziye left for foreign country to study. Yet although he had the courage to implement his will, the Chinese society still foreclosed his dreams: his lover dared not go with him together abroad for fear of public opinion, and reluctantly married a rich relative instead; when he returned to his homeland after graduation, Chinese society did not allow him to advance his career. Instead of teaching the knowledge he studied from the West, he teaches Chinese traditional literature. His flights of anger in the class only release his sense of defeat.

Yan Ziye's sense of powerlessness and enfeeblement is shared by Nie Chuanqing. But the latter's sense of frustration and feeling of anxiety is more serious: not only is he unable to inherit his "real" father's will to break social tradition, but he falls into the social web, where his patriarchal, old-styled, biological father abuses him, and his stepmother spurns him. His Electra complex thus is a search for a model father figure to define his "true" identity. But though he is eager to look for a new socio-temporal order, this world could not be found in reality, so his identity could never be formed.

Thus said, we still need to go a step further by linking the specific temporal and spatial order. The introduction by the narrator at the very start reminds readers that what follows is a sad story related to Hong Kong: "This pot of jasmine tea that I made for you may be too bitter. I am afraid the Hong Kong romance which I am to tell you is bitter—Hong Kong is a fabulous city，but heart-breaking." In addition to creating a critical distance between the readers and the events to be unfolded，this narrative framework has stressed that what follows is a romance closely related with Hong Kong as a wailsome place. As a British colony closed to yet also aloof from its mother country，Hong Kong was at the time a place where many "old fogies and leftovers from the old dynasties"（遗老遗少）lived. Nie Chuanqing's family there is from Shanghai. Like many leftover households in Eileen Chang's story，they never catch up with the tide of the contemporary society.

In this family，Nie Chuanqing has received traditional education since childhood，so his level of Chinese culture supposedly should be higher than his classmates in Hong Kong. Yet even in the Chinese literature history class that Professor Yan Ziye teaches，thanks to his laziness and lack of confidence，he scores low and appears listless and shy. But only when we correlate Yan Ziye's sense of defeat in his concern with the fate of the country，can we understand why he rebukes Nie Chuanqing like this，"If Chinese youth are all like you，China would be conquered long time ago."

But I will go a step further by proposing a hypothesis：would it be more inspirational if we read Nie Chuanqing as an allegorical figure of Chinese juvenile bourgeois class，which，as a new，weak social stratum，was metamorphosed from traditional merchants and gentry-official class？ Because this newly emerged，slowly developing class was despised and abused by the repressive，old-styled，patriarchal regime，a sense of being second-ranked citizens，without an authentic self-identity and protection from an upright forebear，transformed itself into an inferior complex. But while Nie Chuanqing's perplexity with his bloodline，which shows his shame with his ignoble upbringing，can be read as the moral quandary of the bourgeois class towards their direct forebears，his entanglement with the past，indulgence in illusions，and refusal to confront the contemporary situation and reform himself show the inclination of this class towards willful evasion of the reality. Meanwhile，his stubborn obsession with an orthodox lineage，a "real" father，is simultaneously a search for an upright，spiritual father-figure as an idol that he can adore and study from，the duty of which his biological father，who，as a traditional figure addicted to opium, could not perform. Without a solid social-economic power and status, and the ensuing cultural-political confidence of its self-image and identity, this new class lacks virago and stamina. Worse, this anxiety can change itself to an impulse revenging the outside world, in particular the weaker and the more unprotected, for its own inferior complex, as shown in Nie Chuanqing's fascist inclination of sadism, which exposes his possessive mentality that wrangles with the world to claim the justice that he believes he himself owns.

In this light, this story ultimately can be read as a story about two generation of Chinese intellectuals: the May Fourth type of intellectuals such as Yan Ziye, who did not accomplish their dream and found no way to contribute their skills in the face of the retarded, conservative society; and some post-May Fourth youths, such as Nie Chuanqing, who lacked virago or even the will to reform the society as their inferior complex imposed a restraint on them. This obsession with an existential quest for self-identity thus persists in Nie Chuanqing, an allegorical figure of the generation, who now and then feels that "there is no way to escape." This sense of no way out is due to his entrapment in his own flawed vision and his incapability to accept the reality, a result of the stringent social-historical (including the familial) circumstance. As a weak and crippling youth, an allegorical yet personified figure, who owns no vision of breaking out of the predicament by self-reform, his sense of helplessness and doomed destiny is socially and historically conditioned and (over-)determined.

*Heart Sutra* (《心经》) is another story apparently about Electra complex, a pursuit for an idol as well as an object of love by another egocentric, adolescent figure, now a girl. Having an attachment to her father Fengyi, Xiaohan sees herself as a superior goddess. Like Danzhu, she also has a vanity to manipulate men. She not only successfully despoils her father's love on her mother by sneering at the latter's decoration and sign of intimacy, to him but also appropriates the love of her suitor Gong Haili in order to arouse his father's jealousy. To appease Gong Haili's passion, she tries to be a matchmaker for him and her classmate Lingqing (who resembles her in appearance). But against her will, later on she only finds that her father has taken Lingqing as his mistress. It is clear that her father has found a substitute to avoid his incestuous feeling. She also finds that her mother has long ago discovered the affair of his father, yet remained silent to keep the family from breaking apart. Disappointed with the reality, "she suddenly has a strong feeling of disgust and horror. Who is she afraid of? Who does she hate? Her mother? Herself? ... She starts to cry. She has sinned."

What does this story signify? The use of the title "Heart Sutra," which bears a strong Buddhist connotation, implies that the evil quality resides nowhere but in human nature, and we see that self-deception and illusion are harbored by various characters. Xiaohan's father has explained to her that her desire to preserve her security and the memory of his love in her childhood years accounts for her attachment to him. This egoistic consideration is born of her sense of indulgence, and she refuses to be mature enough to enter adult relationship. The failure of her selfish scheme and the defeat of her extreme egocentrism belie the myth of individualism. However, this ethical complexity needs to be brought further into the social arena to be examined; only through this procedure can we understand the social cause of the psychological abnormality.

We first note that what the characters live in is a Western-style apartment building, with "a roof garden, rooms with glass doors, an elevator, and a long stairway." Leo Lee has noted that "a Western-style house or apartment building is often the site of estrangement and disturbance."[①] It means that not only are their psychological tensions strengthened by the architectural designs, but their psychological abnormality is an indirect result of the anxiety and anomie arised by living in a semi-Western locality, where stimulations of erotic desire frequently transpire in the commercialized daily setting. When combined with traditional decadent life-style, the erotic phantasmagoria can yield to a new kind of psychological disorder and incestuous instinct.

But if we go beyond this empirical inquiry and read this story as a social

---

① Lee, L. O., *Shanghai Modern: The Flowering of New Urban Culture in China*, 1930-1945, Cambridge: Harvard University Press, 1999:272.

allegory, then the immature status of Xiaohan, together with her other
friends who are seeking a father-figure for security, as well as her mother's
determination to preserve order without justifying it, all of which can find
their symbolic import from the historical perspective. For instance, in regard
to Xiaohan's Electra Complex, a critic has noted that:

> Her reasoning and lying are both evidence of the…self-deception that she is above
> the human lot, that she is different and superior, that she can put something over on
> the world. In essence, it is to preserve the time in her life that was "the golden age" of
> seven or eight years past, the time of security and unquestioned love.[1]

This nostalgic remembrance of "the golden age," this inextricable
attachment to a father-figure, are a call for a custodian who can take care of
the development of an underdeveloped living being; it is a psychological need
of a sense of security, which is only a result of feeling threatened by alien
others and precarious in its socially unformed identity. Lingqing is eager to
find a man around her age to go out of her unhappy family, yet she is willing
to be Fengyi's mistress due to financial considerations. Xiaohan also once
tells her father, "You should have understood long ago, Dad…as long as I
do not give you up, you will not give me up." This earnest petition is out of
a juvenile sense of reliance and the ensuing uncertainty about her identity.
But this ostensibly personal existentialist quest is merely a displacement of a
social predicament, a substitution of a cultural-political confusion, and a
projection of an economic necessity, with a distinct class nature.

In this light, these adolescents cannot simply be understood as ruthless
people with no sense of shame, but their self-deception and flawed vision
which lead to their degradation should be examined with the historical
context and experience as its subtext and, furthermore, be read as
modernist allegory. Their psychological morbidities springing forth both
from their intellectual/political immaturity and economic dependency, their
psychological and physical reliance on and callings for patron-like figures to

---

[1]    Fung, C. H., Hoyan, *The Life and Works of Zhang Ailing: A Critical Study*,
PhD Dissertation, The University of British Columbia (Canada), 1997:126.

secure their precarious sustenance of life, are an allegorical correspondence to the lack of economic and political power, sense of security, and finally a solid cultural-political identity of a newly developed, yet weak and unprotected, proto-bourgeois class, in an extremely precarious, semi-colonial, semi-traditional society.[①]

## 三、Conclusion

This chapter suggests that the predominant thematic focus of the writer is a matrimonial anxiety, which aims to cash in on any opportunity unabashedly to transcend its class status to secure financial security and boost social status. This archetypal motif of Eileen Chang's stories is leading to, and is also part of the reason for, an anxiety of self-identity. Due to the lack of rationalization of the society, and various domestic and international conflicts that were epitomized as the rhetoric of "war" under the writer's pen, a bourgeois (woman's) subjectivity is difficult to be established. In its response to the crisis of marriage and love as social institution, this anxiety articulates, crystallizes, and projects the social-political dilemma and predicament. When this feminine concern is projected back to the broader social arena, from which the middle-class men's vain struggles to acquire a "normal" bourgeois respectivity or an esteemed class identity are unraveled, the story is often narrated from the peculiar perspective. The feeling that "we have been deserted" articulated by the writer echoes this sentiment of a deeply-entrenched crisis.

---

① Similar analysis can be applied to the story *Withering Flower* (《花凋》), which is a story about a girl with tuberculosis, having youthful dream for life and love, yet is deserted by the guardians, and as a result, her withering, which is also enveloped in a framework of a love story. Living in an unhealthy circumstance, the bud of an infant flower could have little chance to burgeon and develop. The love is limited if not inexistent, with much energy pulled to their interests. Life appears a desolate and unfulfilled dream in the middle-class family originated from the traditional gentry's class. The lack of genuine care and selfless devotion leads to the early demise of a beautiful life. She never has a chance to develop her life form.

# Part IV.

Narrative Strategy under
Middle-Class Consciousness

# Chapter Seven    Double Pitfalls for Chinese "New Women":Mei Niang's Fictional Narrative of the Colonial Society

## 一、Introduction

After Xiao Hong (1911-1942) left the Japanese-dominated puppet-state Manchuria in 1934, female writers remained there continued their literary representation of the historical experience of the people living in the colonized state, among whom Mei Niang (1920-2008) quickly distinguished herself. In 1942, there was a catch phrase "the south has Eileen Chang, the north has Mei Niang" (南玲北梅).[①] The link between the two writers was based much more on their comparable fame at the time—even from a historical vantage point of view, both writers published their major works and thus attained their literary achievement before 1945, when they were merely twenty-more years old—than their compatible literary tastes and features as shown in their works with vastly differing foci and thematic motifs. Compared with other works describing life in occupied areas written by patriotic writers living outside the Japanese's control, which unsurprisingly mostly show tragic sufferings of Chinese citizens there with emphatic nationalistic message, Mei Niang's fictional narrative would appear more "authentic." This is

---

① According to Norman Smith's study, the catch phrase was "coined by Beijing's Madezeng and Shanghai's Yuzhoufeng bookstore after a contest to determine the most popular contemporary Chinese woman writer." See Smith, N., Only Women can Change this World into Heaven:Mei Niang, Male Chauvinist Society, and the Japanese Cultural Agenda in North China, 1939-1941, *Modern Asian Studies*, 2006,40(1):81.

so partially because most of the stories were a recording of what she saw and heard, and even what she personally experienced, which thus offer supplemental material for our understanding of the life in the colonized state apart from what we read from Xiao Hong's "hard-core" narration. As noted, the distinct feature of her works was a strong feminist discourse.① This constitutes a sharp contrast to the other writer in the catch phrase: Eileen Chang, who, though paying no less concern over the destiny of middle-class women, remained a cold distance from the feminist ideal. Why this significant departure?

So far, the authoritative study on this subject focuses on the aspect that "progressive gendered ideals of modernity, as articulated with reference to May Fourth notions of women's individual emancipation, inspired young Chinese women in Manchukuo to take advantage of the opportunities offered them by the Japanese colonial state."② Granted that their insistence on the May Fourth ideal of "new women" substantially challenged and subverted the Japanese promotion of conservative Confucian idea of womanhood which aimed to legitimize their political domination, is this sort of cultural criticism, as a form of resistance, effective in its diagnosis of the symptom of the patriarchal, colonial society with residual yet strong traditional conventions and conceptions? How did the female writers there ingeniously assert their views without incurring the colonizers' suppression? What lessons can we learn from their representation of the colonial society? This chapter, with Mei Niang as a case of study, looks into the achievements as well as the limitations of these writers' practice of literary creation as critical interventions. Rather than merely following the logic of feminism as a theory per se that the writers undertook in structuring their narrative, I try to put the feminist discourse shown in the texts vis-a-vis the social-political circumstance

---

① Norman Smith notes that "from a privileged vantage point, Mei Niang articulated a feminist critique of Japanese colonial ideals." See Smith, N., "Only Women Can change this World into Heaven": Mei Niang, Male Chauvinist Society, and the Japanese Cultural Agenda in North China, 1939-1941, *Modern Asian Studies*, 2006,40(1):83.

② Smith, N., *Resisting Manchukuo: Chinese Women Writers and the Japanese Occupation*, Toronto: University of British Columbia Press, 2007: ⅩⅤ.

to see the twisted relations in the articulation of the May Fourth ideal. I suggest that there is a double pitfall for the Manchurian women in Mei Niang's fictional world: in addition to the conservative ideal about women as "good wife, wise mother" promoted by the Japanese, there was the other one regarding the "modern" idea of a "free-willed" individual. This is a pitfall partially because the individualist assertion of women's right was impossible to be realized under the colonial, semi-traditional social-political and economic conditions, which oftentimes rendered the characters to regard their failure as merely a gender issue.

## 二、A Successful Professional Woman in Manchukuo

Mei Niang was the pen name of Sun Jiarui. She was born in a wealthy local family in 1920. What brought about its fortunes and social distinction is attributable to the legendary career of her father. He was from a small county of Shandong, yet moved to Manchuria for business interests. His ascendance from a person of nobody to a powerful (before the Japanese came) and rich man—a giant regional industrialist—is almost a miracle: working initially as a messenger in a British company, he mastered English, Japanese, and Russian in relatively short time period aside from his busy schedule of errands for the foreigners. Foreseeing the promising prospectus of this ingenious talent, a distinguished warlord introduced his daughter to him for marriage. His experience of getting rich can be seen as a rare, and yet also typical, case of some local talents fighting to ascend to the top of the society with their diligence and wisdom, as well as their well relations with powerful domestic dignitaries and foreign businessmen there.

But Mei Niang's early personal experience reminds us Xiao Hong's: her mother, married to the rich family merely as a concubine, was forced by Sun Zhiyuan's formal wife to death (by suicide) not long after Mei Niang was born. But unlike Xiao Hong who kept an inimical relation with her father, Mei Niang's father treated her kindly and urged her to be independent. Her step-mother was distant to her, though not necessarily always harsh to her.

Typical of the wealthy family at the time, the education the writer received from her early years on was eclectic: it was classical Chinese learning blended with studies of Western culture. Since she entered a junior middle school for girls as late as 1930 when she was ten, the books she had read were mainly works by Chinese May Fourth writers such as Lu Xun (1881-1936) and Bing Xin (1902-1999), by Western writers of classical romanticism [such as those by George Byron (1788-1824)] and realism, and of Soviet's socialist realism [such as works by Maxim Gorky (1868-1936)]. The next year, she transferred to another girls' school. In her historical vantage point, the dormitory life in these girls' schools meant to her a formation of a "strong affection" towards collective womanhood.

After the Japanese's invasion of Manchuria in September 1931 and its immediate occupation of the whole area, a radical change occurred to the Sun family. As a patriotic person, Sun Zhiyuan refused the attractive position of vice president of the Manchukuo Central Bank imposed by the Japanese, and led his family to north China. Yet the economic straitjacket imposed on them due to the Japanese restrictions on capital-exportation from Manchuria forced the family to return to their hometown a year later.

The life in Manchuria was relatively stable compared with other occupied areas at the time. This might have offered the simulacrum of a peaceful society, though the Japanese propaganda of an "earthly paradise" (乐土) was hardly seen as reality. Mei Niang, just like other girls from middle-class families who could afford to attend school, was skeptical and loathe towards the Japanese promotion of womanhood ideals that emphasized obedience and docility in family life, which occupied a ponderous share in the school's curriculum.

The year 1936 marked a turning point for her, as in this year two events happened: her first story collection named *A Young Lady's Collected Works* (《小姐集》) was published; and her father died. She was sent to Japan to pursue further study. Interestingly, Xiao Hong was also in Japan around this time. But though Mei Niang had read her works earlier, the two writers embarked on two vastly differing personal trajectories and they apparently never met each other. In the two years in Japan, though her dream of studying medicine was aborted, nonetheless she read more leftist works such as those by Guo Moruo (1892-1978).

But the more important thing to her seemed to be her love affair with her future husband, a fellow Chinese overseas student who was also studying and working there. The opposition from her family and the threat of discontinuing her financial support forced her to return to Manchukuo in 1938, working as a proofreader for a local newspaper. But the next year, she still refused the family's arranged marriage and lived together with her lover, who followed her there. In 1940, her work of *Clams*(《蚌》) appeared in a Chinese journal sponsored by the Japanese, *Osaka Mainichi Shimbun/ Chinese Osaka Daily*(《大阪华文每日》).

Together with her husband and some friendly Japanese intellectuals, Mei Niang joined a newly formed literary league, Literary Collective(文丛). Her second volume of story collection, *The Second Generation*(《第二代》) was also published by this organization. In its preface, Liang Shanding (1914-1996), a famed male writer, has praised the writer's tendency to "expose reality" against her earlier inclination towards "little girl's love and hate." The writer's more famous works are the three novellas *Clam*(1939), *Fish*(《鱼》)(1941), and *Crabs*(《蟹》)(1941) written shortly later, all of which won several distinguished literary prizes at the time.

The couple moved to Japan in late 1940 because Mei Niang's husbandneeded to work there as a reporter. There, she saw the hardship average Japanese people endured, and also wrote "Fish" and "Crabs" which harbored no serious, though subtle, exposure of harsh reality of the local Manchurian society under the Japanese occupation. In spring 1942, she followed her husband to Beiping, working as editor and reporter for *Women's Journal*(《妇女杂志》).

What is controversial, however, is not merely her husband's role in the North China Writer's Association which apparently was under the Japanese's sponsorship. As noted, her "fame" (or notoriety from a historical vantage point?) had "solidified in conjunction with the establishment of the Japanese-sponsored, Pan-Asian Greater East Asia Writer's Congress,"[1] whereas the

---

① Smith N. "Only Women Can Change this World into Heaven": Mei Niang, Male Chauvinist Society, and the Japanese Cultural Agenda in North China, 1939-1941, *Modern Asian Studies*, 2006,40(1):91.

Congress had unambiguously claimed that it "discusses ways and means of how literary circles … can offer cooperation toward the prosecution of the Greater East Asia War and the creation of literature and art characteristic of East Asia."[①] Because of this political complexion, Eileen Chang had evaded attending its meetings despite the invitation she received from it, and had published a proclamation in newspapers announcing that she had no intention to (and indeed did not) join it though her name appeared there without her own permission. Compared with this political wisdom or misgiving, Mei Niang seemed to quite enjoy her distinction achieved in the Congress. She earned two prizes there: a secondary prize in the second Congress, and with her novelette *Crabs* the "Novel of the Year" in the third Congress.

But what compounds the complexity and adds to the ambiguity of the issue is that, the novelettes which brought prizes to Mei Niang are both works of social critique, and *Crabs* even bears unambiguous anti-colonial and anti-patriarchal message, which are counteractive to the Japanese's fanfare of establishing "peaceful and happy land" and its promotion of conservative Confucian concepts. It is also worthy to note that the awardee of the first prize in the first Congress, the Manchurian writer Yuan Xi (1919-1988), was imprisoned by the Japanese because of his "dark writings" when he had freed to Beiping from that area. What can explain these curious phenomena is that the writings of these writers, mostly works of social realism, remained their semi-autonomy and a distance to the imperialists' policies and demands. By being faithful to the reality as the writers saw it as, these works "naturally" downplay any positive image the Japanese tried to propagandize.

Another ambiguity or mystery is Mei Niang's own attitude towards the Japanese occupation. Obviously in her works she "exposed" the oppressive, dark reality of the occupied area, but not only did her participation in the

---

① This was from a news report on the first Congress held in Tokyo in late 1942. See *The Hong Kong News*, Oct. 29, 1942, p. 1. Cited from Gunn, E., *Unwelcome Muse: Chinese Literature in Shanghai and Beijing*, 1937-1945, New York: Columbia University Press, 1980: 32-33.

activities of the Congress stigmatize her image, but one of her articles appeared just before the end of the war in *Women's Journal* unambiguously called for Japanese women's devotion and sacrifice for the efforts of the "Sacred War."[①] Her husband's role in the wartime is no less bewildering: apparently he led the pro-Japanese writers' association, yet according to Mei Niang's own accounts, he in fact worked for the underground resistance force. Historical puzzles aside, I suggest the key to break the debate about whether her writing is a kind of "resistance" or "collaboration" is to look into the real content of her fictional narrative.

Mei Niang and her husband returned to Manchuria in 1945 and stayed there for three years; after that they went to Shanghai and then Taiwan. After 1949, they decided to return to the mainland to join New China, yet her husband drowned himself mysteriously in the sea during this trip, leaving two daughters and a son, who was still in his wife's body, to Mei Niang. Mei Niang was assigned to teach middle school by the new government and joined Beijing's Writers' Association.

### 三、Female Desire and Thwarted Dream of Women's Liberation

As a member of the generation receiving the baptism of May Fourth New Culture, in particular its message of women's liberation, the writer courageously upheld the banner of women's sexual independence; yet sometimes the characters' assertion of female desire becomes a sort of anarchical self-destruction for themselves.

*Before Operation*(《动手术前》) shows the strong influence the writer received from the May Fourth confessional style of writing. As usual, the person who makes confession is a woman. In this genre, the heroine always delivers her sufferings to a person whom she apparently can trust, usually a man. In this one, the woman is conveying her secrets to the male doctor,

---

① 赵月华:《历史重建中的迷思——梅娘作品修改研究》,《中国现代文学研究丛刊》,2005(1):135-136.

whom she happened to meet once in the day she experienced her traumatic incident.[①] She was seduced to have sex with one of his husband's colleagues and infected venereal disease. What the lesson she learns from this experience, however, is: "Go to hell the so-called virginity! Life is so precious!" and "I will revenge, I will go to work as unlicensed prostitute, to damage those men who play women." And she insists that "I did not do anything wrong" because her husband also plays other women, and what she performs is merely out of women's natural instincts. She declares that "I will unite all those unfortunate women to fight men! I will teach my child, to let him understand that the society is so unfair to women. At least, I hope the second generation would understand and respect women."

This feminist discourse takes the patriarchal society and in particular, men with male-chauvinist consciousness as the enemy and the target of women's liberation, which is in line with the May Fourth feminist diagnosis of the social malaise. Yet what it takes to challenge the patriarchal system is an anarchical impulse and a blind move of (self-) deconstruction; in particular, sexual dissipation is mistaken as a weapon for women's emancipation, which would easily fall into the pitfall set up by the degenerate society.

Sex plays an equally important role in "Fish." Because of this emphasis, although it earned the second prize for literature in the Congress, it was condemned by a contemporary Japanese writer as a piece that is "utterly devoid of values in its portrayal of adultery and despair" and so "among the most degenerate pieces" that he ever read.[②] Compared with the last story, here the writer entrusts more power to the heroine by granting the only narrative voice to her. The dangerous aspect of this narrative perspective is less in its silencing of the other voices, such as those of the male characters,

---

① Because of a quarrel with her husband, she went out to release her anxiety, and happened to see one of his husband's colleagues. He asked her to deliver two books to her husband, which he borrowed from the latter.

② Gunn, E., *Unwelcome Muse: Chinese Literature in shanghai and Beijing*, 1937-1945, New York: Columbia University Press, 1980:37.

than in its overdue emphasis on the psychological trauma of the female protagonist to invite sympathy that would neglect the social-economic overdetermination of the "women's problem."

A confession of a woman in a stormy night unravels the curtain of the story, which is conveyed to her paramour. Gradually we learn her experience, a representative love affair of a May Fourth "new woman." A girl "thirsting for love," she betrays her family to be with the man who allures her heart, yet the latter turns out to be a married man merely enamored of her beauty. As a result, her blind passion costs her a lot. She is pregnant, and the man pays little attention to her and there was oftentimes fighting between them. She finds solace in her husband's cousin who seems to be sympathetic of her experience. Yet after the consummation of this (perhaps not less blind) passion with the latter, she articulates complaints of the same issue: he loves her merely because of her physical attraction. She attributes the cause of the unromantic ending to the patriarchal society that takes women as accessories of men rather than a human being. This is a familiar criticism from the May Fourth tradition of repudiating the "feudal" society; whereas the new focus on women's sexual satisfaction offers no better sign of prospect.

The central imagery of the story comes from the title "fish," whose connotation is explained clearly by the protagonist's deliverance of her inner thought—"I have seen through (the society): the fish in the net can only find a hole to free itself; to wait until it is captured and then put back again into the water. It is more illusion than dream. If it gets an opportunity to free itself of the net, no matter whether it falls into the water or on the earth, it is better." [1] The words show a brave will to break loose from the stifling social network, yet fundamentally it is out of an anarchical passion against anything that obstructs the fulfillment of her desire, and it would easily be quenched by conventional force without much repercussion from the society.

Furthermore, this "new woman" herself acknowledges that she is

---

① 　张泉编：《梅娘小说散文集》，北京出版社 1997 年版，第 79 页.

paradoxical in her feelings. In her confession, she acknowledges that she does not love her cousin, only because the latter consoles her heart physically and emotionally that she develops their affair. Although her first love cheats her and treats her badly, she still wants him back and admits that she still "loves" him. This is not merely due to the weakness of an emotionally-entrapped woman, but should be seen as simultaneously a dilemma for a middle-class "new woman" who has few choices before the reality exposes its true facade. Nevertheless, she insists that she is not wrong in her choice from the very beginning. "What I did was not wrong at all. I needed love, then I loved… I did not hurt anybody, I did not give anyone inconvenience, what I chose to do was the only way that I could take. I still want myself, then I have to follow this path."[1] This lament is not merely an explanation for the sake of her (in)dignity, but the principle she sticks to as shown here, which dictates that any choice is up to the decision of an individual so long as it does not hurt others. That is fundamentally the tenet of the May Fourth individualism and the "golden rule" held by the (Western) middle class, but in the contemporary Chinese society which fell short of a full rationalization process, a dogmatic insistence on this laisse-faire principle could only lead to failure and suffering in reality, especially for women, because the other gender and the society in general oftentimes did not accommodate and cooperate with this belief.

Nevertheless, like the first story, here the author implies that it is desire as an inalienable natural instinct that brings about all the happenings, because the title "fish" in Chinese pronunciation is identical to desire. The pursuit of freedom from the traditional ethical-moral straitjacket which stresses suppression of physical instinct led to a reverse process aimed to chase sexual liberation. Nevertheless, the protagonist here still dares not to expose or articulate this consciousness; rather, she argues that the cause for her series of unfortunate choices is from the outside: "If my family did not oppress me, I will not love Lin Xingmin so carelessly; if Lin Xingmin did

---

① 张泉编：《梅娘小说散文集》，北京出版社 1997 年版，第 109 页.

not bully me so much, I would not accept your consolation."[①] And she can only hope the society will be open enough to accept her extramarital affair: "If this society has one more reasonable person, women will have less bitterness." While she pins down the patriarchal society as the chief culprit, she does not reflect on whether she herself has anything to do with her sufferings.

The author's exposure of the various problems related to "women's issue" from a societal perspective reveals the impossibility of the "New Culture," and she oftentimes attributes it to "men's problem." *A Trip* (《旅》) (1942) records an episode happened in a train from the narrator's perspective. Just before she departs, she hears from her aunt that a whore who kills her husband is in the train with her paramour, and there are a lot of polices waiting there hunting for her. During the trip, this traveler (the narrator) notices a beautiful lady with a handsome man, by their intimate manners she fantasizes that they are the wanted. Yet they are another pair of lover who are also fleeing from the restraint of marriage and the oppression of public opinion. Their destiny is not different from the alleged whore: while we are informed finally that the latter is captured immediately when she is boarding the train, they are found by the man's vulgar wife just before the train stops. By paralleling the two similar cases, and with the comment of an elder man which complains the unreliability of women at the time, the narrative shows that the society habitually attributes the responsibility of problems caused by extramarital relations to women. While "free love" seems not a faraway dream now, the ideal of "New Women(hood)" is still constrained by the customary social opinions on women.

## 四、A Problem Caused by Men?

"Men's responsibility" becomes the more salient motif of the writer's satirical fiction. *Gift at a Dusk* (《黄昏之恋》) lampoons the lust of men, in this way it clearly reveals that the problem lies in men rather than women.

---

① 　张泉编:《梅娘小说散文集》,北京出版社 1997 年版,第 109 页.

Poet Li Liming sees an advertisement in a newspaper about a newly widow who proclaims that she is rich and beautiful and wants to interview any middle-aged man who has the will to marry her. Extremely excited，he immediately plans to visit her though his returned wife from her hometown needs his pick-up. Yet the woman turns out to be a dirty woman with five children. She cries to tell the poet that she flees to the city to evade bandits，and it is her landlord's daughter who "sets up" the scheme for her to get some offers from "sympathetic philanthropists." Poet Li Liming is disappointed，angry，and shifts towards his dry wife whom he has little interests in in order to pry out some money from the latter. From a feminist perspective，the story still implies that ugly man with a lustrous mind is the cause of the social problems.

*The Spring Returns to the Human World* (《春到人间》) similarly exposes the dirty minds of a group of men. This time the game reverses itself：these men pretend to publicly hire some actresses while the real intention is to seduce women；but while they think they have successfully achieved their goal，those girls ask them for money for various reasons：they are also manipulating men by catering to their lustful taste in order to attain their own objective. But the author does not want to show that these girls are mercenary swindlers；rather，their sisterhood and their kind hearts (one girl really needs money to meet expensive expenditures to save her mother) make a sharp contrast to the dirty men who only want their body. That the "women's problem" is caused by men unambiguously becomes the story's central theme. Meanwhile，it is the patriarchal society that forces the girls to sell themselves to maintain a humble life.

Likewise，*Story Inside a Small Advertisement* (《小广告里的故事》) (1943) through the same confessional mode of writing delivers the female narrator's sufferings to her lover：she is manipulated to swindle dowry from men who love her. *Rainy Night* (《雨夜》) describes a scene in which a woman slaughters the man who tries a rape. In all，the author shows that the "women's issues" are all caused by men，or the patriarchal society which privileges men and oppresses women with the concept of virginity.

Although the dignity of women is the core concern of all these stories， when the writer shifts her perspective a little bit towards incidents taken place outside of women's interior arena, the rewards are more fruitful. For instance, she sometimes notices that the problem exists not merely in "men," but in the condition of the "New Culture" itself, which is shown in the metamorphosis of the "New Youths."

*Little Wife* (《小妇人》), written in 1944, is an incomplete novel. In terms of its major plotline which narrates the process of a broken romance of an ideal couple who married against the objection of their relatives—an emblematically successful story of the May Fourth "free love"—it is obviously a post-May Fourth narrative. In the very beginning, this couple is still in their honeymoon and embarks on their journey from Beiping to Changchun, a city in the Manchuria, in order to find a haven there to avoid the persecution of their families. The second section changes the time setting to two years later, when there has been fissures between the two, and the husband beats the "little wife" Fenghuang (which means phoenix) and leaves the family. What happens is that he has an affair with the female master of the school where he works. But he tries to break this extramarital affair as he still deeply loves his wife, and his paramour (the schoolmaster) also understands and accepts quietly his arrangement. The novel ends up with his chance meeting with the family of his nieces in Japan, where he has been there teaching Chinese in order to cool down the intricate relations between him and his two lovers. In this narrative, both the wife Fenghuang and the schoolmaster are "new women." The triangle that shows the complexity of the emotional tangles might aim to underline the psychological weakness of the "little wife." Here, the husband loves his wife, so the problem happened apparently exists elsewhere; in particular, in the troubled relationship in the middle-class world.

In another story, a man and a woman also love each other, but here the writer reveals what causes the tragedy of their romance.*Clams* is focusing on a psychologically besieged young woman. Through her perspective, it presents a dim picture of the local society in which women could not find much hope in living a noble life with dignity, thus it can be read as a story inheriting the spirit of the May Fourth New Literature. The storyline is not complex: Meili, a high-school graduate and a clerk, is in love with her coworker Qi. In this "free love" she devotes her virginity. Yet her parents oppose the trend of "free love," warning her of the alleged immorality of the practice and intending to marry her to a playboy whom she dislikes. Meanwhile, Qi's family also arranges him a marriage with a woman in a compatible household from his hometown. When Meili hears the news, in an impulse to revenge Qi's betrayal which she mistakes it as, she declares that she has another lover and never loves Qi. She also leaves her job which offers merely meager salary for her. Her haste reaction backfires to hurt herself: a chance meeting with a former male colleague in a park is set up by some evil news reporters as a case of immoral affair, and Qi takes it to be the truth and reluctantly accepts his arranged marriage. Meili tries to save her love by going to the train station to stop Qi, yet she misses it. In this unfortunate encounter she is "devastated by the loss of her relationship, her job, and her hope for the future."[①]

Like a typical May Fourth New Literature piece, the story shows that what causes the predicament of women in love is the semi-traditional society: residual yet diehard customary practice of arranged practice, social prejudice against the "immoral" free love, few choices for intellectual women in society save for some low-paid jobs, etc, all of which contribute to the unfortunate "accidents" of the heroine. In terms of all these familiar motifs, the story is not exceptional or fresh enough; what adds to its merits, however, is the detailed presentation of the colonized society.

The heroine lives in the society as a second-rate citizen, for the arrogance of the Japanese appears here and there. Not only is the Japanese train ticket-collector harsh to her and to other passengers, the Japanese soldiers sing obscene song and call girls of Manchuria in the streets bordering on sexual harassment, but even Japanese kids also dare to throw stones to her for fun (the identities of these persons are ascertained through

---

① Smith, N., "Only Women Can Change this World into Heaven": Mei Niang, Male Chauvinist Society, and the Japanese Cultural Agenda in North China, 1939-1941, *Modern Asian Studies*, 2006, 40(1): 93.

nuanced reference to their awkward pronunciation of Chinese characters and their body size and gesture). The several references to the setting sun are also generally regarded as the writer's deliberate depreciation of the Japanese suzerainty. In this occupied society, the collaborators—two patrols—bully their country men (those middle class citizens) which they dared not to do so before the occupation for the latter's official position (as one patrol acknowledges), because now they are only responsible to the Japanese authority.

Under these social-political conditions, the life of middle-class families is inevitably affected; Meili's family is no exception. We are informed that her "family, originally not so harmonious, recently because of the confiscation of its houses and the rationing of foods, has already been a mess," which leads to her parents' eagerness to marry her out to a wealthy family. Her elder brother has complained to her that he has few choices; not a graduate of the colonial military school, he cannot hope to ascend to a higher position; the will to develop his career is also frustrated by the meager payment. Under this suffocating environment, he only wants to immerse himself in physical dissipation by appropriating the inheritance of the residual family fortune. The ugly internal landscape of this extended gentry's household is delineated; many ladies engage in mah-jong; one of her brothers indulges himself in opium and her father in concubine; one of her brothers spends money for prostitutes; there are numerous internecine fights among the ladies and men in the extended family vying for property and fortune, a familiar clan politics abounds in the literature of the period.

Living in this degenerate world, apparently, Meili has internalized the May Fourth concept of "New Women", including its tenet of free love, into her mind. But she still realizes that granted her love with Qi succeeds, the future prospect is not a rosy one [which reminds us the experience of romance in Lu Xun's *Regret for the Past* (《伤逝》)]. She has confessed to her girlfriend her relations with Qi: "We are not different. We knew (each other), fell in love, and only waited to get married. But our future will not be better than yours (that drags on a less than unhappy life)."[1] She attributes this failure of implementing the ideal of May Fourth free love to the prejudice of the society: "In my view, it is only because of the immoral slander of average people. Once a man and a woman know each other and walk together, other people will say a lot of things about their relations. As a result, they could not afford not to get married (to avoid more negative public opinion)."[2] This explanation sees the problem less in the society as a network than in men, which, however, still fails to find out the true cause of the problem with a social nature—it displaces an essentially social problem to be an ethical issue, no matter the target is the "immoral" common people or the other gender.

This is because from the perspective of the narrative which focuses on Meili, the sufferings of the people in the society are examined through the unfortunate destiny of the women; and the hope to break out of this straitjacket is also put on the collective awakening of their feminist consciousness of the women and their will. When Meili talks to her girlfriends: "This society was not prepared for women. Originally (I) thought that I still can study and work, now even this little hope is disappearing. To study? There are three-hour classes on housework in the six-hour daily class schedule. To work? Women are (regarded as) incompetent and merely serve tea (to men)…But we are already fortunate, (because) we have a heart that can feel agonies. If all women feel this pain, then we have the opportunity of salvation, isn't it?"[3] Later on, when she reflects on her loss of virginity to Qi, she complains that Qi does not consider her situation, "the road for women is narrow; in particular, the society still evaluates women based on her virginity." She concludes that "only women can sympathize and understand women, only women unite

---

① 张泉编：《梅娘小说散文集》，北京出版社 1997 年版，第 25 页．

② 张泉编：《梅娘小说散文集》，北京出版社 1997 年版，第 25 页．From the text we can hardly tell this statement is articulated by Meili or her girlfriend Xiuwen. But no matter who says it, Meili obviously accepts the explanation.

③ 张泉编：《梅娘小说散文集》，北京出版社 1997 年版，第 23 页．

together they can save themselves."[1]

The educated background gives Meili a sort of sense of intellectual certainty, but her diagnosis of the problem could not settle the problems within her extended family, which to a great extent bring about her torture and tragic experience; nor can it redress the prejudice and customary consciousness and practice against women's rights in the society. This is the more direct cause of her aborted romance. This awareness of women's rights also has rare opportunity to be realized in the colonial society: the Japanese would suppress it directly with its rhetoric of conservative Confucianism. Therefore, the "collective sisterhood," as a utopia, in this historical circumstance merely gives an illusionary solution to the "women's problem."

On the other hand, the central concern for Meili and her girlfriends is much more on their role in love and marriage than on their jobs which pay them pitiable sum of reward. Xiuwen complains that women's role in family is merely raising children and doing housework. Echoing this view, Meili says she is better to work as a prostitute than to be a wife, merely a plaything for men. This bold assertion subverts the Japanese's promotion of the ideal womanhood, yet it shows more a regret over the lack of social opportunities due to the retarded social rationalization for women, than a clear political consciousness against the Japanese propaganda. Fundamentally in its negative statement, it looks for sympathetic men as the last resort and haven.

Indeed, if the woman finds no way to change the consciousness of average people (so she resorts to the collective sisterhood for potential power, which is an illusory utopia, as said), then she tries to rely on men to address the dilemma. She accepts Qi's rhetoric that as long as they join together, they can flee to the heaven, though earlier she has a clear realization that even they flee to Tianjin, Beijing, Shanghai and Nanjing,

---

① 张泉编:《梅娘小说散文集》,北京出版社 1997 年版,第 45 页.

"everywhere would be the same." [①] Moreover，Qi's rhetoric appears merely a pretext to hoodwink Meili's trust to take her virginity（which happens immediately after the talk）—in its side effect this subtly exposes the hypocrisy of "men"—but Meili later on still holds that she is right in devoting her virginity for the sake of love. Yet in other times，she acknowledges that she is too haste before she knows Qi fully. A deconstructive effect also lies there：free love based on her "free will" in reality might not be so romantic and ideal. Granted she and Qi's love consummated itself in marriage，the final outcome might just like what her girlfriends are experiencing：fighting and divorce.

In this light，although the central message that the story meant to convey is that "Meili's devastation personifies the violence that Mei Niang ascribed to the Confucian ideals that dominated women's lives in Manchukuo，" [②] the preface of the story—which reads："A huge wave throws her into the beach，she was shone to dray. She could not bear more（desire） but open her shell. Yet as soon as she did this，her body was picked up，"— obviously refers to the sexual desire of the women—which，if not seen as the genesis of the problem，at least plays an important function in it. The text conveys a feminist message of sexual liberation irrespective of conventional concept，which seemingly offers the way to solve the "women's issue." But this overarching message is challenged by the side plot of the story itself.

Nevertheless，the reference to the societal network through the heroine's social experience marks a turning to a broader perspective，which led to a more comprehensive portraiture of the semi-traditional and colonial totality. *Flowers That Blossom in the Night*（《夜合花开》），another unfinished novel，is apparently a story that has various layers of contrasts

---

① 张泉编：《梅娘小说散文集》，北京出版社 1997 年版，第 28-29 页. These areas are all occupied areas at the time，perhaps the writer at the time dared not to mention any city in the control of the Chinese government.

② Smith，N.，"Only Women Can Change this World into Heaven"：Mei Niang，Male Chauvinist Society，and the Japanese Cultural Agenda in North China，1939-1941，*Modern Asian Studies*，2006，40（1）：95.

between men and women. All its characters bear typical features pertaining to his/her social status and ideological concepts, which contribute to its representative value of a skit of critical realism. Daidai is married to a tycoon to secure her financial needs while her younger sister Dailin ekes out a hard life with her own perseverance. Daidai's husband Rixin (literally means daily renewed) is a vulgar Babbitt who squanders money coveting an opera actress, a conventional decadence at the time for both the old leftovers and the new rich. A young reporter Han Qingyun, Daidai's former neighborhood, upon a chance meeting with her, plans to seduce her as his concubine and also tries to hoodwink money from her husband. He helps the actress Lingzhu who is coveted by Rixin by assisting her study and daily sustenance, whereas contains in his mind an evil scheme of manipulating her body and heart for his physical and material enjoyment. The ugliness of these two men composes a sharp contrast to Dailin's lover Aiqun (literally means "love the masses") who honestly fights against the hardness of life for the goodness of the family.

Although Daidai, Rixin and Han Qingyun appear either pitiable or despicable, they were all "New Men" and "New Women" that had received the baptism of the May Fourth New Culture. Although Daidai's marriage was founded more upon the stake of money than love, we cannot deny that she also loves her husband and chooses him out of her own choice; and although Rixin splurges money, being a social elite he is not too evil and he loves Daidai tenderly. Han Qingyun is reminiscent of the character Fan Jiashu in Zhang Henshui's (1895-1967) novel *Fate in Tears and Laughter* (《啼笑因缘》), but the kindness of Fan Jiashu now metamorphoses itself to be the evilness of Han Qingyun. These characterizations fundamentally subvert the image of "New Youths" idealized in the New Culture Enlightenment.

Han Qingyun is especially noteworthy. He appears progressive to Daidai, and informs her that although to average people "to survive is a big problem and eating becomes the only objective," he himself believes that "on top of eating, man should have a goal If not, isn't it that life has no meaning at all?" When Daidai asks him what this goal is, his grandiose answer appears illusionary for readers："（to work）for the state，for the people，and for the masses."① The reason that this progressive political slogan shows itself as merely baloney is not merely because we have been informed that Han Qingyun is a selfish man intending to seduce Daidai for ulterior，debased gains，but it is the result of our consideration of the local society in which these youths who had been subjected to the influence of the May Fourth New Culture have to drag out an ignoble life under the colonial oppression and have no way to realize these lofty ideals. His desire for Daidai is partially out of his envy for her husband——a new rich that appears to him vulgar.

Parallel to the paradoxical situation which shows how a seemingly progressive May Fourth youth retrogrades to be a rat，the recipients of this grandiloquent rhetoric of May Fourth ideals are also not enlightened. Lingzhu doubts his teachings "as soon as she begins to associate with rich persons." To her "the force of life outweighs him（his baptism），and it matters much more."② Most of these people had owned sublime social-political ideals. Now more or less they resign to the dire situation which the colonial regime imposes upon them，in which economic necessity surpasses any other concerns.③

What makes the ideals of New Culture impossible，we are informed，is the social circumstance. Dailin has no way but to accept her sister's financial assistance for her ill mother，as the salary of his father，a school principal，could not maintain their life sustenance. She urges her sister Daidai to find a job to keep her dignity，but the plan is mocked by Rixin for its impracticality：the money earned by honest work cannot pay fare for bus，and only the job of working as a prostitute can support oneself at the time.

---

① 张泉编：《梅娘小说散文集》，北京出版社 1997 年版，第 408-409 页.

② 张泉编：《梅娘小说散文集》，北京出版社 1997 年版，第 441 页.

③ To outstrip this burden，Dailin has held "a secret longing，a secret hope among her classmates"——to go to an "ideal place" where "money would lose its power，a place that justice，innocence，and the sublime feelings of the humanity aggregate." 张泉编：《梅娘小说散文集》，北京出版社 1997 年版，第 454 页. We are informed that there are many people around them assigned to help to deliver the youths who want to go that place.

Accordingly, from the broad social network and interpersonal relations we see the correlation among the stringent social-political conditions and the hopeless living situation and the little choice for "new women," thus the futility of the "New Culture" concepts.

If in this story, the disclosure of the degraded colonial society is still conducted through the examination of the "women's issue;" then sometimes we also witness the reverse sort of observation: the latter's problem is embedded in an unfolding of a "family saga."

Although the epitaph of the story "Crabs" (which reads: "The man who captures crabs turns on the light in his boat, then the crabs themselves follow the light. Then, they fall into the net well prepared for them.") reminds us the motif of "men's problem," and it indeed concerns the destiny of women in a traditional society colonized by a foreign subject; its thematic scope is much broader, which offers a vivid picture of a declining extended Chinese traditional family trapped in the net of the colonial society and of its degradation and metamorphosis.

Apparently, the protagonists of the novel are two filles, Sun Ling and Little Cui; but now it does not focus exclusively on the women. Rather, the details in *Clam* related to the family politics of the extended family here received more comprehensive treatment. Containing many auto-biographical elements, we are informed that this extended well-to-do family got rich through its ties to Russians who had powerful force in the local society before they were evicted by the invading Japanese. After that its fortune falls into irrevocable decline. In a colonized society, there were always men from the erstwhile rich gentry's family trying to save their privileges and advance their interests by not only usurping the residual fortune of the family (which precipitates its disintegration), but also cooperating with the colonizers in order to have a share in the latter's colonial adventure. The incarnation of this evil in the novel is Third Uncle, who manages to manipulate the family business by controlling its channel of revenue at the cost of the interests of other family members, most of whom are pitiable nieces and cousins without the protection of their former patrons who now either are died or neglect to take care of the complicated and noisome affairs. He also enters the local tax office controlled by the Japanese. When he sees the daily routine there cannot offer him much money, he joins the illegal business of selling opium, which finally forfeits his fortune.

What is more evil seems to be the behavior of the cattier lackey named Wang Fu. Seeing the irreversible change of fate, he changes his object of loyalty from the elder master to Third Uncle. He does not openly object the latter's ugly plan of marring his daughter Little Cui as concubine, but manages to send her as a gift to the Japanese. But this major plotline is buried subtly under many interspersed plots and episodes. Even the provocative recording of the search of concubines for the Manchukuo "emperor" manipulated by the Japanese which causes misgivings and panics of the local society did not attract much attention. The reason for this calculated description of a by no means flattering picture is quite simple: the major event itself is sufficient enough to invite the Japanese's suspicion and cause a dangerous situation to the author. That the writer not only did not find trouble, but earned a handsome prize from the Congress is probably due to the fact that this realistic piece aimed only to expose the reality "as it is"; and it did it so faithfully that even the Japanese could not find its subversive connotation by its superficial narration. Thus the disintegration of the Chinese family with the disastrous effect of the Japanese appropriation of local fortune by forced conversion of silver to worthless paper currency is vicariously presented. This is done through Sun Ling's stepmother's obsession over her concealed, amassed stash of silver, parts of which nevertheless are cheated away by the merciless lackey Wang Fu in his mission of money conversion entrusted by the widow.

It is under this social-political context-as-subtext that the relentless process of demise of the traditional Chinese world is delivered through the personae of the aged Granny, the impotent and unskilled elder brother, and the frustrated and resigned brother Xiang, who had been an overseas student in Japan and had held entrepreneurship to do business; and under this bleak circumstance the fates of the two lovely girls illustrated. The destiny of

Little Cui is introduced earlier.[①] The other girl, Sun Ling, is the daughter of the second son of the matriarch who nevertheless had passed away (the story implies that her father quits his office as a result of his unfulfilled dream due to the Japanese occupation, because he had informed Sun Ling his will to rejuvenate the weak country). She loves study, yet her educational and career plan is sabotaged by the Japanese occupation. The current curriculum she learns from school is mainly on Japanese cuisine to meet the Japanese promotion of "wise wife, good mother." The message of "new women" ideal is also asserted through her realization that only self-reliance and spirit of endurance can help women in times of hardship. Compared with Little Cui, who is illiterate, the destiny of this "new (intellectual) woman" is more unascertained.

### 五、From Concerns over the "New Women" to the Subaltern

As noted, throughout the colonial period the writer "implicitly argues that the social turmoil that epitomized Chinese life in Manchukuo was induced by Japanese colonialism and patriarchy."[②] The writer would pay more and more attention to the social politics that caused the women's issue in the latter period, but even in her earlier career, she had already had sensitive attention to it. *An Evening's Comedy* (《傍晚的喜剧》), an early story included in *The Second Generation*, for instance, is a farce that exposes the "abnormal" reality of the colonial society that divests the citizens of their sense of dignity.

The title as well as the content of the story reminds us of Lu Xun's famed piece *The Comedy of a Duck* (《鸭的喜剧》), in which a Russian poet raises tadpoesl, but they are all eaten by ducks. The comedy of ducks is the

---

① What has not been mentioned is that when she is assigned by her father to take care of the matriarch Grandma, she has also been coveted or admired by the enfeebled Xiang, who himself is a married man.

② Smith, N., *Resisting Manchukuo: Chinese Women Writers and the Japanese Occupation*, Toronto: University of British Columbia Press, 2007:80.

tragedy of the tadpoles. What it conveys is the weak falling victim to the strong. A vicarious expression of social Darwinism through an allegorical scene, Lu Xun delivers his idea of the importance of self-strengthening of the weak in a ruthless society against the bullying powerful. The similarity of the titles suggests that Mei Niang probably had got her inspiration from the literary master. What she narrates now is a comic episode happened in the colonial society in which the colonized subjects drag out a life without dignity, taking ignoble farce as its daily routine.

The happenings take place in a laundry and in the street. In the beginning, Little Sanzi, an apprentice in a family laundry shop, is scolded by the hostess for his ineptness. He is deeply appreciative of his Korean colleague, a feminine youth and the favorite of the matriarch, who diverts the latter's attention thus absolves the punishment that he would receive. But Little Sanzi is soon forced to leave off his duty again by the matriarch's son to go to the street helping the latter study the skill of driving bike. In the street, the naughty boy has fun with a flirting lady, who returns the mockery to the son by intimating that his mother keeps illegitimate lovers. When the son is about to lose his tantrum, his father Master Wang joins the farce by endeavoring to seduce the attractive woman. At the moment, the hostess arrives with the Korean boy. Witnessing what has happened, in front of the gathering public looking for fun, she vehemently rebukes her husband, scolds the woman, and orders Little Sanzi to go home serving the Korean boy, who is very tired.

There are a lot of concealed messages in the text which make it filled with allegorical connotation. The person who runs throughout the scene is the matriarch, who might be seen as typifying the traditional-styled patriarchal power, as she owns all its main features: keeping extramarital lovers (the Korean boy is probably insinuated to be one of her lovers), being harsh to the lower and subordinated class, arbitrarily managing business, and obsequiously cooperating with and ingratiating the Japanese. The last of which is revealed by her peculiar relations with the colonizers: she can freely enter the latter's headquarters. But this is done by her sending the Korean boy as a gift to the Japanese to satisfy their lust (in Manchuria, many

Korean residents were simultaneously the target of the Japanese). Under her shadow, her husband, the nominal Master Wang, appears incompetent and ludicrous who only knows of seducing women.

The chaotic and farcical ending gives a vivid, symbolic picture of the colonial Manchurian society. The Japanese are the invisible yet omnipresent dark force in the subtext. Under this gigantic shadow, the Chinese as well as all the other nations in the land live a pitiable life. For the middle-class residents, in particular, their ignoble living state shows itself as the inheritance of degenerate traditional conventions and practice which goes hand in hand with an intricate intercourse with the Japanese for favor. The title "an evening's comedy" can be simultaneously translated as "a farce during the sunset," which gives us more hints about its allegorical nature with a political significance.

In the period between she settled down in Beijing in 1942 and the surrender of the Japanese in 1945, Mei Niang's concerns over the destiny of "new women" were unabated. But while she insisted on this agenda, in her objective observation of the real happenings of the society, we see the metamorphosis of the image of "new women." Meanwhile, towards the later period, she broadened her horizon to look into the dignity of the subaltern, joining her feminist stance with the humanitarian inclination towards those suffering masses lived under the life standard of the proto-bourgeois ladies. This new move then sharpens the edge of her critical realism.

*Dwarf* (《侏儒》) from a first-person female narrator's perspective transcribes the tragic life of a dwarf. He is a bastard of her landlord and his mistress. But neither did the enfeebled landlord protect his mistress nor is he responsible for the dwarf who is his son. While the pitiable woman is beaten to death by the landlord's merciless wife, the son lives an abject life in the past ten more years and is subjected to all kinds of prejudice and abuse. He appears ugly and foolish to other persons, nevertheless the narrator feels intimate with him and cares for him tenderly. His pubescent sexual instinct pushes him to touch her, which provokes her impulsive reaction that stuns him. Just before this intimate relation develops, unfortunately the dwarf is attacked by a mad dog and dies on the site. A humiliated and injured boy, he is essentially murdered by the web of the dark society and the ignorant people. In this touching piece the author combines her feminist concerns (over the destiny of vulnerable women) with the destiny of the oppressed and the downtrodden showing that the two issues are closely related, which makes it come close to leftist writings and humanitarian perspective.

*Difficulty in the Road*（《行路难》）(1943) is also a story reminiscent of the writings of leftist writers. It records the psychological metamorphosis of a woman returning home from a banquet in a night. She is scared by a barking dog, and helped by a man to evade it. But immediately she takes this man as a threat as he is seemingly following her. Finding no assistance from a cart driver who is haste to return home and insulted by a drunkard who mistakes her to be a "street angel" (prostitute), she feels that she falls into a desperate situation. The man rebukes her misunderstanding of him, which apparently hurts his sense of dignity. He defends himself as a "civilized man," reproaching the narrator as a woman who "merely knows drinking, card playing, watching movie, and engaging in love," and squanders money for senseless feelings (to avoid the supposed danger, she has promised ten dollars to the cart-driver) but does not know the amount of money would assist a family in which food is not guaranteed and a daughter is seriously ill. To express his indignant sentiment, he claims that he had no intention to rob her, now he takes away her money as he supposes this would not be much harmful to her. In the meantime, he throws her something he holds and asks her to see what destitute men eat everyday. After he leaves, a cart belatedly arrives. The narrator finds that what he throws to her is a dirty peanut cake, which is still demanded by the cart driver who takes it as what the narrator incidentally found in the street. She simultaneously finds a note in the paper enveloping the cake, which indicates that the man is a primary school teacher, and the cake is what he can find for his ill daughter. Feeling incompetent and desperate, he is going to commit suicide. The narrator feels a little solace because her money might help the man temporarily cancel his plan of ending his life.

The story reminds us of Lu Xun's story *A Little Matter* （《一件小事》）, which narrates how a little good deed did by a cart driver made the narrator

realize the kindness of the oppressed subaltern. By contrast, this story
focuses on the dignity of the latter, and "exposes" the superficial and
egocentric lifestyle of the middle-class "new women." If Lu Xun's story
belongs to the category of revolutionary realism, this piece is fundamentally
a critical realistic writing—through a humanitarian concern, it demonstrates
the spirit of liberal humanism. It also shows that the author has tried to find
other unjust social phenomena in addition to the predicament of the "new
women," though she might not have found the intricate relations between
the two.

## 六、Conclusion

This chapter examines Mei Niang's fiction as a case study of the
writings by female writers in the Manchurian society during the period of
Japanese occupation. Living in the colonial society, as noted, the
Manchurian female writers "worked within a weighty regulatory framework
to map out careers, which ultimately undermined the state that staked claim
to their allegiance and sought to contour their self-identities." [1] The
endeavor might be consciously or unconsciously taken by a specific writer,
but undoubtedly that by a somewhat collective effort the female writers
flunked the Japanese agenda of resorting to the rhetoric of "good wife, wise
mother" to realize their intended goal of identification of the colonial identity
which they hoped to impose on the colonized subjects.

Due to the limitation of the living conditions and lack of available
sources offering inspirational political analysis of the social malaise, the
writers' ideal of "new women" that "advocated women's dominion over their
bodies, relationships, and careers," [2] has also certain shortsightedness.
Oftentimes the female writers believed that "women in this society

---

[1]   Smith, N., *Resisting Manchukuo: Chinese Women Writers and the Japanese Occupation*, Toronto: University of British Columbia Press, 2007: xiv.

[2]   Smith, N., *Resisting Manchukuo: Chinese Women Writers and the Japanese Occupation*, Toronto: University of British Columbia Press, 2007: 14.

experience a great deal of suffering and pain that men can't imagine … Only women can change this world into heaven."[①] The cause for women's sufferings was rightfully attributed to the "male chauvinist society"（男权社会）, but the narrative usually did not go further to diagnose the deep roots, the structural overdeterminations of the semi-traditional society and the colonial state apparatus. In short, they staged a feminist critique of the colonial society, which was both valid and effective in terms of its sharp exposure and denunciation of the patriarchal society undergirded by the colonial supra-structure and its conservative ideological framework; and pallid and inefficient in terms of diagnosing the real cause of the "women's problem" and ways to overturn and eradicate the social-political as well as economic roots of the social malaise. As a result, they often attribute the "women's problem" to "men" as a gender issue. But we also see that when Mei Niang with her humanitarian spirits combines the feminist discourse with an analysis of political economy, or the universal rhetoric with concrete social-historical reference, the writings become a sharper weapon bearing more critical edge to fulfill potential and aimed goal of women's liberation.

This argument can be examined from another perspective. Mei Niang's writings look into the state of the New Culture enlightenment in the 1940s. The exposure of the moral degeneration of the various "New Youths" reveals the historical predicament of the May Fourth New Culture project (including the "new woman" ideal) that the writer was persistently in pursuit of. The sympathetic description of extramarital relation shows that the subject matter related to "free love" has extended from the May Fourth struggle for the individual right of choosing one's own lover into a farther area related to the interior arena of intimate emotions and relations, an area closely related to the middle-class world. Because the various characters in the writer's world (compared with the characters in Eileen Chang's fiction) have the potential to reach the state of middle-class women (thanks to the

---

① The words were articulated in a letter, written in 1942, to a fellow Manchuria female writer Wu Ying (1915-1961). It was published in Xinjing (now Changchun). 梅娘：《寄吴英书》,《青年文化》,1943(1):84.

relative stability and developed rationalization process of the colonial society), they own more the fantasies of realizing the middle-class dream of individualism and "new women" ideal (which then constitutes a sharp contrast to Eileen Chang who held a cynical attitude towards the same issues), but the colonial state's policy sabotaged this hope. While the reservation over and the critique of the puppet-state's conservatism adds to their knowledge of the women's problem, when the writers broaden their horizon and ties in this concern with the social network, including the subaltern, a more comprehensive picture is unfolded and a more poignant critique of the colonial society presents itself.

# Chapter Eight　Making a Historical Fable: The Narrative Strategy of *Lust*, *Caution* and Its Social Repercussions

## 一、Introduction

In the year of 2008, the screening of the film *Lust*, *Caution*, which was directed by the renowned director Ang Lee based on his understanding and rendition of Eileen Chang's story produced in the year of 1950, created a big stir, arousing clamorous, heated debates across ranks of the society that lasted more than half a year, making it one of the most sensational cultural events in the year. Indeed, the film is quite unusual in many aspects. To begin with, its reception in the East and the West was vastly different: while its gross in the Chinese world (Chinese mainland, Hong Kong and Taiwan) was huge, it did not receive enthusiastic reception in the United States.[①] The Women Film Critics Circle (WFCC) even ranked it as one of the "Top

---

①　It premiered at the Venice Film Festival on Aug. 30, 2007 and won the Golden Lion Award(Chinese director Zhang Yimou was the jury president). Despite only a heavily-edited version being screened, thanks to its successful prescreening advertisement campaign which publicizes the sex scenes, the film was a huge success in Chinese mainland and grossed $17,109,185 USD, making it the country's third highest-grossing domestic production film of 2007. (See "2007 China Yearly Box Office Results." http://www. boxofficemojo. com/intl/china/yearly/? yr = 2007&p =. htm. Accessed Feb. 1, 2008.) However, its gross in the US was disappointing. It was rated NC-17 and never played at more than 143 theatres in its entire US run and eventually grossed $4,604,982. (See "Top Grossing NC-17 Rated Movies at the Box Office." http://www. boxofficemojo. com/alltime/domestic/mpaa.htm? page=NC−17&p=.htm. Accessed Feb.1, 2008.)

Ten Hall of Shame" of the year，with a derogatory comment "Adam and Eve
in Old Shanghai. Female-assisted destruction of a nation while falling in love
with torturer/rapist."[1] Ang Lee himself，although had premonition of the
difference in box offices, expressed surprise at such a vast gap，and
attributed it to the fact that Americans lack the experience of being occupied
by a foreign regime and hence do not have the concomitant empathetic
feelings. Moreover，it is even controversial as to what the proper genre
should the film be defined：is it an espionage thriller，an art film，or a film
noir? Many film critics made conjectures and had differing opinions.[2]

The only thing that is apparently doubtless is that it is a wartime
melodrama，though the disclosure of the secrets of the filmic content (which
is premised on repeat viewings and freeze-framings) would reveal that its
subtlety and sophistication to the seemingly pulpy themes，with its
extremely lush yet apparently languorous style，are as much the result of its
ambition to be an art film as its intention to make a film noir allegorizing the
historical maelstrom of modern China.

Although many overseas (mostly Chinese) critics hailed the film as a
success that ingeniously deconstructed patriotism,[3] in Chinese mainland it
received vehement critique. However，this critique was articulated not in
mainstream media，but in Internet，and most of which was couched on
nationalist rhetoric. In a domestic poll taken in the cyberspace，the ratio of
the supporters and the opponents to the ban，contrary to what we might
have expected，reached more than 2：1.[4] This quantitative data makes a
sharp contrast to the overwhelmingly positive appreciation of the film in the

---

[1]    See the website of this Association，http：//wfcc. wordpress. com/women-film-
critic-circle-awards-2007/ .Accessed Feb 1，2008.

[2]    See the comments in the famed website of film review "Rotten Tomatoes."
http：//www. rottentomatoes.com/m/lust_caution/ .Accessed Feb 1，2008.

[3]    For instance，see two articles by Chen Xiangyin and Song Jiafu，published in
*Reflexion*(《思想》)，a famed journal in Taiwan，No.8，2008.

[4]    On March 22，the poll reaches around 20,734：9,261，with altogether 29,995
people participated. See http：//comment2. news. sohu. com/255572601/d66587862. html.
Accessed March 22，2008. None of the elite media ever reports the result of this poll.

elite circle. Why this interesting phenomenon?

In this chapter, I will argue that insofar as the filmic content brings about conflicting and contradictory discourses that were subjected to different appropriation for differing purposes, the intricate representation of its cinematic text and the complex reactions of the social context together constitute a rich cultural politics to be deciphered. Through an analysis of the narrative strategy of the film, this chapter argues that, for its specific nature as a rare genre of political film noir, such elements as character designment, plot motivation, and narrative mode, through the mechanism of operation as projection, displacement, and appropriation, interact with and reinforce one another in prescribed ways, which altogether postulate a specific internal order that is underwritten with a particular historical conception and world view. This narrative strategy informs the human experience represented in the work. I suggest that only through this meticulous dissection, can we understand why there were so many diversified, and even antagonistic, audience responses in the Chinese world; furthermore, these contestations themselves show the existence of heterogeneous voices in the society that were competing for cultural hegemony in contemporary China.

## 二、A Précis of the Surface Plotline

A synopsis of the story can hardly explicate all the complicated, multilayered plots, it is still indispensable for our analysis to be unfolded. In the year of 1939, Wong Chia-chi, a transferring first-year college student in Hong Kong and a refugee from Shanghai, was introduced to an acting troupe consisting of college students led by Kuang Yu-min. Kuang Yu-min invited her to join them to put on a patriotic play to rouse morale and gather donations for the resistance efforts, which came out as a stunning success.

However, Kuang Yu-min wanted to achieve more to kill a would-be collaborator Mr Yee. He asked Wong Chia-chi to assume a persona Mrs Ma to worm her way into his confidence. Mr Yee was a defector from the KMT's quarter Chungking, now hiding in Hong Kong preparing for the establishment of the collaboration government. Their plan failed when it just began as soon Mr Yee returned to the hinterland to assume his official service in the regime now set up there.

The film then flashes ahead to 1941. and now we are in Shanghai. Kuang Yu-min, now recruited to be an agent of the KMT government, approaches Wong Chia-chi again. She was brought to an Old Wu, the underground organizer. He demands her to get reinstated in the life and bed of Mr Yee, who now is in charge of secret polices.

Instead of assuming a femme-fatale role, she is first raped and then tortured chronically by Mr Yee. Despite physically and emotionally torn and bleeding, and even though she knows that he betrays his country and executes many resistant fighters, she apparently falls in love with him. In the last moment which is ostensibly an assassination scene, when she sees Mr Yee presenting her a 6-carat diamond with a caring gaze, she blurts out: "Go. Go away quickly." Mr Yee runs downstairs, jumping into his car and slips away. Mrs Mak and her coteries are arrested and executed. But their boss Old Wu, together with his two gunmen, is out of the net.

### 三、Projection of Social Institutions in Historical Representation

There are two parallel love tales that are played out and ultimately meet fatefully together, which are intricately layered, both concealing their most explosive secrets. When examined closely, not only does the scenario of love stories contain a discourse of love that is attached to a particular ideology, but the fable itself is formulated with layers of projection.

The first tale is Wong Chia-chi's emotional attachment to Kuang Yu-min, the idealistic youth; however, instead of developing this passion into a romantic story, Kuang Yu-min forfeits her virginity to the only member of the group who has sexual experience (picked up from hookers), to prepare her to be the paramour of Mr Yee. What is more, three years later he asks her again to reprise the role in their resumed, first meeting. He is too patriotic to be a genuine lover, and so persistent as to willingly use any foul means. By the same token, Wong Chia-chi's acceptance of the arrangement is also much more amenable to the explanation of her own patriotic passion, than the possibility that she loves Kuang Yu-min so much that volitionally follows his will. Patriotism, or the nationalist resistance, drives these people to make cruel and inhuman decisions, which is more than false and ridiculous; for it not only finally proves futile, but also destroys the sprout of genuine love between the couple.

As this plot is based on the historical experience of modern China rather than any ahistorical fairy tale, the scenario itself is subjected to a discussion vis-a-vis the historical probability itself.[①] Put in another way, even though it is a film that is "twice removed, as it were, from an unrecoverable historical experience," as "a fictionalized treatment of an ideological version of past events," it "must nevertheless be judged according to its fidelity to history."[②] Here, "the criterion of historical truth" is "important because, as many discussions about the value of art and literature show, audience often respond to works literally as reality."[③] From this perspective, the story

---

[①]　Insofar as the virginity of a female body is always regarded by the Chinese people as the symbol of integrity, sanctity and dignity of the mother country (just like anywhere in the world), however, this disgraceful action of mercilessly stripping a compatriot's virginity would, by itself, violate the token of sacred national interests. In the mean time, both the historical facts of the Chinese society of the period (which show it to be more sex-enlightened than we might expect) and the literary tradition of the era are at odds with this anti-mainstream narration.

[②]　Feuerwerker, Y. M., *Ding Ling's Fiction: Ideology and Narrative in Modern Chinese Literature*, Cambridge, Mass, and London: Harvard University Press, 1982:139.

[③]　Feuerwerker, Y. M., *Ding Ling's Fiction: Ideology and Narrative in Modern Chinese Literature*, Cambridge, Mass, and London: Harvard University Press, 1982:139.

might appear barely credible in reality in consideration of the historical experience,[①] as some critics have pointed out. These critics believe that this plot is not a "realistic" one in terms of either the "poetic truth" or the "historical truth" of the Aristotelian categories.[②]

But a historically "unrealistic" plot is not totally irrelevant, for we can study it in terms of its narrative strategy and the message it meant to send forth.[③] This rite of sexual initiation introduced by a rogue-like figure, which is showed vividly in minute details, is not devised to be a spy comedy, as some critics have surmised. Rather, to substantiate the probability, the film offers another elusive thread of plots, with the only other girl in the group, Lai Xiujing, as the protagonist. She loves Kuang Yu-min secretly, yet the latter never has feelings for her. Many shots in the film present her in the

---

①　The cinematic plot comes from the original short story, yet the writer Eileen Chang herself has claimed that as early as in her teens, she had been familiar with traditional Chinese pornographic novels and knew adult matters. Meanwhile, ever since the May Fourth Movement (1919), and especially in the 1930s, the enlightenment efforts by the intellectuals had also brought about a "sexual revolution" by helping the society to be familiar with "sexually enlightenment" pamphlets, if not sheer pornographic fiction, by writers like the nicknamed "doctor of sex" Zhang Jingshen (1888-1970) and "triangle affairs expert" Zhang Ziping (1893-1959). Moreover, for Kuang Yu-min's restraint towards love, modern China's literary history and historical record would also offer quite a different picture: before the period depicted in this film (late 1930s) and ever since the middle of 1920s, for a whole decade the stories with the so-called "revolution plus love formula" were prevalent, which exerted great influence on the youths; many of whom, because of that influence, went to pursue the revolutionary path. This is especially true after the outbreak of the full-scaled Resistance War in 1937. Here the film adopts an anti-mainstream narrative—the latter being the staple of the works from both the Nationalist persuasion and the Communist one—for its thematic purpose.

②　See Aristotle, *Poetics*, Oxford: Clarendon Press, 1968.

③　Allegedly the plot of the original story was derived from a hearsay that the writer Eileen Chang had acquired from her husband about a similar silly action practiced by patriotic students in Beijing. But as her husband is a collaborationist who was hostile to, if not directly suppressed, the anti-Japanese resistance, the hearsay cannot by itself be taken for granted as historical fact. Furthermore, the incident, even if it is true—which is scarcely possible—was too rare to assess any typicalities.

same frames with Wong Chia-chi, in which her complexion always seems to show a genuine care to the latter. Yet only from the film script can we know clearly the implied storyline: because Kuang Yu-min is attracted to Wong Chia-chi, she then sets all the traps for the latter throughout—including instigating this initial act of sacrificing her virginity (in order to deprive her opportunity of acquiring Yu-min's love), and furthermore implicating her into the new job again three years later. In all, it appears that this treacherous person is the cardinal figure responsible for the tragedy.

However, as Lai Xiujing's nice complexion disguises her intention, and so the impression the audience gets is that she is not evil at all in her nature, at most the only blamable entity inside of her is her vanity and desire to win Kuang Yumin's love. Put in another way, even for those smarter viewers who have perceived Lai Xiujing's evil scheme, compared with the vulnerable humanity itself (she did it for her love!), it is still patriotism that is the key to this Paradise Lost: only due to blind passion, the students accept her vicious proposal; and only because of Wong Chia-chi's vanity, she consents to it.

This discourse of human nature, or the correlation between inhumanity and patriotism, can be subjected to an examination through narratology. The decipherment of the political as well as aesthetic encryption embedded in these cinematic details requires the decoding of another shocking scene: after their first attempt ends up fruitless, Mr Yee's lackey Old Cao threatens the students with exposure. The extortion results in an impulsive, awful murder: they take turns stabbing him with seven knives, but still cannot end his life. Then Kuang Yu-min miraculously remembers some knack and twists off Cao's neck in one blow. Who teaches him this execution skill? This protracted, brutal murder scene poses a big enigma, which not only puzzles many ordinary audience, but also perplexes some seasoned film critics, "Where did that come from? Who knew he had it in him? What does it mean?" Eric Snider is amazed and eager to know.[1]

As a symbolic ritual, this extraordinary scene is intended to work as

---

[1] Snider, E. D., "Review." http://www. ericdsnider. com/movies/lust-caution/. Accessed March 21, 2008.

another initiation rite into the horrific, atrocious political world—so that the
director admits, the design of this horrible scene is "to expose the horrors of
violence, to show that once the patriotic students cruelly murder a people,
they unrelentingly follow a path that would slaughter numerous innocent
peoples."① Notwithstanding its apparent narrative purpose, the scene itself
has a fissure that could hardly be sutured by the narrative, which also
unexpectedly answers the lingering doubt: the cruel execution rite, to the
extent that it could only be carried out with a skill derived from special
training, would only be possible from an experienced agent, but scarcely
possible from these innocent, idealistic youths: the horrible scene is only
made out of a mechanism of projection.

But there is still a second layer of projection in the narration. Many of
the Western audience complained that Wong Chia-chi's moral inspirations
into the scheme are as unelaborated as the cruel crimes of the collaborator
Mr Yee against his homeland.② But for the latter, the film does offer an
explanation, which appears as a tangential remark uttered by Mr Yee's wife
in the mah-jong party, in which she laments: "I said to Old Yee, your
government (the collaborationist regime) could not even put on a
presentable show: no matter how many good deeds you have done for the
people, they would not buy what you have done for them." They feel greatly
wronged, because the Chinese people in the occupied area, constrained by
narrowed nationalist sentiments, do not appreciate their kind intentions
while accepting their offers of protection.

As well known, this ratiocination itself was the staple excuse of the
collaborationists. We will not evaluate it per se, but will go on to tease out
the layered secretes of the cinematic texture. In terms of the narrative itself,
the decryption of the protracted mah-jong scene in which this statement is
uttered will contribute to our comprehension of the cinematic information it
gives off—although only through a word-to-word anatomy of the gossip as
well as their facial expressions by technically slowing them down, can we

---

① 郑培凯:《色戒的世界》,广西师范大学出版社 2007 年版.

② This was expressed in the numerous reviews in *Rotten Tomatoes*.

get the message the characters communicate: most of these ladies have affairs with Mr Yee, Mrs Yee not only knows about these affairs, but conspires to bring them about, including the one with Mrs Mak.[①]

These privileged, powdered and pampered wives of the collaborators slap down the mah-jong tiles to relieve their boredom. Their suffering under the occupation is minimal, unlike those countrymen starving in the streets as one or two shots show (which meant to remind us that survival was the utmost concern at the time). These mah-jong scenes suggest their politics pertain to the preservation of their lifestyles. They (these ladies and their husbands) are classified as the Chinese comprador class, a section of the privileged upper-level bourgeois class that was metamorphosed from traditional landowning gentry class, the latter of which formed the crucial component of modern Chinese middle class developing the capitalist mode of modernity in modern China.

When examined in this angle, the game between Mr Yee and Mrs Mak, essentially the bourgeois play of adultery, would yield new knowledge for our appreciation of the story. Here, it is not that Wong Chia-chi plays the two tenuous halves of her personality, but she is now entrapped in a changed identity: one is a patriotic, petit-bourgeois student; the other is a middle-class leisure lady trying to become a member in the aristocratic circle. When she is unable to distinguish her real self from the fictional one, she has misplaced her body and her psyche in a class that she does not belong to, and her true nature is distorted by the role she is assigned.

Thus said, the three sexual episodes in the film are worthy of further analysis. The coarse, explicit rape is shockingly presented to us when we are

---

① Here it is no space for me to give a full account of the words and subtle countenance of these ladies fighting for the affections of Mr Yee. But a Chinese e-friend with a nick name "Spanish eyes" has done an excellent job in this respect. See his analysis in "The Secrets of Mrs Yee," posted in the website http://cache.tianya.cn/publicforum/content/filmtv/1/211079.shtml. Accessed Feb 3, 2008. Meanwhile, various actresses playing these ladies also confirm this point in their interviews or personal blogs. See, for instance, an entry of Joan Chen's (who plays Mrs Yee) blog at http://blog.sina.com.cn/s/blog_48fbb60e01000bkw.html (accessed Feb 23, 2008), which affirms this fact.

lulled by the film's languid pace. But Mrs Mak seems to enjoy this, and a few days later when they meet again they immediately embrace each other, with Mr Yee lying down in her arm like a baby. As for the second sexual encounter to be followed immediately, Michael Wood has described it like this: it is "the visual set piece, with four pairs of limbs all over the place, as if the couple were trying to compose a difficult fleshly jigsaw puzzle rather than have sex." Roland Barthes' remark is quoted here to illustrate the theoretical puzzle: "Complexity of combinations, contortions of the partners, everything is beyond human nature."[1] The crosscutting between the lovemaking shots and shots of an open-eyed vigilant police dog can be read as conveying the message that sex is the most sensual enjoyment in a circumstance imbued with white terror, yet the parallel editing also helps the audience to read the intercourses as the most inhuman, bestial behavior at the time of national humiliation, both metaphorically and metonymically—and under the surveillance of an invisible force, just like the dog is being drawn by its master whose face is not shown.

The "jigsaw puzzles," which try to display the couple's respective attempts at gaining power, are also baffling in their effect on Mrs Mak. And so in the third sexual encounter showed in the film, when Mr Yee practices the missionary position, the film completes its goal of narration: a love is produced by, or emerged from, the raw sex—she falls in love with this cruel traitor in the face of the Grand Phallus. This worship of the patriarchal symbol of the Name of the Father initiates her, through a discourse of love, into the "symbol of order" of the traitors. Here, the key to the ultimate mystery (or rather, a myth) of "love" comes from an ideological core: she is turned on by his domineering fascist-aristocratic power-entitlement. The hieroglyph of the fetal curl, as well as the image of Grand Phallus, points to the fact that it is primitive passion, or lust, that finally counts. All the human's cultural adornments, and love as a genuine emotion, when measured with this "primitive pleasure," pale and are stripped away.

---

① Wood, M., At the movies: *Lust*, *Caution*, *London Review of Books*, 2008, 30 (2):31.

This discourse of love takes power-play as love potions that lead to lust, but not love as a romantic emotion. Nonetheless, since this experience sickens Mrs Mak to the core as she complains bitterly to her boss, and she is informed by her director that under the same situation Mr Yee had killed two other women spies, her headlong plunge into love with the devil is hardly persuasive.

As an ideological effect, this discourse of love was popular in a certain period and among certain class strata, which points to love as a historically conditioned (and so historically ever-changing) social, cultural, and finally psychological institution. A patriotic petit-bourgeois girl Wong Chia-chi can hardly "fall in love" with a collaborator, no matter whether she physically enjoys sex or not, but a middle-class lady Mrs Mak, without much nationalistic consciousness, might do that. But since change in class consciousness (from Wong Chia-chi's to Mrs Mak's) needs years of habituation, not by a sudden metamorphosis (thus some critics have pointed out that the delicate flirtation with and intricate seduction of Mr Yee by Mrs Mak is unrealistic, given the latter's real identity as a lower-level, naïve fille),[①] this scenario of love is not only "just a movie" for its thematic purpose, but also constitutes the second layer of projection.

## 四、Displacement of Party Politics by Sexual Politics

When the film's brooding meditation on the unnerving power and terrible cost of emotional (and political) masquerades finally exposes its authentic concern, it will show the sex politics of loyalty and betrayal is only a displacement of the national (party) politics, which is accomplished through setting up multiple moralistic paradoxes.

Like Wong Chia-chi, the erstwhile idealist Kuang Yu-min has two widely differing identities. While his sacrifice of Wong Chia-chi when he was a progressive student is hardly credible, when he is assimilated into the KMT's secret agency, he assumes a new personality. In face of the tough

---

① For instance, see Wood, M., At the movies: *Lust*, *Caution*, *London Review of Books*, 2008,30(2):31.

Old Wu, who requires Wong Chia-chi's blind allegiance to unreservedly play her sex-toy role, he often remains silent (though protests once, but when he is reproached, he recoils). He can not help her, but also feels a mix of guilt and jealousy. Although, from a veiled plot which is only deducible from their ambiguous dialogue in the phone-call, finally he bursts out by planning the fateful sabotage without permission from his boss to release her burden, with the cooperation of Wong Chia-chi. He is not loyal anymore, for his love of Wong Chia-chi he betrays the inhuman order of the domestic regime.

For the heroine, there is also a paradox of loyalty and betrayal. She deludes herself by living an illusory life, and gets lost in this simulated role. But this is an argument for the sake of the storyline. In the original story by Eileen Chang, Mrs Mak never loves Mr Yee, but only in the last moment's psychological turmoil she mistakenly takes Mr Yee's care as a gesture of love. And Mr Yee believes she must hate him in the execution site. The re-creation in the film again invites deeper consideration of the concept of the "realistic," both in the sense of faithful to the probable and faithful to the historical fact, and reminds us of the film's idiosyncratic narrative strategy, which is pertaining to its ideological theme.

Like Wong Chia-chi, Mr Yee is also playing roles within roles. Extremely guarded and suspicious, he figured out her real identity immediately after their association. Though, turned on by her lust, he veils his sadistic impulses behind a pretense of propriety. With the true nature of a political chameleon due to his fear of terror imposed by the Japanese invaders as well as the underground resistors, he also clandestinely flirts with top KMT leaders. Meanwhile, his opponent Old Wu, who seemingly suppresses all his feelings except a passionate devotion to the cause, in fact is also not loyal to his mission. He hates Mr Yee to the marrow because of a family feud. When he receives the petition from Kuang Yu-min to supervise Mrs Mak's meeting with Mr Yee, he immediately realizes that Kuang Yu-min wishes to kill Mr Yee to relieve his lover. As this is a good chance to take revenge without shouldering the responsibility, he not only agrees to the plan, but also offers Kuang Yu-min two gunmen.

Many teasing layers of guile, secrecy, and cool impersonation played out here are not merely for the sake of the genre of espionage, but correlate closely with their thematic purposes which design these many moral riddles in the first place. The whole story leaves us the impression that loyalty or betrayal is never a black and white question, but this deliberately bewildering arrangement of plots has led many uninformed critics to complain that the story calls "for a powerful nation to depend on a young, inexperienced woman to help win a war."[①] The complaints are due to a lack of historical knowledge of modern China during the Anti-Japanese War, when China was by no means a powerful nation, as well as a want for knowledge of the war strategies that the KMT government had adopted, which relied on a weak regular army. Without proper education, their soldiers were drafted from poor villagers by coercion and force, and to prevent them from escaping they were often chained together during this process; therefore the army often lacked military efficiency. It also should be noted that it is for the same reason that Wang Jingwei (1883-1944), who led the KMT deserters to pursue the so-called "Peace Movement" and set up the collaborationist government, fell into desperation when he saw the KMT crack troop hopelessly defeated in the first few months after the full-scale war unraveled.

Another similarity shared by these two factions is that they put apivotal emphasis on the role of the secret service to assassinate their political enemies. In the movie the impudent means taken on by the KMT side are illustrated with vivid details (though the message is only conveyed very subtly). Historically, they recruited inexperienced citizens (such as those unfledged college students) to assume dirty tasks (such as the badger game) and undertake assassinations that would require special long-term

---

① Review by Marcy Dermansky. http://worldfilm. about. com/od/chinesefilms/fr/lustcaution.htm. Accessed Feb 7, 2008.

*professional training*;[1] and often disregarded their safety and ruthlessly sacrificed their lives (Old Wu arranges his gunmen and himself to run away, while leaves the youth group there unattended). Thus we can understand why in an interview, the director said that in showing in these details the specific historical facts, the film expressed his disillusion with the politics of the KMT in the Resistance War that the KMT propaganda had imposed upon him during his childhood.[2]

While exposing this dirty history, the film leaves out showing the torture and executions of patriotic resisters performed by the collaborators. Instead, as noted, it shows that Mr Yee takes care of his work dutifully, politely drops in to greet the guests, and has no interests in money.[3] It makes us feel sympathy for a man whose schizoid nature is but an outcome of the grim political circumstances, a man whose cruelty is almost dissolved by the cool and subtle humanity he shows now and then. In a nutshell, he is at worst a pitiable victim of the inclement era, rather than a shameless traitor and merciless executioner.

His redefection to the KMT side means to emphasize this point: the motivation is revealed by the confession he admits to Mrs Mak, "When the war with the American began, they (the Japanese) knew the War would soon come to an end." The US declared its war with Japan on September 10, 1942 following the Pearl Harbor Incident. Mr Yee feels his doomsday approaching. The syuzhet of the film happens in one day Oct. 27, 1942, as the signature of the document Mr Yee signs for the execution of the resistors indicates. It was the second day of the battle of the Santa Cruz Islands, when the Americans won a decisive war.

What this narrative detail subtly conveys is that, it is the meddling of

---

① For historical background, see Frederic, W. Jr., *The Shanghai Badlands: Wartime Terrorism and Urban Crime*, 1937-1941, Cambridge: Cambridge University Press, 1996; and Brook, T., *Collaboration: Japanese Agents and Local Elites in Wartime China*, Cambridge, Mass: Harvard University Press, 2005.

② The interview was conducted in Chinese in a TV program by TVG, dated Oct. 27, 2007.

③ 张系国:《政治不正确的老易》,《中国日报》,2007 年 11 月 11 日.

the Americans, rather than China's resistant efforts, that transforms the fate of the originally doomed resistance, and as a consequence also the mind of Mr Yee. If the Japanese had not attacked Peal Harbor, the Americans probably would not intervene and there would be no chance for China to win the Resistance War; and so the ensuing implied message that the "Peace Movement" efforts would appear more patriotic, as the latter prevented China from being ruled by the Japanese and let the country still be ruled by them as "Chinese." Who would know that contingent incidents would unexpectedly change the course of history? "When I review that period of history, a word always comes into my mind: fear…Man's calculation is never comparable to the nature's mystery," the director lamented in the same interview conducted in Los Angeles.[①]

Thus we can understand why there are so many "moral riddles" here—ultimately they come from this historical belief, and why the fear of Mr. Yee would metamorphose into a sadist/masochist drama. It does not mean that Yee is either emotionally or physically ineffective, but only alludes to the death of his soul. When Mr Yee throws out the confession: "I know better than you how to be a whore," in responding to Mrs Mak's remarks that he wants to keep her as a harlot, he is disclosing his true nature. However, compared with the ending of the original story, when the writer has Mr Yee allude to a phrase to pinpoint the relationship between him and Mrs Mak (now dead): "Alive, Wong Chia-chi is his woman; dead, she is his ghost"; which apparently underscores his inexorable cruelty, the finale of the film does not stage Mr Yee as a dead man who was psychologically raped and killed by the Japanese, but represents him as dying for love: after he signs the execution document, he steps into the room reserved for Mrs Mak, sits on the bed caressing the velvety sheet. When the bell rings, he steps out, tears in eyes, and sentimentally pays a last tribute to the bed: his shadow is cast on it—symbolically he becomes the ghost of Mrs Mak.

If we do not take in the political rhetoric of the collaborators, the film

---

① The interview was conducted in Chinese in a TV program by TVG, dated Oct. 27, 2007.

might not be read as delivering a special patriotic message. And, when in the execution scene the camera cranes up in a dizzying speed to show the depthless cavern the resistors face in a kneeling gesture and are howling to meet their destiny, and when the voice-over from the screen in the theater during the rendezvous between Kuang Yu-min and Mrs Mak urges us: "Sister, let us go home. Mother is still waiting for us." "How can you be here?!", the message that it enforces upon us is also clear. But the ostensible tragic love story to certain extent glosses over its ulterior motive, whereas what is easily neglected is that its emphasis is placed less on Kuang Yu-min's unfulfilled love (as a strong emotion of regard and affection), than on Mrs Mak and Mr Yee's consummated lust (as fundamentally animalistic instinct). In this story about transformation—by war, politics, and sex—the sexual politics played out communicates, or rather, displaces, passionate ideological commitments, which are fundamentally underwritten with a class-based party politics.

This politics is class-bound and is furthermore suggested by the film's representation of the role that women assumed in the War in particular, and in the society in general. Around the time that Mrs Mak works as an erotic spy in Mr Yee's bed, Old Wu sends two other female agents to seduce Mr Yee, but they are found out, raped and executed; according to Old Wu, they are even forced to submit a long name-list. This plot already transmits the message that women could not play any constructive role in the resistance, as they have no intellect. Worse than this, Old Wu uses Mrs Mak just as a sex toy and does not count on her to earn valuable information. Mrs Mak's weakness and lack of intellect cost many lives. This conservative misogyny extends to the cardinal plot. Mr Yee gives her no reason to love him, but the actress gives a seemingly haunting expression to her conflictive feelings and sense of entrapment. In this perspective, Mrs Mak's seemingly strong will, as shown by her initiative towards performing intercourse and her remorseless countenance in the execution site, is only a patriarchal ruse.

The nature of this make-up could be more fruitfully explained by a real cultural difference, with two scenes underwritten with historically Chinese literary figures. One is a popular bard song sung by a girl accompanied by a one-string fiddle, in a tavern where the ladies meet. The song laments the destiny of an imperial concubine and an emperor in the Tang dynasty (618-906). The emperor was forced to order his concubine to commit suicide because he was threatened by his generals who believed it was the concubine who caused the national chaos, for the emperor was infatuated with her and neglected the governance of the country. To maintain his power and status, the emperor succumbed, on the pretext of sacrificing his concubine for the country. The film evokes this parallel reading to suggest that Mr Yee likewise has to sacrifice his beloved for his tough mission, as the woman is really a trouble. The other similar message could be found in the imagery (as a result of the mise-en-scene) in which Mr Yee embraces Mrs Mak in his arms and she offers him a song-dance—an image that recalls a famous moment out of Chinese history, when the Conqueror Xiang Yu (232 BC-202 BC) bid farewell to his concubine before she killed herself to avoid the trouble she would have inculpated him when he was entrapped.

This concept of love, as displayed in these two stories, requiring innocent women to willingly sacrifice their lives for powerful men, is a traditional (in the sense of being aristocratic or feudal), patriarchal ideology that the conservative regime had embraced: [1] Mrs Mak is sent to death by her master even though he "loves" her, and she never regrets—not to say hate, but feels self-assured and happy.

## 五、Appropriation of Historical Allegory through Identity Deconstruction

This insinuation of party politics finally points to the problematic of national identity, which is the ultimate crux of the movie. When Mr Yee buys a diamond for the heroine, she is confused, oscillating, and finally

---

① The KMT had promoted itself as the authentic inheritor of essential Chinese culture. The first image of Mrs Mak's thoughts of flashback is a close-up shot of Wong Chia-chi with her hair handsomely waving in the air, which is a typical aesthetic imaginary of the KMT's discourse of neo-traditionalism.

betraying her mission and her country. Her personal and national identities are shattered. This action itself, as well as the film in general, becomes a symbolism in which lust (rather than love) prevails.

The more important implication of this ideological message, however, is that it speaks to an idiosyncratic representation of history. As a film determined to be a microscopic mapping and allegorical rendition of modern China's history, there is another plotline in the movie which is deeply embedded in the text yet is rarely exposed. It involves the supply of ammunition, which is sent by the US to the KMT government as war time assistance and is intercepted by Mr Yee. In their meeting, Old Wu informs Mrs Mak that the Japanese are currently also inquiring about the whereabouts of it. Where is it? To whom does Yee give it? Right in the beginning of the movie, Mr Yee asks Secretary Zhang to kill the captured KMT spy before the Japanese interrogate him. Why does he try to kill the informant? Obviously he wants to keep some of his secrets.

The conundrum can only find its answer by a correlation with the historical experience as the subtext. When we examine all the existent forces at that time, this hidden force that covets weapons could be none other than the CCP army: The KMT's propaganda always portrayed the role of this power-force during the Resistance War as at best passively fought the Japanese, and at worst sabotaged the KMT's resistant efforts while actively strengthened itself. It is only from this perspective can we understand why the director states at the film's premiere in Japan, on Dec. 4, that, "The movie ostensibly is about the war between the Chinese and the Japanese; in the truth it is about the domestic war between the KMT and the CCP."[1] Cast in this light, the CCP, as the force behind the curtain, is the most treacherous historical actor: it sabotages the resistant efforts by secretly working with the traitors to steal away the advanced weapons the United States exports to the KMT government; it is due to the mission of ferreting out this vicious domestic enemy that Mrs. Mak as well as numerous KMT

---

[1]   This is from a news story reported in a Taiwan media. See the link http://www.im.tv/VLOG/Personal/236326/3235095. Accessed March 3, 2008.

agents sacrifice their lives.

As a standard picture offered by the cold-war narrative of conspiracy theory, this account itself, held by few historians today, is opened to debate and wants historical documents to certify. The partisan viewpoint aside, from this perspective, China's Anti-Japanese War was doomed to lose without American intervention; partly also because the resistant efforts of the two political powers (the KMT and the CCP) were both half-hearted, fooling their people yet dallying with the enemy. This narrative is indeed a far cry from the historiography of either the KMT's or the CCP's, and comes very close to the collaborationists'. But the allegorical dimension extends even further: besides the American assistance cued by the ammunition, the other global power at that time, the Soviet Union, is not left out here. There are rich verbal as well as visual hints throughout the film insinuating the Russian presence,[①] which imply that the Soviet Union is the black-hand meddling in China's politics that would lead to the civil war. Again, this is a traditional story provided by the cold-war rhetoric.

In a nutshell, these narrative details convey that in the turmoil of the country's political crisis, the dangerous game of deception is a dueling set of power plays. What is special in this particular narrative, however, is that the collaborators, such as Mr Yee, are only out of their league when it comes to locking horns with global geopolitical powers. As a victim of dirty domestic party politics and global geopolitical power-play, he has a tragic fate because he has to execute Mrs Mark whom he "loves": his secretary Zhang is assigned to oversee him and has known the identity of Mrs Mak for a long time and keeps close watch.[②] Like the tragic heroes in the two traditional Chinese imaginaries that I analyze, Mr Yee has to sacrifice his

---

① White Russian prostitutes walk around the street corners, two Russian chefs ostensibly look over Mrs Mak when she makes calls, etc.

② The agents in the diamond shop are not Kuang Yu-min's assassination group but are sent by him to safeguard Mr Yee's safety. As early as he sees Mrs Mak for the first time in Mr Yee's house, he suspects her—the film cues us with several single shots and two-shots (with Mrs Mak) of him—and sets off to investigate.

lover for a greater, sublime cause.

By presenting a "tragic" story of a collaborator and a traitor, this presumably ethnography intends to be a national allegory of the history of modern China, as well as a global allegory of the world political power-transactions played out in the country. For this motif, it presents an allegorical place in which the concepts of oppression and treason were tacked onto universal human needs like love and desire. But this is also why it fails to make the political goals of Mr Yee cogent and compelling, because its expression that irrational emotion wins out over tidy political abstraction is merely an ideologically preemptive motive that sets out to manipulate a barely plausible narrative to start with.

Furthermore, a closer examination of the cinematic texture reveals it much less a symbolism of the power of lust than an allegory of the failure of history. "The supersession of the symbol by the allegorical," Fredric Jameson informs us, "would thus dramatize the overcoming of some first naïve and representational immediacy...with a reflexivity that demystifies that immediacy and identifies its constituents as purely literary and linguistic realities."[1]

Allegory is the result of a process of reading. As Paul de Man says, it designates a temporal process: "In the world of allegory, time is the originary constitutive category."[2] In the film, the failure of history means the failure of the resistance efforts of both the populace (represented by the students) and the official regime (as Old Wu stands for the resistant endeavors of the KMT government). It even signifies the failure of the collaborators (typified by the treacherous political chameleon Mr Yee). Therefore, when reading the film as an allegory of the history of modern China, it shows the failure of all the three major forces in play. Meanwhile, there are no clean players in history: all historical actors, even those who claimed to be on the just side, are ignoble partners.

---

① Jameson, F., *A Singular Modernity: Essay on the Ontology of the Present*, London; New York: Verso, 2002:107.

② Man, P. de., *Blindness and Insight: Essays in the Rhetoric of Contemporary Criticism*, Minneapolis: Minnesota University Press, 1997:207.

Yet would not this allegory of failure only lead to the conclusion that history is absurd? Indeed, as life is presented as tragic, pointless and absurd here, the entire story is an exercise in absurdity; or the absurdity was played as a drama. Such absurdity apparently points to the infructuous efforts of the patriotic resistance, which, manipulated and used by the party politics, forfeited so many innocent lives.

But when assigning a woman (in particular her body) to assume all the weight of history, this woman's body again becomes a symbolic space. Hence, this allegory of the failure of history is only the other side of the same coin of a symbolism, a symbolism of the supremacy of lust, which means this is a pseudo allegory—because insofar lust is treated as one that owns the preemptive power, simultaneously it already means the failure of all the others—patriotism, love, and history.

The failure of history is on the surface brought about by the base means the various actors apply. But for the spirit of allegory defined by Fredric Jameson and Paul de Man, this ethical concern needs to be placed in its historical situation, to be seen as a response to an essentially social dilemma, and we need to translate it into political terms: insofar as this allegory of (historical) failure is not historically tenable for the Chinese nation, I would argue that it is at most a workable one for a particular class; that is, it is an allegory of the failure of the politics of this comprador class.

Moreover, I will go a step further to suggest that this scheme of historical fable is derived its inspiration from the history of a particular area that the film producers (the director and the script writer) come from; that is, the ultimate understanding of the filmic text should take the social text of Taiwan's cultural politics into account, which makes the film essentially an appropriation of another set of historical allegory.

This is because, to the extent the film script shrinks the larger geopolitical conflict of the Second Sino-Japanese War to the experience of a young, traditional Chinese "good girl" who has become a war orphan and loses her national identity, the film is simultaneously very amenable to another allegorical reading in reference to the history and national identity of modern Taiwan. For, when it is devised that Wong Chia-chi's mother is dead, this can be interpreted as an allusion to the death of traditional Chinese culture for modern Taiwan (as well as Chinese mainland, to be sure. This figurative expression is a common phrase in the Chinese world); and when it is schemed that Wong Chia-chi's father flees to England with her brother and abandons her, and when a figure like Old Wu (as a merciless surrogate father) uses her as a tool and sex toy to cater to the enemy,[①] it could be read as imparting the message that Taiwan's mother country—China—had abandoned her and used her as bait to satisfy the Japanese by signing the secession treaty in the wake of the defeat in the Sino-Japanese War in 1895. In this light, the fact that the heroine's national identity is shattered and co-opted simultaneously then finally becomes a perfect fable of the formation of an "ambiguous" Taiwanese identity, the discourse of which is popular in the area.[②]

Indeed, as a visual reconstruction of the national memory, this epic/anti-epic film noir inserts itself, through a representation of body, gender, and revolution, in the public consciousness as a point of reference for intellectual discussion of the historical experience of Chinese modernity. In the climactic moment of the film, the heroine's national identity is shattered and deconstructed. The deliberation of its social-phenomenological import could be pursued through a study of the discursive changes of China's national identity.

The history of modern China is a history that the Chinese sought to forge their modern national identity through a strenuous process of nation-state building, in which the Resistance War also made a substantial contribution. The founding of the People's Republic of China in 1949

---

① These plots are not contained in the original story, where she still seriously trusts the mission.

② When this reasonable speculation is associated with contemporary political events—when the then—DPP regime's policy of de-Sinicization ousted Chiang Kai-shek from the altar, it is Chinese mainland's alleged communist regime that simultaneously demolishes the Maoist doctrine as well as the socialist infrastructure and follows the developmentalist policy that the KMT had adopted, and boosts the status of Chiang Kai-shek in historical writing—it inevitably leads to our contemplation: are these the ultimate "historical absurdities" that are projected back to the displaced allegorical time-space?

established its national identity, as the new leaders claimed, as the one that was based on a concept of class-nation, a discourse that asserted that the Chinese people were now citizens in a socialist country, with the working class as the leading class and the alliance of workers and peasants its foundation. Fundamental changes have taken place since the late eighties. Now the government resorts to traditional, cultural source (especially a Confucian one) to define what the Chineseness is, which, as some critics believe, is fluid and unsubstantial, with no solid foundation to back up. It also tries to promote nationalism to replace the former state ideology. Accordingly, the national identity that it erstwhile proclaimed was fragmented and dispersed. The state is anxiously being co-opted into the world market-system and to join the trend of globalization. In this light, the central motif of the film-betrayal-echoes a prevalent social sentiment among the populace in contemporary China.[1] The massive transformation, or the abruptly turning fates of different classes within China, also invests some with the feeling that history is a process of absurd, purposeless transmigration.

While the narrative strategy can make any sort of historical representation, the historical experience per se would not lend itself to any specific use indiscriminately. So the dialectics also subject this allegory of failure of history to its opposite through a deconstructive reading. With a realist surface and a new political fervor, the film intends to present an enclosed world "as it was" (though it has also been dressed up to a great extent). This effort also leads to some revelations it might not have expected, and brings out some jarring, incoherent discourses: the patriotic play the students put on probably means to satirize a CCP's propaganda play

---

① In early 2008, there was a mobile-phone short message phrase that was very popular in cyberspace, which reads: "After viewing *Lust, Caution*, I feel women are not reliable; after watching *The Warlords*, brothers neither; and after seeing *Assembly*, I only realize the organization is the most undependable." (Here "the organization" in China historically and literally refers to the CCP.) The three movies mentioned here rank the top three in the box-office list in the year of 2007. It is generally accepted that this phenomenon reflects the crisis of mutual trust and the lack of sense of security in the society.

*White-Haired Girl* (as the meticulously equivalent mise-en-scene suggests),
for in reality Kuang Yu-min (who plays the solider) cannot save Wong Chia-
chi (who acts the peasant girl), unlike the rosy picture narrated by the
original drama. But the very fact that Kuang Yu-min cannot achieve the goal
of liberating the people and his lover also poses a historical alternative for
the other road to national salvation. In addition, the resplendent, enticing
scenes with colorful light effects, tawdry embellishments, yet are filled with
emptiness and boredom, intrigues and deceits in the inhumane mah-jong-
room, are a constant reminder of the political-economic truth—content
underneath the frivolous ornamentation and indulgence of the bourgeois life.
Thus, by presenting a distorted mode of life as it was, the film discloses the
decadent, treacherous life world that anticipates a new world. Furthermore,
the content or implications of this new world can be found in the ephemeral
scene of the authentic, simple-hearted genuine emotions (a token of sincere
love) and encouragements (to fight the invaders unswervingly) exchanged
between this peasant girl and the soldier. Meanwhile, the audience's
passionate calls for national salvation in the theater also emit the message of
an unyielding resistance. In other words, in its efforts to deconstruct
patriotism, the film simultaneously—in an unconscious and unintentional
way—articulates the discourses of genuine love as affectionate emotion and
uncompromised resistance as fearless devotion.

In short, the unwittingly juxtaposed scenes present a hybrid ("semi-
colonial, semi-feudal" and multi-layered classes) society and its overlapping
social, ideological, and moral orders, which is made explicit by the various
characters' vastly different political attitudes towards the Japanese
imperialists. In this light, the ontological passion of the film becomes its
dialectical opposite: it not only stands for an ideological reification and
fantasy, but also paradoxically speaks to an alternative historical imagination
and aspiration.

## 六、Conclusion

By scrutinizing the many aspects of the cinematic narrative, from its selection of theme and subject matter，concepts of character，notions of causality and plot，to its use of setting and metaphor，style and language，as well as choice of narrative mode，I propose that the film aimed to be a closely-knit，coherent yet subtly concealed political film noir subservient to a particular ideological demand，but its multiple-layered narrative also unwittingly contains contending and antithetical discourses that trigged differing responses.

To be more specific，the passionate desire to reconstruct collective memory and rewrite national history finds its genre objectification in a film noir disguised as an erotic thriller，in which the juxtaposition of the melodrama and the epic is the crux of this cinematic artifact. The melodrama covers up the political supplement of the epic，and the epic unravels the political sublimation of the melodrama. In a series of operations of displacement and projection，denial and reaction formation (the utterance of fear)，as well as rationalization and identification (of defeatism)，the cinematic artifact endeavored to undo anxieties and compensate for unfulfilled desires. But the film meant to flatten out this endeavor by its artistry of an unobtrusive narration，seamless editing and camerawork. The visual and narrative logic of the cinematic language，such as framing，editing，sound effects (like music，drum-beating in the sexual scenes，etc.)，and in particular the heavy uses of the POV shots，eye-line matches，shot/reverse-shot patterns，reflect its orientation towards manipulation of audience response towards an imaginary reality，one that possesses a semblance of coherence and wholeness，which constitute a representative example of suture theory.[1]

The living room of the rising Chinese urban middle class is the imagined

---

[1] Stacy Thompson has distinguished two sorts of "sutures." One is "imaginary suture" which sutures spectators with characters，whereas "symbolic suture" sutures the "world-views" represented by films with us. *Lust，Caution* typically exemplifies both the operative mechanisms. I would add a third kind "practical suture" which comes before "imaginary suture" and uses shot/reverse-shot to make the psychology and deportment of the characters more credible and "realistic." Cf. Professor Rob Nowlan. "What Is 'Suture'?" http://www.uwec.edu/ranowlan/suture.html. Accessed March 4，2008.

space in which a meta-historical critique of Chinese revolution, or
resistance, as traumatic experience, is to unfold. Conservative ideology
(assuming itself as liberal humanism) rejuvenates by venturing into this
terrain of time and memory. The preponderance of flattering acclaims of the
film in the Chinese mainstream media (all with the same expressions:
"excellent representation of profound humanity, a great art film"; etc.),
shows that in Chinese elite strata, the nationalist sentiments, which are
generally viewed as rampant in the society, in certain times could easily be
outweighed by a new class consciousness. This class consciousness, if not
yet comes from a class stratum that is substantively formed, then at least is
in the process of formally institutionalizing the habitus, or the
"subjectivity," of a unfledged middle class—the reason for this easy
transformation is that contemporary Chinese nationalism is only premised
upon a robust consumerism backed up by the same emerging class stratum.
This group is easily subjected to the influence of an idiosyncratic code of love
and universal humanity: "True love is blameless," as an aggressive slogan
propagated by the advertising organ of the film's producer, which is largely
accepted by this elite group.

Although it is within this general ideological, or cultural-political
framework that a misplaced historical drama plays out, just as the film also
sets in motion the fundamental discrepancies, conflicts, and the coexistence
of different systems of value, culture, and social codes of conduct, it also
turns out that history still goes on, and not necessarily towards "the end":
Though in various public elite media, positive reviews were overwhelming,
in Internet space the movie was also subjected to numerous criticisms. But
these repudiations are mostly couched in nationalist rhetoric: "How can a
patriotic girl turn into a traitor falling in love with a collaborator?"
Ironically, it is in the context of the rapid reshuffling of class structures that
the perspective of class analysis is obsolescent.

Yet the acknowledgement of the ban by few of mainland Chinese also
should not be regarded as an endorsement of the administrative measure;
but it merely shows their spontaneous opposition to the film's class-bound
ideology. In this light, the conflicting responses to the movie in the Chinese

society finally become a mirror-house of the post-socialist China: it reflects the existence of all the heterogeneous elements among differing social forces—they are vying with and competing against each other to claim their political legitimacy and cultural hegemony in the ongoing development of Chinese (post-)modernity.

# Part V.

## Peasants' Habitus and "National Form"

# Chapter Nine "Problem Stories as Part of the National Form:"Rural Society in Transition and Zhao Shuli's Peasant Stories

## 一、Introduction

Yi-tsi Mei Feuerwerker has said of the famed modern Chinese "peasant writer" Zhao Shuli (1906-1970) that had he not existed, "he would have had to be invented, and perhaps to a great extent he was."[①] Does this mean that "the model peasant writer was an ongoing joint creation of the living writers and party ideologues"?[②] Instead of following this view that Zhao Shuli's writings "seemed to have been tailored-made to meet its (the Party's) specific requirements"[③]—which apparently implied that he somewhat arbitrarily "made" stories to "represent" the Party's policies—I will take a different perspective in examining how his efforts coincided, as well as being perhaps sometimes in conflict, with the Party's mandate of creating a "new direction" for society. I will seek to understand why Mao Dun (1896-1981) praised his works as "a milestone on the way to national form,"[④] and why Zhou Yang (1908-1989) extolled his stories as evidence that Mao Dun's idea

---

① Feuerwerker, Y. M., *Ideology, Power, Text : Self-Representation and the Peasant "Other" in Modern Chinese Literature*, Stanford:Stanford University Press, 1998:100.

② Feuerwerker, Y. M., *Ideology, Power, Text : Self-Representation and the Peasant "Other" in Modern Chinese Literature*, Stanford:Stanford University Press, 1998:100.

③ Feuerwerker, Y. M., *Ideology, Power, Text : Self-Representation and the Peasant "Other" in Modern Chinese Literature*, Stanford:Stanford University Press, 1998:100.

④ 茅盾:《论赵树理的小说》,载郭沫若主编:《论赵树理的创作》,新华书店(苏南)1949 年版,第 43 页.

of a "people's literature" was on its way to realization.[①]

The discussions of his stories reveal the general historical experience of a rural society in transition in the "liberated area." There are two major themes:social improvement under the intervention of the new regime, and the "standing up" of the subaltern peasant class. These two elements oftentimes overlap, and sometimes there is a hybrid work which combines the two themes, such as the novel *Changes in Li Village*(《李家庄的变迁》). The last section will briefly discuss the supposed paradox of Zhao Shuli's "direction," its contributions to representing and educating the masses, and its limitations in implementing the Party's long-term ideological goal of reforming the peasants' ethical-moral world.

## 二、Rural Society in Transition Ⅰ:Social Dynamic and the New Regime

In the first category of stories, the writer shows the intricate relations between the social dynamic which propels rural society's transformation and the new regime. One of his most famed stories, *Little Blackie Gets Married* (《小二黑结婚》) is nevertheless quite simple, concerning the resolution of a love tangle. Xiao Erhei and Xiaoqin are two young rural peasants in love with each other. However, Xiao Erhei's father, Second Zhuge, a master necromancer, through his superstitious practices comes to believe the couple are an unpropitious match, and Xiaoqin's mother, Third Fairy, an old-fashioned shaman and a coquette, wishes to keep Xiao Erhei as potential prey for herself. These two parents both oppose the marriage of the couple. Meanwhile, some local bullies who covet Xiaoqin's beauty threaten the young lovers. Through the intervention of a higher authority, the bullies are punished, the parents yield to the youngsters' wishes, and the marriage finally goes ahead.

Many separate motifs in the story make it difficult to determine a central theme. It can be said that it is a tale that debunks the peasants' superstitious mindsets and their "feudal consciousness" (the patriarchal

---

① 周杨：《论赵树理的创作》,《解放日报》,1946 年 8 月 26 日.

habitus that establishes older people's right to determine the affairs of the
younger members of their family). Zhao Shuli, however, does not spend
time exposing the flawed internal logic of these superstitions. Right at the
beginning, when his narrator introduces the origin of the nicknames of Third
Fairy and Second Zhuge, the invalidity, inefficacy, and fraudulent nature of
their traditional practices are disclosed as being well-known to the local
community.[①] They are local laughing stocks, whose obstinate persistence in
their archaic practices is evidence of the inertia of rural society.

The historical subtext is that the traditional cosmology and
epistemology which supported such traditional beliefs have already collapsed.
Rural China, after two decades of development since the establishment of
the Republic, though still more or less ignorant of modern concepts of
science and technology, had grown more enlightened about superstition, and
such residual traditions as these were no longer very persuasive. Therefore,
rather than a tub-thumping presentation of the motif of battering down
feudal superstitiousness, which had been common in the New Literature of
earlier decades (usually exposing the dire human costs resulting from such
practices), the falsity and stupidity of superstition is taken for granted and
merely serves as the starting point for the story. Nevertheless, by
highlighting the perversity and absurdity of these traditions, the story helps
to instill an anti-superstitious mentality in its readers.

These two backward characters, with their comical and eccentric
mannerisms, make a stronger impression than the young couple, who are
lackluster "new heroes." For example, Third Fairy's outlandish appearance
is portrayed vividly. Her sartorial and cosmetic excesses are not merely

---

① "Fairy" (仙姑), in traditional Chinese folk tales refers to a female spirit that has
certain powers. The woman is called a fairy because she pretends to have the supernatural
power of allowing herself to be possessed by the spirits of the dead, who can purportedly
transmit messages to the living through her. Zhuge refers to the famed character Zhuge
Liang in the traditional novel *Romance of the Three Kingdoms* (《三国演义》), who in
traditional belief possessed such superior wisdom that his status was godlike. Yet the man
acquires his nickname because his divinations seem weird and even ludicrous to the
villagers. The two nicknames are both ironic parody.

presented for comic effect, but are intimately related to her personality and behavior. Her immaturity is revealed to be the result of the psychologically traumatic experience of being forcibly married to a burly peasant at the age of just 15. After a quarrel with her uncle, she had fallen into a coma, and when she awoke from it, she became a medium. Through this ruse, she felt she could still gain the attention of young men, but she did not realize that after twenty-odd years she had lost her youthful beauty.

In the New Literature, this experience would probably have been elaborately described to expose the cruelty of rural society in smothering young people's love, but here it is only briefly introduced. This is not because the writer lacked the skill or knowledge to follow the style of the New Literature. His decision is attributable to the psychological habitus of his intended peasant audience: they would not be receptive to a sympathetic description of this woman, or to an "enlightenment" drama promoting a feminist message. In their eyes, the woman was simply ignoble, and had challenged the ethical-moral system of their world.

The graphic and lively portrayal of these two comic figures seemingly offers typical examples of two unenlightened peasants. Typicality, in the terminology of literary realism, means "the truthful reproduction of typical characters under typical circumstances," as Friedrich Engels proposed.[1] In other words, whether a certain character is typical or not depends on whether he or she faithfully represents the historical experience of a particular "moment." Such a representation does not merely present reality "as it is," as if it is a photocopy, but is a representation of "the real" which highlights the direction of historical development.

The two comic characters, though exaggerated to a certain extent, are not totally distorted figures. They are a genuine representation of the "typical circumstance" of the historical moment. Along with the local bullies, they embody impediments to social progress, and as such they are the cardinal protagonists of the story. That it is the comic parents rather

---

[1]  Engels, F., "Letter to Margaret Harkness." Quoted from Travers, M., *European Literature from Romanticism to Postmodernism*, London: Palgrave Macmillan, 1997: 123.

than the evil bullies that are focused on might again be to cater to the literary taste of the peasants; although more descriptions of the bullies could add more drama to the story. The two young peasants, as a catalyst of the dynamic change taking place in rural society, are also protagonists, yet readers feel unimpressed by their personalities. The writer obviously pays less attention to their portrayal, again, perhaps, in deference to the tastes of rural peasants, who tend to prefer more action elements in a story than individual characterization of ordinary, familiar characters.[1] More character description might have been warranted, but we should note that the thematic focus of the story is the social dynamic, rather than any individual character.

Here, the idea of "personality" itself needs reconsideration. If "personality" is shown more vividly in the comical parents than the youngsters, it is because the latter are submitting to a historical momentum for which their personal struggles are merely a medium, and also perhaps because their personalities are in the process of formation during these struggles. Their individual love story represents the fight against unfair social institutions such as the "feudal" patriarchal practice of arranged marriages, and against the kind of bullies who manipulate and control local affairs. This is a kind of "typicality," or better, "representativeness," showing a typical event that happened in a typical historical situation. Without changes in the village, the young couple's love would have ended tragically rather than happily. Thus, their story exemplifies the dynamic of social progress.

This dynamic of social transformation first manifests itself in the change of personality of Third Fairy and Second Zhuge. Under the pressure of public opinion and the new regime, they relinquish their arbitrary, patriarchal arrogance and acquiesce to their children's choice, and they are forced to give

---

[1]   We should note that although to a certain extent they are "new youths," they are not the traditional type of hero that the peasants are familiar with in their folk culture. The defiant spirits of the two youngsters are, in the eyes of the elder peasants, merely out of childish immaturity.

up their public display of superstitious practices. The social dynamic also shows itself in the younger generation, which is often mistakenly viewed as a central concern of the narrative. The youngsters' rebellion against their parents is not merely a result of their authority being delegitimized by their lack of popularity. Their spontaneous spirit of defiance is analogous to the young intellectuals of the May Fourth Movement, whose influence, under the new historical situation with the new regime seeking to mobilize the peasants to undertake social revolution, was now spreading to the rural areas. They are struggling for individual rights and freedom by breaking out of patriarchal relations. This fight, with the blessing of the new regime, involves overturning the existing social order.

What brings this into the category of "problem stories" is the local bullies who assume administrative positions in the new regime, and try to abuse their power to punish those who disobey their will. It is only because of the intervention of higher authority that the case is finally settled in a happy ending. When the ruffians accuse the youngsters of adultery and drag them off to trial, the district government supports the couple and penalizes the hooligans. This narrative of justice being done is another individual motif. The new regime ultimately plays a crucial role here.

The prevalent use of such a deus ex machina in the writer's stories is often attacked as being propagandistic. However, the ideological component here is not so much promoting the Party as simply reflecting the traditional—largely unconscious—political concerns of Chinese peasants: what they yearn for is a fair and capable ruling power that can right wrongs for them, provide safety, and prevent them from being bullied. Thus, the happy ending to the story satisfies both the will of the Party and the political-aesthetic habitus of the peasants. When the peasants themselves were not yet awakened and mobilized, and were incapable of bringing about their own liberation, such a positive ending was necessary to show them the direction to go. The author's intended audience/readers were primarily peasants and local cadres.

This can be read as a story about a new society in its struggle to establish its own laws and self-image in opposition to the traditional patriarchal system and its ideology. It is the new marriage law introduced by the Party that sanctions and endorses the couple's will. And it is the intervention of the higher authority of the new regime that secures a just conclusion. The story demonstrates a new social dynamic in which the ruling power supports the will of the people. It is a story about a society in transformation: individual peasants, interpersonal relationships, and the local regime are all seen to undergo fundamental changes.

This ultimate thematic motif is conveyed with the help of a comedic spirit, which is both an asset and a burden. The sobriquets the two comic characters are given are full of folk color, with traditionally comic connotations. These figures have been compared with the classic alazon in Western culture.[①] The following comic features are stereotypical—almost universal—in agrarian society and are also incorporated in various characters in the writer's later stories:

> ...the nicknamed women impress the observer as overbearing and calculatedly, even vulgarly, self-centered, wreaking havoc in their homes as well as disturbing the peace in their society. The nicknamed men, by contrast, are ingenuous drolls in their eccentricities and express their self-centeredness in more subdued, if tenacious, manners. While the women are virulent, the men are merely deluded. While the women exhibit repugnant personality flaws, the men manifest quaint recalcitrance.[②]

They are comical because their behavior transgresses agrarian society's

---

① Josephine Alzbeta Matthews describes the alazon "the obstructing character of the comic mythos." Characters of this type "all scheme to prevent their respective children from marrying the person of their choice," and they "play the role of obstructionists to a smooth transition to a new society, one in which people organize themselves into collective labor arrangements." Meanwhile, "all of them make themselves conspicuous in their society by talking or behaving in a manner inconsistent with society's expectations." In particular, "in their role as imposters, the women are often unabashedly vocal, employing a decibel level that draws to them a concentration of attention greater than that normally encountered in small village life." Josephine, A. M., *Artistry and Authenticity: Zhao Shuli and His Fictional World*, PhD Dissertation. Ohio State University, 1991:275-276.

② Josephine, A. M., *Artistry and Authenticity: Zhao Shuli and His Fictional World*, PhD Dissertation. Ohio State University, 1991:277.

expectations—its conventional concepts and moral-cultural institutions—thus creating farcical effects. The story can be said to uphold the conventional ethical-moral structure, which ensures its entertainment value to its peasant readers, but distances it from the Party's long-term objective of reforming traditional society and its outmoded ethical-moral order.

Problems occurring in the transformation of society are subtly examined here, but they are more thoroughly treated in *The Just Prevails* (《邪不压正》), published in October 1948. This story again deals with an arranged marriage, but it now concentrates on the corruption of some local party cadres implementing land reform. They infiltrate and usurp the power of the local administration by pretending to be activists, and by bribing weak-minded party cadres. These rogues not only abuse their public office for private gain; but also coerce the disempowered peasants into marriage contracts. Still, justice finally prevails, not as a result of the peasants' revolutionary consciousness or their democratic participation in the administration of local affairs to become the "masters of their own life" (当家作主). It is only with the arrival of a higher official who discovers their wrongdoings that the bad situation is redressed. Nevertheless, when the peasants claim that "this is really a place where reason can be asserted," it implies that they have realized that this is a new age where they can hope for justice.

Another example of a story dealing with this new social dynamic is *The Tale of Li Youcai's Rhymes* (《李有才板话》), which was published in the same year of "Little Blackie Gets Married", and enjoyed similar popularity. Susan MacDonald has argued that the central theme of the story is "the contrast between the styles of two political workers."[1] This argument is seemingly substantiated by the writer's own argument that he wrote it because "some enthusiastic young colleagues, who did not understand the real situation in the rural villages, were misled by some superficial

---

[1]　MacDonald, S. S. H., *The Tale of Li Youcai's Rhymes*, Cambridge: Cambridge University Press, 1970: ⅩⅤⅱ.

achievements." ① It is a "problem story" highlighting faults and errors, but its central theme is the new regime's struggle to overcome obstacles on the road to the ultimate victory of the masses. The Party had to overcome many difficulties, including internal enemies, to validate itself as the "people's regime" (人民政权). The contrast of the working styles between the two party workers merely provides the material of the overriding plotline.

Li Youcai is a poor peasant but he is also a "clapper talker," a kind of folk artist expert in composing spontaneous rhymes, a form of local satirical verses called "快板". Such rural poetry was usually considered outside the realm of literature, both by Party officials and May Fourth intellectuals. The author here integrates Li Youcai's rhymes with modern fiction technique, using them as a device to recapitulate on the preceding story or comment on characters and ongoing events.

The first section, "The Origin of the Book's Name," simultaneously introduces Li Youcai and sets up his relationship to the story's first person narrator:

> From the time of the Anti-Japanese War, many changes had taken place in Yanjiashan, and Li Youcai made up some new clapper talks about them. This got him into trouble. I want to talk about these changes, and have copied down some parts of his clapper talks during those changes for your diversion. As a result, this book was written. ②

This recalls the narrative voice at the beginning of Lu Xun's *The Diary of a Madman*. The difference is that what this narrator sets out to record is not simply the protagonist's actions and psychological motivations, but "the changes" in society—an ongoing historical process in which he is not merely a transcriber but a mediator.

However, contrary to this initial promise, the first person narrator immediately gives way to a third person narrator. The story "revolves

---

① MacDonald, S. S. H., *The Tale of Li Youcai's Rhymes*, Cambridge: Cambridge University Press, 1970: ⅩⅤⅱ.

② Feuerwerker, Y. M., *Ideology*, *Power*, *Text*: *Self-Representation and the Peasant "Other" in Modern Chinese Literature*, Stanford: Stanford University Press, 1998: 128.

around the struggle to establish grass-roots level political power through the election of a village head." This major plotline exemplifies the important historical experience of the rural areas at the time, "the movement for the reduction of rent and interest announced in January 1942."[①] Like previous stories, it presents a situation in which reactionary feudal forces still manipulate local power structures. Although the wicked village head has been removed by higher authority, in the following election Yan Hengyuan, a local landlord, holds on to power by fooling the party cadre, the young and inexperienced Comrade Zhang, with a wily stratagem. Moreover, he corrupts two other important local cadres, Xiaoyuan and Ma Fengming, by cajoling them into accepting his favors and forsaking their obligation to safeguard the peasants' interests.

Yan Hengyuan and his lackeys cheat the new regime by applying false methods to measuring the land in order to conceal the real extent of their properties. Li Youcai makes up some new verses to expose their scheme. This leads to his land being appropriated while he himself is expelled from the village. The arrival of a higher party official finally restores moral order.

The last-minute deus ex machina this time is embodied in the person of Comrade Yang, the chairman of the County Peasant Association with rich experience, who was himself a poor peasant and thus familiar with rural realities, in sharp contrast to Comrade Zhang, a naïve bureaucrat easily fooled by appearances. An idealized party cadre, Yang investigates local affairs by living with and working with the masses, and is able to bypass the influence of the local bullies. He not only embodies the Party's ethic of following the "mass line," but represents the traditional type of an honest, upright, and perceptive official—an incarnation of sovereign power and reliable authority. However, unlike traditional exemplars, he is from the lower classes, and he joins with, or rather, is at one with the masses. Like Bao the master, who is a representative figure familiar to the Chinese

---

① Feuerwerker, Y. M., *Ideology*, *Power*, *Text : Self-Representation and the Peasant "Other" in Modern Chinese Literature*, Stanford:Stanford University Press, 1998:128.

peasant world, he takes vigorous action after he discovers the wrongs the village has suffered. He dismisses incompetent local officials and summons district cadres to hold a mass struggle meeting, which brings down the chief villain Yan Hengyuan and restores local administration to a healthy order: Yan Hengyuan and his associates are forced to return land and extorted money to the peasants. The final scene sees Li Youcai, at Yang's request, composing a new song to celebrate this victory.

The peasants in this story, with the help of Party cadres acting as the catalyst, have their revolutionary consciousness raised, and are seen to be capable of assuming an active political role, participating in the revolution, and collectively overthrowing the local power structure. This story is thus a development of the theme of the new social dynamic under the new regime, and it comes close to articulating the second major theme of Zhaoshuli's stories: the liberation of the masses.[①] Its presentation of the "mass line" in a natural manner, unlike the formulaic descriptions of dogmatic party cadres in later propagandist works, provides a good lesson for local cadres.

While sharing some of the features of traditional Chinese stories of legal cases involving a sagacious judge remedying injustice by punishing the wrongdoers, it differs from them in focusing on the process of establishing a democratic government at the lowest level of society. (After the peasants have experienced a sham democracy manipulated by the residues of the old power structure, they create a regime by themselves.) Through this popular and engaging tale, the author achieves the aim of both entertaining the peasant masses and educating them about their rights and interests. By presenting a new but realistic "legend" about the realization of a collective dream, the story articulates the political unconscious of the peasants and satisfies their deep yearning for social justice. It also instills in them a new

---

① Cyril Birch said that "the real and astonishing achievement" of the Party's work as represented by the Communist fiction of this period is that the peasant "was goaded into… believing that he was being guided, not directed, by the Communist Party to a position of control over his own destiny." See Birch, C., Fiction of the Yenan Period, *The China Quarterly*, 1960, (4):8.

passion for individual rights，which simultaneously means collective rights，as they are a subaltern class.

Moreover，this liberation is accomplished with the assistance of a new language—the Party speaks. Edward Gunn has highlighted some of these new terms，such as "status，identity"（身份），"organize"（组织），"importance"（重要性）and "significance"（意义）.[①] They appear in the letter of introduction for Comrade Yang，explaining the Party's mission to "educate" the peasants to recognize their "identity" as members of a community but also as members of an oppressed class，and to recognize the need to "organize" themselves and to understand the "importance" and "significance" of this action. Only through acquiring this new language，and thereby equipping themselves with a revolutionary class consciousness，can the peasants learn to stand up for themselves by taking charge of their own affairs，speaking out in struggle meetings and overthrowing existing power structures. However，the same vocabulary is seen in the bureaucratic party worker Comrade Zhang's high-flown speech. Therefore，whether this modern language is useful or not，abstract or concrete，still depends on the extent to which it can be integrated with the peasants' own language through following the "mass line."

Despite the potency of Li Youcai's "clapper talk，" the story suggests that promoting the language and art forms of the peasant masses is not enough on its own，and is not a primary goal of Party policy. It is only through studying the new revolutionary language，and using it to reform the old，folk language and the traditional consciousness embedded within it，that the peasants，with guidance of the Party，can attain their will. It is no surprise that in later Communist stories，these two aspects are emphasized simultaneously：the Party's teaching and education of the unenlightened and oppressed peasants，and the Party's close connection to and indispensable assistance from the peasants. It becomes increasingly common to typify this two-way transaction in the figure of a model party worker. Zhao Shuli's

---

① Feuerwerker，Y. M.，*Ideology，Power，Text：Self-Representation and the Peasant "Other" in Modern Chinese Literature*，Stanford：Stanford University Press，1998：132.

story can be seen as a forerunner of this pattern of writing.

That Li Youcai's traditional verse is framed within the narrator's modern narrative can be seen as symbolic of the intellectuals' mediating function between the peasants and the Party. As a mediator, the narrator's voice assumed an apparently neutral yet actually authorial voice, helping to integrate three strands of discourse: the folk artists', the average peasants', and the Party's.

## 三、Rural Society in Transition Ⅱ: The "Standing up" of the Subaltern Class

In the second category of stories, Zhao Shuli emphasizes that the social dynamic represented by the theme of justice being done by the new regime involves the liberation of an entire class, the peasantry, and also of an entire gender, women, from the straitjacket of traditional feudal/patriarchal society. This theme is often expressed in a new term from the Party's jargon, "翻身", which literally means "turning over" or "standing up."

*Meng Xiangying Stands Up* (《孟祥英翻身》) was completed in 1944, some months after Zhao Shuli attended a conference of model party workers of the Taihang area. The titular heroine was someone he met there. The text apparently blurs the distinction between reportage, short story, and biography. The difficulty in assessing the fictionality of this piece is typical of a group of literary works of that time, both in the KMT-controlled area and the "liberated area," which reflects a fundamental change in the historical experience. Zhao Shuli indicated that the events he narrated "were prevalent in the society of those days," and that he "had been used to seeing them."[1] What distinguishes this story from similar earlier works is that the protagonist/role model is now not a courageous fighter, but "an illiterate, impoverished, and oppressed peasant woman."[2]

---

[1]   Feuerwerker, Y. M., *Ideology, Power, Text: Self-Representation and the Peasant "Other" in Modern Chinese Literature*, Stanford: Stanford University Press, 1998:124.

[2]   Feuerwerker, Y. M., *Ideology, Power, Text: Self-Representation and the Peasant "Other" in Modern Chinese Literature*, Stanford: Stanford University Press, 1998:124.

A model party worker, the heroine has mobilized the women in the village to unbind their feet (the description of her large feet reveals her unconventional spirit of rebelliousness and non-conformity, because bound feet were traditionally regarded as the norm of femininity), to attend literacy classes to transform their illiterate status (since traditional Chinese women were praised for their illiteracy as a token of virtue, this is a laudable move), and to undertake agrarian labor such as gathering wild plants to stave off famine. The writer focuses on how she has been "liberated from under the oppression of the forces of old society" because he believes that "how a person changed from not ever being a hero into a hero was also what everyone would like to know."[1]

The story is divided into ten sections, each narrating one episode. A large space (the first three sections) is devoted to depicting the miserable life that Meng Xiangying endured during the old days: she was maltreated by both her cold husband and her hostile mother-in-law in the "honeymoon phase"; and although she had tried to fight back courageously, the cruel flogging she met destroyed her spirit and she had twice attempted suicide. In this way, the "dynamic of dominance and suppression" in the family "replicates in microcosm" the society's macrostructural pattern of oppression.[2]

Meng Xiangying's mother-in-law's verbal abuse is highlighted, but the physical violence that Meng Xiangying is subjected to by her husband is not portrayed in graphic ways. This has provoked protests from some scholars, who accuse the story of "sexism."[3] This criticism neglects the historical subtext: in the rural areas at this time (in fact, for thousands of years),

---

[1] Feuerwerker, Y. M., *Ideology, Power, Text: Self-Representation and the Peasant "Other" in Modern Chinese Literature*, Stanford: Stanford University Press, 1998:124.

[2] Matthews, J. A., *Artistry and Authenticity: Zhao Shuli and His Fictional World*, *PhD Dissertation*. Ohio State University, 1991:191.

[3] Feuerwerker, Y. M., *Ideology, Power, Text: Self-Representation and the Peasant "Other" in Modern Chinese Literature*, Stanford: Stanford University Press, 1998:125.

tense and awkward relations between mothers-in-law and daughters-in-law had often resulted in bitter feelings and tragic consequences. This centuries-old problem was a priority issue for a new regime aiming to bring in a new social order. And the writer does allude to the brutality Meng Xiangying endures from her husband, references would be all too clear to his peasant readers/audience. More graphic descriptions might have been more dramatic, but would potentially have alienated the intended audience, since this topic was still something of a taboo. After Meng Xiangying becomes the leader of the Women's National Salvation Association under the aegis of the Party, her life changes. The empowering efforts of the Party help her to "stand up" before her husband, her mother-in-law, and society as a whole. This transformation, however, is only briefly introduced: through her participation in the revolutionary process, she sees the power of the mass movement. The narrator tells us, "after the struggle meeting, she became bolder."

This story only depicts the most prominent episodes in the whole process of transformation, but it does not show the heroine's acquisition of revolutionary consciousness, nor does it describe how she underwent such a profound change in her psyche. This might make this piece seem less persuasive to intellectual readers, and somewhat primitive in comparison to the worker-peasant-soldier literature of a later period. However, by witnessing her personal transformation, although no psychological metamorphosis, nor revolutionary consciousness, is presented here, peasant readers could still realize that a great social revolution was taking place and become mobilized to support it. Put in other words, in showing that a poor woman peasant can be empowered to transcend herself and contribute to collective goals, the piece demonstrates to the peasants that their personal destinies are bound up with the collective goal, and that the assertion of their individual rights, including women's rights, is intimately connected with the validation of the political value of this subaltern class.

The role of the narrator, who "assumes the stance of a chatty oral storyteller in giving out occasional background information," and "records *events as they unfold,*"① is effective enough for this purpose. The motif of liberation also manifests itself in the character of a social pariah. The story *Fugui*（《福贵》）covers the life of the protagonist from the age of 12 to his middle age. Fugui becomes a pariah not because of his indulgence in pernicious habits, but because of social oppression. This is a familiar figure in many stories written by leftist writers since the May Fourth period, from Lu Xun's Ah Q to Lu Ling's Luo Dadou. Zhao Shuli, however, describes this type of figure and his experiences from a different perspective. Rather than stressing the dejected spirit and ignorant mentality of people to expose their bad "national character," the writer shows the social-political circumstances that Fugui is trapped in, and the unfair social prejudices that he is subjected to. He even ascribes some virtue to the miserable outcast himself: though Fugui's reputation is destroyed by unfeeling society, he still shows love and care towards his wife; and though his misfortune has stripped all his material property, he still has the courage and tenacity to fight against the odds as best as he can. Many urban intellectuals, proudly proclaiming the "enlightenment" mentality of the May Fourth Movement, produced naively one-dimensional representations of the suffering yet fatuous masses. Zhao Shuli's story is told from the perspective of the subaltern class themselves. This does not mean the "enlightenment" agenda is discarded or replaced, but it is sublimated into a higher program of education that aims to propel the peasants to a realization of their collective interests and rights. Readers see that Fugui as a social pariah is avoided and despised by everyone, including those of his own class. They also see his virtue and perseverance persisted even in this most wretched existence, and learn about the cause of his degradation. This helps the peasant readers, who might have shown the same derogatory attitude towards social pariahs in their communities, recognize their fault.

A bright and diligent young lad, Fugui had been a popular figure in his community, a fine performer in the local opera troupe. His downfall comes

---

① Feuerwerker, Y. M., *Ideology, Power, Text: Self-Representation and the Peasant "Other" in Modern Chinese Literature*, Stanford: Stanford University Press, 1998:126.

from his virtue and his hope of living a decent life. Two events before he
crossed the threshold of adulthood threw him into a never-ending cycle of
debt: a marriage and funeral service. His dying mother had urged him to
marry the bride that she had arranged for him in childhood ( a
commonpractice in rural areas then). This wedding and shortly after his
mother's funeral ceremony, both demanding extravagant expense, forced
him to borrow money from a usurer.

The rapid growth in his interest payments year by year soon caused him
to forfeit his small parcel of land. Hard work simply could not pay back the
debt. Insolvency weakens his incentive to cultivate his land, and hunger
propels him to gambling and thievery, and then to undertake the socially
disrespected profession of laying out the dead for funerals. Thus, it is
ingrained social institutions of superstition, prejudice, cruelty, and
hypocrisy that divest him of his human dignity and force him to such
miserable extremes.

Wang Laowan, the loan shark responsible for Fugui's misery, is also a
familiar figure in the gallery of modern Chinese literature. A revered clan
leader, he pretends to be a higher morality, and maintains his own
reputation by exploiting the popular belief that the fall of the social pariah is
the result of the latter's own turpitude. However, he is not described as
thoroughly villainous in nature. His "typicality" as a representative of the
cardinal class consciousness and the behavioral patterns of the "power class"
is not emphasized, but his representation of the general dynamic of this
society is more than clear. Not only does he teach his children that "to earn
money by (lending) money is much faster than making money," but he also
assumes the mask of a guardian of the ethical-moral order of this world. His
sense of righteousness in his non-guilty exploitation of the disadvantaged is
attributable to existing customs and institutions of the patriarchal society.
Though he is not the "typical" villain—increasingly personified as an
incarnation of pure evil in Communist literature—he is still manipulated by
the imperceptible forces of the social-economic system and sanctioned by its
power-structure. Here the writer maintains the left-wing tradition of critical
realism.

When Fugui learns that Wang Laowan is planning to lynch him for his alleged crime of besmirching the Wang clan, he flees. The process of Communist reform in the village is not introduced, but when we see him again eight years later, this process has been completed, and the threat to his life has thus been eliminated. Because the Party's reforms help such social outcasts, he is able to live a new life by farming land reclaimed for him. The story's finale is unusual, and rarely seen in earlier leftist works. In a village meeting, Fugui "stands up," speaking out boldly to Wang Laowan to complain of the unfair treatment he has suffered at his hands. What he asks for in restitution is not property or goods or money, but his reputation, and "the right to exist as a free man with all the rights and privileges normally accorded to members of the human race."[1] He is demanding from his class enemy the restoration of his dignity and his "authentic self"—his innate property as a man that had been denied him by the "power class." Now, he regains it through "standing up" with the help of the new regime.

In this story, the writer's description of the peasants' predicament is a departure from the narrative of the May Fourth era. Instead of stressing the implicit connivance of the passive peasantry with the powerful to perpetuate the existing system, it shows that a social tyrant is a "function of the system, both drawing nurture from it and in return helping to perpetuate it," or there is a "symbolic relationship between a tyrannous system and the tyrannical individual."[2] It also shows that the "power class" needs such social pariahs, the existence of a despised "other" helping to maintain the "normal" ethical-moral world and ultimately the political order of society. In placing the tragic life of the poor peasants in a political world in which antithetical relations dominate the social space, the story is an early example of what would become an increasingly common theme in Communist literature—the conflict between social tyrants and the masses. At this point,

---

① Feuerwerker, Y. M., *Ideology, Power, Text : Self-Representation and the Peasant "Other" in Modern Chinese Literature*, Stanford : Stanford University Press, 1998 : 289.

② Feuerwerker, Y. M., *Ideology, Power, Text : Self-Representation and the Peasant "Other" in Modern Chinese Literature*, Stanford : Stanford University Press, 1998 : 290.

the masses have not become a united community, as Fugui is despised by his fellow villagers. Zhao Shuli's story is more a criticism of the system as a whole than simply of the class enemy. Thus, it is a work that falls between critical realism and revolutionary realism in critical terms, or in ideological terms, between the New Culture Enlightenment discourse (which stressed the ignorance of the peasants) and the New Enlightenment discourse (which emphasized class politics, or the progressive class consciousness of the subaltern class).

## 四、*Changes in Li Village* and Zhao's Horizon of Social Change

Among the writer's works in this period, there is a hybrid story that combines the two motifs—social dynamic and class liberation—in a panoramic portrait of a society in transformation, spanning a long period of time. *Changes in Li Village* is said to be "the first modern realistic novel written specifically for a peasant audience."[1] In deference to its intended readership, this "modern novel" still bears many of the marks of the traditional "story" genre.

As its title suggests, the story is about the social dynamic in a northern village, but viewed over a long period. This lively world is filled with antagonistic relationships between ordinary villagers and local villains, or as Josephine Matthews aptly notes, between the force of good and the force of evil. This antagonism can also be characterized as the struggle of the populace and the collective hero versus the power class and the collective anti-hero.[2] At one end of the antithetical spectrum is Li Ruzhen, head of the village, and his two nephews: Chunxi and Xiaoxi; at the other end is Zhang Tiesuo, a poor peasant. The theme is thus one of emancipation through social struggle. What makes this story unusual among the writer's works is

---

① Feuerwerker, Y. M., *Ideology, Power, Text: Self-Representation and the Peasant "Other" in Modern Chinese Literature*, Stanford: Stanford University Press, 1998:229.

② Feuerwerker, Y. M., *Ideology, Power, Text: Self-Representation and the Peasant "Other" in Modern Chinese Literature*, Stanford: Stanford University Press, 1998:230.

that it encompasses the whole process of liberation, including the origins of the revolution. Its diegetic time runs from 1928 through the next two decades to the end of the Resistance War, a total span of 17 years. It is divided into three time periods, representing three distinct stages of development.

At the beginning of the story, Zhang Tiesuo is a mid-level peasant owning his own house and a small amount of land, which enables him to maintain himself without becoming a tenant. However, this happy state is destroyed by an incident which immediately deprives him of everything he owns, a typical instance of the unjust seizure of peasants' lands by landlords. A false accusation of property destruction is made by Chunxi, backed by his uncle, the village head Li Ruzhen, and his relative Xiaoxi, who serves a powerful warlord. The large amount of remuneration demanded from him costs Zhang Tiesuo's lands, house, and savings. Moreover, fearing Zhang Tiesuo's wife may dare to petition to a higher authority for justice, the villains contrive to have her jailed on a fabricated charge of conspiracy to murder. The force of evil is so strong that injustice prevails. Such events demonstrate the persistence of the traditional power structures in rural areas. The allies of the despotic village head are an army officer and a school teacher, traditionally considered members of the gentry class.

In the second stage of development, Zhang Tiesuo comes to Taiyuan to seek employment. He encounters Xiaoxi there and becomes his batman for one year. Though he earns nothing in his job, he meets the student Xiaochang, who is a Communist Party worker, and who answers his numerous questions about the unfair treatment he has suffered. He regains some faith in life after this experience, but unlike later Communist stories in which party member(s) have to take the initiative in seeking to inspire the masses with revolutionary awareness, here it is Zhang Tiesuo who approaches Xiaochang in his quest for answers.

The third stage is the most crucial in the development of the story, or rather, of Zhang Tiesuo as a character. After he returns home, he is imprisoned by the authorities because Xiaoxi has learned that he has been spreading the ideas he learned from Xiaochang—that the oppressors need to be overturned. Released after the establishment of the united front, he again

meets Xiaochang and helps the latter to mobilize the masses. What follows is
an example of the "problem story" that we are familiar with: Chunxi and
Xiaoxi manipulate local party workers and usurp the power of the
government organization. With the assistance of the masses, Xiaochang
recognizes their scheme and redresses the problem.

The story thus far seemingly is a Bildungsroman, because it focuses on
the life experience of Zhang Tiesuo, but from here on, we rarely see him
again. It is often argued that when he attains a mature, "awakened"
revolutionary consciousness, he merges into the revolutionary collectivity,
and thus he as a person can fade into the background. However, Zhang
Tiesuo does not seem mature enough: for example, he does not recognize the
strategy the villains employ to cajole the cadres. The story thus appears to
be an incomplete and unsuccessful account of Zhang Tiesuo's intellectual and
political maturation, perhaps hindered in this regard by the preference for
describing the events of his life from his own perspective. This narrative
strategy is dictated by a concern for the intended peasant readers, who were
more likely to identify with such a portrayal. The writer does however
provide a thorough exposition of the revolution through Xiaochang's speech
to the peasants, in which he describes the mission of the resistance
movement, and explains in colloquial language the relationship between the
resistance efforts and the people's awakening to their rights-rent-reduction,
freedom, and democracy.①

What follows is the development of the ongoing social-political
momentum. Although the villains, having become Japanese collaborators,
had been subjected to temporary disciplinary measures by resistance
fighters, they were protected by the warlord Yan Xishan. Later, they stage

---

① Likewise, at the end of the story, the writer arranges the new villager to make a
speech detailing the contrast between the new and the old life as a concomitant result of the
resistance work, with the conclusion: "The world here is not their world anymore! This
world has completely become ours." All these plot arrangements, although not organic
enough to fit into the texture, meant to emphasize the message of the correlation between
the anti-Japanese work and the project of nation-building.

a coup，murdering those who oppose them，and burying Xiaochang alive. The arrival of a large Communist army finally brings about Li Ruzhen's capture，and he is then beaten to death by angry peasants determined to take revenge for their sufferings.[1] Chunxi takes refuge with the warlord and Xiaoxi with the Japanese，so justice has not been fully done. Soon afterwards，the new world is disturbed by new threats，and so the story ends up with an epilogue that is no less important：at a celebration party，Zhang Tiesuo announces the KMT's outlawing of the Party，and rouses the villagers to join the army. The final scene is a warm send-off for the newly expanded army，in which Zhang Tiesuo's wife encourages her grown-up child to emulate his father in bravely fighting against reactionaries. This is an elaboration of the formula of disturbance-intervention-restoration in the writer's earlier stories，prefiguring a direction that would be followed by other Communist writers，such as Ding Ling.

To fit in with the Party's "new democracy" policy of seeking to unite all patriotic elements in the resistance efforts，the novel also describes an enlightened member of the gentry class，a senile Wang Anfu. He is a large landowner in his sixties，and has suffered greatly during the recent turbulent decades. After being educated by Xiaochang，who allays his misgivings about the alleged radicalism of the Party，he voluntarily introduces rent reductions and makes contributions to the resistance. Because of this，he too is ill-treated by the reactionary villains. The inclusion of this new element not only shows the author conscientiously devotes his writing to anti-war enterprise，but also reveals that he is seeking a broader readership than before.

To cater to the peasants' taste for stories，the writer blurs the distinction between genres ( though probably unconsciously )，melding a Bildungsroman and a resistance novel with traditional "problem stories." The thematic focus of the novel is the defeat of the villains and the

---

[1] The mob dismemberment of Li Ruzhen might look gruesome，but contemporary readers were probably impatient for this late stroke of justice. This model inspired many later stories about land reform.

establishment of the new regime under changed social-political institutions. In the midst of this great momentum for social progress, Zhang Tiesuo and Xiaochang are only a facilitating medium of the historical process, not individual heroes; while the villains of the "power class" are obstacles to the process. To meet the purpose of representing the ongoing great historical experience, the writer develops his literary craft in this novel, skillfully expanding or compressing his narrative: the events of six months are dealt with in detail in three chapters, while a span of seven years can be skipped over in just two chapters. He also uses a variety of narrative techniques, which have been perceptively analyzed by Josephine Alzbeta Matthews.① In particular, he employs multiple narrative perspectives, deftly switching between a "telling" mode with an external point of view, which can speed the passage of time, and a "showing" mode with an internal point of view, which can emphasize the role of individual characters within the flow of events. ② Descriptions of the environment are not included for their own sake, but to clarify the characters' perception, and to serve to reveal their personalities by showing what intrigues or interests them.

## 五、The Paradox of Zhao Shuli's "Direction"

Zhao Shuli realized that the New Literature that sprang from the May Fourth Movement was not effective enough to achieve the goal of sweeping away feudal culture. He believed that China's "literary altar" (文坛) was "too high for the masses to clamber up to"; it had to be torn down and be replaced by "literary mat," literally the type of small mat that market

---

① Matthews, J. A., *Artistry and Authenticity: Zhao Shuli and His Fictional World*, *PhD Dissertation*. Ohio State University, 1991:229-268.

② Josephine Alzbeta Matthews has cited A. W. Friedman's description of his narrative perspective: "At times he may approach omniscience, at others provide only occasional explication of the internal realities of those within his province, at still others become little more than a roving reporter ... a 'camera' eye." Quoted from Matthews, J. A., *Artistry and Authenticity: Zhao Shuli and His Fictional World*, *PhD Dissertation*. Ohio State University, 1991:233.

vendors spread out on the ground to display their wares. He recognized that to weaken the dominance of the feudal culture and dispel the "feudal consciousness" among the masses, progressive works had to "crammed into *A Whole Forest of Jokes* and *Seven Heroes and Five Gallants*"—traditional stories that were popular with the peasant masses and would appear frequently on vendor's mats. [1] The influence of his works is said to have eventually surpassed that of these old tales. It was his ability to attract peasants towards the world of fiction, with realistic stories modeled on their own experience, that has led to Zhao Shuli's works being praised for being a perfect vehicle of the "national form" and for promoting the "new (democratic) culture."

The subaltern class of the peasantry was now being represented from the perspective of the peasants themselves. This is most obviously seen in "Fugui," where the narrator stands on the same level with the protagonist, rather than above him, and seeks to understand his hard life and his inner feelings, rather than merely exposing his ignorance.

Zhao Shuli's stories are largely based on real incidents. His adaptation of true events points to the later development of socialist realism. For instance, the scenario of "Little Blackie Gets Married" is derived from a real-life murder case in which a young man who provided the model for Xiao Erhei was beaten to death by malicious rivals who had usurped power in the local government. [2] A decade earlier, the May Fourth "Enlightenment" agenda would have encouraged Zhao Shuli to employ a critical realistic mode of writing, to make this tragedy a "typical" case exposing the ignorance and cruelty of rural peasants. Zhao Shuli instead transformed a real-life tragedy into a social comedy in order to appeal to the aesthetic habitus of the peasant masses. He also toned down his depiction of the ingrained "feudal consciousness" of the peasants in the story—showing them as taking a neutral position, rather than a cold and cruel stance—so as not to risk alienating his intended readership. According to the Party's new doctrine,

---

[1]　陈荒煤:《向赵树理的方向迈进》,《人民日报》,1947 年 8 月 10 日.

[2]　董均伦:《赵树理怎样处理〈小二黑结婚〉的材料》,《文艺报》,1949 年第 10 期.

the backward consciousness of the masses was susceptible to change, and what mattered was not to expose their ignorance and even cruelty while under the sway of old feudal concepts, but to deliver them out of this ignorance. In "Meng Xiangying Stands Up," Zhao Shuli depicted the villagers' reaction towards the title character's tragic life with a light touch, which has led some scholars complain that it "creates a curiously discordant effect."[1] However, his narrator states that "according to the 'old rules,' there was no need to ask why a man had hit his wife," a statement which clearly distances him from the patriarchal tradition and pours scorn on its legitimacy. When a work is intended for the masses to read, to educate them, it requires subtlety in approaching its subject matter. Zhao Shuli's stories follow Mao Zedong's injunction "not to expose, but to teach." He therefore aimed to make his stories compatible with the "structure of feeling" of the peasant world, so that they could assert a positive influence. This approach entailed a gradual yet fundamental change in, or rather, a supplement to, the notion of "typicality," and contributed to the new concept of "representability": his stories encapsulate the "spirit" of the historical moment, prefiguring the change that must occur in the near future.

Zhao Shuli also skillfully utilized and adapted folk language and style. It has been said that his "The Rhymes of Li Youcai," was "above all a response to Mao Zedong's call for the use of national or folk forms, a practical example of the writer speaking to and for the masses in their own language." However, this is not necessarily a conscious "response to," but might be an incidental echo of Mao Zedong's idea.[2] Li Youcai in the story is

---

① Feuerwerker, Y. M., *Ideology, Power, Text: Self-Representation and the Peasant "Other" in Modern Chinese Literature*, Stanford: Stanford University Press, 1998: 125. The example she presents is the reaction of the villagers towards the mistreatment that Meng Xiangying has been subjected to from her husband: when the latter hacked a bloody wound on her forehead, the villagers "were only saying that he had hit her in the wrong place: nobody asked why he had hit her."

② Feuerwerker, Y. M., *Ideology, Power, Text: Self-Representation and the Peasant "Other" in Modern Chinese Literature*, Stanford: Stanford University Press, 1998: 130.

like a model Party writer, transvaluing popular folk entertainment and shifting the "conventional associations of such rhymes with the risqué and ribald release of sexual tension … to new associations with political activism and ultimately political panegyric, to express the will of the Communist leadership on behalf of the peasantry."[1] Traditional folk arts such as "clapper talk" are now "detached from their folk origins, revised and adapted to new use"[2] and appear to meet Mao Zedong's call for a "lively (national) form that is catering to the taste of the people."

The story affirms the intuitive wisdom of the peasantry as personified by Li Youcai. His superior vision, knowledge, and literary skill call to mind the Party's promotion of the rights and intellect of the peasants, in contrast to the outlook of the May Fourth intellectuals who regarded them as ignorant and in need of being "enlightened." Li Youcai, a capable, resourceful, and almost omniscient character, yet a fully integrated member of masses, in this light provides a role model for the new generation of intellectuals. Zhao Shuli's story thus efficiently presents the Party's "mass line," that revolutionary action should be integrated with the reality of the masses' lives, that "investigation and study"（调查研究）of rural society should become the "tool"（工具）for furthering the revolution.

The Party plays a leading and authoritative role in the story: the wise cadre Comrade Yang redresses the wrongdoings of the local despots, and, with the help of the local peasants, restores order and rebuilds their local government. When everything is done, he encourages Li Youcai to compose a celebratory rhyme and praises it as "summing up the whole business!" The voice of the Party is heard, its authority imposed, its victory eulogized. Yet the victory is arrived through letting the peasants speak up for themselves. In short, the authority of the Party goes hand in hand with the empowerment of the subaltern. The narrator in this story acts as a mediator

---

① Feuerwerker, Y. M., *Ideology, Power, Text : Self-Representation and the Peasant "Other" in Modern Chinese Literature*, Stanford: Stanford University Press, 1998:130.

② Feuerwerker, Y. M., *Ideology, Power, Text : Self-Representation and the Peasant "Other" in Modern Chinese Literature*, Stanford: Stanford University Press, 1998:130.

"between the village community and the broader readership 'out there,' between the two languages of folk idiom and 'official speech'—that is, standard Chinese," and "remains in charge of plot action," but does not comment directly on unfolding events; this latter function is left to the "clapper talker" Li Youcai.[①] Put in another way, although the narrator is an outsider, he is simultaneously an insider—because he has been integrated into the peasant world and has assimilated its grammar. The intellectual writer has finally "joined the people"; he does not merely "represent" them.[②]

The language of the story is a mixture of folk dialect, colloquial language, and modern literary language, which produces a new, lively style. As Yi-tsi Mei Feuerwerker notes:

> The author/narrator incorporates local idioms and strives for a folksy down-to-earth style himself, seeking to make his own language and vision converge with that of the folk artist's ... The juxtaposition of two genres of different language and compositional forms—one more literary, intellectual, and modern, in spite of its adoption of the oral story-teller's voice, the other folk and traditional—within this joint narrative enterprise enables them to interact and create a relationship of mutual endorsement in the text.[③]

This brings in a popular style of writing, which is entertaining to the rural masses who were the intended readers, and not too vulgar for urban educated readers. Some veteran writers such as Guo Moruo saw this

---

① Feuerwerker, Y. M., *Ideology, Power, Text: Self-Representation and the Peasant "Other" in Modern Chinese Literature*, Stanford: Stanford University Press, 1998:130-131.

② Yi-tsi Mei Feuerwerker points out that the modern narrative structure links Li Youcai's clapper verses and provides them with a framework in which "the people will appear to have their say; their wisdom, their true perceptions of the world, are given a vocal presence." Feuerwerker, Y. M., *Ideology, Power, Text: Self-Representation and the Peasant "Other" in Modern Chinese Literature*, Stanford: Stanford University Press, 1998:131.

③ Feuerwerker, Y. M., *Ideology, Power, Text: Self-Representation and the Peasant "Other" in Modern Chinese Literature*, Stanford: Stanford University Press, 1998:131.

combination as creating a possibility for an alternative literature that could build a "new culture."

On the other hand, it was due to this self-imposed goal of accommodating his writing to the ethical-moral as well as the aesthetic parameters of his peasant audience, that Zhao Shuli fell short of attaining the more ambitious goal of fundamentally changing their ethical framework and moral cosmos. The Party ultimately aspired for the peasants to acquire a revolutionary consciousness and become "a class for itself," to enter into a higher ethical-moral, to participate in building a new society or constructing an "alternative modernity." Zhao Shuli's deferential approach to his readers limited his ability to realize such a far-reaching mission. Zhao Shuli's "problem stories" show that the overturning of the old hierarchy with the economic disenfranchisement of landlords and rich peasants, and the introduction of the social leveling process, do not on their own fully achieve the goal of social justice. Without sufficient education for the peasants and an effective democratic process, the new regime itself is easily penetrated by reactionary former powers. The correction of such problems still often relies on the deus ex machina of intervention by a higher authority. These stories depict the "democratic" operation of the new regime, and the final victory of the masses under the blessing and leadership of the new regime. Yet in terms of the ideological mission of awakening revolutionary consciousness and of mobilizing the masses to become the masters of their own lives, they are only of a limited success. For instance, the couple in "Little Blackie Gets Married" never have realized that power should be in the hands of the people; they retain the traditional consciousness, looking passively to an authority that can issue fair judgment for them (no matter what ideology this authority might assume).

Although the story debunks the "feudal consciousness" in regard to superstitious practices, it still leaves the traditional social mores and ethical concepts of the peasant world intact. Once the bullies are punished and the abnormality redressed, ethical world seemingly goes on as before, blessed by the new patrons. The fact that Third Fairy's behavior—attempting to seduce young men even at the age of forty-five when her beauty has faded away, and trying to frustrate her daughter's genuine love—is vilified as inappropriate by the local ethical-moral norms is because adultery undermines local order. Therefore, her giving up of her gaudy make-up and coquettish manner is a submission to the ethnical norms. The local bullies' behavior also outrages long-ingrained ideas of fairness and justice; the intervention of a higher government authority restores a peaceful world. The story is satisfying the political unconscious and the political-aesthetic habitus of the peasants. Thus, while the happy ending signifies "the desirability of the individual's unqualified subordination to the proclaimed interests of society,"[1] the society is not a new one. Therefore, this story does not fit the template of socialist realism. The characters here still lack "typical" characteristics or class consciousness. Generally speaking, they are still a class that needs to be represented, incapable of representing themselves.

This lack of revolutionary consciousness is seen both in Party members and in the masses in Zhao Shuli's other stories. For instance, although Meng Xiangying is a model Party worker, a figure who could encourage oppressed women, her lack of political consciousness makes her less a satisfactory role model. In "Little Blackie Gets Married," there is no guidance from the Party. Nor is there any "class subjectivity" in this writer's fictional world. Although "Fugui" depicts a dichotomous world which is fundamentally political in nature,[2] thus implying that the class hierarchy could only be overturned through a wholesale reform of society, it does not show how the Party liberates the peasants or how the tyrant is brought to submit to the power of the new regime. Though the actions of the tyrant are seen to be malignant, the illness of the old system can only be inferred. "Changes in Li Village" is specifically about the theme of proletarian emancipation, but it contains neither a model hero nor a revolutionary collectivity. The social

---

① Feuerwerker, Y. M., *Ideology, Power, Text: Self-Representation and the Peasant "Other" in Modern Chinese Literature*, Stanford: Stanford University Press, 1998:283.

② Matthews, J. A., *Artistry and Authenticity: Zhao Shuli and His Fictional World*, PhD Dissertation. Ohio State University, 1991:292.

dynamic finds no personified class hero or revolutionary leader (aside from the vaguely delineated and short-lived Xiaochang) to represent its direction and ethos. The "enlightenment" of the oppressed class first comes not through the active efforts of the Party worker Xiaochang but through the peasant Zhang Tiesuo's taking the initiative to ask questions. The description of the oppressed class is also not "typical": Zhang Tiesuo can cooperate with his oppressor, even running to buy opium for him, essentially becoming a debased and degraded lackey, which can be seen as contradictory to his "class identity." This sort of story-telling might be keeping with social-political conditions in which peasants, and even many Party workers, were still in the process of acquiring revolutionary ideology; but with the development of the revolution and the rise of the radical political consciousness it demanded, this mode of writing would soon have to catch up with the social tide.

The same paradox applies to the literary form. Although the writer's "subordination of his literary craft to the masses" validates "his own credentials as a revolutionary writer,"[①] his stories, having much more of a flavor of folk art, appear naive and less refined for those with an urban or Western educational background, and are not so appealing to metropolitan tastes. The question of Zhao Shuli's "alternative modernity" mirrors the dilemma of the "new democratic culture" that he endorsed and passionately endeavored to create.

## 五、Conclusion

Zhao Shuli's strong attachment to rural culture proved to be both an asset and a burden to him. His constant identification with the peasantry restricted him from writing about things other than the rural subjects. His dedication to the peasantry was laudable, but the "new culture" he envisioned for the peasants could not by itself bring about the foundation of a

---

① Matthews, J. A., *Artistry and Authenticity: Zhao Shuli and His Fictional World*, PhD Dissertation. Ohio State University, 1991:131.

new nation. His "direction" in this sense can be said to refer to his emotional identification with the peasant masses rather than the intellectuals.

The predicament of Zhao Shuli's creative impulse is also the ultimate paradox of modern Chinese culture: Zhao Shuli believed the writer/ intellectual had the obligation to communicate in a style amenable to the linguistic competence as well as aesthetic preference of his audience (the peasants); it was not the duty of the poorly educated masses to try to understand and appreciate the writer/intellectual. While his efforts in this regard are understandable, his practice obviously fell short of Mao Zedong's education ideal for cultural policy—to elevate the cultural-political level of the masses. Indeed, this was apparently not a priority of the Party at this juncture when the focus was on mobilizing the peasants to undertake the revolution, and thus the simplicity and clarity of cultural works was the first requirement. However, society is forever moving on, and even the peasants' lives and society are changing in the process of modernization after the success of the revolution. Literature needed to progress with these changes, to reach wider audiences.

## Chapter Ten From "Use of Old Forms" to "Establishment of a National Form": A Re-Evaluation of Mao's Agenda of Forging a Cultural-Political Nation

### 一、Introduction

The debate on the "use of old forms," which became a hot issue soon after the full-scale outbreak of the Resistance War in the year of 1937, sprang from two political regions with diverse (though overlapping) phenomena as its targets. In the KMT-controlled areas, many of which were metropolitan cities, popular magazines and newspaper supplements aimed at a mass audience (offering "fictional entertainment, frivolous words and idle talk") swamped the market. To intellectuals of sophisticated tastes, especially those who preferred the May Fourth New Literature, these texts, almost exclusively catering to the tastes of literate urban dwellers, still contained highly commercialized and hackneyed—and often cheap and vulgar—contents, although they often had "new and progressive" themes such as patriotic resistance and free love. On the other hand, wartime propaganda works cloaked in traditional Chinese art forms (such as local opera and folk music) also appeared backward to them. Therefore, for the intellectuals in these cities, "there was a widespread feeling that the great wave of Resistance War propaganda in old forms threatened the very survival of the New Literature and the May Fourth tradition."[1] Apparently, in these

---

① Holm, D., *Art and Ideology in Revolutionary China*, Oxford: Clarendon Press, 1991:52.

areas, the "old forms" came from two major sources: vulgar commercial culture and traditional folk art. The intended audience of both were mostly urban residents. In the CCP-controlled areas, mostly located in the countryside, the priority for works of art was educating and mobilizing the peasants. Here, "old forms" often referred to folk genres and traditional literary forms. Ideas about whether or how to use the "old forms" in creating contemporary literature were hotly debated among intellectuals of diverse aesthetic habitus and political inclinations.

The debate assumed a new orientation in the wake of Mao Zedong's call for "national form" (民族形式) in 1938, i.e., it now revolved around the relations between "old forms" and this unspecified "national form." The contention over a "national form" was not only an integral part of the debates on the Party's cultural policy and practice (both among its cultural workers in the CCP's base areas and among leftist intellectuals in the KMT-controlled areas), one with substantial political and ideological ramifications at the time; it also had significant repercussions throughout the early decades of the People's Republic of China, as many of the points brought out in the debates were crystallized in Mao Zedong's "Yan'an Talks," which laid the foundations for the Party's subsequent management of cultural matters.

For these reasons, this chapter intends to re-examine this important debate. It first discusses the contemporary referents of the "form" and "content" in the term "national form," then explores the intricate relationship among literary language use, class consciousness, and a new national culture. It suggests that Mao Zedong's agenda of creating a "national form" was not merely a means of achieving popularization, but an end aimed at creating a revolutionary culture to facilitate the establishment of a highly homogenized society, or to forge a hegemonic cultural-political nation.

## 二、The "Form" and "Content" of Modern Life

As David Holm points out, the debates in Yan'an "reveal deep divisions of opinion not only…between Party critics and Party writers, but also within the CCP's cultural leadership itself." To be sure, there was a certain consensus; for instance, many agreed that "the New Literature would have to become more Sinified, but also the revolutionary tradition of the May Fourth New Literature Movement should be reaffirmed. All agreed that the use of 'old forms' was an indispensable part of the effort, but also that these forms…would have to be substantially 'refashioned.'"[①] But we will start our analysis from another consensus or premise underlying the various arguments put forward by these party critics, which was also frequently articulated in their statements: according to the Marxist dialectics, form is determined (or better, over-conditioned) by content, so the form to be used should correspond to the expression of the (new) content. But anyway, what was the "content" and what was the "form," the two key words in the debates? From this perspective, one rarely discussed by critics thus far, we can unravel the multi-layered veils of "form" covering the inner core of "content."

There can be no doubt that all the "contents" the participants spoke of referred to modern life. But if they were talking about modern metropolitan life with its new social relations and customs, it is obvious that the May Fourth-type New Literature was better than the indigenous "old" forms at the task of showing modern sensibilities. But the native forms were still convenient in, and valid for, portraying rural life, because out of China's lagging industrialization, the vast Chinese countryside to a great extent still maintained the traditional form of life, the soil in which the "old" local folk art forms had grown. This socio-economic situation was so marked that some critics in the discussion, such as Ai Siqi (1910-1966), a Party philosopher, even believed that "the forms of art popular among the common people actually had certain advantages over the new forms of the

---

① Holm, D., *Art and Ideology in Revolutionary China*, Oxford: Clarendon Press, 1991: 54.

May Fourth tradition when it came to portraying the lives of the people."[1]
Here, "the lives of the people" has a specified referent, but Ai Siqi seemed
to be unconscious of it, or at least avoided talking about it in more detail.

If, however, it is "revolutionary struggle," including resistance efforts,
that are the "content," then the indigenous forms are still viable as a
medium portraying such scenes—though, because of long-term cultural
differentiation among various classes and in different areas, they catered
more to the tastes of the rural masses than to urban residents. To be sure,
the May Fourth Literature is also pertinent in this respect, but it appears to
have been more congenial to urban readers.

Now let us examine the same issue from another perspective—that of
"form." If "old forms" refers to existing local rural art forms, it is clear that
unadapted, they were too coarse and unrefined to appeal to urban audience;
if, on the other hand, it refers to the forms of traditional "high culture,"
such as classical poetry and drama, it had a highly restricted capacity to
convey modern sensibilities and describe sophisticated social relations. It
seems that only the last categories of "old forms"—the May Fourth New
Literature and Revolutionary Literature (the "critical realism" promoted in
the 1930s), and even the popular Mandarin Duck and Butterfly works—were
candidates that were up to the mission of delivering the socio-economic and

---

① Holm, D., *Art and Ideology in Revolutionary China*, Oxford: Clarendon Press,
1991:57. Ai Siqi made a distinction between genuine realism (现实主义), referring to
certain Chinese forms of art believed to offer a true reflection of social reality, and the
classical nineteenth-century European realism (写实主义), which, he contended, was
merely a specific stylistic effect but not necessarily more faithful to reality. Meanwhile, he
also referred to the realism of old Chinese forms as a sort of "special method" that gave
exaggerated and stylized expression to characters and social institutions. For him, "the
function of art did not originally require a minute and exhaustive delineation of reality, but
only demanded that it could forcefully grasp reality." On the other hand, he also saw a
contradiction here: although the exaggeration of old forms reflected reality forcefully, this
stylization also "represents the conservative aspect of Chinese society" because of its
routinization. We surely cannot see this argument merely as a sort of nationalistic rhetoric,
and we need to note that the realities in the two forms refer to two differing ways of life. 艾
思奇:《旧形式运用的基本原则》,《文艺战线》,1939,1(3):17-20.

emotional structures of modern society. But with their Europeanized language，they certainly appeared too sophisticated and difficult for the broad masses，especially (and predominantly) the peasants who constituted more than ninety percent of the population and who were the targets of the CCP's mobilization.

In this brief survey，we see clearly that this dialectic of content and form is tied in with the relations between literary form and historical content/experience. This was the ultimate reason for their differing priorities. But also at stake were their differing audience and their various cultural distinctions. All these differences were dictated by the polarized urban-rural division. Therefore，although some discussants had contended that new content would naturally change "old forms" into "new forms," this transformation was limited and its efficacy doubtful if we take all "the people" into consideration—because of social stratification and the urban-rural opposition，a real-life solution to this predicament was hard to find.

Thus we see the following four sides in the discussions，with "indigenous forms" and "May Fourth Literature" being the two coordinates. Where "old forms" refers to indigenous popular art forms，especially folk art，some believed that it should be creatively refashioned into the basic source of a new national culture. A representative of these ideas was Chen Boda (1904-1989). Even though he was the first to propose the term "national form," he directly identified it with "old forms," and argued strongly for the "combination of new cultural content with old national form."[①] In this way，one could "pack (new content) into the old form and give it appropriate refashioning."[②] In addition，May Fourth New Literature could offer supplementary assistance—Chen Boda takes works of the New Literature to be components of the "national form," provided that they have the ability to move the masses.

Some critics [such as the Poet Xiao San(1896-1983)] are on the side of "old forms" yet are against the May Fourth tradition (Ai Siqi，as we

---

① 陈伯达：《在文化战线上》，生活书店 1939 年版，第 92-93 页.
② 艾思奇：《旧形式运用的基本原则》，《文艺战线》，1939，1(3)：69.

mentioned above, also holds this view). Apparently, the audience in the minds of these writers and artists was mainly the peasant masses, for the merit attributed to the "national form" in the models of China's "old forms" (mainly folk literature) was that it could tap into the structure of feeling of the masses and move and inspire them.

The audience implied in the arguments of the other direction on the scale points to different sections of "the masses." This other direction prioritizes Westernized art forms and more or less decries indigenous forms, especially folk art. This tendency is represented by Zhou Yang (1908-1989), head of "鲁艺" (the Lu Xun Academy of Art, the most famed institution of higher education in Yan'an), who preferred elevation to popularization. He suggested that the May Fourth New Literature should be the point of departure, with the assistance of indigenous art forms if necessary. For him, because the Europeanization of the New Literature Movement had answered the real needs of China at the time, it had "become an organic part of the Chinese people's blood and flesh."[1] These "new forms" were held to have a "higher ideological character and artistic quality" than the old forms; the "old forms" (local folk art), "owing to both subjective and objective factors, generally still can only be a lower form of art." This distinction of backward/advanced form is founded upon a one-to-one correspondence of content and form, a seemingly Marxist base—superstructure determinism that sees "conflicts and struggles between advanced content and backward forms."[2] In this teleological schema, "old forms would eventually entirely give way to new forms."[3]

Another spokesperson for this direction is Xian Xinghai (1905-1945), a famed music professor in the same institution, whose argument, like Zhou

---

[1]　周扬:《对旧形式利用在文学上的一个看法》,《中国文化》,1945,1(1):34-39.

[2]　He says, "Particular forms are suitable for particular kinds of content; they came about in the midst of the old social structure, had their roots in the old world outlook, and already have their own old set of images." 周扬:《对旧形式利用在文学上的一个看法》,《中国文化》,1945,1(1):37.

[3]　Holm, D., *Art and Ideology in Revolutionary China*, Oxford:Clarendon Press, 1991:63.

Yang's，is also predicated on a rigid content-form determinism which refutes the idea that "old bottles can hold new wine," though he also acknowledges that the masses cannot accept new （Western） art forms quickly or naturally.[①] Essentially，his theory was "to Westernize Chinese music，and thereby 'win a place in international music'."[②] He Qifang （1912-1977），head of the Literature Department there， supports this view. His rationalization is also premised on a cultural Darwinian framework. To him，"European literature is more advanced than China's old literature or folk literature. Hence the continued growth of the New Literature must still rely primarily on the reception of these relatively healthy， lively， and rich nutrients."[③] For him，indigenous tradition has given sufficient nutrition to New Literature，so the latter is already an integral portion of Chinese culture. On the other hand，although he acknowledges not having explored

---

① He says，"Old forms and old content，though they can work for each other harmoniously，are absolutely not appropriate today. New content and old form are a little bit incongruous. New content set to new form is not only harmonious but also very necessary，though oftentimes the masses cannot accept it very quickly and naturally... I propose that we let content determine form，and apply a modern，advanced viewpoint to produce new content." Clearly，this rigid content-form determinism is also premised on a teleological point of view. Somewhat contradictory to his strong argument，however，is the fact that he also praised the achievement of the Chinese musical tradition and proposed to combine Chinese and Western musical instruments in a special kind of Chinese symphony orchestra. His rhetoric reminds us of the enduring formula of Chinese intellectuals："Western knowledge as the essence，Chinese knowledge for the use （or raw materials）." 冼星海:《论中国音乐的民族形式》,《文艺战线》,1939,1(5):1.

② See Holm，D.，*Art and Ideology in Revolutionary China*，Oxford：Clarendon Press，1991：60-62. He comes to the conclusion that "there is little evidence in this essay... that Xian Xinghai paid very much attention to the musical tastes of the Chinese masses per se." Holm D. *Art and Ideology in Revolutionary China*. Oxford：Clarendon Press，1991：62. In his artistic creation，Xian Xinghai thus typifies the direction preferred by this group of intellectuals："Rather than starting from Chinese opera and then modernizing，Xian and his colleagues worked in the opposite direction，reworking Chinese musical material and fitting it into a Western operatic structure." Holm，D.，*Art and Ideology in Revolutionary China*，Oxford：Clarendon Press，1991：70.

③ 何其芳:《论文学上的民族形式》,《文艺战线》,1939,1(5):11.

old forms thoroughly, he believes that old forms have great intrinsic limitations. As he was working in an institution which stressed elevation, his urging that actual practice should be "best left to those who have done some work in this field" amounts to insinuating that it was best to follow the injunctions of Westernized specialists.

The most radical view on this side, however, is held by the literary critic Wang Shiwei (1906-1947), who thoroughly repudiated folk tradition for the reason that it contained feudal consciousness. Notwithstanding the lip service paid to the usefulness of old forms for the masses, the implied readership/audience on this side of the debate was in the main obviously intellectuals, or the literate "masses."[1] To be sure, it is probable that the critics in this group would not have acknowledged this publicly; instead, they stressed that the ordinary masses were also a potential audience for the new literature. Nevertheless, in their evaluation, the "old forms," in a universal scheme of teleological evolution, was inferior in themselves and at best valid only for temporary, makeshift use. It is perhaps because this view was popular in Yan'an that Mao Zedong felt the necessity to stand out again and redirect the direction of the debates.[2]

---

[1]   So Zhou Yang could say that the contradiction between advanced content and backward form "can even elicit the laughter of an experienced readership or audience during a tragic scene." 周扬:《对旧形式利用在文学上的一个看法》,《中国文化》,1945,1(1). David Holm aptly comments, "Such incongruities might not have been so obvious to the mass audiences for whom such works were presumably intended." Holm, D., *Art and Ideology in Revolutionary China*, Oxford:Clarendon Press, 1991:64.

[2]   David Holm points out that "One result of this was that the ringing phrases and activist slogans proclaimed by Mao in October 1938 were gradually surrounded by a conservative exegesis which neutralized them and deprived them of any clear implications for practice. It was this process which eventually led to further interventions by Mao in 1940 and again in 1942." Holm, D., *Art and Ideology in Revolutionary China*, Oxford:Clarendon Press, 1991:55.

### 三、The Problem of National Language

Before we discuss Mao Zedong's vision of "national form," including his view on the "use of old forms," we have to make a brief study of the canonization of, and discontent over, the "May Fourth tradition," which occupied so large a share of the arguments of all sides and was itself the subject of an important re-evaluation by Mao Zedong.

Although the May Fourth proponents of a "白话"(Vernacular) literary language vociferously denounced the old classical literary language, they also repudiated the pre-modern vernacular and regional vernaculars seen in popular fiction. The vernacular they promoted was a special language, Europeanized in grammar and utterance. In some of the early writings of the May Fourth writers, we see that even peasants speak this awkward language. Therefore, this literary form was unpopular. Contrary to its proponents' intentions, the so-called "new literature" written in this language was influential only among a small circle of Westernized intellectuals and students. It was still difficult for ordinary Chinese to access it.

This problem was later defined by the CCP as a class issue. Ever since then, the discussion of language or literary form has been inexorably linked with the notion of class and class analysis. Unlike the dichotomy posed by the May Fourth New Culture Movement between aristocracy and plebeian, this antagonism was now taken to be between bourgeois and proletarian (language and culture). The Party openly denounced the fact that the implied readers of this new language were urbanites with a bourgeois background, while the literature written in this medium did not reach the masses of the lower class. Qu Qiubai (1899-1935), the early CCP leader, in a 1932 article "The Question of Popular Literature and Art," rebuked this May Fourth elitism and Europeanization, referring to the new Westernized vernacular as a "new classical language." He charged that because May Fourth intellectuals uncritically accepted Western bourgeois ideology and propagated its hegemonic culture, their motives and actions did not take China's realities into consideration and could not serve the interests of the working people.

Qu Qiubai's critique of the hegemony of Western cultural modernity does not mean that he viewed modern bourgeois culture negatively. He acknowledged its progressive function in creating the modern capitalist mode of production in Western Europe. He also did not deny that the May Fourth Enlightenment had achieved laudable success in combating "feudal tradition." But he said that because it was primarily a bourgeois cultural movement, its elitist and European inclinations divorced intellectuals from Chinese reality: "They do not have a common language with China's working class, and they are almost foreigners to the middle-and-lower ranks of the people."[①] Even after leftist writers underwent a "Marxist turn" after the Nationalist massacre of Communists and their sympathizers in 1927, Europeanization still remained a problem unresolved.

The language they used, he said, was a hybrid: "Neither a horse, nor a donkey," but "mule-like." Therefore, it was a "new classical language" mixing archaic and aristocratic literary language with Europeanized idioms.[②] But here Europeanization should not be taken merely as style or syntax that was "unfamiliar" to the Chinese working class; it needs to be decoded as a word for Western bourgeois cultural hegemony. That is, in his view, works with a Western style and European syntax not only made awkward prose, but also brought with them the stigma of bourgeois hegemony/ideology. Consequently, they relentlessly severed the ties between these May Fourth petit bourgeois intellectuals and the masses.[③]

As an alternative, he then called for making use of "the modern vernacular spoken by living Chinese…especially the language spoken by the proletariat." He contended that because of modernization, this language is used by the proletariat, or common language (mandarin), "contains aspects

---

① 瞿秋白:《瞿秋白文集(第 2 卷)》,人民文学出版社 1953 年版,第 856 页.
② 瞿秋白:《瞿秋白文集(第 2 卷)》,人民文学出版社 1953 年版,第 596 页.
③ 瞿秋白:《瞿秋白文集(第 2 卷)》,人民文学出版社 1953 年版,第 880-888 页.

of a variety of local dialects while eliminating the obscure localisms of those dialects."[①] In the same vein, this language was closely tied to the class issue.

Although Qu Qiubai advocated developing a revolutionary national-popular culture for the proletariat, he still mainly targeted on urban readers, because the proletariat here refers solely to the urban proletariat (mainly industrial workers) who were seen by Qu Qiubai (then Party leader), on the basis of orthodox Marxist precepts, as the motive force of the socialist revolution. The peasantry was excluded from this parameter. Only from this perspective can we understand why Qu Qiubai says the language of rural people is primitive and obscure. And we can also see that the language he talks about here is ultimately still a literary, written language.

With regard to the problem of mass illiteracy, a Romanization movement had tried to develop a Romanized system to replace Chinese characters between 1933 and 1936, and there had been various discussions of this project by CCP intellectuals. However, after Mao Zedong took power in the Party, the focus changed completely. Great attention was now paid to the mobilization of the peasants as the revolution itself shifted its locus to the rural areas. The discussion of language was still couched in terms of the effectiveness of propaganda, but now the effective medium was taken to be the local, familiar language of the peasants. It was this pragmatic approach to popularization that necessitated new attention to different local languages or dialects.

The outbreak of full-scale war with Japan in 1937 ignited a nationwide passion for the popularization of literature, now that the message to be communicated was much more one of united resistance than the class struggle promoted earlier. How was this resistance consciousness and patriotic zeal to be conveyed to the utmost number of people? The problem of popularization now fell on both the language medium to be used (dialect or the common language) and literary style. And again, the outstanding

---

① Qu Qiubai. The question of popular literature and art. P G. Pickowicz, Trans. Berninghausen J. and Huters T. eds. *Revolutionary Literature in China: An Anthology*. White Plains: M.E. Sharpe, Inc., 1976: 49.

problem was closely related to the relationship between intellectuals and the masses (the peasants). But "national form" was not entirely a language issue; rather, it was tied closely to a new national culture Mao Zedong envisioned.

## 四、National Form and National Culture

It has been noted that "Mao's call for 'national form' in October 1938 was in part an attempt to change the terms of this debate." [1] His replacement of "old forms" with "national form" was to dispel the negative connotation of the prefix "old." But what is more, he essentially changed the term from an issue of literary genre or style to one that pertained to the political realm. If Chen Boda's proposal for "national form" was made out of pragmatic considerations (whether the form used could mobilize the masses), then Mao Zedong's appropriation of the term contained his vision of a new national culture.

The term appeared the first time in his call for a "Sinified Marxism." In his address entitled "The Role of the Communist Party in the National War" at the Sixth Party Plenum in October 1938, Mao Zedong said:

> Being Marxists, communists are internationalists, but Marxism can only be realized through a national form. There is no abstract Marxism, there is only concrete Marxism. By concrete Marxism we mean the Marxism with national form, and to apply Marxism to the concrete struggles in the concrete circumstance of China, rather than applying it in the abstract. [2]

This sinification of Marxism "will endow every manifestation of Marxism with a Chinese character, that is to say, applying it according to China's characteristics." For this imperative, Mao Zedong called for repudiation of anything which conflicts with this requirement: "Foreign

①   Holm, D., *Art and Ideology in Revolutionary China*. Oxford: Clarendon Press, 1991, 52.

②   Mao, Z., On New Democracy, *Selected Works of Mao Tse-tung* (Vol. 12), Beijing: Foreign Language Press, 1967: 209-210.

'eight-legged essays' must be abolished, chanting of the vacuous and abstract tunes must be reduced, dogmatism must be put to rest." He dictated the alternative: "They must be replaced by the refreshing, lively Chinese styles and airs that are palatable to the taste and ears of the common folks."

A close inspection of these phenomena and styles that Mao Zedong either castigated or promoted will reveal the incoherence of the different categories. "Foreign eight-legged essays" refers to those articles with stereotyped language and form, i.e., style of writing; "vacuous and abstract tunes" can refer either to style of writing or to empty policy without detailed content, i. e., work style; and dogmatism, insofar as it points to Mao Zedong's political opponents who either followed Soviet Union's orders or stuck to Marxist dogma that denied the possibility of a communist revolution in China, was a political term. All of these, whether referring to style of writing or way of working, were delivered at the political level. After bringing out the aforementioned evils as targets, Mao Zedong's ultimate objective was "Chinese styles and airs." Therefore, rather than merely being a way of reforming the awkward existing prose language and creating a new literary style, the content of "national form" should also be examined from the political perspective.

The key to understanding this famous paragraph lies in the import of the "sinification of Marxism." In my view, this does not simply mean applying Marxist theory to Chinese society, nor does it mean Mao Zedong's famous strategy of undertaking revolution by mobilizing the peasants to "encircle the cities from rural areas." But it probably implies Mao Zedong's preliminary consideration of the idea of breaking away from orthodox Marxist doctrine which dictates a teleological route to socialism via capitalism. This supposition can be partially substantiated by Mao Zedong's emphasis on China's own "laws of development." Several sentences preceding this paragraph indicate this point:

> Another mission of study is to study our historical heritage, and to summarize it critically by the Marxist method. The several thousand years of history of our great nation has its own laws of development, its own national characteristics... We are

Marxist historicists, and we should not cut off history. We should sum up and inherit the valuable legacy from Confucius to Sun Yat-sen. Inheriting this legacy will then bring out a method, which will significantly help us in guiding the great movement of the present.

Marxist historical materialism is a dialectics that calls for attention to both the universal and the particular. While there is a general movement towards the liberation of the whole humanity, the process of attaining it is subject to the particular social, political, and historical conditions of differing countries/regions. In this light, the "method" to be generated after studying Chinese history (to "help us in guiding the great movement of the present") was Mao Zedong's anti-teleological thinking of exploring a Chinese path to socialism. Although this seems to be a challenge to orthodox Marxist dogma, it was also consistent with the CCP's analysis of modern China's history. This reasoning was put forward more clearly in Mao Zedong's "On New Democracy," written in 1940.

In this significant treatise, Mao Zedong started by proposing to use the Marxist principle of historical materialism to analyze the contemporary historical juncture. He contended that there was an antinomy: on the one hand, the time was yet not ripe for socialism; therefore, to "clear away the obstacles to the development of capitalism," which was essentially the task of the bourgeois revolution, remained the "objective mission" of the people. On the other hand, oppressed by feudal forces and imperialism alike, the weak national bourgeoisie was incapable of leading this revolution, so that the burden fell on the proletariat, who had to "participate in the leadership or take up the leadership" and lead the masses to wipe out the feudal forces and evict the imperialists. This would ensure that the struggle would not lead to a bourgeois state ruled by the bourgeois class, but to a "new democratic society" founded on a coalition of the various classes participating in the revolution.

Although this new democratic society was essentially a capitalist one, and in the original version of the treatise Mao Zedong also indicated the inevitability of capitalism as a historical stage, he also specified that this "new democratic society" was a transitional stage leading to the second stage, a socialist revolution. Perhaps he hesitated at the time to break away

from the historical determinism of classical Marxist precepts.[①] Yet whatever
the truth may be, endowing the proletariat with the leadership role in the
(bourgeois) revolution already exemplifies Mao Zedong's efforts at the
sinification of Marxism. As "a local (or vernacular) version of a universal
Marxism," it restructured Marxism "to accommodate the questions thrown
up by this multidimensional historical situation."[②]

For Mao Zedong, because China was subjugated by the oppression of
the imperialist powers, "socialism was not merely an alternative to
capitalism, but an alternative that promised national liberation from
capitalist hegemony, and the possibility of entering global history not as its
object but as an independent subject."[③] This was probably what was in his
mind when he composed the awkward sentences quoted above, which mix up
history, politics, and culture. In this light, "national form," as a code word
for the concretization of Marxism on Chinese soil through the transformation
of Marxist economic determinism, simultaneously becomes the political
statement of a "Chinese Marxism."

In a like manner, though in the beginning Mao Zedong acknowledged
the classical Marxist view that economic factors "determine" culture since
the latter "reflects" political and economic life, he immediately turned to
deliberation on revolution in the ideological, political, and cultural areas. In
particular, the "new democracy," as a new regime, was for him premised on
a "new democratic culture."

---

① The other rationalization after Mao Zedong had determined to bypass capitalism
and the "new democratic society" to arrive at socialism would be that as the aforementioned
harshly disadvantageous conditions precluded the possibility of bourgeois revolution and the
development of capitalism in China, national liberation must go hand in hand with social
revolution to liberate the peasants from exploitation and oppression by the landlords.
Therefore, China would bypass capitalist development and go directly to socialism. See
numerous articles of Mao Zedong in the early fifties.

② Dirlik, A., *Marxism in the Chinese Revolution*, Lanham, Md: Rowman &
Littlefield Publishers, 2005:78-79.

③ Dirlik, A., *Marxism in the Chinese Revolution*, Lanham, Md: Rowman &
Littlefield Publishers, 2005:80.

What was at stake in proposing this cultural blueprint and portraying its features should be considered in the light of the specific historical juncture. The Resistance War was commonly understood by the populace at the time to be a pivotal moment for China's destruction of its residual yet still strong feudal social relationships and the overhauling of contemporary national cultural consciousness. The CCP seized on this general will. Mao Zedong understood that he must build a theory to map the contours of a new culture so as to win the battle in the ideological field. For him to win over the minds of intellectuals and the society in general, he had to exhibit the superiority of this revolutionary culture and politics. Therefore, he saw this mission as being a primary task comparable to the military one (and thereby endowed with a metaphorical military rhetoric work on the "cultural front.")

In order to accord with the anti-Japanese united front, this new cultural formation was a mixture of such divergent cultures as the bourgeois, the petty bourgeois, and the working class. But the problematic of class and class analysis by no means became irrelevant or unimportant (at least for Mao Zedong, who frequently criticized other high-ranking Party leaders for failing to notice this important issue when carrying out united front policy). Mao Zedong repeatedly reiterated that the Party had joined the united Resistance War for the whole nation, and first and foremost for the laboring masses. Therefore, the content of this new democratic culture was defined as:

> …the anti-imperialist, anti-feudal new democracy of the popular masses led by the culture and thought of the proletariat. This kind of new democratic culture is national…National in form and new democratic in content—this is our new culture of today. [1]

To be more specific, this "'new' democratic culture" should be "national, scientific, and popular." For this culture to be national did not mean blindly advocating nationalist chauvinism, because it would not only "oppose imperialist oppression and uphold the dignity and independence of

---

[1]   See Mao, Z., On New Democracy, *Selected Works of Mao Tse-tung* (Vol. 12), Beijing: Foreign Language Press, 1967: 174-206.

the Chinese nation" and be endowed with national characteristics, but would also learn from Western progressive culture. For it to be scientific did not mean proposing a scientific discourse, because it not only called for "opposing all feudal and superstitious ideas," but also demanded the "unity of theory and practice," which meant that it saw "practice" (the code word for "revolutionary struggle") as important as "theory." Finally, the imperative of "popular" or "for the masses" did not mean promoting populist thinking, as it not only called for "serving the toiling masses of workers and peasants who constitute more than 90 percent of the national population," but also stressed that this new culture can only "gradually become the masses' culture." In other words, although this new culture was intended to be formed from the best of both foreign and Chinese culture, and in particular from their classical traditions, it was also imperative for it to be understood by the masses and appreciated by them. Insofar as socialism promises liberation of the oppressed laboring masses and equality among all the people, the nature of this "new democratic culture," with its objective of being "for the masses" and its function of being "led by the culture and thought of the proletariat," already had a socialist inclination. In short, this statement implies its true nature as (at least a preparation for) a socialist revolutionary culture.

The creation of this "new democratic culture," according to Mao Zedong, was pioneered by the May Fourth Movement. As a man of the May Fourth generation, Mao Zedong also gives a high evaluation of this movement. But his appraisal is made from a rigorous class perspective: before the May Fourth era, the New Culture Movement was led by the bourgeoisie and directed against the "old culture of the feudal class." It was the May Fourth Movement, with its newly ignited anti-imperialist passion, that added new elements to it. Now, having changed to the leadership of the proletariat, the culture was being re-directed to be for "the broad masses of the people." "There had never been such a great thorough-going cultural revolution," he claims.

Indeed, "cultural revolution" is a key concept in Mao Zedong's thought and the core of his vision of a new culture. In particular, seeing the May

Fourth "New Culture" as inadequate to address the needs of the Chinese masses, Mao Zedong saw the construction of a new culture as a way to achieve the success of a political (as well as social) revolution and an alternative modernity. In this regard, culture was both a means (as an ideological weapon) and an end (the outcome of a cultural revolution). In this vision, culture and aesthetics play a significant role in China's passage into a "new modernity." Accordingly, the establishment and development of "national form" were a cultural revolution which would replace the existent and dominant culture in a revolutionary hegemony and become an outstanding feature of Mao Zedong's vision of socialist modernity.

To further understand Mao Zedong's vision of a "new democratic culture" premised on a new "national form," we need to understand that this new culture is both a result and a facilitator of the "proletarian revolution." First and foremost, in a backward agrarian society in which industrial workers were only a tiny number in a few cities and were lacking in active class consciousness, where could revolutionary forces be found to undertake socialist revolution? Unlike the Russian revolution led by Lenin, which was in accord with orthodox Marxist doctrine—city-based, led by a revolutionary vanguard of ideologically sophisticated elites who mobilized a mature urban proletariat (in short, essentially a political revolution), the Chinese revolution was led by a politically immature party leadership which frequently drastically changed its policies (at least until Mao Zedong assumed leadership in the mid-1930s). In this country, where the urban proletariat was small and the capitalist mode of production was embryonic, the vast class of the peasantry was ignorant and waiting to be instilled with political consciousness to become "a class for itself." That is, for the Chinese revolution to be successful, it would have to be simultaneously a political, a social, and a cultural revolution.

In other words, bereft of the fully fledged urban proletariat and a correspondingly mature and advanced revolutionary consciousness, the Chinese revolution had to create a revolutionary agency in the process of making revolution. Mao Zedong found in the numerical predominance of the peasants the main latent force. Seeing the political inertia of the masses, the

CCP became more and more aware that the revolution in China had to be created. To do this, the precondition was a revolution in consciousness, or more broadly speaking, in culture. Mao Zedong says in "On New Democracy,"

> Revolutionary culture is a powerful revolutionary weapon for the broad masses of the people. It prepares the ground ideologically before the revolution comes and is an important, indeed essential, fighting front in the general revolutionary front during the revolution.[1]

A new culture was to be desired, especially considering the two most important components of the revolutionary forces, the peasants and the (revolutionary) intellectuals (the former, in Mao Zedong's rhetoric, fought with guns; the latter with pens). In Mao Zedong's analysis of China's social strata, both of these classes were from a petty bourgeois background. Thus, the purpose of creating a national form was to enable a cultural revolution to instill class consciousness in the peasant class and convert intellectuals to the revolutionary forces. Accordingly, the problematic of class consciousness was also intimately tied in with the issue of national form.

## 五、The Problematic of Class Consciousness

The difference between Marx's way of conceptualizing consciousness and Hegel's lies in Marx's practice of historical dialectics. Situating revolutionary consciousness in history by tying it in with the development of proletarian consciousness, he sees it as coming into being when the proletariat transforms from an inert class-in-itself to a class-for-itself in terms of its political self-awareness in comprehending itself as a class in history and setting out to realize its historical mission. In this light, revolutionary consciousness is the articulation of proletarian self-consciousness. It thus endows its agents, the revolutionaries, with the mission of delivering to the proletariat the message of liberation and

---

[1] See Mao, Z., On New Democracy, *Selected Works of Mao Tse-tung* (Vol. 12), Beijing: Foreign Language Press, 1967:382.

assisting them to achieve this objective through fulfilling their potential. To carry out this task, revolutionary activity plays the indispensable role of dialectical mediation. This theoretical generalization comes from Marx's observation of and participation in the revolutionary events of his time.

Lenin lays more emphasis on the aspect of subjective agency in Marx's revolutionary theory. From Russian reality, he realizes that revolutions did not happen spontaneously but were produced by the conscious activities of revolutionaries. Spontaneous social movements of classes did not always bring revolutions into being; it was only through the actions of political organizations that they could finally be induced. Thus, unlike Marx, who links revolutionary consciousness with spontaneous proletarian consciousness, Lenin assigns revolutionary consciousness to the attributes of revolutionaries. In other words, the proletariat was now seen as the object of education by revolutionaries; the latter now became the subject of revolutionary activity, and thus of history. This theoretical redefinition of the historical subject released Marxist revolutionaries from the burden of anxiously waiting for this history to arrive on its own.[1]

Like that of his two predecessors, Mao Zedong's theory also emerged from his praxis in revolutionary domestic practice, assuming the form of a new synthesis of Marxism and Leninism. Like Marx, his concept of revolutionary consciousness was a kind of class consciousness, but he also shared Lenin's emphasis on revolutionary agency, which dictates that proletarian hegemony should be articulated with reality. For Mao Zedong, this reality was Chinese society. The proletariat here was both the subject and the object of the Chinese revolution. Mao Zedong puts forward the idea that the Chinese revolution has a two-fold goal: "to change the objective world and at the same time to change the subjective world."[2] This process of changing the people's consciousness did not simply refer to reform of world

---

[1]   Dirlik, A., *Marxism in the Chinese Revolution*, Lanham, Md.: Rowman & Littlefield Publishers, 2005:132.

[2]   Mao, Z., On New Democracy, *Selected Works of Mao Tse-tung* (Vol. 12), Beijing:Foreign Language Press, 1967:308.

outlook; it was simultaneously a process of making a new nation by creating a new culture.

As noted, Mao Zedong's sinification of Marxism (to make it fit in with the Chinese situation) was a process of localization. But Arif Dirlik has further incisively observed that

> What made Mao's Marxism authentically radical (and not just an excuse for nationalism) was his insistence on integrating Marxism into the language of the masses, which he believed should reconstitute China as a nation; in other words, localizing it within the nation at the level of everyday life.[1]

Constituting as it did "a certain way of life and thought" that would be dominant across all ranks of society, for Mao, this new culture should be radically different from the culture either of the past or the present, either domestic and traditional or imported from abroad. By forging modes of everyday life and constituting the everyday practice of cultural institutions, this new culture contributed to the formation of a new nation.

## 六、Mao's Agenda in Forging a Cultural-Political Nation

But to construct a revolutionary new culture, to forge a link between the leader and the led, a class has to "nationalize" itself to produce a "national and popular" culture. To nationalize means to repudiate the heterogeneity of Marxist revolutionary consciousness as regards the national culture, in a national environment that was not materially mature enough to welcome it.

"National form" thus pertains to this creation of a new democratic culture. "National" does not mean that it is filled with parochial nationalist rhetoric, but signifies that it is adapted to the features of the national character and its tradition and that it serves the nation—a class nation with the broad masses as the historical subject. This idea can be elaborated with Gramsci's concept of hegemony.

---

[1] Dirlik, A., *Marxism in the Chinese Revolution*, Lanham, Md.: Rowman & Littlefield Publishers, 2005:96.

Gramsci also believes that revolutionaries should win the battle for revolutionary consciousness among the people before they can win the revolution. Thus he developed his well-known idea of hegemony. In expounding this seminal concept, Gwyn Williams has noted, it is

> ...an order in which a certain way of life and thought are dominant, in which one concept of reality is diffused throughout society in all its institutional and private manifestations, informing with its spirit all taste, morality, customs, religious and political principles, and all social relations, particularly in their intellectual and moral connotation.[1]

Gramsci's vision was premised on his reflection of the failure of the Communist revolution in the European setting out of the robust bourgeois civil society, which is different from the situation of modern Chinese society in which a bourgeois civil society was too vulnerable to bring about a hegemonic consensus among the populace. Yet in terms of the competition with the various players (the KMT being the foremost one) to vie for the cultural-political leadership in the united front during the Ani-Japanese War and later to educate the masses as well as the intellectuals to win the proletarian revolution, Mao Zedong's thinking about a new culture perfectly echoes his idea. Mao Zedong strove to win the ideological war for the legitimacy and hegemony of the new culture, as "ways of life and thought," against the opposing classes and their ideologies. But we need to differentiate his strategy in accomplishing this goal in the 1940s from that used after he won the war, which seems to be more characterized by coercion than persuasion. This entails that we put his practice into its historical circumstances, in which a "new democratic revolution," led by the proletariat (given China's real situation, this was a code word for the Communist Party) and uniting all patriotic elements, was called for and practiced. This particular historical situation confirms Arif Dirlik's observation of the three features of a "hegemony class." First,

---

① Gwyn, W., The Concept of "Egemonia" in the Thought of Antonio Gramsci: Some Notes on Interpretation, *Journal of the History of Ideas*, 1960, 21(4):587.

a hegemony class must of necessity incorporate into its interests, the interests of other classes (or articulate the interests of other classes through its own interests) in order to universalize its economic domination. Second, it must incorporate into its culture elements of its cultural context in order to universalize its culture. It follows, third, that a hegemonic class must be a national class.[1]

The first principle found its expression in the New Democracy policy. In the Resistance War, to establish a united front to attract as many of the patriotic forces as possible, the CCP adopted a new policy, the "Three Thirds System," to reorganize the government in areas they controlled. This dictated that one third of government positions should be kept by the communists, who represented the interests of the peasant masses, another third should go to the nationalists, and the remaining third should go to enlightened gentry members and landlords who were willing to fight the Japanese. To win support from the "rural gentry" to deal with the Japanese, they also accommodated the interests of landlords and rich peasants. Culturally, for this "hegemony class," to incorporate "elements of its cultural context" "into its culture" and make it universal, Mao Zedong pledged to absorb all the "democratic elements" of Chinese traditional culture and Western bourgeois culture.

Yet ultimately, what Arif Dirlik's argument that "this hegemonic class must be a national class" meant for Mao Zedong's political thought is that Mao Zedong envisioned a new historical subject in the class of the "proletariat." This "proletariat" would not only be a national hegemonic class, but should also represent all Chinese as a "class nation."

But what would be the culture of this new "class nation"? It certainly was not the existing culture of the "national class"—the peasantry. Yet this problem is the key to this new historical subject, because hegemony, according to Gwyn Williams, is

a whole body of practices and expectations over the whole of living: our senses and assignments of energy, our shaping perceptions of ourselves and our world. It is a

---

① Dirlik, A., *Marxism in the Chinese Revolution*, Lanham, Md.: Rowman & Littlefield Publishers, 2005:139.

lived system of meanings and values—constitutive and constituting—which as they are experienced as practices appear reciprocally confirming.

Gwyn Williams has perceptively pointed out that Gramsci's definition essentially abolishes the Marxist division of base/superstructure, seeing culture as a materialized constituent element of social life.

> It thus constitutes a sense of reality for most people in the society, a sense of absolute because experienced [as a] reality beyond which it is very difficult for most members of the society to move, in most areas of their lives. It is, that is to say, in the strongest sense a "culture," but a culture which has also to be seen as the lived dominance and subordination of particular classes.[①]

A ruling class can enforce its class interests and ideology on society, but a genuinely hegemonic class, as a leading class of society, can only join other classes' interests (apart from antagonistic ones, that is, the enemy's) to its own. At least, it needs to come to terms with other cultures. As the "national class" endeavors to restructure society to advance its own interests and to win the status of a hegemonic culture, it must articulate its own class interests and revolutionary consciousness in the language and society of the (other) culture that it attempts to transform. Thus a "national form" is called into service, as both a weapon and a trophy.

## 七、Conclusion

This chapter suggests that Mao Zedong's vision of establishing a "national form" was not merely a means to achieve popularization, but an end aimed at creating a revolutionary culture to facilitate the establishment of a highly homogenized society. Thus popularization through a national form was simultaneously a process of political, ideological, and moral transformation, with the latter also being both a means and an end in itself. In this light, Mao Zedong's agenda was ultimately an effort to forge a

---

① Williams, R., *Marxism and Literature*, Oxford:Oxford University Press, 1977: 110.

hegemonic cultural-political nation.

For Weber, a modern "political nation" is formed through political participation on the widest scale to shape the national political identity of people. It aims to develop a set of well-developed mechanisms to facilitate the political process and to ensure that the political community is involved in national politics. At the same time, in this process, the characteristic of a modern mass political party is that it promises that any political activity will not be confined within a particular group; rather, it is committed to communicating with different classes and different groups with partial interests in different regions, and thus fostering a national consensus on the overall interests of the community.[1] From this perspective, Mao Zedong's efforts to establish a "national form" follow exactly the same approach. This agenda now needs re-appraisal, especially in terms of contemporary China, where differing interests and newly-divided classes make the national consensus highly vulnerable. Meanwhile, although Mao Zedong's vision of creating a homogenous society is seemingly out of fashion in today's post-modern society, where calls for "the politics of difference" are in vogue, we cannot afford to neglect the fact that the first world itself usually appears highly homogenous in terms of class structure and manipulation of the mass media. In addition, how to foster a new culture that will be germane to a national community of differing aesthetic dispositions and will realize its interests and able to uphold the claim of representing "universal values," is again an urgent question for intellectuals from the third world countries as they encounter the hegemonic challenges of the first world to their indigenous cultures and life forms. Mao Zedong's historical agenda, in this perspective, brings us inspiration and lessons in terms of both its achievements and its vicissitudes.

---

[1]  Weber, M., *Political Writings*, Cambridge:Cambridge University Press, 1994.

# Conclusion

# Some Thoughts on the Origin of Modern Chinese Literature

Literary Historian Chen Pingyuan had said, in modern China "in the eyes of both experts and ordinary readers, popular fiction is not real 'literature'." For him, "this common bias against popular literature is rooted in the 'myth of literature' that was constructed during the May Fourth era."[1] If it is really so, how should we understand this phenomenon, and how can we "deconstruct" the myth? Furthermore, how can we understand the position-takings of high-brown literature and low literature? Are the definitions something to do with the technical supremacy of a literary text, such as its stylistic quality, structural cohesiveness, sophisticated phraseology?

Apparently, a work of "high literature" to a certain extent more or less has a "high" quality in terms of these criteria, or it seems to be so for us. However, it is not merely a technical issue, for a mediocre work can hold all such superb adjectives, yet no matter how sophisticated a structure of a text might be, the conventional idea could still hold it to be a piece of "low literature"; for instance, the most renowned Chinese classical novel *Dream of the Red Chamber* at the time of its birth. But even the literary quality of a text is not so high compared with its superior peer at the time, and in terms of today's standard, it can still be seen as being in the category of high literature, such as many "rhyme verses" (曲) of the Yuan dynasty. This

---

① Chen, P., Literature High and Low: "Popular Fiction" in Twentieth-Century China, In Hockx, M., ed., *The Literary Filed of Twentieth-Century China*, Honolulu: University of Hawaii Press, 1999:116.

necessarily poses us the question: since the criterion is always changing over the time, in a particular space-time, what is the criterion in evaluating the high and the low (literature)? And what is the middle brow (literature) which apparently is situated between the two? This chapter aims to offer a new way of thinking on the definition of "high," "low" and "middle brow" fiction/literature in modern China through theoretical deliberations of, and a dialogue with the existing scholarship on, the birth and development of modern Chinese literature. As a research note, it does not intend to offer detailed analysis of particular works as case studies. It finds that there are three standards evaluating what modern Chinese critics have meant by "high" and "low" in terms of the nature and quality of a literary work, viz. (1) high is politically or morally serious literature, low is entertainment literature; (2) high is literature appreciated by intellectually high-class people, low is literature lower classes like; (3) high is intrinsically better art, low intrinsically less-good. But for the latter two standards, there was a complicated issue, as the alternative modernity envisioned and practiced by the Chinese Communist Party (in particular Mao Zedong himself) called for utilization of "low" or popular, folk art to create a mass-oriented literature and culture which was assumed to be better (politically and culturally) than the ones produced by the high class.

## 一、Canonization, Legitimacy, and Cultural Hegemony

If a literature is high or low that is not merely an issue of the "literariness," then is it something related to the "attitude" and "goal" of writers when they lend their pens to paper? Some scholars held this point.[①]

---

① For instance, Chen Pingyuan argues that "fiction written by Liang Qichao and others is not very accomplished, but because it stresses the expression of own ideas and feelings and de-emphasizes readability and entertainment, it bears distinct similarities to existing traditions of literati narration (文人叙述). It was this 'serious' aim of writing that led Zhu Ziqing to acknowledge that these writers 'can be traced to the same origin as the new literature movement.'" Hockx, M. ed, *The Literary Filed of Twentieth-Century China*, Honolulu: University of Hawaii Press, 1999: 125.

Within this horizon, frivolousness and the objective of entertainment promise the works' preclusion from "high literature." But should this be the standard, why the high-handed moralism and didacticism of the "old school," which are serious enough, were repudiated by the May Fourth writers as popular literature of the worst kind? And why some works of Western modernism, playfully created, morally controversial, or even directly attacking moral conventions, are nowadays regarded as "high literature"?

To be sure, this is something related to the process of canonization, but I will suggest that the more fundamental aspect is related to the issue of legitimacy and cultural hegemony, which, ultimately, boils down to the problematic of historicity. Jameson's teaching "Always historicize!" is not a relativistic thinking. We can better understand this point when we review Chinese literary history. Traditionally, Chinese "high literature" had merely referred to classical poem, and rhyme verses (词) and Yuan Songs (元曲) had been regarded as vulgar creations, but gradually the latter two genres were accepted to the grand palace of literary pantheon. The writing of stories for thousands of years in China had been treated as trivial and in most cases, morally suspicious. It remained so until the late Qing when Liang Qichao (1873-1929) launched the movement of "revolution of fiction," which drastically raised its position in the hierarchy of literary genres. In the May Fourth period, the "literati literature," which till then was held to be "high literature," was derided as moribund, aristocratic culture. In particular, the "literati literature" of the Saturday School and Butterfly fiction was repudiated as "low" cultural products catering to vulgar tastes.

While on the surface, the issue is merely pointing to a shift of the readers' tastes; or in more sophisticated terms, a transformation of their aesthetic habitus and disposition: they are changing with the historical transformation of the society's moral-ethical conventions, customs, and cultural concepts; the effect of defamiliarization by the epochal-spatial distance, which adds to unfamiliar feelings over literary languages, also facilitates the process of canonization; yet the ultimate reason lies in the change of the cultural hegemony of the dominant culture of a society, which usually happens with the change of cultural institutions（both in terms of relations of production and cultural-political concepts）. Apparently, the latter appears to be a process of democratization：the turning from the "feudal" society to the capitalist world witnessed the alteration of aesthetic tastes from the aristocratic habitus to a bourgeois one. Gradually, the "old" culture（a "high" culture at its time）, which was repudiated as "reactionary," "moribund" and thus "low" by the emergent culture（the latter holds cultural legitimacy and consolidated cultural hegemony）, would gradually become canonized to be "classical" and once again "high." In this later stage, whether a text is worthy to be canonized depends more on whether it "reflects" the "epochal spirit" of the era than on its level of reaching the aesthetic criterion of its own era. We can understand this point through examining modern Chinese literary history to see the legitimization of fiction as a genre and its ascendance to the highest literary hierarchy by usurpation of the cultural hegemony, and the following vicissitude of modern literature as a social and cultural institution.

The inexorable breakdown of the feudal type of imperialist ideology since the late nineteenth century was exacerbated by the 1895 fiasco of the Sino-Japanese War. The feelings of great shock by the failure in the war stimulated intellectuals like Liang Qichao and Yan Fu to more whole-heartedly pursue modern Western ideas. Then, there was a fundamental epistemological shift from the "Heavenly Principle"（天理）to the "Axiomatic Principle"（公理）,[①] which entailed and triggered the replacement of the whole set of conceptual ideas on cosmological, ethical, moral, political and social relationships. It is well known that Chen Yinke has said it was a time of "fundamental change the sort of which had not occurred over the last three thousand years." Seeing the national salvation though technical improvement in the "Westernization Movement"（洋务运动）could not succeed, the intellectual-gentry class was galvanized to pursue modern concepts and institutions. Liang Qichao founded the journal *New Fiction*（《新小说》）in Yokohama in 1902 and proposed a "revolution of fiction."

---

① 汪晖：《现代中国思想的兴起》,生活·读书·新知三联书店 2004 年版.

If one intends to renovate the people of a nation, one must first renovate its fiction. Therefore, to renovate morality, one must renovate fiction; to renovate religion, one must renovate fiction; to renovate politics, one must renovate fiction; to renovate social customs, one must renovate fiction; to renovate learning and arts, one must renovate fiction; and to renovate even the human mind and remold its character, one must renovate fiction. Why is this so? This is because fiction has a profound power over the way of man.[1]

In this proclamation, "profound power over the way of man" is taken as the legitimacy for inversion of traditional generic hierarchies. The burst energy after the emergence of a unique world of fiction after this declaration saw an avalanche of massive output of fiction unimaginable before. It dealt specifically with the collapsing culture and introduction of the Western new ideas, especially political ideas that called for more enlightened and equal political-social relationships, for which the novel was promoted as an efficient means of social engineering.

In this process, satirical novels which criticize corruption, bureaucracy, myriad social injustices were taken to be serious and high literature. Yet with the rapid disintegration of the ruling regime, such novels tended to degrade into vulgar "scandal literature," and sentimental novels influenced by Western romanticism changed to be "Mandarin Ducks and Butterflies Fiction" with conservative motives and overt-sentimentalized tears and cries; commercialization also brought about tabloidization. At the same time, the vernacularization was also difficult to proceed further. All these symptoms show that there was a deadlock waiting for breakthrough.

The quantitative experiments with new ideas and new forms contributed to a qualitative change. In an article originally published in *New Youth* in January 1917 titled "A Preliminary Discussion of Literature Reform" (《文学改良刍议》), Hu Shi advocated for a (new) literary revolution of the era which aimed to replace scholarly classical Chinese in writing with the vernacular spoken language, and to cultivate and stimulate new forms of literature. He

---

① Liang, Q., On the Relationship Between Fiction and the Government of the People, Denton, K., Trans., *Modern Chinese Literary Thought : Writings on Literature*, 1893-1945, Stanford: Stanford University Press, 1976:74.

emphasized eight guidelines for this purpose，among which are the instructions that writers should not imitate the ancient literature（but rather write in the modern style of the present era）；not use allusions，and not use couplets or parallelism，all of which were taken to be the golden rules for creating a high literature before. He also proposed to use popular expressions or popular forms of characters. In short，modern literature should be written in vernacular，rather than in classical Chinese，which was taken to be allusive，artificial，and divorced from contemporary reality. In the same time，Chen Duxiu published his article *On Literary Revolution* (《文学革命论》) in the same journal，offering three suggestions：(1) to overthrow flowery language of aristocracy and establish plain language of people；(2) to overthrow stereotypes and classicism and establish "fresh，sincere，realist literature"；(3) to overthrow obscurantism and pedanticism and establish "plain，popularized，social literature." Apparently，the new literature proposed in the May Fourth from the very start intended to create a popular literature. Yet the word "popular" here has an ideological connotation in addition to being plain and obvious. Thus we see that in the same year，Lu Xun published his story "Diary of a Madman," which，for its profound spirit of iconoclasm and enlightenment inspiring modern individualism，as well as its westernized style and language syntax，brought about a shaking repercussion from the society and unraveled formally the curtain of a new literary revolution，in which the new vernacular literature was canonized by this newly established cultural hegemony. In 1919，the vernacular language of Beijing was adopted as the national language (国语). With the fast process of political-adicalization，we witness that

> What the May Fourth advocates of new literature called "old school fiction" was nothing else than the continuation of late Qing new fiction. That the once so innovative new fiction ended up being ridiculed as old-school fiction is not just a matter of generational change，but a manifestation of the way in which cultural trends as a whole shifted from "reform" to "revolution."[①]

---

① Denton，K.，*Modern Chinese Literary Thought：Writings on Literature*，1893-1945，Stanford：Stanford University Press，1976：124.

Yet soon the New Literature group itself disintegrated. Lu Xun and his cohort insisted on literature's responsibility of social engagement, whereas some other writers dreamed of playing with literature for amusement, or went to the cultural market producing commercialized works catering to the tastes of urbanites. This has something to do with their understanding of the nature of the cultural institution of literature, which was further premised on their sense of intellectuals' position in the market economy and commodity society; and it is also tied in with their competition for cultural legitimacy and hegemony. Shortly later, the left-wing writers refused to acknowledge the legitimacy of creating leisure literature and took it as debased and low (whereas the latter in the 1990s was enshrined to be high literature in the secularized society out of the ubiquitous middle-class cultural milieu). Influenced by Marxist thoughts including Marxian artistic views, some new literature writers observed the society from the historical materialistic perspective and their works were taken to be serious, high literature (such as Mao Dun's).

What we witness is that since the mid-twenties, modern Chinese literature as a cultural and social institution has underwent another dramatic change. The concept of New Literature established in the May Fourth Literary Revolution had emphasized an individualistic orientation as an iconoclastic gesture against the tyranny of tradition. This agenda now gradually lost its urgency and appeal. Instead, because of the deepened crisis of the Chinese society, the idea that saw literature as instruments "for society," "for the nation," and "for the state" gradually became the mainstream. As this collectivistic reorientation was premised on and propelled by the worsened class conflicts and imperialist threats, the leftists requested the new literature to represent the epochal spirit, in particular to portray the lives of the suffering masses and the spirit of the awakening "proletariat." They called this as a shift from the "Literary Revolution" to a "Revolutionary Literature." Works of the latter were taken by the readers as high and serious, whereas the entertainment fiction of the Shanghai School (海派) (including the new sensationalist school now canonized) and the so-called "popular modernism" (Wumingshi and Xu Xu) was taken to be low, although the latter studied and adopted some techniques of the new literature and foreign literature. (Again, since the 1990s, they have been elevated to the high position of cultural hierarchy thanks to the changed attitude towards literature.) The newly emerged revolutionary literature regarded the new literature as "new classical literature" (洋八股) which "simply provided the Europeanized gentry with yet another sumptuous banquet to satisfy their new tastes while the laboring people were still starving."[1] The left-wing writers then tried to produce mass-oriented literature, which, however, did not succeed due to the political circumstance and social environment in which the masses could not access to their texts. In the following years, the utilization of folk art and popularization of elite literature gained more legitimacy during the Anti-Japanese War, but they only fully established their cultural hegemony and received whole-hearted praxis in the liberated areas in the 1940s, when Zhao Shuli's works such as "Little Blackie Gets Married" were canonized soon after they were popularized. The connotation of high vs. low literature has received its new content since then, which led to another drastic turn of modern Chinese literature after 1949, when socialist literature was gradually enshrined as the only legitimate culture under the sway of "proletarian cultural hegemony."

On the other hand, while the chronological understanding calls for observing the "historicity," a synchronic observation stresses more on the hierarchy of cultural capital and genre difference. In a society, a genre that was pandering to the needs and tastes of the lower class would usually be regarded as vulgar and "low," while the genre that fits in with the dispositions of the higher class would be taken to be "high."

Again, the history of modern Chinese culture offers a representative case study: the Butterfly fiction and Saturday School, with highly refined classical phrases and poems that satisfy the needs of gentry class literati, would be seen as "high" literature after canonization is completed in contemporary literary world. However, because fiction was despised at the time, it did not enjoy such a status then; and also because the epochal-

---

① 瞿秋白：《大众文艺的问题》，《瞿秋白文集（第 3 卷）》，人民文学出版社 1989 年版.

spatial distance is still not long enough to make a full defamiliazation process take effects, it has not arrived at the pantheon of canons now. Worse, at its own time, it was regarded by the emerging May Fourth culture (which, with its high moral ground and cultural capital of importing Western, and thus "modern," culture, soon usurped the cultural legitimacy and hegemony) or proto-bourgeois intellectual class as inscribed with feudal consciousness and its value system, such as chastity and filial piety (as well as unconditional loyalty to the superior) embraced by the leftovers of the imperial class and degenerate gentry class, thus "reactionary" and "low."

The more complicated issue is still pertaining to the particular situation of modern China, where in a relatively short period various "new cultures" vied for the cultural hegemony. The May Fourth New Culture agenda was soon to be attacked by a more radical intellectual trend as being "bourgeois," or serving the interests of the emergent, new "aristocratic" class—the bourgeois class—while neglecting the cultural needs of the broad masses, namely the working class and the peasants. This repudiation does not necessarily mean the direct rejection of the ideal of the New Culture; but this radical trend saw itself as a sublation of the former; it not only demanded the liberation of the newly emerged bourgeois class from the "feudal" domination, but also called for the liberation of the downtrodden from the oppression of the "reactionary" regime and the imperialist forces. Thus it necessitated a deeper level of equality: an equality not only between the middle class (which was metamorphosed from the gentry-landlord class) and the aristocratic class (the residual imperial class and the official stratum), but also between the subaltern and the middle class. Therefore, in modern China, the perspective of class (analysis) was also closely correlated with the issue of literature of high vs. low, serious vs. popular.

## 二、Class, Popularization, and "Common People's Literature"

To begin with this new round of inquiry, we first need to understand what the word "popular"（通俗）in "popular literature"（通俗文学）means in Chinese context. For one thing, "popular" implies that it is not "serious"; but the more important thing is to look into the etymology to understand what in the Chinese "popular" means. The word signifies that it is catering to the common knowledge（通）and vulgar（俗）taste（and it is easy to understand, as the word is oftentimes immediately followed with another word "易懂"—easy to understand—to become a set phrase）, which then primarily refers to the aesthetic disposition of the lowest class—the peasants—with little educational background, who was entrenched in a long-term tradition of folk literature and art that was popular in vast rural areas. Sometimes it also refers to the urban commercialized forms of arts and literature which pander to the tastes of merchant class, small proprietors, and working class, whereas traditional Chinese literati had consistently despised. To be sure, some works of "popular literature" today are simultaneously "serious literature"; or even though they are still sort of "common knowledge," they no longer look "vulgar." But this fact only points to the fact that the populace today (in the Western world) is a highly homogenous community with much less hierarchy in terms of aesthetic disposition, if not also in class status. Put in another way, the populace are endowed (or imposed) with a highly homogenous aesthetic taste and political stance. Whereas in the "pre-modern" or "early modern" China (and even in today's China), the situation was vastly different.

In modern China, writers and intellectuals heeded to this situation and paid special attention to the relationship between class and literature. For instance, while Liu Bannong (1891-1934) has defined the notion of popular fiction as "fiction common to the upper, middle and lower class,"[1] Guan Dalu（？－？）differentiates fiction "for the upper classes"（为上等人）from fiction "for the lower classes"（为下等人）. In more specific terms, Xia Zengyou (1863-1924) divides literature into two departments: "One caters to the needs of scholars

---

① 瞿秋白:《大众文艺的问题》,《瞿秋白文集(第 3 卷)》,人民文学出版社 1989 年版,第 117 页.

and literati, the other to the needs of women and coarse folk."①

When turning to the content of fiction, Liu Bannong also has words to say, which boil down to the same problematic of class. In his view, popular fiction is "not for the exchange of ideas and ambitions by philosophers and scientists, nor is it fiction meant for literati and scholars to vent their complaints and show off skills." Obviously, this definition by exclusion is hardly to be accepted, as some of the novels included in his example of the first category, such as *Water Margin*(《水浒传》) and *Dream of the Red Chamker*, and his second category, such as *Regret over Flowers and Moonlight*(《花月痕》), were clearly seen as popular fiction in those days. Chen Pingyuan aptly points out that "apart from emphasizing the point that popular fiction featured an element of entertainment and that it was appreciated by the general public, Liu Bannong also assumed that it did not contain profound thought."② But in modern China, we witness that some popular novels which were exactly aimed for exchanging "ideas and ambitions" and venting "complaints and show-off skills," and which apparently "contain profound thought," were popular and belonging to the category of middle brow fiction. Liu's conclusion also appears problematic: "In the future, when mankind's knowledge has progressed and everyone is able to read fiction of lofty content, popular fiction will naturally perish…"③ Clearly, Liu Bannong sees popular fiction as something not having "lofty content," or something that has vulgar content and nasty tastes, for some ones who have no much knowledge, especially for those readers who were from lower class and had less educational background. However, the literary genres of tanci（弹词 storytelling to the accompaniment of stringed instruments）and song texts（唱本）that he discussed in his second lecture

---

① 瞿秋白:《大众文艺的问题》,《瞿秋白文集(第 3 卷)》,人民文学出版社 1989 年版, 第 118 页.

② Hockx, M., *The Literary Filed of Twentieth-Century China*, Honolulu: University of Hawaii Press, 1999:117.

③ Hockx, M., *The Literary Filed of Twentieth-Century China*, Honolulu: University of Hawaii Press, 1999:117.

which are entitled "China's Lower Class Fiction", and were well received in the low society of the time, today is regarded by ordinary readers as "high-brow" literature.

As Chen Pingyuan succinctly summarizes, the literature that Liu Bannong envisioned was one that "considered the needs of 'the lower classes,' while at the same time advocating 'common people's literature' (平民文学)."[①] Here, it is clear that "common (or ordinary) people" is not identical with "people of the lower classes." In fact, this problematic is one of the key issues for us to understand the tension between high literature vs. low literature and serious literature vs. popular literature in modern China, which persists to this day.

It is well known that there was a general attitude for Chinese intellectuals during the May Fourth period, if not more earlier, to oppose "aristocratic literature" and advocate a literature for ordinary people. Chen Duxiu called for creating a "国民文学", which is generally rendered as "national literature"; but since the literary translation of "国民" is citizens, so the phrase is better understood to be "literature of the citizens." But for a new republic, what did the "citizens" refer to? This vague notion [together with Hu Shi's more ambiguous term "living literature" (平民文学)] was then reasonably superseded by Zhou Zuoren's proposal for establishing a "common people's literature." This move might be seen as an echo of Liu Bannong's view, but Zhou Zuoren elucidates the term more clearly. However, although all Chinese session-chapter novels were "specifically meant for the common people," Zhou Zuoren took them to be drastically departing from his ideal of "common people's literature." How is that so?

This is because for him, "common people's literature" is "definitely not popular literature" and "definitely not philanthropist literature," whereas Chinese session-chapter novels "contain elements of playfulness and exaggeration." This argument directly dispels the suspicion of any populism

---

① Hockx, M., *The Literary Filed of Twentieth-Century China*, Honolulu: University of Hawaii Press, 1999:118.

contained in his proposed project. In his mind, the "popular literature" at the time was "feudal" in nature and contradictory to the New Culture agenda that he was in pursuit of. For instance, he decried such famed Chinese traditional novels (though at the time they were "popular", today they appear rather high-brow and "classical") *Water Margin* and *Journey to the West*(《西游记》) as "books about bandits" and "superstitious books about ghosts" that "obstruct the growth of human nature and destroy humanity's peace," thus being "inhuman literature."① In his view, "common people's literature" should serve as a "prophet"(先知) or "guide"(引路人) to uplift the readers and raise their capability of appreciation and intellectual taste, rather than cater to their original aesthetic habitus. The representative of this literature that he praises is *Dream of the Red Chamber*.②

As Chen Pingyuan aptly notes, this unusual appraisement is made because Zhou Zuoren "consciously judged Chinese fiction from the perspective of Western literary theory."③ Or, to be more precise, whether they fit in his ideal of the New Culture; for instance, whether a novel's "attitude" towards women is misogynic or not, whether it is "hypocritical" or it has a "human spirit." The Enlightenment discourses of benign human nature and peaceful humanity become his standard to evaluate a seemingly alien culture. Accordingly, the apparently anti-elitist attitude of Zhou Zuoren turns out to be elitist in his literary sense, for he stands in the position of an enlightened intellectual repudiating any "popular fiction" that "suits the mentality of the lower class" and/or "provides entertainment or teaches a lesson."④ Nonetheless, what he calls a "human's literature" or "common people's literature" is exactly intending to teach a lesson, or to "enlighten" the human nature of the lower class. The difference then

---

① Hockx, M., *The Literary Filed of Twentieth-Century China*, Honolulu: University of Hawaii Press, 1999:118-119.

② Hockx, M., *The Literary Filed of Twentieth-Century China*, Honolulu: University of Hawaii Press, 1999:119.

③ Hockx, M., *The Literary Filed of Twentieth-Century China*, Honolulu: University of Hawaii Press, 1999:119.

④ 周作人:《日本近三十年小说之发达》,《新青年》,1918(5).

apparently lies in what should be promoted: whether it is about feudal morality that the "popular literature" at the time still advocated or the bourgeois enlightenment value-system that the "common people's literature" that he advertised.

His position also naturally raises the question: whether the educator himself should be educated? If the answer is yes, who would be the educator? Or is he someone who owns absolute knowledge and supreme intellectual power as an unchallengeable jurist? This becomes the problem even when the "common people" (平民), referring mainly to literary urbanites, broaden its scope to include—and itself was replaced by—the masses (大众), referring to the working people and the broad rural residents of peasants, many (or most) of whom are still illiterate. In the late 1930s, Guo Moruo contended that "mass literature" is not "literature of the masses," but one that "guides the masses." It implies that this literature is to be created by the knowledgeable intellectuals rather than the "ignorant-and-waited-to-be-enlightened" masses themselves. Clearly, this raises the issue about (who owns) the right to represent the "other." It is more than apparent that Guo Moruo stands by the position of the intellectuals and believes that he holds the unquestionable qualification to lead the masses. Whereas he gradually shifted this position in the 1940s, some other intellectuals [such as Hu Feng (1902-1985), another distinguished intellectual] had clung to this view unyieldingly till the end of their lives.

This elite position is challenged today by the postmodern ethics, which charges it as the fundamental spirit of modernity that relentlessly makes the dichotomy between the subject and the object. Whereas this contemporary new ethics calls for a sort of inter-subjectivity that fuses the subject and the other, seeing the two as equal partners; in modern China, the enlightenment intellectuals' elite stance in fact had been interrogated ever since the New Culture Movement, and they were called to study from the "masses" and create a newer "literature of the masses" (人民大众的文学). If Zhou Zuoren essentially promoted a new ethics different from that of the "popular literature," then what the enlightenment-minded writers should study from "the people" (as well as the content of this new literature being envisioned) must also have a new value system differing from that of the "New Culture." This was discussed by the left-wing writers in the 1940s and systematically explicated by Mao Zedong in his treatises of "On New Democracy" and "Yan'an Talks."

Mao Zedong's "Yan'an Talks" proposed a transformation of literature and art based on a changed literary and artistic practice, which was predicated on a changed political allegiance of writers and artists and also a fundamental change in their social position. By calling for the writers and artists to put aside their professions (at least temporarily) and go and live among ordinary working people for an extended time, Mao Zedong aimed at a profound transformation of the writers and artists in order to produce a very different literature and art. Thus various forms of cultural productions—fiction, poetry, drama, and fine art—of the period all show the influence of rural northern China in the incorporation of indigenous folk literary and artistic elements. To respond to Mao Zedong's deliberate call to develop "Chinese style and manner, of which the Chinese masses are fond"[1] in artistic works, a host of productions, which utilized forms resuscitated from popular, folk, and local literary traditions, appeared. It should be kept in mind when we analyze the cultural works in the liberated area that the communists' project was targeted at the lower-level masses (worker-peasant-soldier and their cadres) which were the majority of the population in order to create a literary style that is modernity-oriented, allegedly more democratic and having more "national flavor." This second-time radical transformation of the political/cultural legitimacy of modern Chinese literature as social institution points to the further development of the socialist, "worker-peasant-soldier literature" after 1949.

## 三、What is Middle-Brow Literature in Modern China?

Having discussed high literature and low literature, then what is

---

[1] Mao, Z., Talks at the Yan'an Forum on Literature and Art, *Selected Works of Mao Tse-tung* (Vol.3), Beijing: Foreign Languages Press, 1967.

"middle-brow" literature in modern China? Literally, it means that it is neither "high" nor "low," but meeting the needs of the middle-leveled readership with its mediocre quality. In *Oxford English Dictionary*, when the middle-brow is referred the quality of an artistic work, it is defined as "of limited intellectual or cultural value; demanding or involving only a moderate degree of intellectual application, typically as a result of not deviating from convention."[①] Pierre Bourdieu argued that "middle-brow" culture has a reverential relationship to "legitimate culture" and is the taste of the middle-class, falling short of intrinsic qualities.[②] But why is it mediocre? In the Chinese academic world, there is oftentimes a tendency to take some middle-brow literature to be a belletristic literature that breaks through the boundary between "high (-brow) literature" and "low (-brow) literature." In the following section, I will take the Mandarin and Butterfly literature as the object of analysis and suggest that the ultimate cause for a literary work to be "middle brow" is that it resorts to moralistic discourse in order to evade social-political and economic explanation of social problems, though this not necessarily is done consciously.

The efflorescence of the Butterfly fiction was witnessed in the first and the second decades of the twentieth century, which was generally regarded as brought about by "the rapid growth of the popular press, the spread of literary, and the emergence of a large middle-class readership in China's urban centers."[③] Leo Lee has regarded Butterfly writers as "treaty-port journalist-litterateurs" who endeavored to the efforts of "popularization of

---

① Simpson, J., Weiner, E., *Oxford English Dictionary*, Cambridge: Oxford University Press, 1989.

② Bourdieu, P., *Distinction: A Social Critique of the Judgment of Taste*, Routledge and Kegan Paul, 1984.

③ Lee, H., All the Feelings that are Fit to Print: the Community of Sentiment and the Literary Public Sphere in China, 1900-1918, *Modern China*, 2001,27(3):321; also see Link, P., *Mandarin and Butterflies: Popular Fiction in Early Twentieth-Century Chinese Cities*, Berkeley: University of California Press, 1981.

sentiment as the central mode of existence."① And Haiyan Lee has focused on this "mode of existence" and inferred that it was "grounding self-identity in sentiment as opposed to…in kinship or native-place ties."②

Haiyan Lee also applies Habermas' theory of the bourgeois "literary public theory" to analyze this school. She summarized his ideas as the follows, "what he called 'the literary public sphere,' consisting primarily of journalism and fiction, provided a forum or 'training ground' wherein individuals shared their private experiences and mutually affirmed a new form of subjectivity-universal humanity." In particular, she notes that "Habermas stressed that the domestic novel and the kindred genres of letter, diary, and autobiography… were the primary training ground of bourgeois subjectivity."③ Apparently, here Haiyan Lee pays particular attention to the correlation between the formation of subjectivity, self-identity, and sentimental emotions of humanity. This correlation is described as the follows: because in the literary public sphere "the private experience was from the very beginning a public matter-something to be talked about, shared, and scrutinized" by "the discursive community of authors, editors, critics, and readers," therefore, through this communication of emotional experiences "the bourgeois individual recognized and ascertained his (and sometimes her) humanity," which, furthermore, "provide the conceptual basis on which the bourgeois made their political claims." This is so because "their shared self-image as human beings whose parity was founded on the abstract notion of universal human nature inspired them to demand political and legal rights on equally abstract and general grounds."④

---

① Lee, L. O., *The Romantic Generation of May Fourth Writers*, Cambridge, Mass: Harvard University Press, 1973:216.

② Lee, H., All the Feelings that are Fit to Print: the Community of Sentiment and the Literary Public Sphere in China, 1900-1918, *Modern China*, 2001,27(3):292.

③ Lee, H., All the Feelings that are Fit to print: the Community of Sentiment and the Literary Public Sphere in China, 1900-1918, *Modern China*, 2001,27(3):293.

④ Lee, H., All the Feelings that are Fit to print: the Community of Sentiment and the Literary Public Sphere in China, 1900-1918, *Modern China*, 2001,27(3):293.

Apparently, this idealistic description, which is bereft of any substantial (which means social-political) account, is only a partial story about the formation of bourgeois self-identity during the process of transformation of relations of production (from the feudal-mercantilist one to a liberal-capitalist form). But what intrigues our interests is how she correlates Habermas' theory with Chinese reality. She first contends that some historians are convinced that "elements of a loosely defined civil society and public sphere had emerged and played an undeniable part in social and political processes" in late imperial and early republican China; then, she stresses that "one of these elements was the rise of the popular press," which reminds us of the similar situation in Habermas' case study of the conditions of seventeenth- and eighteenth-century Europe. Furthermore, she notes that for the Butterfly writers, these "journalist-litteratures" also "enjoyed an unmistakable esprit de corps"; lastly, like the European case, here "authors and readers" also "related to one another not as producers and consumers so much as like-minded individuals who were interested in 'what was human,' in self-knowledge, and in empathy."[1] Through the comparison of all these identical facts, Haiyan Lee arrives at the conclusion "Butterfly literature played an indispensable role in the formation and consolidation of bourgeois identity."[2]

In fact, her key argument is that "by making sentiment foundational to human bonds, morality and virtue, and knowledge and truth, sentimental fiction provided the ethical and epistemological basis of self-definition for the urban middle classes."[3] I will challenge this conclusion by analyzing the concrete procedure that she undertakes to substantiate this argument.

When making this argument, Haiyan Lee denies the popular view

---

① Lee, H., All the Feelings that are Fit to print: the Community of Sentiment and the Literary Public Sphere in China, 1900-1918, *Modern China*, 2001, 27(3): 294-295.

② Lee, H., All the Feelings that are Fit to print: the Community of Sentiment and the Literary Public Sphere in China, 1900-1918, *Modern China*, 2001, 27(3): 296.

③ Lee, H., All the Feelings that are Fit to Print: the Community of Sentiment and the Literary Public Sphere in China, 1900-1918, *Modern China*, 2001, 27(3): 321-322.

(mainly circulated in the critics from Chinese mainland from a vulgar materialistic perspective) that sees the literature as merely "a byproduct of capitalist development," and "Butterfly writers as catering to the taste of a fast-rising urban (petit) bourgeois."[①] But she does not discuss what the taste of the latter class was. In her conclusion, she fundamentally follows Habermas' way of thinking that regards holding the concept of universal humanity (manifested as sentimental emotions of love, empathy, etc.) as the inalienable route to and essential component of a bourgeois subjectivity and identity. This idealistic thinking prevents her from delving into the deeper relation between the emergence of this literature and the formation of a new (social and political) subjectivity and identity, although she apparently cites Perry Link's sociological study of the class structure of the readership of this literature.[②] In this way, her analysis becomes a kind of "vicious circle," or circulatory argumentation: "Their worldviews, values, and political consciousness surely were affected by their experience in the

---

① Lee, H., All the Feelings that are Fit to Print: the Community of Sentiment and the Literary Public Sphere in China, 1900-1918, *Modern China*, 2001,27(3):296.

② According to Perry Link's study that Haiyan Lee summarizes, "it is generally assumed that 'petty urbanites' and secondary school and college students constituted the bulk of the Butterfly readership, which also included well-to-do merchants, landlords, bankers, and industrialists and their families, as well as intellectuals." Lee, H., All the Feelings that are Fit to Print: the Community of Sentiment and the Literary Public Sphere in China, 1900-1918, *Modern China*, 2001, 27 (3): 296. See Link, P., *Mandarin and Butterflies: Popular Fiction in Early Twentieth-Century Chinese Cities*, Berkeley: University of California Press, 1981:190. She also quotes Yeh Wen-hsin's study and points out that "particularly noteworthy is the fact that secondary school students were the largest and most avid group among the consumers of popular fiction. Most of these students on completing or quitting school probably became 'vocational youths'—members of the middle school and lower middle classes as clerks and apprentices in trade, manufacturing, the professions, and the service sectors." Lee, H., All the Feelings That Are Fit to Print: The Community of Sentiment and the Literary Public Sphere in China, 1900-1918, *Modern China*. 2001,27(3):296. See Yeh Wen-hsin, Progressive Journalism and Shanghai's Petty Urbanites: Zou Taofen and the Shenghuo Enterprise, 1926-1945, *Shanghai Sojourners*, Berkeley: University of California Press, 1992:205-214.

'training ground' of bourgeois subjectivity—the literary public sphere."
Here，not only is the Chinese "literary public sphere" taken for granted as
"the 'training ground' of bourgeois subjectivity" without substantiation，
but also the process in which "being influenced by the bourgeois sentiments，
they become (to acquire a) bourgeois (identity)" is a hasty argument. The
circulatory argumentation becomes more apparent in her last point：
"Butterfly sentimentalism helped create an affective community within the
literary public sphere whereby bourgeois individuals exchanged private
experiences and fashioned themselves as men and women of sentiment."[①]

The key to the problem，obviously，lies in what "their worldviews，
values，and political consciousness" were，and how they were affected by
their reading，if not social，experience. The scholar apparently ignores this
issue，which is shown in her argument："As material from the Butterfly
popular press abundantly demonstrates，the private self enters the literary
public sphere not to unfold an a priori subjectivity but to be constructed as a
subject by the ideology of universal humanity."[②] Here，the "private self" is
assumed to be one without "a priori subjectivity" but whose "subjectivity"
has to be constructed by a (new) ideology，whether the latter is alien to
him/her or not is not questioned.

The crux lies in the priori belief，which is an ingrained one in the
postcolonial theory that the scholar subscribes to，that sees subjectivity as a
discursive construction. Thus we read the following argument："Bourgeois
subjectivity and its putative origin—the conjugal family—were discursive
constructs of the literary public sphere."[③] Sometimes，she disavows this
origin，nevertheless she affirms the discursive function："Bourgeois
subjectivity does not originate from the privacy of the conjugal home，as

---

① Lee，H.，All the Feelings that are Fit to Print：the Community of Sentiment and
the Literary Public Sphere in China，1900-1918，*Modern China*，2001，27(3)：321.

② Lee，H.，All the Feelings that are Fit to Print：the Community of Sentiment and
the Literary Public Sphere in China，1900-1918，*Modern China*，2001，27(3)：299.

③ Lee，H.，All the Feelings that are Fit to Print：the Community of Sentiment and
the Literary Public Sphere in China，1900-1918，*Modern China*，2001，27(3)：297.

Habermas maintained; rather, it is fashioned and refashioned in the public sphere of the world of letters." Sensibility, sentimentality, humanity, subjectivity, and finally (bourgeois) identity are essentially all identified as the one, which is particularly witnessed in the following argument: "As readers contemplate the intensely emotional 'tableau' that crowds the landscape of sentimental narratives, they also contemplate the plenitude of their own subjectivities. Their inclination to shed tears ensures them of their sensibility, which in turn points to their humanity, endowing them with an identity that is at once uniquely individual and universally valid." This individual sentiment and identity, furthermore, are equated to be a collective one: "Through the experience of reading and weeping, the readers are transformed into private individuals capable of coming together to form a public—a sentimental community."[1]

Rather than following this "idealistic" argumentation, I propose the other way of thinking: individual sentiment, subjectivity, and identity are collectively formed, or rather, transformed; they are not a discursive construction, rather, they are socially and politically over-conditioned; the sentiment was not being fomented in the literary world, or the literary public sphere whatsoever; rather, the agony and anxiety were brought out by outside force, which were refracted in, distilled and purified by, and dispelled from the literary world.

To be more specific, if "the eighteenth century cult of sensibility represented a progressive force in the early phases of the Enlightenment, industrialization, and transition from aristocratic to bourgeois society,"[2] then the Butterfly writers' passion in sentimentalism was a symptom of the fallen gentry-landlord class, which was sandwitched between the corrupted late imperial (and later on the republican) regime and the realistic and potential threat of the foreign imperialistic forces located in an embarrassed

---

① Lee, H., All the Feelings that are Fit to Print: the Community of Sentiment and the Literary Public Sphere in China, 1900-1918, *Modern China*, 2001,27(3):301.

② Lee, H., All the feelings that are fit to print: the community of sentiment and the literary public sphere in China, 1900-1918, *Modern China*, 2001,27(3):301.

niche in a historical conjuncture that relentlessly trekked from a traditional "mode of organization" (or rather, "relations of production" if not "mode of production") to an alien one. The democratization of social space and commodification of social relations did not bring sense of bliss, but feelings of pains and anxiety. If in the West, "by making natural feeling the basis of progressive civil society, religious faith, and aesthetic judgment, sentimentalism brought religious, moral, and aesthetic realms into a homologous relationship," then in China, sentimentalism only signified the merciless disintegration of the religious, moral, and aesthetic realms (which then became heterogeneous). If in the West, "by placing sensibility at the base of human nature, as the grounding of morality and virtue, the bourgeois is able to promulgate the universal equality to humanity, challenge the aristocratic ideology of birth and bloodline, and thereby lay the conceptual foundation for its hegemony"; then, in the Butterfly literature, although tears also bore testimony to the writers' sense of "sensitivity, moral superiority, and common humanity," they did not endow them with a sense of the "'natural' right of the bourgeoisie to economic and political power," rather, the tears only signify their sense of vulnerability, helplessness, loss in the confidence of claiming economic and political power. If in the West, "as an agent of social change, literary sentimentalism constitutes a site of contention between radical and conservative ideologies," then in the Butterfly literature, the sentimentalism was a secluded haven for a conservative ideology, which delved in traditional "structure of feeling" to protect a traumatized heart. To be sure, like the sentimentalism in the West, the latter also "affirms the innate sociability of humanity," but the humanity it upheld is mainly referring to two central traditional values: chastity and filial piety, which underscore social hierarchy, rather than equality and individual autonomy; and this "social solidarity" is for a particular class—the gentry class which contained doomed feelings. If in the West, "sentimentalism pioneered the triumph of the Enlightenment dialectic of subjectivity and sociality, of individualism and civil society," then in China, the sentimentalism heralded the defeat of the traditional form of subjectivity and sociality, of the Confucian worldview and its patriarchal social-class hierarchy.[1]

In short, what Haiyan Lee misses is the historicity (the differing social-political, economic elements) that accounts for the different nature of similar historical phenomena. Accordingly, although she stresses that "judging literary texts on whether they challenge its (Confucian) basic tenets obviously misses the dynamism of historicity,"[2] what she errs is on the same principle. Thus, although her observation that "the late imperial cult of Qing (sentiment) was already transforming Confucian ethics from within by placing sentiment at the foundation of all virtues" is cute,[3] she does not explain why this happened, and her argument that " the sentimentalization of virtue, I submit, is the defining elements of what may be called… ' the Confucian structure of feeling '" is an ahistorical overgeneralization that takes a particular phenomenon in a specific historical era as the overall principle of Confucianism for all periods (the neo-Confucianism in the Qing period, for one, was quite stringent in demanding an unyielding obeisance of its tenets; many times it was also not " sentimental "). Granted the critic's description of the ostensible manifestation of Butterfly sentimentalism is apt, she does not look into the social-historical overdetermination of these phenomena: why "it takes a keen interest in the subjective ramifications of moral behavior, appropriating venerable Confucian virtues to elaborate private, affective experiences"; and why "Butterfly texts invite the readers to an engrossing contemplation of what characters inflict on themselves in an effort to transform themselves

---

① Lee, H., All the Feelings that are Fit to Print: the Community of Sentiment and the Literary Public Sphere in China, 1900-1918, *Modern China*, 2001,27(3):302.

② Lee, H., All the Feelings that are Fit to Print: the Community of Sentiment and the Literary Public Sphere in China, 1900-1918, *Modern China*, 2001,27(3):304.

③ Haiyan Lee. "Love or Lust? The Sentimental Self in *Honglou Meng* (*Dream of the Red Chamber*)." Quoted from Lee, H., All the Feelings That Are Fit to Print: The Community of Sentiment and the Literary Public Sphere in China, 1900-1918, *Modern China*, 2001,27(3):304.

into ethical subjects." ①

## 四、Sentimentalization and Moralization of a Political Issue

In fact, the author has to acknowledge that the Butterfly literature is conservative as "the subject is always situated within a specific Confucian configuration of human connectedness," and she reluctantly admits that "the objective effect may be to reaffirm orthodoxy." ② But she tries to gloss over, or at least to lessen the severity, of this conservatism by saying that "the plural subjective realities" that were explored were significant. Moreover, she endeavors to contend that the literature is "radical" "because the subject is ultimately recognizable as a universal being—the man or woman with feeling—and because the act of devotion or sacrifice ultimately honors feelings, not codes." However, this argument is not persuasive at all: firstly, a subject in any literature, if he/she is not an evil beyond rational explanation, is recognized as a "universal" being, or a man or woman with feeling; secondly, without further analysis, we are not sure whether it "ultimately" honors feelings or codes—the act of separation between feelings and codes itself is a dubious, priori preclusion.

One argument that supports her validation of Butterfly moralism is an historical (which means metaphysical) viewpoint that "morality… provides not so much foundational principles as a pliant tool for defining 'who we are'." ③ As well acknowledged, neo-Confucianism that the Butterfly writers still subscribed to at the time was exactly playing the function of "fundamental moralism" that severely circumscribed the action and psychosomatic feelings of the populace, making them still fall into the

---

① Haiyan Lee. "Love or Lust? The Sentimental Self in *Honglou Meng* (*Dream of the Red Chamber*)." Quoted from Lee, H., All the Feelings That Are Fit to Print: The Community of Sentiment and the Literary Public Sphere in China, 1900-1918, *Modern China*, 2001,27(3):304.

② Lee, H., All the Feelings that are Fit to Print: the Community of Sentiment and the Literary Public Sphere in China, 1900-1918, *Modern China*, 2001,27(3):304-305.

③ Lee, H., All the Feelings that are Fit to Print: the Community of Sentiment and the Literary Public Sphere in China, 1900-1918, *Modern China*, 2001,27(3):305.

straitjacket of traditional "structure of feelings" and could not break out of it to access to the modern world together with its principles. That it is a "tool for defining 'who we are'" is at the same time working as the "foundational principles."

Indeed, Butterfly moralism, as Haiyan Lee contends, "seeks to delimit a new community by simultaneously invoking a timeless Confucian moral tradition and pitting itself against the contemporary social morass."[①] What the Butterfly writers mistook is that they took the Confucian ethic codes that are always pliant and susceptible to the historical dynamic and ideological demands of changing regimes (for instance, some codes of the neo-Confucianism are vastly differing from the Confucian tenets of earlier periods) to be a "timeless" "moral tradition," and they tried to safeguard the "fundamental principle" that was subjected to the outside challenge, especially the onslaught of modern (which at the time means the Western) morality that stresses not so much chastity and filial piety as individual autonomy and freedom. The so-called "contemporary social morass" in my view refers not so much to the corrupted "officialdom" (it is certainly one of its "depraved other," though) than these "degenerate" new morality that in their minds led to the paradise lost. For instance, as Haiyan Lee aptly observes, "'free love' or 'free marriage,' is denounced as a euphemistic pretext for disobeying parents and a license to debauchery."[②]

An essentially political issue about the loss of legitimacy of the traditional polity then, in the conservative minds of the Butterfly writers, was refracted to be the loss of moral fundamentality (or, in Haiyan Lee's words, "a matter of moral bankruptcy, a betrayal of the basic Confucian paradigm of rule by moral principle."[③]) This is not a single phenomenon

---

① Lee, H., All the Feelings that are Fit to Print: the Community of Sentiment and the Literary Public Sphere in China, 1900-1918, *Modern China*, 2001, 27(3): 305.

② Lee, H., All the Feelings that are Fit to Print: the Community of Sentiment and the Literary Public Sphere in China, 1900-1918, *Modern China*, 2001, 27(3): 308.

③ Lee, H., All the Feelings that are Fit to Print: the Community of Sentiment and the Literary Public Sphere in China, 1900-1918, *Modern China*, 2001, 27(3): 306.

seen in the Butterfly literature, but the conservative perspective held by most writers of the time. The mediocrity of the so-called "scandal fiction" (黑幕小说), expose fiction (谴责小说) precisely lies in their equation of the ultimate bankruptcy of state legitimacy with the apparent loss of the virtues of rectitude, or the betrayal of the principle of rule by virtue.

Although Haiyan Lee fails to pinpoint the cause for the Butterfly's sentimentalism, her observation of the ostensible overarching storyline of most Butterfly literature is keen: "The heroes and heroines who populate their stories are more likely to be of humble origins and display their steely virtues in grievous destitution"; and her designation of the function of this literature is sometimes on the point: "Sentimental fiction's inverted hierarchy, based on feeling rather than rank, offers both an explanation for and utopian solution to the benighted social world as portrayed in political exposes."[1] This argument points to a more fruitful direction to go: an ideological analysis of the texts would yield to a conclusion that sees the ideological reification of the Butterfly moralism as simultaneously a utopian yearning for a more equal society (including a more equal gender relations) that would break the boundaries of the Confucian ethics that circumscribes the fulfillment of the happiness of the heart-stricken lovers and prevents the interventions of state politics by the politically inferior class. It is in this sense that we can read Haiyan Lee's argument in a new light "implicitly, it declares that the hope lies with 'us'—the educated middle and lower classes, the unique breed of men and women of sentiment who are chaste, filial, and capable of pitying the suffering masses."[2] Put in another way, its ideological side-effect is to amass empathetic and sympathetic feelings from the readers, who are from the same classes, to bring into a sense of being a community—an essentially new class, yet with traditional habitus, dispositions, tastes, morality, ethics, that defies the onslaught of the

---

[1]  Lee, H., All the Feelings that are Fit to Print: the Community of Sentiment and the Literary Public Sphere in China, 1900-1918, *Modern China*, 2001,27(3):307.

[2]  Lee, H., All the Feelings that are Fit to Print: the Community of Sentiment and the Literary Public Sphere in China, 1900-1918, *Modern China*, 2001,27(3):307.

"depraved" new Western value systems. Fundamentally, then, it points to the difficult yet unyielding struggle of the Chinese traditional (middle and lower) gentry class for a metamorphosis towards a new identity of middle class "bourgeois."

This is to say, just as the Butterfly literature is something of a "leftover" phenomenon taken by a transformative class in metamorphosis in a transitional era, there were also progressive elements in its generally conservative perspective. This not only refers to the fact that their repudiation of the idea of "free love" is based on the observation that it "merely lifts the floodgate of lust," which also points to some real happenings at the time, but it more relates to the issue that the writers poignantly felt the pains imposed on them by the traditional practice of arranged marriage, so in presenting the agonies and tragedies out of the latter, they essentially exposed, if not attacked, the conventional customs. They also attacked polygamy, but this attack, as admitted by Haiyan Lee, is "based not so much on the principle of gender equality as on the desire to stamp out what is seen as a hotbed of vices." [1] As a result, as observed, they can reconcile to the fact of patriarchal polygamy, insofar as it is supposed to "reconcile an arranged marriage··· with the other model of marriage that Butterfly lovers all dream of—the companionate marriage." [2]

It is here that again Haiyan Lee sees the comparability between Chinese and Western sentimental fiction: "By insisting on the primacy of the conjugal bond, sentimental fiction is in effect ushering in the modern notion of the family as primarily an affective unit, a sphere of intimacy insulated from the laws of the market and relations of power." [3] But this comparison is somewhat misleading, because for the Chinese "family as primarily an

---

[1]  Lee, H., All the Feelings that are Fit to Print: the Community of Sentiment and the Literary Public Sphere in China, 1900-1918, *Modern China*, 2001,27(3):307.

[2]  Lee, H., All the Feelings that are Fit to Print: the Community of Sentiment and the Literary Public Sphere in China, 1900-1918, *Modern China*, 2001,27(3):307.

[3]  Lee, H., All the Feelings that are Fit to Print: the Community of Sentiment and the Literary Public Sphere in China, 1900-1918, *Modern China*, 2001,27(3):307.

affective unit" is not a "modern notion" at all，the values of filial piety and familial solidarity and harmony（伦常之乐）precisely underlie this point；and the polygamous practice also directly violates the "modern notion" of love and marriage based on the institutionalization of nuclear family. To be sure，the emphasis on sentiment and especially love would lead more to a love and marriage between a man and a woman，thus instrumental to the formation of the conjugal bond，which is generally seen as the foundation of the bourgeois（or middle class）identity.

Nevertheless，this love is never transcendent beyond—in fact more often than not subservient to—the value of filial piety，thus the stories become "sentimentalization of filiality," which Haiyan Lee acknowledges that it "is indeed highly problematic."[1] But again she tries to tone down this problem by saying that "for a Butterfly writer，filial stories，like romantic ones，are narratives of virtue."[2] Although she notes that later on，the May Fourth writers "would radically revise this scenario so that filiality becomes the egotistic resentment that stymies romantic as well as broader social feelings," again，she does not explain why this occurred. In fact，the eulogies of filiality as a virtue becomes so problematic—hackney and fake—that brought about its own demise，and invited the backfire from the May Fourth radicals. The Chinese traditional，patriarchal extended family system was on its way to disintegration under the new social-economic momentum，which，together with its lingering influence on the budding of new gender relations（including "free love" and new marriage practice not based on parental arrangement），was the cause for the traditional-minded Butterfly writers to stress filial piety，as a psychological substitution for their sense of loss of virtue in the modern world. The emphasis on the ideal of a sentimental bond between parents and children points to its shortage in the real world；the same rule applies to the idealistic picture of the unity

---

[1]　Lee，H.，All the Feelings that are Fit to Print：the Community of Sentiment and the Literary Public Sphere in China，1900-1918，*Modern China*，2001，27（3）：309.

[2]　Lee，H.，All the Feelings that are Fit to Print：the Community of Sentiment and the Literary Public Sphere in China，1900-1918，*Modern China*，2001，27（3）：309.

between amatory love and filiality. But while Haiyan Lee sees "contestation and miscegenation" in "Butterfly fiction's dual pursuit of romantic love and filial piety," she does not look into the implied tension and real conflicts "between the imported discourse of individualism and the indigenous valuation of filial bonds."[1] It seems that she is too identified with the surfacial rhetoric and ostensible plotline of the Butterfly fiction, taking its ideology of the underlying unity between chastity and filial piety for granted.

What needs to be pointed out here, however, is that at the time when the writers wrote their fiction, the modern atomistic individuals had not fully come into reality; individuals were still embedded in social and familial web. This was so because the slow change of social relationship (though a fast and relentless process of capitalist social rationalization was ongoing) helped to perpetuate the tenacity of traditional ethic-moral concepts, especially the ones regarding family values,[2] which contributed to the superfacial resemblance of the central value that the Butterfly fiction sanctioned with what the modern, Western novels validated: it "affirm(s) a mode of existence centering on familial affections, constructing the domestic

---

① Lee, H., All the Feelings that are Fit to Print: the Community of Sentiment and the Literary Public Sphere in China, 1900-1918, *Modern China*, 2001,27(3):312.

② Lee H points out that "sociologically speaking, the conjugal model with the wife as homemaker was far from dominant even among the bourgeoisie in the early years of the Republic. The phenomenon of long-term urban sojourning pointed to the tenacity of the traditional family structure." Lee, H., All the Feelings that are Fit to Print: the Community of Sentiment and the Literary Public Sphere in China, 1900-1918, *Modern China*, 2001,27(3):314. She even notes that "an encyclopedia published in 1918, All-Purpose Household *Encyclopedia* (Jiating wanbao quanshu), primarily targeted the extended family and its moral and economic well-being, giving advice on how to coordinate the nettlesome interpersonal relationships in a big family even as it supported family reform." Lee, H., All the Feelings that are Fit to Print: the Community of Sentiment and the Literary Public Sphere in China, 1900-1918, *Modern China*, 2001,27(3):314. But she again does not delve into the issue and bypasses it completely.

world as an emotionally rewarding realm within the larger community of sentiment."[①] For instance, in the autobiographical novels of Chen Diexian, a veteran Butterfly writer, "romantic love is never allowed to impair the integrity of the family."[②] But this is more often than not from the patriarchal, male point of view; later on we would see that from the women's angle, the picture would appear wholly different, such as what we have read from Eileen Chang's stories.

In one story *The Money Demon*（黄金祟）that Haiyan Lee discusses, a woman refuses the male narrator's proposal to be his second wife, choosing to be his mistress instead for her independence. This triggers the resentment of the conservative narrator: "Because of all of Koto's (the woman) money, she has no need to rely on anyone for support, nor need she have any concern about her family. She looks upon money as her lifelong support, so I can think of no better name for her than 'money demon'."[③] Obviously, here the conservative narrator refutes the modern concept of individual

---

① Lee, H., All the Feelings that are Fit to Print: the Community of Sentiment and the Literary Public Sphere in China, 1900-1918, *Modern China*, 2001, 27(3):314. It is also alarming that she says that when the encyclopedia "denounce(ed) the practice of keeping large members of concubines and maidservants…the implied ideal seems to be the nuclear or stem family as a sphere of affection and virtue." It is well known that traditional Confucian moralists had repudiated the same phenomena centuries years ago, and it is nothing to do with the ideal of the modern nuclear family. When she says "in entries devoted to women in their role as 'able wives and good mothers'（贤妻良母）, contributors invoked the Confucian spatial metaphor of gender segregation to articulate the bourgeois ideology of separate spheres," it is still well known that the ideal of "able wives and good mothers" is a traditional Chinese principle regarding a married woman, and the "Confucian spatial metaphor of gender segregation" is exactly a conservative morality seen as reactionary then and has nothing to do with bourgeois ideology. It seems Haiyan Lee is too haste to find example to support her argument that there was abundant progressive bourgeois ideology in the otherwise conservative Butterfly fiction, which helped to found a bourgeois identity.

② Lee, H., All the Feelings that are Fit to Print: the Community of Sentiment and the Literary Public Sphere in China, 1900-1918, *Modern China*, 2001, 27(3):319.

③ Lee, H., All the Feelings that are Fit to Print: the Community of Sentiment and the Literary Public Sphere in China, 1900-1918, *Modern China*, 2001, 27(3):320.

autonomy, including women's independence, and pursues unabashedly his own interests and happiness regardless of women's feeling. Because "Koto is a bit too modern…taking the unversalist ideology of the bourgeoisie to its logical conclusion,"[1] at the end of the story, the male narrator gives up Koto and returns to his family mastered by his mother and his subservient wife (who helps to manage the house affairs). In the facade of a "bourgeois genre" of autobiography, what the story affirms is nothing more than the conservatism of the Butterfly fiction. This ideology is fundamentally derived from the conservative Confucian ideology that stresses the dominance of men's rights over women's, and the repudiation of any monetary interests which is seen as impairing the integrity of a man of virtue (which is also shown as rejection of commercial activities and the merchant class), both of which are at odds with modern bourgeois ideas. It is here that Haiyan Lee's comment appears poignant: "Butterfly writers' attitude toward money, at least as reflected in sentimental fiction, is symptomatic of their split identity as custodians of Confucian morality and as professional writers necessarily implicated in the bourgeoning capitalist economy."[2] This "split" personality shows little more than their fundamentally unreformed, deeply ingrained traditional identity of gentry class that was struggling and negotiating with the modern, bourgeois ideology in the emerging capitalist world. His identity as a "man of sentiment who has reined in his wild passions for the sake of hearth and home—the moral sanctuary where filiality and conjugality jointly smooth over the vestigial delusions of the bourgeois individual" thus

---

① Lee, H., All the Feelings that are Fit to Print: the Community of Sentiment and the Literary Public Sphere in China, 1900-1918, *Modern China*, 2001,27(3):321.

② Lee, H., All the Feelings that are Fit to Print: the Community of Sentiment and the Literary Public Sphere in China, 1900-1918, *Modern China*, 2001,27(3):320.

stops short of acquiring a new, bourgeois subjectivity.[①] The metamorphosis of the characters in the Butterfly fiction, together with the ideological message that the plotlines of the stories transpire, is slowly developing with many traumas, reluctant compromises, and uncompromising insistence in their hearts and minds. This painful process transmigrates to become the tearful lamentation of unfulfilled love, attributing it to the merciless outside social impediments and relentless interpersonal intervention. The middle brow nature of this fiction is intimately correlated with this sentimentalization of an essentially political issue, a displacement of social-economic elements, and a moralization of conservative motive.

Through theoretical engagement with existing scholarship on Chinese literature in lateimperial China and examination of the birth and development of modern Chinese literature, we have witnessed that the criterion of categorizing "high (-brow) literature" and "low (-brow) literature" is a historically changed one which is intimately tied in with the problematic of canonization, legitimization, as well as cultural hegemony which is clearly witnessed in modern China when there was a fast shift of cultural legitimacy and hegemony, and the latter was also closely related with political legitimacy and hegemony. This historical fact shows the intricate interplay between culture and politics in the period.

Meanwhile, the criterion is also pertinent to class distinctions and tastes in a period of time. In addition, the so-called middle-brow literature in modern China is essentially moralization of political and social issues, which

---

① Lee, H., acknowledges finally that Butterfly writers' "sentimental, theatrical displays of virtue eclipsed rational, critical conversations...the commitment to the family set a limit to individual rights; and the logic of domination and exclusion undermined the universality of the sentimental community." But these facts do not lead her to the knowledge that the Butterfly sentimental fiction does not lead them fruitfully to a bourgeois identity, but only make her derive the conclusion that more often than not "Habermas's narrative of the literary and the political public spheres" did not work itself out in China, though sometimes it did. Lee, H., All the Feelings that are Fit to Print:the Community of Sentiment and the Literary Public Sphere in China, 1900-1918, *Modern China*, 2001, 27 (3):322.

is a move of displacing social-economic elements and political motivation, usually done by a glorification of conservative ethical-moral points of views. The reason that this phenomenon is frequently witnessed in modern China is that the nation-state painfully metamorphosed itself from the traditional world to a modern one, in which various political and cultural forces vied against each other for the political as well as cultural hegemony and the right of claiming for the nation's future. Because of this, literature as a cultural and social institution rapidly changed its nature and feature, and various definitions of high vs. low literature emerged to replace one another.

## 六、Subjectivity, Class Consciousness, and Identity Politics

The chapters of the present book have efficiently substantiated the fact that in modern China, the search for a new subjectivity was undertaken through conquering the identity crisis of the "new man" and "new women"; meanwhile, in the writing of stories, the manipulation of the form is simultaneously a symbolic action that articulated the intellectuals' anxiety of becoming a new, modern Chinese. The first argument yields to a notion that this search for a new identity is premised upon the establishment of a new subjectivity; and we have seen that the creation of "subjectivity" was an integral part of the various projects of "new cultures." Moreover, since the "new cultures" had diversified versions and visions, various subjectivities had also been pursued that were taken as, or promoted to be, the subjectivity/identity for modern Chinese. Therefore, the second argument leads to the point that this symbolic action is closely correlated with differing class consciousness: the diverse ways to negotiate with or to design the "new cultures" that the writers faced, via the refraction of their class consciousness, were expressed as and incarnated in the form and the content of their stories. A brief discussion on this problematic between class consciousness, subjectivity and identity, as shown in the writers' writings and their literary career, is thus necessary.

It is well acknowledged that the May Fourth intellectuals held exuberant individualism, or "put their priority on an affirmation of the self, championing the individual's energies and emotional needs," and believed that "it was only in fulfilling the individual that society could thereafter accomplish its renewal, reform, and salvation."[①] However, this individualism subsided in the writers of the 1940s. As my analysis of Eileen Chang's stories show, her stories as a whole demonstrate that individualism—the cardinal principle of the middle-class world—was in a deep crisis, and this is because the social-historical reality—the semi-traditional, semi-colonial situation—restricted and constrained the expressions of the "human nature," which has a historical and class-bound feature. Therefore, for many writers, "their doubts that individual needs could be attained and their concern with the theme of self-delusion, upon which both individual ambitions and social institutions were based,"[②] could only find their explanation from the social-historical context as the subtext of the fictional texts.

As suggested, Xiao Hong's personal tragedy, a result of the ruthless conditions of the society but also a side effect of her own numerous miscalculated choices out of her weak capability of political judgment, was also symptomatic of the besieged "new women," which shows the predicament of liberal-humanist intellectuals in the transformative era, and the dilemma of the New Culture agenda in general. While her early stories generally can be read as leftist stories that contain strong doses of class conflicts, what also stands out is a humanist concern. This should be understood in conjunction with her life experience. The sympathetic feeling for the social outcast was derived from her own wretched experience thus far, which contributed to her sense of merciless class division and oppression. This pre-theoretical recognizance did not necessarily lead to revolutionary thoughts, but it undoubtedly led to her pro-leftist inclinations with strong humanitarian sentiments. Nevertheless, because she was weak

---

① Gunn, E., *Unwelcome Muse:Chinese Literature in Shanghai and Beijing*, 1937-1945, New York:Columbia University Press, 1980:270-271.

② Gunn, E., *Unwelcome Muse:Chinese Literature in Shanghai and Beijing*, 1937-1945, New York:Columbia University Press, 1980:271.

in political thinking, in particular the perspective of class analysis, while her novel *Field of Life and Death* had helped to promote the patriotic, anti-Japanese sentiment of the populace, the multiple thematic concerns in it are not coherently connected but are subtly in conflict with each other, contributing to its thematic incoherency. I suggest that this was a result of the author's unclear differentiation of the priority, and her incapability to look into the innate correlativity, of the three major social contradictions of the time: patriarchal gender inequality, class conflicts, and national resistance. Also because of her little theoretical knowledge of class politics, later on she stopped short of exploring further areas apart from what she observed within her own (somewhat narrow) life circle—the latter of which, furthermore, mainly comes from her childhood experience. Without a broadened social experience in her avoidance of taking part in the dramatically shifted social reality, the largely unchanged pattern shows a predicament difficult to break through, which is also confirmed by the mediocrity of her "resistance stories." Her last work *Tales of Hulan River* retreats from her earlier social-political analysis in a culturalist perspective predicated on the discourse of the New Culture enlightenment. All in all, holding little political belief and refusing to enter an essentially political world, she was ultimately a humanist and an individualist who had tried to seek "a room of her own" for personal security and pleasure, yet the relentless Chinese society amid wartime circumstance did not allow her to do so.

For Eileen Chang, there was another picture. The connection between her apparent "transcendence of politics" and a profound cynicism and nihilism grew out of her privileged yet disoriented life as a marginalized member (partially also because of her gender) of the cultural establishment of the Republic. Her egocentric self-consciousness and her "aesthetic" attitude towards life could not be dissociated from the aristocratic tradition of the pre-modern Chinese gentry class. By meticulously yet coolly documenting and codifying the daily trivial details of private quotidian experience, she tried to define a sustainable pattern of "living appropriately" for middle-class women, which as both utopia and fantasy of that awkward social group，bordered on the explicit abnormality and brutality of the social conditions in the 1940s' China. For the female characters in her stories，the agonies and troubles caused by marriage and love show the predicament of these social institutions at the time，which in general reveals a deep crisis that the May Fourth individualism had been trapped in，and the impossibility of the "new woman" project in the historical conjuncture. The identity complex as demonstrated in her works not only shows an unsuccessful transformation of a class identity，but also belies the seemingly apolitical nature of her "boudoir literature." This "existential" cultural-political anxiety brings out a fictional style which is a hybrid of traditional taste and Western techniques，as an elaborate mechanism to absorb the frustration and shock she experienced internally，and a labyrinth of symbols and images collected to fend off assaults on vulnerable individuals from a hostile environment. Since it was not merely a personal identity，but simultaneously a class and a national one；thus we sometimes witness that the crisis of the identity of this particular class would transmogrify itself to (yearn to) be a (fake) ethnography，as shown in her story *Lust，Caution*.

If those middle-class women writers in the occupied areas at worst submitted to the politically high-handed pressure and struggled for a humble life of dubious personal happiness amid war time turmoil—for whom there was no place in their minds for the ideal of the New Culture to be propagated，and at best promoted the modern women's virtues which were part of the New Culture ideal；then we also witness that some male writers in the Nationalist-controlled areas still laboriously designed and invented various ways to achieve the ideals of the enlightenment dreams of the May Fourth era，though the latter could not be transmitted openly. In Wumingshi's novel circle *Book without a Name*，the hero Yin Di，after experiencing ups and downs in the society，finally believed that he had at last found a genuine way to achieve a bright future，based on a new culture that combines the cultural essences of both China and the West，for him and for the nation. The writer's other stories were oftentimes cast in a similar vein with Xu Xu's "modern tales about the strange," and most of them share similar thematic concerns of a culturalist deliberation on "human nature," love, beauty, and cosmopolitanism.

I have suggested that the two writers' "novel of conception" has a particular nature. Lost in the faith in the intellectual revolution of Chinese enlightenment that aimed to promote and institutionalize progressive political agenda, they were immersed in the fantasy of fundamentally changing the mentality of the people, especially the nature of the rulers, to be peace-loving, thus to solve the irrevocable social contradiction. The stylistic mannerisms of their works were not only strategies of self-positioning in a rapidly-shifting sociological space, but more importantly, ways of expressing a nascent national bourgeoisie that found itself caught between ruthless class struggle and ideological conflicts that defined modern China. Although their cultivation of fine taste and elaborate style fit in with the agenda of making a vulnerable individuality sustainable, they failed to recognize the collective reality—the once defeated yet persistent mass movement that propelled radical social change, thus their self-positioning revealed a cultural crisis and intellectual dilemma. Their project was at once populist and elitist, as neither the socio-economic condition of modern China nor its political-legal culture endowed concreteness to their culturalist discourse of salvation. Thus while the male characters in the two writers' stories apparently hold substantial subjectivity and firm identity, the oftentimes pseudo-Bildungsroman in a "spiritual conquest" betrays its flimsy nature and vulnerable character.

These contradictions were to a great extent seemingly solved by the writers from the CCP-controlled areas. In close scrutiny, however, we find that there are still tensions there. It is due to the capability of attracting the peasants towards the fictional world based on their own real life, that Zhao Shuli's stories were regarded as a perfect vehicle of following Mao Zedong's call for establishing a "national form" for promoting a "new democratic culture." First and foremost, rather than merely to "expose" the ignorance of the peasants, the subaltern is now being represented from the perspective of himself to show his life and feeling. Secondly, Zhao Shuli's stories are mostly adaptations from real incidents. The ways of adaptation point to the later development of "socialist realism." It is not distortion in the normal sense, but an adaptation for the sake of educational effectiveness. Because now the author/narrator's consciousness is supposed to stand at the same level of, or be identical with, the "proletariat's," the function of the narrator also accordingly changes. Although he is in charge of plot action, many times he does not comment on unfolding events directly, the latter being yielded to the diegetic peasant character. He is an outsider, but simultaneously an insider—because allegedly he has been integrated with the peasant world and has acquired its grammar. The intellectual writer now does not "represent" the subalterns, but he let them speak up for themselves.

For this purpose, the language of the story is an integration of folk, colloquial language with modern, literary language, which produces a new, lively style. This contributes to a popular style of writing, which is both entertaining to the masses and appearing less vulgar to the urban educated readers. But on the other hand, it is also due to this self-imposed goal: to accommodate the ethical-moral as well as aesthetic parameters of the peasants in order to entertain and educate them, that Zhao Shuli fell short of attaining a more far-reaching imperative which intended to fundamentally change the peasants' ingrained mentality, to educate them to acquire a revolutionary consciousness to be "a class for itself," in order to usher them into a higher ethical-moral realm that aimed to build a new world, or to construct an "alternative modernity." Thus the subjectivity of the peasants is ambiguous or amorphous, and the narrator could not assume a personae of a mediator, nor could he provide a model party member with higher revolutionary morale to instill further revolutionary message into the implied readers. The same paradox applies to the literary form. For those with urban- and Western-educated background, these stories catering to the tastes of peasants, having much more flavor of folk art than metropolitan tastes, still appear naive and less refined.

If the subjectivity of the peasants is merely undergirded and blessed by the Party in Zhao Shuli's stories, then in Ding Ling's works this subjectivity sometimes curiously asserts itself without any outside assistance. Tani Barlow has pointed out that Ding Ling "belonged to the May Fourth generation, a group of academics, writers, politicians, and cultural revolutionaries who acted as brokers between imperial and socialist China." As to the background of this "group," she continues, "many belonged to the new social category of educated people, the zhishi fenzi (知识分子), or intellectual class."[①] But Ding Ling apparently repudiated thoroughly the intellectual habitus of this class, and metamorphosed from an uncompromised individualist to a revolutionary fellow traveler, and finally became a firm party intellectual, which she took to be identical with the identity of the people's critic.

The four stages of development she experienced before 1949, both in her personality and in the style of her literary works, were simultaneously a shifting process of her intellectual commitments and identity (trans-) formation. These differing identities not only show her drastically shifted subjectivities in her efforts to conquer her sense of alienation, but also correspond to four shifting notions of literature, or literature as social-cultural institutions. The contemplation of the "women problem" ran throughout her creative career. Briefly speaking, in the changes from a feminine woman to a social critic, through being a cultural worker (for the masses and following the direction of the Party) to the last stage of an ambiguous role of the people's critic/a party intellectual, the literature she writes simultaneously changes its nature: from a "bourgeois," "boudoir" literature to critical realism, through revolutionary realism she finally approached socialist realism.

In most stories of her last period, the subjectivity of the peasant class is presented to be their desire to acquire their land. The incapability to describe the "proletarian consciousness" as the class subjectivity of the peasant masses is not due to the writer's shortsightedness, but it was fundamentally conditioned by the Chinese historical reality: the revolutionary ("proletarian") consciousness did not exist in modern China in reality as the case might be of some industrialized Western countries, in which the

---

① Barlow, T., *I Myself Am a Woman: Selected Writings of Ding Ling*, Boston: Beacon Press, 1989:2.

"proletariat"—the industrial workers—had cultivated for a long time a class consciousness which is supposedly identical with the revolutionary consciousness. Consequently, the failure to present a collective subjectivity goes hand in hand with a weak representation of an ambiguous, or amorphous, new individual subjectivity. This dilemma of forming a class subjectivity—in both the two levels—is also correlated with the predicament of establishing a new culture, the latter of which is both its premise and its outcome.

The dilemma of this "new democratic culture" predetermined its own sublation and development in the "socialist culture" after the establishment of the People's Republic. But at this moment, for this "new (democratic) culture" as envisioned and tested by Ding Ling, the allegedly historically new "subject"—the peasant "proletariat"—still had to be represented, but could not represent itself; and the intellectuals who were to represent them themselves needed to be educated by the revolutionary theory and the Party—thus their own subjectivity and identity were still not yet solidly formed, which brought about many conflicts, tensions, and agonies.

To sum up, from the death of a "new woman" Xiao Hong, to the "rebirth" of a self-styled "intellectual of the people" Ding Ling, we witness the various cultural forces and trends of intellectual thoughts which coexisted, vied and interacted with each other in the same historical juncture to claim their cultural hegemony. Through a practice of political hermeneutics of fictional texts and social-historical subtexts via an analytical detour of exploring the relationship between class consciousness, subjectivity, and identity, this book intends to show that social modernity and literary modernity in modern China were intertwined and interacting with each other in the development of modern Chinese literature.

# References

## Works in English

Adorno T W, Horkheimer M. *Dialectic of Enlightenment*. Edmund J. Trans. Stanford:Stanford University Press, 2002.

Anderson M. *The Limits of Realism: Chinese Fiction in the Revolutionary Period*.Berkeley: University of California Press, 1990.

Appiah K A. Cosmopolitan Patriots. *Critical Inquiry*. 1997,23(3):617-639.

Aristotle. *Poetics*. Oxford:Clarendon Press, 1968.

Barlow T. *I Myself Am a Woman:Selected Writings of Ding Ling*. Boston:Beacon Press, 1989.

Bergere M. *The Golden Age of the Chinese Bourgeoisie*, 1911-1937. Lloyd J. Trans. New York: Cambridge University Press and Maison des Sciences de l'Homme, Paris, 1989.

Best S, Douglas K. *Postmodern Theory: Critical Interrogations*. Houndmills: Palgrave Macmillan, 1991.

Birch C. Fiction of the Yenan Period. *China Quarterly*. 1960,(4):1-11.

Bourdieu P. *Distinction:A Social Critique of the Judgment of Taste*. Routledge and Kegan Paul, 1984.

Brook T.*Collaboration:Japanese Agents and Local Elites in Wartime China*. Cambridge, Mass:Harvard University Press, 2005.

Chang Y S. *Literary Culture in Taiwan:Martial Law to Market Law*. New York: Columbia University Press, 2004.

Chang Y S. Revisiting the Modernist Literary Movement in Post-1949 Taiwan. http://www. soas. ac. uk/taiwanstudies/eats/eats2008/file43157.

pdf. Accessed June 23，2012.

Chen P. Literature High and Low："Popular Fiction" in Twentieth-Century China. In：Hockx M，ed. *The Literary Filed of Twentieth-Century China*. Honolulu：University of Hawaii Press，1999.

Cheng S. Themes and Techniques in Eileen Chang's Stories. *Tamkang Review*. 1977,8(2):169-200.

Chow R.*Primitive Passions：Visuality，Sexuality，Ethnography，and Contemporary Chinese Cinema*. New York：Columbia University Press，1995.

Chow R.*Woman and Chinese Modernity：The Politics of Reading between West and East*. Minneapolis and Oxford：University of Minnesota Press，1991.

Chow T.*The May Fourth Movement：Intellectual Revolution in Modern China*. Cambridge，Mass：Harvard University Press，1960.

De Man P. *Blindness and Insight*. Minneapolis：University of Minnesota Press，1997.

Dermansky M. Review of *Lust，Caution*. http://worldfilm.about.com/od/chinesefilms/fr/lustcaution.htm. Accessed Feb 7，2008.

Denton K. *Modern Chinese Literary Thought：Writings on Literature，1893-1945*. Stanford：Stanford University Press，1976.

Denton K. *The Problematic of Self in Modern Chinese Literature：Hu Feng and Lu Ling*. Stanford：Stanford University Press，1998.

Dirlik A. *Marxism in the Chinese Revolution*. Lanham，MD：Rowman & Littlefield Publishers，2005.

Dirlik A. Contemporary Challenges to Marxism：Postmodernism，Postcolonialism，Globalization. *Amerasia Journal*. 2007,33(3).

Doleželová-Velingerová M.*Selective Guide to Chinese Literature* 1900-1949(vol.1). New York：Brill Publishers，1988.

Eagleton T.*The Ideology of the Aesthetic*. Oxford：Basil Blackwell，1990.

Feuerwerker Y M.*Ding Ling's Fiction：Ideology and Narrative in Modern Chinese Literature*. Cambridge，Mass and London：Harvard University Press，1982.

Feuerwerker Y M. *Ideology, Power, Text: Self-Representation and the Peasant "Other" in Modern Chinese Literature*. Stanford: Stanford University. Press, 1998.

Gibbs D A. Dissonant Voices in Chinese Literature: Hu Feng. *Chinese Studies in Literature*. 1979-1980,(1):947-974.

Giddens A. *The Consequence of Modernity*. Stanford: Stanford University Press, 1991.

Gunn E. *Unwelcome Muse: Chinese Literature in Shanghai and Beijing*, 1937-1945. New York: Columbia University Press, 1980.

Hansen M B. The Mass Production of the Senses: Classical Cinema as Vernacular Modernism. *Modernism/Modernity*. 1999,6(2):59-77.

Hansen M B. Fallen Women, Rising Stars, New Horizons: Shanghai Silent Film as Vernacular Modernism. *Film Quarterly*. 2000,54(1):10-22.

Hegel G W F. *Phenomenology of Spirit*. Miller A V. Trans. Oxford: Clarendon Press, 1977.

Hockx M. *Questions of Style: Literary Societies and Literary Journals in Modern China*, 1911-1937. Leiden and Boston: Brill Publishers, 2003.

Holm D. *Art and Ideology in Revolutionary China*. Oxford: Clarendon Press, 1991.

Hsia C T A. *History of Modern Chinese Fiction*. Bloomington: Indiana University Press. 1999.

Hsia C T. Forward. In: Pu N. ed. *Red in Touch and Claw: Twenty-Six Years in Communist Chinese Prisons*. New York: Grove Press, 1994.

Huang N. *Women, War, Domesticity: Shanghai Literature and Popular Culture of the* 1940s. Leiden and Boston: Brill Publishers, 2005.

Fredric J. *A Singular Modernity: Essay on the Ontology of the Present*. London: Verso, 2002.

Fredric J. *Political Unconscious: Narrative as a Socially Symbolic Act*. Ithaca, NY: Cornell University Press, 1931.

Fredric J. *Marxism and Form*. Princeton, NJ: Princeton University Press, 1974.

Jung C G. *The Archetypes and the Collective Unconscious*. Hull R F C. Trans. 2nd ed. Princeton, NJ: Princeton University Press, 1980.

Larson W. Review: the Sublime Figure of History. *Comparative Literature*. 1998,50(2).

Lee H. All the Feelings That are Fit to Print: the Community of Sentiment and the Literary Public Sphere in China，1900-1918. *Modern China*. 2001,27(3):291-327.

Lee H. *Love or Lust*? The Sentimental Self in *Honglou Meng*.*Chinese Literature:Essays，Articles，Reviews*. 1997,(19):85-111.

Lee L O. *The Romantic Generation of Modern Chinese Writers*. Cambridge，Mass.:Harvard University Press，1973.

Lee L O. *Shanghai Modern:The Flowering of a New Urban Culture in China*，1930-1945. Boston:Harvard University. Press，1998.

Lehan R.*The City in Literature*. Berkeley and Los Angeles:University of California Press，1998.

Link P. *Mandarin and Butterflies:Popular Fiction in Early Twentieth-Century Chinese Cities*. Berkeley:University of California Press，1981.

Liu J. Gender Geopolitics:Social Space and Volatile Bodies，1937-1945. *Journal of Modern Literature in Chinese*. 1998,2(1).

Liu K. *Aesthetic and Modernism:Chinese Aesthetic Marxists and Their Western Contemporaries*. Durhem and London:Duke University Press，2000.

Liu H L. *Translingual Practice:Literature，National Culture，and Translated Modernity—China*，1900-1937. Stanford: Stanford University Press，1995.

Mao Z. Talks at the Yenan Forum on Literature and Art. *Selected Works of Mao Tse-tung*(Vol.3). Beijing:Foreign Languages Press，1967.

Mao Z. On New Democracy. *Selected Works of Mao Tse-tung*(Vol.12). Beijing:Foreign Languages Press，1967.

Mao Z. On New Phase. *Collected Works of Mao Zedong*(Vol.6). Hong Kong:Po Wen Book Co.，1976.

Mao Z. On New Democracy. In: Takeuchi M ed. *Collected Works of Mao Zedong*(Vol.7). Hong Kong:Po Wen Book Co.，1976.

MacDonald S S H. *The Tale of Li Youcai's Rhymes*. Cambridge: Cambridge University Press，1970.

Matthews A J. Artistry and Authenticity: Zhao Shuli and his Fictional World. PhD Dissertation. Ohio University, 1991.

Mote F W. *Imperial China*, 900-1800. Cambridge, MA: Harvard University Press, 1999.

Nowlan R. "What Is 'Suture'?" http://www. uwec. edu/ranowlan/suture.html. Accessed March 4, 2008.

Porter T E. The Magna Mater: the Maternal Goddess in O'Neill's Plays. *Eugene O'Neill Review*. 2005, (27).

Qu Q. The Question of Popular Literature and Art. Paul G. Pickowicz. Trans. In: Berninghausen J and Huters T eds. *Revolutionary Literature in China: An Anthology*. White Plains: M.E. Sharpe, Inc., 1976.

Roddy S J. *Literati Identity and Its Fictional Representations in Late Imperial China*. Stanford: Stanford University Press, 1998.

Schwarcz V. *The Chinese Enlightenment: Intellectuals and the Legacy of the May Fourth Movement of* 1919. Berkeley: University of California Press, 1986.

Shih S. *The Lure of the Modern: Writing Modernism in Semicolonial China*, 1917-1937. Berkeley: University of California Press, 2001.

Simpson J and Edmund W. *Oxford English Dictionary*. Cambridge: Oxford University Press, 1989.

Smith N. *Resisting Manchukuo: Chinese Women Writers and the Japanese Occupation*. Toronto: University of British Columbia Press, 2007.

Smith N. "Only Women Can Change this World into Heaven": Mei Niang, Male Chauvinist Society, and the Japanese Cultural Agenda in North China, 1939-1941. *Modern Asian Studies*. 2006, 40(1): 81-107.

Snider Eric D. "Review." http://www. ericdsnider. com/movies/lust-caution/. Accessed March 21, 2008.

Sypher W. *Loss of the Self in Modern Literature*. Westport, Conn.: Greenwood Press, 1979.

Travers M. *European Literature from Romanticism to Postmodernism*. Houndmills: Palgrave Macmillan, 1997.

Wang B. *The Sublime Figure of History: Aesthetics and Politics in Twentieth-Century China*. Stanford: Stanford University Press, 1997.

Wang B. *Illuminations from the Past：Trauma，Memory，and History in Modern China*. Stanford：Stanford University Press，2004.

Wang D D. *Fin-de-siecle Splendor：Repressed Modernities of Late Qing Fiction*，1849-1911. Stanford：Stanford University Press，1997.

Wang D D. *The Monster That Is History：History，Violence，and Fictional Writing in Twentieth-Century China*. Berkeley：University of California Press，2004.

Wang D D.*Fictional Realism in Twentieth-Century China，Mao Dun，Lao She，Shen Congwen*. New York：Columbia University Press，1992

Wang D D. A Report on Modern Chinese Literary Studies in the English Speaking World. *Harvard Asia Quarterly*. 2005,9(1/2).

Wang J. *High Culture Fever：Politics，Aesthetics，and Ideology in Deng's China*. Berkeley：University of California Press，1986.

Wakeman F Jr. *The Shanghai Badlands：Wartime Terrorism and Urban Crime*，1937-1941. Cambridge：Cambridge University Press，1996.

Weber M. *Political Writings*. Cambridge：Cambridge University Press，1994.

Williams R. *Keywords：A Vocabulary of Culture and Society*. New York：Oxford University Press，1985.

Williams R.*Marxism and Literature*. Oxford：Oxford University Press，1977.

Williams G. The Concept of "Egemonia" in the Thought of Antonio Gramsci：Some Notes on Interpretation. *Journal of the History of Ideas*. 1960,21(4).

Wood M. At the Movies：*Lust，Caution. London Review of Books*. 2008,30(2):31.

Woolf V. *The Death of the Moth*. London：Hogarth Press. 1947.

Yeh W and Fredric W.*Shanghai Sojourners*. Berkeley：University of California Press，1992.

Chang E. *Love in a Fallen City*. Kingsbury K S. and Chang E. Trans. New York：New York Review of Books，2007.

Zhang X.*Chinese Modernism in the Era of Reforms：Cultural Fever，Avant-Garde Fiction，and the New Chinese Cinema*. Durham：Duke

University Press，1999.

Zhang X.*Postsocialism and Cultural Politics：China in the Last Decade of the Twentieth Century*. Durham：Duke University Press，2008.

Zhang X. Shanghai Nostalgia：Postrevolutionary Allegories in Wang Anyi's Literary Production in the 1990s. *Positions：East Asia Cultures Critique*. 2000,8(2).

Zhang X. *The Politics of Aestheticization：Zhou Zuoren and the Crisis of Chinese New Culture* (1927-1937). PhD Dissertation. Duke University，1995.

Zhang Z. *An Amorous History of the Silver Screen：Shanghai Cinema*，1896-1937. Chicago：University of Chicago Press，2005.

**Works in Chinese**

艾思奇.旧形式运用的基本原则[J].文艺战线,1939,1(3).

陈伯达.在文化战线上[M].上海:生活书店,1939.

陈荒煤.向赵树理的方向迈进[N].人民日报,1947 年 8 月 10 日.

陈平原,夏晓虹编.二十世纪中国小说理论资料[M].北京:北京大学出版社,1989.

丁玲.梦柯[J].小说月报,1927 年 12 月 10 日.

丁玲.丁玲选集[M].上海:万象书店,1936.

丁玲.丁玲文集[M].长沙:湖南人民出版社,1983.

丁玲.丁玲选集[M].成都:四川人民出版社,1984.

丁玲.我的创作生活[D].创作的经验.上海:天马书店,1933.

丁玲.一点经验[D].作家谈创作.北京:中国青年出版社,1955.

董均伦.赵树理怎样处理《小二黑结婚》的材料[J].文艺报,1949 年第 10 期.

甘阳.走向"政治"民族[D].将错就错.北京:生活·读书·新知三联书店,2002.

耿传明.轻逸与沉重之间:现代性问题视野中的新浪漫派文学[M].天津:南开大学出版社,2004.

郭沫若.论赵树理的创作[M].苏南:新华书店,1949.

何其芳.论文学上的民族形式[J].文艺战线,1939,1(5).

胡风.胡风评论集[M].北京:人民文学出版社,1985.

胡风.胡风回忆录[J].新文学史料,1989(1).

梅林.梅林文集[M].香港:力生书局,1955.

瞿秋白.瞿秋白文集[M].北京:人民文学出版社,1953.

王瑶:中国新文学史稿[M].上海:新文艺出版社,1953.

汪晖.现代中国思想的兴起[M].北京:生活·读书·新知三联书店,2004.

无名氏.绿色的回响[M].广州:花城出版社,1995.

无名氏.野兽、野兽、野兽[M].台北:黎明文化事业股份有限公司,1995.

无名氏.塔里的女人[M].香港:新闻天地社,1976.

无名氏.金色的蛇夜[M].台北:新闻天地,1977.

无名氏.海艳[M].广州:花城出版社,1977.

吴晓东,倪文尖,罗岗.现代小说研究的诗学视域[J].中国现代文学研究丛刊,1999(1).

吴义勤.徐訏与中外文学渊源[J].中国现代文学研究丛刊,1933(3).

冼星海.论中国音乐的民族形式[J].文艺战线,1939,1(5).

萧红.永久的憧憬与追求[J].报告(创刊号),1937年1月10日.

萧红.萧红卷[D].傅光明编.西安:太白文艺出版社,1997.

萧红.萧红全集[M].哈尔滨:哈尔滨出版社,1991.

徐訏.吉卜赛的诱惑[M].安徽:安徽文艺出版社,1996.

徐訏.风萧萧[M].广州:花城出版社,1990.

严家炎.中国现代各流派小说选[M].北京:北京大学出版社,1986.

张爱玲.张爱玲短篇小说集[M].台北:皇冠出版社,1984.

张爱玲.传奇[M].上海:杂志社,1944.

张泉编.寻找梅娘[M].香港:明镜出版社,1998.

张泉编.梅娘小说散文集[D].北京:北京出版社,1997.

张系国.政治不正确的老易[J].中国日报,2007年11月11日。

赵月华.历史重建中的迷思——梅娘作品修改研究[J].中国现代文学研究丛刊,2005(1).

周杨.论赵树理的创作[J].解放日报,1946年8月26日.

周扬.周扬文集[M].北京:人民文学出版社,1984.

周扬.对旧形式利用在文学上的一个看法[J].中国文化,1945,1(1).

周作人.日本近三十年小说之发达[J].新青年,1918(5).

梅娘.我的青少年时期:1920—1938[D].载张泉编.寻找梅娘.北京:明镜出版社,1998.

梅娘.寄吴英书[J].青年文化,1943,1(1).